DRIVING LESSONS

A YOU KNOW WHO GIRLS NOVEL

D1534005

Visit us at www.boldstrokesbooks.com

Praise for
The You Know Who Girls: Freshman Year

"I sure wish I had gone to high school with *The You Know Who Girls*! Annameekee Hesik has created smart, sassy, sweaty, sexy characters who tore down the basketball court and leaped into my heart. Readers of all ages will absolutely love this book."—Lesléa Newman, author of *The Reluctant Daughter* and *Heather Has Two Mommies*

"It's not easy to write humorously about lesbian adolescence. It's a gift and a talent, and Annameekee Hesik, a Santa Cruz teacher and the author of The You Know Who Girls series, has both."—*Curve Magazine*

By the Author

The You Know Who Girls: Freshman Year

Driving Lessons: A You Know Who Girls Novel

DRIVING LESSONS

A YOU KNOW WHO GIRLS NOVEL

by

Annameekee Hesik

A Division of Bold Strokes Books

2014

Credits
Editor: Ruth Sternglantz
Production Design: Stacia Seaman
Cover Design by Sheri (graphicartist2020@hotmail.com)

Acknowledgments

Thank you so much to my official editor at Bold Strokes Books, Ruth Sternglantz, for her guidance and encouragement, and thank you to my expert readers, AJ Reyes and Alyssa Pierce, for their thoughtful feedback. Thank you to my incredible students who continue to amaze and inspire me. Thank you to my kitty, Matisse, for always making sure my wrists were warm as I attempted to work on my laptop, and thank you to my doggies, Jax and Aggie, for contributing to the manuscript with their surprise paw smacks and nose typing. Thank you to my BFF and webmaster extraordinaire, Casey Chafouleas, for being the most awesome creator of all things graphic-design related and webby. Thank you to my wonderful family for always loving me no matter what. And, as always, thank you to Mary, my most favorite you-know-who girl of all.

To All the You Know Who Girls All Around the World

Chapter One

I think I killed a man," I confess to Kate as I drop my backpack on the locker-room floor and spin in my PE lock combo.

Kate, my ever-reluctant BFF for the past seven years, has already changed in the bathroom stall to make it clear to everyone that we are not an item. And to fully emphasize her straightness, she averts her eyes as I strip off my shirt and change into my sports bra. "Abbey, how have you not figured out that driving simulator yet? It's been three weeks since school started. Are you even past the parking-lot level? I swear, you're going to be the first sophomore in Gila High's history to fail driver's ed."

I shrug. "It's very possible."

"Hair," she reminds me as I'm about to slam my locker shut. She can pretty much handle it if I'm gay, but a jacked-up hair style is where she draws the line.

I gather my long blond hair and position my ponytail at what I think is the most trendy placement possible. I'm pretty sure I get it wrong, but she nods her satisfaction, and we walk out to join the rest of the class in the gym.

"Score?" Mrs. Schwartz asks us as she pauses at our court. She's the only teacher I know who can basically operate her class with one-word phrases.

"Twenty-one to zero," Kate says proudly. "Abbey spiked it three times," she adds, bragging about my net play. Then before realizing how stupid it would look to high-five about a pointless game of PE volleyball, Kate raises her hand.

I happily slap it because I love it when she has these momentary lapses and acts like her pre-high-school self again.

"Rotate," Mrs. Schwartz says.

We move up to the next court with the rest of our assigned volleyball team. It was Kate's serving that actually won us the last game, so we choose her to start this game, too. And since my limbs resemble those of a giant praying mantis, I take my usual spot at the net to smash down any balls that might try to make their way over to our side. Basketball is definitely our sport of choice, but I'm beginning to reconsider this whole volleyball thing. I like blocking shots at the net, and it doesn't hurt that the uniforms consist of tank tops and spandex undies. I think I would die if I had to wear that out on the court, but it wouldn't be so bad seeing other girls in them. Now I'm wondering if there are any you-know-who girls on the volleyball team or if they only play basketball. Garrett, my authority on all things lesbian, says there are rarely any on the volleyball team, but I'm willing to do my own research on this one.

We're waiting for our opponents to arrive, so I bend down to retie my Nikes. That's when I see her walk onto the other side of the court, her enforcers of evil in tow. "Crap," I whisper to myself.

Her name is Nicky, or Knuckles if you're afraid of her, which I am. I don't know if it's her curly blond hair that stays crunchy and stiff all day, the mysterious scar on her neck, or the smell of cigarette smoke that engulfs you after she walks by, but something about her oozes meanness. Maybe it's the fact that she instigates some of the bloodiest fights at school without ever throwing a punch. Like a mob boss, she's the one who makes bad things happen.

"Serve!" Mrs. Schwartz yells at my team and walks away, but Kate's got the ball between her knees while she fixes her hair, which I can guarantee was perfect already.

Nicky and her cronies aren't into sports—or anything having to do with being at school, for that matter—so they linger in the back of the court in a wide half circle. Then while waiting for Kate's serve to sail over the net, I lose my mind and accidentally make eye contact with Nicky. Our eyes lock and there I am, trapped in a really awkward and dangerous staring contest with the most notorious psychopath on campus. And because I am the dumbest smart girl I know, I make things a thousand times worse and I smile at her.

Nicky scowls and flips me off.

My smile quickly fades.

Even though our exchange only lasts a few seconds, during the stare down, smile, and finger flip, Kate also serves the ball. The sound of the volleyball smacking Nicky Knuckles in the head echoes through the gym. Not even her helmet of hairspray softens the impact.

Not laughing would have been impossible, but I try. And because of my immense effort, the noise that comes out of my mouth sounds like a coyote's yelp. I cover my mouth to ensure nothing else will escape.

"You bitch!" Nicky yells after she recovers from the blow. She's on the move and she's heading my way.

Wait, why is she yelling at me?

"You distracted me on purpose," she says, dipping under the net. I step back, but she pushes my shoulder anyway. I'm a goner.

"Do you even know who I am?"

I blink and see the short film of my life play on the insides of my lids. But when I open my eyes, I'm still alive and Nicky is still standing there. I should have said, *What is your problem? It's Kate you want to kill, not me.* But of course I wouldn't throw my best friend under the bus like that. So instead, I whisper, "S-sorry."

I quickly look over my shoulder for backup, but my team is lined up along the service line pretending I don't exist. Thankfully Kate's got the sense to try and find Mrs. Schwartz. At least I think that's where she's disappeared to. If my good, and more importantly, badass pal Mia were here, she'd have my back in an instant. But no, instead she's halfway across town going to Cholla High School because her mom moved out of district.

"Look, dyke"—Nicky's smoker's breath hits my face and I force myself not to grimace—"I'm not interested," she says and shoves me again for emphasis.

Her friends laugh. I don't seem to be breathing at all anymore, so I make no noise. It's not like she's wrong about me. I mean, I'm a total cow, which is what we call ourselves because we like to travel in herds in the hallways and on the basketball court.

I grip my fists, readying myself. She's at least a foot shorter than me, but my skinny arms are about as strong as twigs. Plus, there's the fact that I have never been in a fight in my life. Do you punch with thumbs in or out? Should I just fall to the ground and curl up like a pill bug and try to protect my face?

"Look at me again," Nicky says, interrupting my manic strategy-planning session, "and you'll be kissing the floor while I kick your ass." Her left eye is twitching, so I look away and focus on the yellow tint of her teeth instead.

"What's going on over there?" Mrs. Schwartz yells, exerting more energy than usual saying all those extra words.

Nicky whispers, "Go ahead," but what she really means is *One word and I'll grate your face on the asphalt like a chunk of cheddar.* Mrs. Schwartz finally arrives to investigate further. "Problem?" Kate's behind Mrs. Schwartz, mouthing, "Tell her," but I stay silent.

"No problems here, Mrs. Schwartz," Nicky says. "We just couldn't remember the score."

I look down at the scuffed court and nod to confirm the lie.

"Irrelevant," Mrs. Schwartz says to us and blows her whistle. She yells out "Time!" at the rest of the class, and that's that. We all head back to the locker room. For now, Nicky seems to be over it, but I race ahead to make sure I'm out of there before she changes her mind.

❖

I kick the kitchen door closed behind me and throw my bag on the couch. "I'm home!" I yell as I open the fridge to scan my options. Instead of the almonds and yogurt Mom always suggests, I grab a natural soda and the jar of pickles and head for my room. Maybe my mom will take the hint and not bother me for a while. I rush by the living room and say, "Hi, Mom. Can't talk. Gotta eat. Love you," without looking up.

At first I pick the Tegan and Sara/Ani/Butchies mix that Mia made for me before school got out last year, but I want something harder and louder, so I opt for Sleater Kinney. I put in my earbuds, crank up the volume, and fall back onto my bed. Peace at last.

After thirty minutes of music therapy, I unplug and get to work on some chem homework until there's a knock.

"Abbey Road?" my mom calls from behind my closed door. She always uses my dad's nickname when she thinks I need a little extra love. Sometimes it bugs me because it makes me think of him, but this time, it makes me feel a little better.

I'm in the middle of downing another pickle spear, so I grunt for her to come in.

She peeks her head in. "Is it safe?" she asks and smiles. Her glasses are askew and her long blond hair is up in a tight bun. This is her making-art look, so she must have been at her easel when I speed walked by. "Have you had a chance to digest the live goat I tied to your cage?"

My hunger is a lot easier to explain than the scare I had in PE, so I play along. "Yes, I am subdued for now."

She steps inside my room. "Good girl. You're doing homework."

"Yep." I tap my pencil on my notebook. Something feels awkward. She puts her hands on her hips, assessing my room like she's seeing it for the first time.

I look around, too, making sure I haven't left any hints of gayness out. I think she knows and I think she knows I know she knows, but that's as close as I am to being out to her, so when she acts like this, I freak out and start to sweat. Is this it? Is she finally going to ask me?

I think I'm in the clear, but then she asks, "Is that new?" and points to the Tegan and Sara poster I bought this summer.

"Um, not really." I look at her carefully. "Why?" The poster's hands down the gayest thing in my room, but she would never know that. I mean, it's just two girls standing side by side.

"Oh, I hadn't noticed it, I guess. They're sisters, right?"

How did she know that? And if she knows that, does she also know they're lesbians? Did she Google them? I should have never shown her how to do that. My heart races. I sit up and busy myself folding the clean laundry my mom dumped on my bed earlier today. "Mom, why are you in my room?" I finally dare to ask.

"What. I can't stop by and say hi?"

"Sure. Hi." I wave at her and smile. Yet she lingers on. Okay, maybe she doesn't want me to come out to her, but something is up. She's acting like I do when I want to ask her for something that I'm afraid she'll say no to. "Anything else?"

"Have you been studying for your permit?"

I roll my eyes. I'd almost rather she out me than ask about that damn test again. "Why are you so eager for me to get my license, Mom? I mean, who cares?"

"Abbey, I think you're avoiding it, and I don't want you to be afraid of driving just because…" She sits next to me on my bed. "Your dad would have wanted you to learn how to drive, honey."

She's clever to use the ol' your-dad-would-have-wanted line. Nicely played. Besides, she's right, I've been afraid to get behind the wheel. I know it's stupid, but there it is. He died, so I assume I will, too. "I'll study, Mom. Okay?" I say and grab my chem book to signify that our talk is over.

She pats my leg. "Okay, my Abbey Roo. Dinner in an hour. Taco Tuesdays."

"*Bueno.*"

She shuts the door behind her, and I fall back onto my bed and stare at the map of the US that I tacked up there when I was nine. All the cities I want to visit are circled in red. When I did that, I imagined I'd take a wild cross-country road trip with Kate after our senior year and visit each place. Ha. At the rate I'm going, I'll never even get to Phoenix with her.

I close my chem book and pull the *Arizona Driver License Manual* out of my bedside table. The thought of bumming rides from my mom or riding Suntran for yet another year is enough motivation. That and the insight that Garrett told me at lunch: learning how to drive is like investing in sex insurance. I'm not really sure what she means by this, but I'll take her word for it. Being a junior and the most experienced you-know-who friend I have, she's usually right about these kinds of things.

Chapter Two

Before Garrett pulls her Corolla into our usual spot, she flips off a carload of students for taking too long to get out of her way. "Effing permit driver," she says and yanks up the emergency brake even though there's no risk of rolling down a hill at Gila High, or hardly anywhere else in Tucson for that matter.

I feel the need to defend the new driver who is at least further along than me in his skills. "Hey, we can't all be as good as you at everything, G."

"So true," Garrett says and smiles. She's only a year older than Kate and me and she's on the varsity basketball team instead of JV like us, but her confidence makes her seem like a college student. I bet she would have thrown the first punch if Nicky had been in her face. If not, her girlfriend, Tai, would have done it for her. Yep, Garrett has it all: a car, a girl, sex appeal, and she's out to her mom. I want to be Garrett when I grow up, and I'm sure she knows it.

"So, freshie"—Garrett whips her thick hair into a perfect bun and looks at me—"what are you going to do about Knuckles?"

"Sophomore, remember?" I say pointing to myself.

She shrugs as if there's some doubt. "So, about that idiot bully on your case."

"Oh, we already have that worked out," Kate says as she does some last-minute prep in her compact mirror. "Let's hear the steps one more time, Abbey. Ready? Go."

I flip down the visor and pretend to care what I look like. *Same freckles, different day.* I flip the visor up again. "This whole thing is stupid. I'm sure Nicky is over it."

"Just do what I said," Garrett says. "Tell Ms. Morvay. Problem solved."

"Step one," Kate says loudly from the backseat because she is constantly trying to compete with Garrett. It used to be Kate's advice that I sought, but Garrett's my number one source on all things homo, so she's trumped Kate for the past year. I can tell it drives Kate nuts. "Never go into the locker room alone," Kate continues, as if I am on the edge of my seat. "Step two: do not make eye contact with her no matter what. Step three: if she starts to come at you, run to the nearest classroom. Got it?"

"Yeah, sure, Kate," I say, but Kate is insane if she thinks logic and smart planning are going to protect me from someone who has already served time in juvie.

When the bell rings to signal the start of our school day, Garrett and Kate grab their bags and get out. I don't. Instead I stare glassy-eyed at the brick façade of the school. Each week of our first month of school, the student government kids have hung up giant posters that are supposed to get us excited about waking up at six in the morning and giving up our summers. There's one that says *Go get 'em, Gilas!* and one that says *Welcome back, Monsters!* This morning, however, it reads *Welcome back, Monsterbators!* This would make me laugh on any other morning, but not this morning. I feel fried like a Twinkie at the state fair.

Today's new ASB banner reads *Make this your best year yet!* and I don't know why, but I already feel like I've failed. But maybe it's not too late. After all, I've got 156 days to turn things around.

After getting my books from my locker, I make my way to first period without getting my ass served to me on a platter by Nicky. So the day has had a stellar start, and I award myself two points that mean absolutely nothing. Now I just need to get through chem and my next five classes.

I casually nod at my lab mates and plop down on my assigned stool. They can't tell, but I'm newly resolved that this *will* be my best year yet. Then somewhere between the bell and Mrs. Stum taking roll, I push *play* on a new daydream that has been in my head nonstop since the start of the school year. It's about my mom and me. I tell her I'm a girl-loving girl, and she decides to throw me a coming-out party complete with balloons, cake, and a dance floor so I can make a boldly choreographed entrance to that "I'm Coming Out" song that plays on the old-school music station Mom listens to sometimes. I'm just about to fling a rainbow boa over my head and do the splits when I feel a hand that does not belong in my daydream grab my arm and raise it up for me.

"Here," Jake says in a girly voice while shaking my arm to alert Mrs. Stum. Everyone, except for Mrs. Stum, laughs because it's Jake, and everyone loves Jake. Jake Simpson also happens to be the only boy I've ever come close to going on a date with. He plays guitar a thousand times better than me and has an easy smile and black curly hair that always smells clean. He's probably the nicest guy at Gila, and I'm thankful he doesn't hold my weirdness from last year against me.

"Thanks," I whisper.

He pats my shoulder. "No problem, rock star."

"Are you Abbey Brooks?" Mrs. Stum is looking at me over the rims of her glasses and raising her eyebrows expectantly. Clearly I have made absolutely no impression on her since she still doesn't know who I am. Maybe this is a good thing, though.

"Yes. Sorry. Here."

"In this class, Ms. Brooks, you need to pay attention. There are open flames and chemical reactions, young lady. You could lose an eye. Do you understand?"

"Um, yes," I say. "Sorry, Mrs. Stum." I say her name very slowly with perfect enunciation because I am deathly afraid of calling her Mrs. Dumb instead, since that's how she's referred to outside her classroom. Then I wonder how many kids have actually lost an eye in school because, nine out of ten times, that's the go-to warning we get from the grown-ups here. Where does this irrational fear come from?

"Sorry isn't going to save you from third-degree burns or asphyxiation."

"I understand, Mrs. Stum." Do I say sorry one more time? It can't hurt. "Sorry…again."

She grunts and moves down to the next student on her roll list. "Marcus Cox?" Someone laughs, and Mrs. Stum gives the kid a perfected teacher death stare, taking the heat off me for now.

I look over at Jake to make a face like *What the hell is her problem?* but his head is down and he's intently drawing something. When he's done, he makes sure Mrs. Stum isn't looking our way and passes it to me. The doodle is a stick-figure girl. I assume it's me by the obscene length of her limbs. She's missing an eyeball, which she's holding in her hand. Her hair is on fire. The caption underneath reads: *When good chemistry goes bad.*

I hide my laughter behind my book, fold the drawing, and put it in my back pocket. Things are looking up.

❖

When I see my PE locker at the start of second period, my stomach drops to my knees, and all I can say is, "My mom can never hear about this."

"Abbey…" Kate whispers then stares hard at my locker, as if she's trying to erase the word with her eyes.

She's mortified, and I know it's somewhat for me, but it's mostly for herself. Even though she's moving along on the spectrum of acceptance and actually agreed to ride in the same car with two known you-know-who girls, Kate doesn't linger too long in the halls when Garrett, Tai, and I are together. I mean, I guess I get it, considering how the rumors last year included lies about Kate and me being together. She's straighter than Interstate 10 and always will be, but everyone else around here wants to clump people together in some sort of organized fashion. Maybe I'm guilty of that, too.

"I wonder how many people have seen this," Kate says.

"I don't know, but it's no big deal," I say, so she won't freak out. But let's be honest here. Seeing the word dyke scrawled in giant red permanent marker on your PE locker is at least a medium deal.

Mari, who is one of our Geek Pack friends from middle school, comes over to see if we're ready to walk out to the gym. "*Chale*," she says. "I'll get Mrs. Schwartz."

Even though I'm pretty sure Mrs. Schwartz will find a way to blame me, I don't protest. I mean, I can't just leave it like this.

Other girls are walking by now and whispering. One girl actually takes a pic with her phone and laughs, which feels like bullets from a BB gun—not deadly, but painful enough to leave a lasting mark. I look over at Kate. Her color has shifted to a deep scarlet. I feel guilt settle in my chest.

"You can go, Kate. I'll deal with it," I say because even though she's my BFF, I know she can't take standing here much longer.

"'Kay, I'll see you out there," she says and bolts for the nearest exit.

After Kate makes her escape, Nicky, Naomi, and Rachel stop at the end of my row of lockers. For the second time in one week, I stupidly make eye contact with Nicky; so much for Kate's plan. I don't have anywhere to run, so I hold my ground and stand tall like my dad told me to do when I'm surprised by a dangerous animal in the wild. She stares me down with her arms crossed in front of her, and I wonder how someone who used to wear Hello Kitty socks ends up like this.

A door opens nearby. I pray to the universe to let it be a grown-up.

"Pull that crap on me again," Nicky says before the footsteps round the corner, "and I won't be as nice." Nicky's stupid friends stand behind her and laugh like Scar's hyenas in *The Lion King.*

She takes a step toward me, but then Mrs. Schwartz arrives. I've never been so happy to see a teacher in my life.

"What is the meaning of this, Abbey? I just got these lockers painted last summer." Mrs. Schwartz must have seen all sorts of mean things written on her lockers before, so this one gets no reaction from her. Then she reads it out loud. The word sounds even worse coming from her. "And who did this?" she asks, as if it's a silly prank by one of my teammates or something.

"I don't know, Mrs. Schwartz." Nothing would make me happier than Nicky getting caught, but it's not going to be because I narc'd on her.

"Unacceptable," Mrs. Schwartz barks. Then she turns to Naomi, as if she's somehow qualified to be a locker vandalism investigator. "Did you see who did this?"

"No, ma'am."

"Nicky?"

"Gosh, I have no clue, Mrs. Schwartz. Abbey, you sure you don't have any ideas?"

Mrs. Schwartz flips to a blank paper on her clipboard and writes a note to herself. "Go ahead and get changed, Abbey. I'll let the custodian know. And you girls"—she points at them with her pen—"have exactly five seconds to get on your numbers before I mark you tardy."

After everyone leaves, the echoing silence creeps me out, so I grab my PE uniform from my locker and walk to the bathroom stall to change. Even though I'm still shaken up, I'm relieved because I don't think my mom will find out. It'll be gone by Monday and maybe so will Nicky's grudge.

❖

"Come on, freshie," Garrett says on the other line. "It's Saturday night and I know you don't have other plans." Garrett's right, but that's not the point.

"I'm just really tired, G." This is only partly true. The second part of the truth is that my bedroom is the only place where I feel really safe. Here I can be me entirely. I don't have to pretend to like boys or pretend to care how my hair looks or even pretend to not be as smart as I am. I guess all that pretending gets exhausting.

"Dude, Nicky doesn't even hang out at Cosmos Coffee. And if she does show up, Tai will pounce on her, and I don't mean in a good way. You should have seen how mad she got after I told her about your locker."

"Yeah?" I switch my cell to the other ear and start to doodle just like my mom does when she's on the phone. Instead of my usual flowers and squiggles, I press hard on my paper and draw a bunch of jagged edges, like the mouth of a great white. This could be because the third part of why I don't want to go out with her has finally been introduced, which is that I've managed to develop a slight crush on Tai. But I know I can make it pass. I just need to stay away from her for a while. "So Tai is for sure going to be there?" I ask. "I mean, to protect me."

"Do lesbians collect cats? Do gay boys love their Speedos? Do Republicans…"

"Okay, G. I got it." Now I have to turn her down again without it looking like it's because of Tai being there. "Hang on, let me ask." I drop my cell on my bed but don't leave the room. Instead, I click through the channels on my tiny TV to see if anything good is on. After an appropriate amount of time, I come back to the phone. "Hey, I forgot my mom asked me to help her clean out the garage tonight. Sorry."

"That's lame."

"Yeah, she's totally OCD."

"Well, I bet if your mom knew you were a baby dyke in training, she'd totally understand why you need to hang out with a couple of lezperts like me and Tai."

Dyke sounds a lot better coming from a friend. "Yeah, probably. Maybe I'll come out to her soon. I better go."

"Oh, hey. One more thing, Abs."

"What?" Like a desperate stranger in a new place, I hang on every word Garrett says because sometimes she can say the simplest thing that makes all my worries disappear.

"What do you call a lesbian with big fingers?"

I have a feeling this is not going to be one of those times. "I don't know. What?"

"Well hung." She laughs.

I laugh, too.

Now it's ten o'clock and my Saturday night has consisted of eating Mom's dinner, which was some veggie-meat pronounced Satan, and I think I know why, alternating between *Teen Mom* and old-school '90s sitcoms on TV Land, and lounging on my bed reading my assigned pages from *Julius Caesar* for honors English. I'm in the middle of another endless soliloquy, barely able to understand what Cassius is pontificating about, when I hear the sound of crunching gravel outside my window. I freeze and stare at my shutters. My stomach tenses. The last time I heard footsteps out there was in June when Keeta came by for a final visit. It's not easy getting over your first love, especially when she's the hottest, most romantic, yet most unbelievably impossible person to figure out, but I somehow managed to ignore her at my window the last time she knocked. Do I have the strength to blow Keeta off again? I'm thinking no. But am I ready to see her? Up until this moment, I thought I was, but this simple sound is making me doubt everything. The idea that it could be a rapist or a rabid coyote crosses my mind, and part of me hopes that I find one of these two possibilities rather than her beautiful smile.

"Are you there?" a girl whispers.

My body shifts into hyper-sweat mode. Was that her voice? It's been months, but I'm pretty sure it was, or am I hoping? I adjust my ponytail and crawl across my bed. I grab hold of the shutters' handles and brace myself for our first face-to-face since we last said good-bye.

CHAPTER THREE

O uch! Damn cactus."
Relief and disappointment hit me at once. "Mia?"

"You were expecting Ellen DeGeneres?"

"No," I whisper, "I was just…I'm just surprised to see you. Did you take the bus?" I don't dare tell her who I was expecting. She never liked the idea that I was dating Keeta, or whatever Keeta called what we were doing. Maybe I should have gone on a date with Mia when she asked me out in study hall last year and saved myself from the Keeta drama, but now we're friends—good friends. It would be too weird, I think.

She tries to move closer to the window but her shirt gets caught on an ocotillo stem. "Geez, how the hell did Keeta get so much action from this window?"

"Screw you, Mia."

"Aww, too soon?"

"Whatever," I say but think yes.

Mia detaches herself from the prickly plants that stand guard outside my room and casually leans her elbows on the windowsill. I can see her face now and it's a refreshing sight. Her blond hair is short and spiky again, the tips are pink, and her nose piercing winks at me when the light from my room hits the gem.

"I know I didn't make a reservation," she says slyly, "but I thought I'd show up to see if there was room in your orgy for one more."

"Gross, Mia. But seriously, what are you doing here? I called your house a million times since school started, but the number was disconnected."

"Yep. We're back at my sister's. Thank God. So I'm a Gila monster again. Go, Gila," she says with a hand gesture meant to mock the cheerleaders. Then she gets serious again. "Don't get me wrong, though, I'd do a cheerleader."

I nod in agreement.

We both ponder that idea for a second, and then she asks, "Anyway, what are you doing?"

I look over my shoulder because I think I hear my mom, but it's way past ten and I know she's already probably dozed off watching *The Daily Show*. "Reading *Julius Caesar*. Why?"

"Get dressed and come out with us."

I look out into the night to see who this *us* is, but she appears to be alone. That's beside the point, though. I'm pretty sure my mom would seriously ground me until graduation if she caught me sneaking out. "Can't. I'm trying this new thing where I don't get in trouble until I get at least one semester of school under my belt."

"Unacceptable," Mia says, impersonating Mrs. Schwartz perfectly. "Now saddle up the horse and giddyap, cowgirl."

Stupidly, I actually consider it. My mom does sleep harder than cement, but there's a slim possibility that she might wake up and check in on me. It would totally freak her out if I was gone. Plus, I don't feel like socializing with strangers. "Umm…"

Mia presses her head against the screen. "Aww. You're wearing that Ani tank I gave you last year? Still looks great on you."

I cross my arms over my chest because I'm not wearing a bra, not that it would make much difference. "Flattery will get you nowhere, Mia. You're insane if you think I'm coming with you to do God knows what with your invisible friends."

"Oh, Abbey," she says and shakes her head, like I'm the crazy one here. "The best memories I have are of doing the things I shouldn't do. I'm willing to bet it's the same for you."

She's got me there.

"I'll have you back by midnight."

"I could get into so much trouble."

"On the flip side, you could have the time of your life."

"Midnight?"

"Not a second later, Cinderella. I promise." Then she sticks out her lower lip. "I miss you."

With that simple declaration, she activates the part of my ego that makes all my mom guilt wash away. "I hate you. Let me get dressed." I close the shutters for privacy and grab the clothes I wore today from the hamper. As I slip on my shorts, though, I have a moment of hesitation. Why should I risk it? I had to work overtime to get my mom to trust me after my craptastic academic performance last year. I look over at my report cards that I posted on my closet door as a reminder of my journey from failing loser back to straight A student. I should at least leave a note.

> *Mom, don't freak out. I went out with a friend who really needed me. I'll be back by midnight.*
> *Love,*
> *Your Abbey Road*

That should help, I tell myself, but my worry is not waning. "Mia?" I whine.

"Yeah?" she says from behind the shutter.

I almost say, *I can't*, but the truth is I've missed Mia and wouldn't mind getting out into the night air to get my mind off everything. "I really, really hate you, Mia." I turn off my light and remove the screen. "Move over. I'm coming out."

"It's about time," Mia says and holds out her hand to assist me on my dismount from the window.

Even though I have loads of experience sneaking people—well, one person—into my room, I'm new to sneaking out. This is why I nearly get a cactus to my face and then trip on the water spout poking out of the house. I fall hard on my knee.

After Mia manages to stop laughing, she helps me up and we run away like escaped convicts until we slam into the side of a red car, parked four houses down the block. I don't know if it's the laughter filling my lungs or the quick jog to the car, but I feel exhilarated.

Mia opens the passenger-side door, pulls the front seat forward, and pushes me in the back. I fall onto a girl I don't know. I know it's a girl because one of my hands lands on her breast and the other slips between her legs. "Oh my God!" I shout and quickly reel in my long arms like fishing line. "Jesus, Mia!" I shove the front seat where she's sitting. "I'm so sorry," I say to the girl and try to take up as little space as possible in the backseat.

"She said sorry, Dev," Mia says, and in the light from the streetlamp I can see Mia using sign language as she talks.

The girl I just hand-mauled is deaf? For some reason, this makes me feel even more embarrassed.

The girl laughs and says, "That's okay," to me. Her voice is definitely different, but easy to understand.

"Well, aren't you special? Dev doesn't usually talk to strangers," Mia says.

The girl sticks out her hand to shake mine. "Devin."

"Abbey!" I yell as I take her hand.

"Dude," Mia says to me, "she's deaf. You do understand what that means, right?"

"Oh God. Sorry. I just…" I say to Devin and then scowl at Mia. I want to melt into my seat and disappear.

"I have a feeling I know what sign I need to teach you first," Mia teases. "Here it is," she says and then shows me a sign. "Sorry. Got it?"

I try it out. "Like this?"

"Yep, that's it."

I turn to Devin and sign my first sign since learning the manual alphabet and a few basic signs in third grade. She signs something back, and from her barely visible facial expression I can tell I am forgiven.

"Other intros," Mia says and flips on the dome light in the car.

Devin's face is fully illuminated now and I'm embarrassed all over again because:

1. I feel like a moron for yelling at her.
2. She is unbelievably cute.
3. I've already been to second, maybe even third base with her.

"Hi," I say to Devin and wave.

She pushes her wavy brown hair back behind her ear, tilts her head, smiles, and waves back.

Oh, how easy I fall.

"Yes, you've met my cousin already," Mia says, grabbing my head and positioning it so I look forward. Mia pats the head of the red-haired girl sitting in the middle of the front bench seat. "This is Shortie."

"Howdy," Shortie says and stretches her arm back toward me and we shake hands. She's wearing sunglasses even though it's dark out.

"And, of course," Mia continues, "Shortie's main squeeze and our driver, Diego."

Diego turns around slightly. "What's up?" he says with a nod.

"Not much," I say, trying to be cool.

"All right, let's go," Diego says. Then he asks Mia, "Any cars in front of us?"

"Nope. You're golden."

"How far to the stop sign again?"

My eyes widen. Wait. What's going on?

"About fifty feet, Captain," Mia says.

"Got it," he says and starts the engine.

"All buckled in?" Mia asks me.

I grab the ragged lap belt and frantically feel around for the buckle, accidentally groping Devin's butt in the process, solidifying my third-base status. I can't find anything to click into, so I wrap the belt around me and sit on its end as if this clever move will save my life in a head-on collision. Then thinking of head-on collisions makes me think of my dad. And now I'm thinking about my mom. I can't go out like this. She wouldn't survive losing us both. If this is some sick hint from the universe to study for my permit test, I get it. Message received.

Mia signs something to Devin and they have a good laugh, but I can't imagine what could possibly be funny at this moment. I wish I were back on my bed with *Julius Caesar*. No one ever died or even lost an eye while reading Shakespeare, I'm sure of it. I try to think of some excuse for why I need to jump out of this deathtrap but can't think of a polite way to say I prefer not to be driven across town by a blind guy. I need to say something, but my throat has closed up and all I can do is scrunch up my face like I'm about to descend from the scariest roller coaster on the planet. I only open my eyes when I hear Shortie talk.

"She freaking out, Mia?" Shortie asks, as if she can feel the shift of anxiety in the car. "They always do the first time. If it makes you feel better, Abbey, he's just barely legally blind."

Mia looks at me, then says and signs, "I didn't think she could get any whiter. I was wrong."

Diego seems more sympathetic to my stress, however. "I promise you, Abbey. This isn't our first time at the rodeo. We've got this down to an art." I appreciate his reassurance but still have my hand on the back of Mia's seat, ready to push it forward and escape.

Then Devin signs something to me, and I shake my head because I have no idea what she's saying. I look to Mia for help.

"She said you're safe."

"Why don't one of you drive?" I whisper to Mia, forgetting that most blind people can usually hear quite well, actually.

"Oh, Dev's dad won't let her learn because he's an asshole."

Devin nods in agreement.

"And," Mia continues, "I'm not allowed to touch the wheel after the Whataburger drive-thru incident last summer."

"What a disaster," Diego mutters. "Never again."

"Exactly," Shortie adds.

Mia shrugs her shoulders. "I'm more of a verbal driver, I guess."

"I can't do this, Mia. I'm sorry." The only thing keeping me from crying is I'm sitting next to Devin. Had I not been instantly attracted to her, I'd be sobbing.

"Dude," Mia says. "How about this? We'll drive three blocks. If you still think you're gonna die, I'll let you out. You can walk home. Deal?"

In the most messed-up way, it seems like a good compromise. Then Devin nods at me as if to say *fair deal*.

"Okay," I finally say, then add, "no offense to you, Diego," because the last thing I want to do, besides die in a car crash, is insult someone I just met.

"None taken. Ready, Mia?" Diego puts the car in drive.

She turns off the dome light. "Clear for takeoff."

The car begins to roll forward as Diego accelerates.

We drive pass Mr. Mulvaney's house, and then the Hazens', and then the Clarkes' and hope they don't see us and call my mom.

Mia starts to give more directions. "Slowing down, Diego…stop sign in twenty feet…ten…and…stop."

I swallow down my screams as he approaches the stop sign, but he stops right where he's supposed to. I guess this really isn't their first time, but I still feel compelled to backseat drive and ask, "We're not taking Grant, are we?"

"Abs," Mia says after giving Shortie the go ahead to put the right blinker on, "we got this. Trust me, okay?"

I say okay because of all the friends I have, I think I trust Mia the most. She's never lied to me or slept with my girlfriend or made me feel stupid for being new at this whole liking-girls thing. I take a deep breath and fake a smile at Devin. I can see that Mia, Shortie, and Diego are a good team. Mia gives the orders, while Diego works the gas and brake pedals and steering wheel. Shortie's job is to operate the blinker. Devin gives me an A-OK sign and I relax a little, but that doesn't mean I'm not imagining the KGUN 9 Sunrise News story about five stupid teenagers who thought it was a good idea to have a barely legally blind guy drive.

"So, are you in or out?" Mia asks as we idle at the third block, my last chance to escape.

I swallow the lump in my throat. "I'm...in."

As we drive across town, taking side streets as much as possible, the only sounds in the car are Mia giving directions and Shortie giggling every time she works the blinker. Then Devin taps my shoulder.

"Hi," I sign again because that's all I've got besides sorry and the few signs for animals and school supplies, but I'm guessing monkeys and pencils aren't going to come up naturally in our conversation tonight.

She pulls out her cell phone and raises her eyebrows as if to ask if I have one, too. I do, but I forgot it in my hasty escape. I shake my head and sign, "Sorry."

Devin types me a message on her phone and hands it to me. *You look familiar. Where do you go to school?*

Gila High. You look a familiar, too, I type back, though it's a lie. I would definitely remember seeing her before. *Where do you go to school?*

ASDB. I thought that was pretty obvious. LOL.

I guess she's right. I should've figured out that she, Diego, and Shortie are all students at the Arizona Schools for the Deaf and Blind.

"Turn it left about fifteen degrees," Mia says to Diego. "Give me five more. Two more. Good. Stay there. Ten degrees right. Okay, big curve coming up."

I look up from Devin's cell when I hear this and think about how sad it is that I'll die a virgin.

The car begins its path on the sharp curve, and I'm unable to contain my fear any longer. "Oh my God!" I drop Devin's phone, and then without meaning to, I grab her leg. My other hand is gripping my unfastened belt, so there's no way to sign *sorry* this time.

Instead of pushing my hand away, though, Devin holds it tight until we make it through the curvy part.

"Twenty right. Go to fifteen," Mia directs. "Ease out now...easy, okay. Perfect. Approaching a red light, D. Slower, slower, easy now, and stop."

Devin releases my hand and starts to type again. *It's scary the first few times, but once you get used to it, it's pretty cool.*

I'm not sure if my heart is pounding because of my death-defying experience or because of Devin's comforting touch. Either way, my hands are too sweaty to type back, so I nod and smile.

"You okay, Abbey?" Mia says after helping Diego park the car in front of Coffee X-Change.

"Uh-oh, did she pass out?" Diego asks.

I clear my throat. "I'm fine, thank you very much." Mia releases the front seat and I crawl out. I almost collapse once my feet hit the asphalt, so I grab hold of Mia until I get my land legs back. "I hate you." Mia laughs. "Doubt it."

Diego's cane snaps open and I look over. "Queen Shortie," he says, offering his hand to help Shortie out of the car. She laughs and takes his hand and I'm envious that they have each other. Will I ever be with someone who loves me like Diego seems to love Shortie? I hope so. It's what I want more than anything.

Mia throws one arm around my shoulder and her other around Devin's. "Let's get our grub on, ladies."

We are quite a posse of misfit teenagers walking into the crowded café. The place is packed, but we get lucky and snag a table in the corner. I'm the last to take a seat, so it's just a happy coincidence that the last spot is next to Devin. She scoots over, and I squeeze in next to her on the red vinyl seat.

I know some deaf people can read lips, so I say, "Thanks," in a normal voice. I think she understands me because she signs something that seems like, "You're welcome."

Mia and Devin open their menus and I do the same. "She's not one of us, Abs," Mia says from behind her menu. "So you can stop smiling at her like an idiot."

The heat from my face could have melted the polar ice caps. I open my mouth to defend myself, but I only end up saying half of *whatever*, combined with a weird hissing sound, so it comes out, "Wha-*pshhh*."

"Mia, be nice to our guest," Diego chimes in while pretending to wipe his face with his napkin. "It's an honest mistake."

"Well, I thought I felt some chemistry coming from the backseat," Shortie adds.

Mia rolls her eyes.

Meanwhile, Devin is hidden behind her menu deciding on her late-night snack, and I am dying of humiliation.

"I think I know my cousin better than all of you."

I finally manage to say, "Got it, Mia. Don't get mad."

The waitress finally comes over. Devin looks up from her menu and signs her order to Mia, who tells it to the waitress. Diego, Shortie, and Mia order a plate of nachos to share and three shakes. I order a chili fry, but can't decide on a drink. "Um, and I'll have the…" I quickly look at my options.

Devin taps my shoulder and she's pointing to the Donnie Darko. She raises her eyebrows and points to me, then at herself, making it obvious she wants to share.

I nod, but then look over at Mia. She's glaring at me with her arms crossed.

For a split second I consider defying Mia, but because I've got the backbone of a newborn, I say, "Actually, I think I want a Rico Suave Strawberry instead," and point to it on the menu. Devin shrugs and signs Mia to order her the coffee drink.

After the waitress leaves, there is a lull in signing and conversation. I feel a compulsion to fill the void. "What's it like going to school at ASDB?"

Mia, who seems to have recovered from hating me, helps with translations.

I find out that Devin's been going there since she was ten. She stays there during the week, and then her mom or dad—they live in Green Valley—comes to get her for the weekends. Diego and Shortie started boarding there when they went into ninth grade. It blows my mind that they get to live in dorms like college students. No parents. No chores. What a relief that would be. Then Mia starts to retell and sign an entertaining story about how Shortie and Diego snuck out of their dorms to secretly meet, but then accidentally ended up walking into the teachers' lounge.

Our food arrives and while everyone adds their condiments, Devin secretly hands her cell to me under the table. *So, do you play on Mia's team?*

I stare at the message and panic. Is she talking about basketball or something else? Wouldn't she know that Mia doesn't play basketball? But Mia and I did both run track last year, and track is a team. But you don't really *play* track. Urgh, what does this mean? One bad thing about this crazy-making gay world is there are a thousand codes for everything. Like, if you want to know if a girl you're checking out is a lesbian, you could ask, Is she family? Or, Does she have her scuba-diving certification? Maybe, Does she work on cars? If Garrett were here, she'd be slapping the back of my head and saying, "Come on, freshie, she's so obviously a cow!" But Mia said she wasn't, and Mia would know.

The lock of hair between my fingers is getting tangled from my twirling, so I type the only thing I can think of saying: *Do you?* I slide the cell back to her.

She reads it and raises an eyebrow, but before she has a chance to write back, Mia starts to sign to her. While they chat, Shortie and Diego fold me into a debate they're having about how tuna make babies. Shortie thinks there's a nest of some sort, like in *Finding Nemo*. And she's positive there's no way they go at it like dogs—too slippery. Diego is convinced, however, that the two fish find a cozy, slow-moving current and hold on to each other's fins until the deed is done. Thanks to my recent binge on Discovery Channel's *The Ocean*, I know the truth, but I keep it to myself. Their theories are much more fascinating.

Mia gets Devin caught up on our conversation, and Devin laughs so hard her mocha almost shoots out her nose. When she recovers, she signs something to Mia.

"Diego, Dev wants to know if there's romantic music in the current, too. To help them, you know, get in the mood."

"Sure, the whales are harmonizing nearby," Diego says with a straight face. Devin laughs again, which makes me laugh, too.

After that we get on a would-you-rather tangent.

"Would you rather be rich, famous, and lonely or poor with great friends?" Diego asks.

We all agree that friends trump fame and money.

"Would you rather be Spider-Man or Superman?" Shortie asks.

Only Devin and I choose Spider-Man so obviously we are meant to be together. Then an image of Devin in a tight Spidey suit pops into my brain. She does have great legs and, from what I felt in the car, a nice butt, too.

"Your turn, Abbey," Diego says, jolting me out of my fantasy.

I think hard, but the only thing that comes to mind is *Would you rather kiss a girl or a boy?* because that's all I really want to know about Devin right now. Instead, I ask, "Would you rather die from a bee swarm or an alligator attack?"

"Geez," Mia says. "Talk about a buzzkill."

"Oh, I see what you did there," Diego says and laughs.

"Sorry, that was a dumb one," I say.

"Definitely alligator attack," Shortie says, trying to make me feel better. "The sound of the bees would drive me crazy."

During the ride home, I am less frightened but even more awkward sitting next to Devin. She doesn't attempt to talk to me via her cell phone. In fact, she looks out the window the whole time, and I feel like

I totally blew it with my stupid message. She was obviously talking about basketball, Abbey.

At exactly 11:59, Mia walks me over to my window to give me a boost in.

"Thanks, Mia. You were right. Good times were had."

"Yeah, I can tell. Remember, I know how you look when you flirt."

"Whatever." I push her shoulder. "I wasn't flirting. But since you brought it up…" I lean on the windowsill to look more casual.

"Dude, I already told you. She's, like, in love with that vampire actor and talks about boys all the time. She's seriously straight, so drop it."

"Okay, okay. Well, thanks again, Mia." I hug her good-bye. "You always bring out the delinquent in me, and that's why I love you so."

I step on her knee, but being the Amazon that I am, I don't need too much help getting into my window. I wriggle my way through and fall on my bed, but not before knocking my lamp and alarm clock off my bedside table.

"Smooth," Mia says.

"I'm fine. Thanks for asking." I pick up the window screen and secure it in place.

I change back into my tank top and boxers and peek out my bedroom door to make sure my mom isn't up. It's dark and quiet in the house. I'm safe.

Since majorly screwing up last year, I'm not allowed to have my computer in my room, so I tiptoe down the hall and into my dad's old office to check my account before bed. I'm not addicted to it like most of my friends, but once in a while I sneak a peek even though I usually only get messages from Kate. Tonight she wrote, *Abbey, why aren't you answering your damn cell. Call me. It's urgent. I am in love.* I roll my eyes. When isn't she in love?

But then I see something I don't get too often: a friend request. I click on the tab and there she is. The picture shows off her beautiful— and, I'm assuming, super soft—brown hair, hazel eyes, and that smile that will be forever imprinted on my brain. Devin Carter wants to be my friend. I click accept and write, *Thanks for the add. I had a lot of fun with you tonight*, but then take off the last part in an attempt to appear nonchalant and mature. Then I click through her pictures to see if they tell me more about her. It's mostly just Devin with other girls, but that doesn't mean anything. I also find a picture of that actor who was in *Twilight*, whatever his name is, with Devin's comment next to it: *So hot!* I deflate a little. Could she be bi like Garrett? I search a little more. Then, halfway through her list of likes, I find a major clue. She likes the movie *But I'm a Cheerleader*, which is only the sweetest, sexiest girl-meets-girl movie I have ever seen.

Maybe Mia's wrong about her cousin, and maybe my gaydar was right. Maybe, just maybe.

CHAPTER FOUR

"There are three basic ways to come out, Abs," Garrett says after she's gulped down half her orange Gatorade, "so listen carefully." It's almost October, a week before basketball practice starts, and we're resting on a patch of yellow grass next to the outdoor basketball courts at Gila. It was her idea to start conditioning for the season early, so she showed up at my door at nine this morning and demanded I get dressed. I'd much rather be in my pj's and reading in bed. Yet here I am.

Garrett rolls up her T-shirt sleeves to avoid a farmer's tan, then continues. "First, there's the right way."

"You mean the way you did it?" I don't remember asking for Garrett's advice on how to come out to my mom, but that's how these conversations with Garrett usually go—unsolicited advice is her favorite kind to give me.

"Shut it and listen to me, freshie. Second—"

"You don't get to call me that anymore."

"Then don't act like one," G says snottily, just like a junior would.

"And you can stop with your list," I say, looking at her through my squinted eyes. The sun is already frying us like two strips of bacon sizzling in a pan. "I know the right way. The right way would be I tell my mom I'm a little ol' lezzie on my own terms. Been there, failed miserably."

I really have tried a million times, but as soon as I open my mouth, the words won't come. The last time this happened, Mom was at her easel and I was on the couch. We hadn't fought in over two days, and the glow in the house from the sunset combined with a Hallmark movie marathon playing in the background really seemed to set the scene for a great coming-out moment. So I leaned over the back of the couch and said, "Mom, there's something I need to tell you." But the second she looked up at me with what seemed like hope in her eyes, I chickened out and said, "I really don't like that tofu thing you made last night." Her disappointment was obvious and I felt like the worst daughter in the world. Not because I lied—that tofu crap was awful—but because I could tell she thought it would be a great moment for me to come out, too.

"And then there's the wrong way," Garrett continues as if I'm still listening.

And I am, even though now I'm thinking about Devin again. This morning I raced to the computer to see if she messaged me. She hadn't, but she did comment on my profile pic, which is a picture I posted of six-year-old me dressed up as Laura Ingalls from *Little House on the Prairie*. Devin said I looked super cute and that I should wear my hair in braids like that all the time, which of course is why I'm sitting here now in two long braids. Maybe I should ask her for her number and we can text. But then again, my mom got me the cheapest texting plan available, so I probably wouldn't get too far that way either.

"Now, the wrong way would be your mom catching you in a big gay lie or, worse, catching you mid-mack with a *mujer*."

My stomach sinks and I make a face as I remember how I was almost caught when Keeta accidentally fell asleep in my bed after sneaking in my window one night last year. Thank God I locked my bedroom door before we dozed off, and thank an-even-bigger God that I had a large enough closet to hide my lesbian non-girlfriend in. But considering I haven't dated since my heart was crushed last spring, I'm not too worried about this one. Garrett likes to remind me, though, that despite my freakish growth spurt this summer, which only served to enhance my Gumby body shape and Shaggy strut, I am bound to find another girl to hook up with. I have my doubts. First of all, where would I actually meet someone new? I already know all the lesbians at Gila and am friends with all of them. Maybe that's why I'm too eager to flirt with Devin. Then there's the underlying fear/hope quandary: maybe this whole *I'm a lesbian* was a one-time thing. It's not like I've had sex with a girl. What exactly makes you gay anyway? Is it the feelings or the acts? Does making out count, or do you have to go all the way to earn your lezification?

"Thirdly," Garrett says and shoves her three fingers in my face to make sure I'm listening.

I push them away. "No one cares," I say and get up before I get too itchy from the sweat and grass combo. But if there's one thing Garrett knows about me, it's that I care.

"Thirdly"—she grabs her basketball and dribbles it as we walk onto the court—"there's the dumb way. Or as I like to call it, the Abbey way."

I reach out to try and get the ball, but she does a quick spin move and bounces it between her legs to her other hand. "You're slower than my grandma, Abs." She passes it between her legs a couple more times to show off, then goes back to a simple dribble. "Anyway, the Abbey way is when you continue on like you have been, and maybe, just maybe, if the obvious can't be ignored any longer, your mom will be forced to ask you directly and then…" She shoots a three over my head.

I jump to try and block her shot but miss. I get the rebound and pass the ball to Garrett since she sank the shot, and finish her sentence. "And then I'll say, *Why yes, Mom. I am gay. Thanks for asking. Let's get ice cream!*" I try to block her second shot and miss again. "I wish it were that easy, G."

"Well, if you ask me—"

I put my fingers in my ears, close my eyes, and scream, "I can't hear you!"

When I finally stop screaming, she says, "And you wonder why I still call you freshie? Anyway, forget I said anything. It's your life. Ruin it at your leisure. Who am I? I mean, I'm just trying to help."

I have the ball now and attempt to dribble, but I'm about as graceful as Margo Dydek. "It's not knowing that for sure everything is going to be okay between us once I say it. That's the part that freaks me out. You're lucky your mom is so cool. She doesn't care at all."

Garrett shrugs. "There's a difference between not caring that I'm gay and not caring about me in general, Abs."

I shoot a jump shot and then look at her. "What do you mean? She even let Tai move in with you."

"Yeah, my mom let my obsessive girlfriend move in to my bedroom without even asking me what I wanted."

"Really?"

"Yeah, they decided it one day when I was at practice and Tai showed up at our door with a trash bag full of clothes after her stepmom kicked her out."

"I thought you liked having her there."

"It was fun for, like, a month, but now I feel like I'm married. And it's not like we get to have sex whenever we want or anything. Or, like, ever. I mean, my mom's room is across the hall."

The idea of having sex in my house with my mom in the room next to me gives me the ickies. No, thanks. But then where would I have sex? Doesn't *everyone* have a parent in the next room? And my mom works at home. Things do not look hopeful for me. Plus, I always fantasize that my first time will be on a rose-petaled, satin-covered bed with candlelight dancing on the walls and soft mood music in the background. Maybe I should lower my expectations.

"I mean, we used to do it like three times a week, at least."

Is that a lot? I wonder, too embarrassed to ask. It sure sounds like a lot of sex to have.

"But now," Garrett continues, "I'm coming down with a bad case of blue ovaries. Seriously."

Oh no. Thoughts of having sex with Tai are flooding my brain. So instead of thinking about things that are forbidden, I wonder exactly what blue ovaries means, but there's no way I'm asking about that either. "That sucks," I finally say and take a shot from the top of the key. I brick it because I can't concentrate on basketball and sex at the same time.

Garrett dribbles the ball to the three-point line again. "Anyway, I can't ask her to move out. She has nowhere to go."

"Oh," I say and remind myself that things aren't always as easy as they seem. "So what are you—" I am interrupted when Garrett rushes up to me.

"How do I look? Not too sweaty, right? My hair good? Teeth?" She exposes all her teeth at me, and I quickly inspect them.

"You're good." I have never, ever, ever seen Garrett worry about how she looks, so I look over my shoulder to see who's coming our way but only see a couple of the boys' varsity basketball players walking toward the court. "Why do you care? What's—"

"Just don't say anything stupid," she whispers to me and then drives around me to shoot a layup. She makes it, of course.

The guys are on the court now. One is Bryan, a guy from my chem class, so I nod to him and he nods back. The other I don't know, but it seems like Garrett does because she bounce passes her ball to him. I get instantly annoyed. I don't want to share the court or Garrett.

He catches the pass and easily palms the smaller girl-ball. "What's up, Garrett," the dude says as he spins the ball on his finger, like it's hard or something. "You up for a game?" I look at Garrett to share a look of *oh, please*, but she's smiling.

"You're on." Then she turns to me. "Abbey, you take Bryan. I'll get Jordan, 'kay?"

What the *what* is happening here? Why is *she* acting so stupid? I stare at her, making sure I give no visible commitment to a pickup game.

Jordan takes off his shirt. He's built like the Greek-god-like gay guys in *Out* magazine, and even I can't help but be slightly wowed. Then I realize there's a half-naked guy who appears to be trying to impress us. But why? I mean, we're just a couple of girly gays over here. He must know that, right? Everyone else knows it.

"Any chick rules we should know about?" he asks after tossing his shirt on the half court line.

I find my voice finally and turn to Bryan to tell him my only rule. "Take off your shirt and I am out of here."

He salutes me.

"Good," I say quietly. It's not like playing with guys is new to me, but their bodies are hard, more sweaty, and less predictable than a girl's, and I don't like it. Plus there's the part where I feel like they're just trying to cop a feel when they play defense on me.

"Yeah. We have a few rules," Garrett says. "First, don't go easy on us. We play girls twice your size who could pulverize you on the way to the hoop."

Jordan raises his eyebrows, but then nods. "All right. Cool."

"And"—Garrett marches over to him and smacks her ball out of his hands and kicks it onto the grass—"we use the guy ball, so you won't have any excuses when we beat you."

"Oh, okay. That's how it is?" Jordan asks, and then he and Bryan bust up laughing.

"Last rule," Garrett says, then peels off her shirt and tosses it on the grass. Now she's standing in her hot pink sports bra, and the three of us are all stunned into a state of stupid until she speaks again. "No cheap fouls," Garrett says with both hands on her hips.

"Oh, I think we can guarantee a clean game." Jordan looks to Bryan and so do I. His look says, *We got this in the bag, bro*, but my look is saying something like, *Touch me and die.* At least, that's the translation I hope Bryan makes.

Meanwhile, back in Abbeyland, I'm wondering if Garrett's horny home situation is playing a role in her willingness to not only play with, but flirt with, Jordan.

"First to fifteen," Garrett says and checks the ball to Jordan.

"Sounds good to me," Jordan says and bounce passes it back.

No one asks me how many points I think we should play to, so I take my position in front of Bryan, avoiding touching him like he's contagious. He does the same when he defends me. And the whole time we play, I'm wondering what Garrett is up to and if I should feel bad for being a part of it.

We lose by ten, but Garrett looks more satisfied than I have seen her in a while. And as we walk away from the courts, Garrett fully clothed again, I officially feel guilty, especially when she makes me swear not to tell Tai about how she asked for Jordan's number, and how I swear I won't.

❖

"As far as underhanded mom moves go, I think this is your best work yet," I say to my mom as we wait in line at the DMV.

"You've studied that book long enough, Abbey Road. It's time to take the test."

I sigh. "What's next? Are you orchestrating an arranged marriage, too?" Despite my anger with her for forcing me to get my driver's permit, I'm also relieved. She's right; it's about time I grow up. Of course, saying you're right to my mom would be as dangerous as saying it to Kate.

I pass with 100 percent and am awarded a blue piece of paper that says I can practice with other licensed drivers. In my opinion, this is probably the most dangerous piece of paper they hand out to teenagers, but who knows. Maybe I'll be a natural.

Two blocks away from our house, my mom pulls over. "Okay, show me what you got, kid."

I stare at her. "Sorry. Huh?"

"You've been taking driver's ed. Come on, your turn." She unbuckles her seat belt and gets out. She's at my door, and before I can protest, she drags me out and takes my place.

I cross my arms and refuse to move, but then she reaches over and honks the horn. She knows I hate to draw attention to myself, so it's a smart move on her part.

"You're evil," I say as I buckle myself in. "You'd give Mrs. Stum a run for her money, and that's no compliment, Mom."

"Foot on the brake," she says, apparently ignoring me, "and then ease it into drive."

I take a deep breath to accept my failure at winning this battle. "I know," I say as if I didn't forget, then wipe my sweaty palms on my jeans before gripping the gear shift and sliding it down to drive. Then we sit there, car idling, going nowhere fast.

My mom takes a calming breath. "It's going to be okay," she says, I think to me, but maybe to herself. I'm probably not instilling the most confidence in her. "Whenever you're ready, Abbey Road," my mom says in her most encouraging voice, but all I hear is *hurry the hell up, Abbey.*

I wipe my hands again and grab the wheel as if I'm holding it in place. My knuckles turn white.

Then my phone rings. I reach for it, but my mom beats me to it. "We talked about this, Abbey. No phones in reaching distance when you're behind the wheel." She silences it and tosses it on the backseat.

"Can you at least tell me who it was?" I look in the rearview mirror, trying to get a glimpse of a name on the screen, a name that perhaps starts with *K*. Maybe Kate?

"Abbey, I'm right here. I'll always be here," my mom says and reassuringly pats my shoulder. "You can do this. I know you can."

She's smiling and nodding. I have to trust her. And maybe I should learn to trust myself.

I very carefully release the brake. We move forward slowly and I apply the gas, but since we're still half on the gravel driveway, we spin out slightly. I freak out and slam on the brakes. My mom grabs hold of the door and the roof but still manages a smile. "Good, honey. Maybe press down a little slower on the gas next time."

I'm laughing because the alternative is hysterical crying. "Got it, Mom," I say once I catch my breath. "Here we go…" I press down the gas, slower this time, and the Volvo accelerates at a normal rate down our street. "Like this?" I ask for reassurance.

She's released the oh-crap bar and the door. "Perfect, honey. Ready to turn right?"

"Yep." But I don't take my foot off the gas. I flash to my first ride with Diego, Shortie, and Mia as my pilots. It was at this stop sign that I was given the choice to stick it through or abandon ship. I stayed.

But why did I stay that night? Just because Devin was cute, or was it because Mia said I could trust her?

"Abbey, slow down," she yells, but I'm already turning.

As far as distractions go, my phone has nothing on my brain. I guess that's why I take the turn too fast and hit the curb hard with the two wheels on my mom's side. "Sorry," I yell back and slam on the brakes.

She tries to calm down but fails. "You need to pay attention to your speed, Abbey. Driving is serious."

"Mom, I know, okay? I'm sorry."

"People can get hurt," she says, her voice still raised.

But it's all I can take, so I throw the car in park and get out. "Fine, you drive!" I start walking down the street. I don't want her to see me cry.

A minute later she pulls up alongside me. "Abbey, honey, I'm sorry. Get in the car."

I wipe the tears off my face. "No, I wouldn't want to hurt you."

"I'm sorry. Let's try again."

Mr. Mulvaney waves at me as I walk by. I wave, but inside I'm dying of embarrassment as my mom and I, the two-woman parade, make our way down my street.

I stop walking and she stops next to me. "I'm getting in, but I'm not driving ever again," I say but don't really mean it. What I mean is I'm never driving with her.

CHAPTER FIVE

The bell just rang for first period, and I'm stuck in a bathroom stall on the second floor with an unexpectedly heavy gift from Mother Nature—we're talking massacre—and no tampons. There isn't a scrap of toilet paper in the whole place, and the school doesn't let us have paper towels anymore since the Great Paper Towel Incident last year.

Texting someone is out of the question because they'll probably get their phone confiscated, thus leaving me in here, still trapped. I could wait for someone to come in, but the chances are pretty slim since I chose the bathroom that no one ever uses because, even after a year and two months of being at Gila under my belt, I really hate going to the bathroom here.

I could try to race to another bathroom, but there's a good chance I'll get caught by the hall supervisors who are utterly unsympathetic. Then I'll be escorted to chem, where I will bleed out and die of shame.

I consider calling my mom, but then I picture her walking into the office and announcing in her proud-to-be-a-woman voice that she has tampons for her daughter, Abbey Brooks.

I dig into the front pocket of my backpack one more time. I usually carry a just-in-case spare, but I gave it to Garrett the other day and forgot to reload. Then thinking of Garrett makes me think of Tai. That's it! She's an office aide first period. I quickly scroll through my contacts, find her name, and push send. Please answer.

"Well, well, well," Tai says slyly. "And why aren't you in class?"

"Tai. I need you," I whisper.

"Anything for you, girl. What's up?"

"I'm in the second-floor bathroom in the math wing, and…" I can't say the rest.

"Yeah?" she says with a full mouth. "Well, I'm in the teacher's lounge eating Mr. Zamora's PB and J."

"Can you bring me some, you know, some toilet paper and personal things?"

She laughs. "Like a diary?"

"Tai, come on. You know."

"Yeah, yeah. There's a bunch in here. Hang on." I hear her get up and open a door.

Then someone enters my bathroom. I stop breathing and freeze, then quietly lean down and inspect her shoes, as if they'll help me determine her level of friendliness. She's got on well-worn black Cons with hot pink patches on them. Friend or foe? Too hard to tell.

Now the girl is in the stall next to me. She shuts the door, but then I guess she realizes there isn't any toilet paper and opens the stall door again. I hear a lighter, then smell cigarette smoke. The girl exhales and walks over to my stall. "Abbey freaking Brooks?" Knuckles says and laughs.

I quickly whisper, "Nicky is here. Please hurry, Tai," and hang up. I shove my phone in my shorts pocket so I have both hands free to defend myself. I'm still sitting, so I use one leg to block the door in case she tries to kick it in.

"I thought I recognized those giant-ass feet and the smell of dyke in the air." She takes a long draw from her cigarette and then blows the smoke into my stall through the space between the door and wall. "Fancy meeting you here," Nicky says, pressing her head against the stall so I can see a slice of her face in the crack. She's smiling like that guy from *The Shining*. "Got yourself in a little predicament?" she whispers.

I'm quickly trying to figure out which would be worse: standing up and bleeding all over myself or sitting here and letting her punch me until I bleed. I quickly stand up and pull up my shorts but stay in the stall. "Get out of here, Nicky. Tai's coming." I know Tai's all the way across campus, and even if she ran in a full sprint, it would take her at least two minutes to get here. By then, I could be dead, but Nicky doesn't know that.

"Oh, don't worry. I've got better things to do," she snarls and then steps back. Her lit cigarette flies over the door, but before I can bat it away it lands in the hood of my sweatshirt.

I smack at my back frantically. "What the hell is your problem?" I yell. "What did I ever do to you?" She doesn't respond but instead grabs my backpack from the floor of my stall. I react, but like always,

I'm too slow. All I can get ahold of is the thin black strap that slips through my fingers. "Nicky, give it back!"

I hear her run out, and by the time I've found the cigarette and tossed it in the toilet, she's long gone.

"Damn it," I whisper to myself, then start to cry.

Footsteps arrive again and I almost puke from fear.

"Abs!" Tai says, leaping onto the next stall so she can see down into mine. "You okay? She didn't touch you, did she?"

Still without a piece of TP, I wipe my nose on the sleeve of my hoodie. "No. My backpack." I point to the floor to indicate where it was last seen. "She took it."

"But you're okay?" she says, out of breath, sweat dripping down her forehead. "Jesus, I got here as fast as I could."

I nod. Her worry and sweetness cause that sneaky crushing-on-her feeling to creep into my body again. I swallow it down along with another round of tears.

She hops down, realizing I might need some privacy, and holds the supplies over the door. "Here."

As I take the toilet paper and the month's supply of tampons, my swooning for her is quickly replaced with humiliation. "Thanks, Tai."

"I'm going to get your bag back. Don't worry," she says. "In fact, I'm going to print out her schedule as soon as I walk you to class. And her home address and—"

"You don't have to do that." But I'm glad she's not going to leave me yet.

She turns on the sink and I hear her splashing her face. I think she leaves it on extra long to make some noise while I get myself situated.

I finally exit the stall I have since decided to call The Cubicle of Doom. I wash my hands and shake them off to dry. I'm too embarrassed to look her in the eyes.

"You okay?" She lifts my quivering chin so we're face-to-face. She looks as relieved as I feel. "Aw," she whispers, then pulls me into her and hugs me. "I got here as fast as I could," she says again.

I hug her back and fight with all my strength not to cry. I lose that battle.

"It's okay, baby D." She pets my hair and I relax into her. She smells so good—not sweet and fruity like most girls, but whatever it is, it's intoxicating. Her long arms easily wrap all the way around me. Her comfort and strength warm me. "I got you," she says.

I remember the secret I'm keeping from Tai and feel guilty. How can Garrett mess with this? If I had Tai as a girlfriend, I'd be so glad that she wanted to protect me and love me all the time. I force myself to open my eyes and I step out of her arms. "I'm okay. Really freaking late for first, but okay."

"Well, I definitely got your back on that." She whips out a pad of hall passes and a pen from her pocket. "Where to?"

I remind myself again to somehow get a position as an office aide before I graduate Gila. "Mrs. Stum. But I don't know, Tai. She's scary."

"Come on. That's an easy one. I've gotten G out of Mrs. Dumb's class a million times. Let's see, whose signature should we use today?" She taps the pen on her forehead. "Got it. Mr. Ikers. They haven't talked since she accused him of eating her gorgonzola pasta. Totally me, by the way." She scribbles some fake details on the form and explains what I am supposed to say when I hand it to Mrs. Stum. "We might want to put those in your locker on the way," she says and smiles, pointing to the brown bag.

Remembering my backpack is gone sends me into a state of panic again. "What about my books? My homework? Why does she hate me so much?"

"She's all kinds of messed up. I think it's because of her brother, you know"—Tai's fingers take the shape of a gun and she puts it to her forehead—"killing himself like that."

"Yeah, I heard about that. I guess that does explain a lot. But still. Why me?"

Tai puts her arm around me and leads me out of the bathroom. "Don't sweat it. I'll take care of it."

By the time I walk into chem, everyone is almost done with the lab. The goggled eyes of my classmates follow me as I approach Mrs. Stum with my hopefully believable forged pass. I hand it to her and swallow loudly. "Sorry I'm late, Mrs. Stum. My backpack got stolen this morning. Mr. Ikers was helping me look for it."

She reads it quickly. "Figures *he* would keep you out of class this long." She tears up the pass and tosses it into the trash bin. I'm relieved that the evidence of Tai's deception has been destroyed. "Join your lab group. You have ten minutes to get caught up. No makeups. Good luck."

"But it wasn't my fault," I protest. "It was stolen. I had to look for it."

She's reading something on her computer screen now, so instead of looking at me or responding, she points to the only classroom rule posted in her room. *There's no crying in chemistry.*

❖

"Are you sure it was her?" Mia asks, as if I had a case of mistaken identity.

"Of course I'm sure." I left out the part about the mess between my legs and the part where I let myself sink into Tai's arms for comfort, but I definitely filled Mia in on all the scary details of my near-death experience. "Why would you think it wasn't her? She's insane." I'm still a little shaky from the whole thing.

"I just can't believe she doesn't have anything better to do, that's all. I'm sure she'll leave you alone now, though. You told Ms. Morvay, right?"

I put her on speaker and start to curl my hair, just to see if it would look good and to procrastinate working on the pile of homework staring at me. "Yeah, I did, but Nicky just lied about it and there was no proof, so whatever." I release my hair and like the way the curl bounces. What I wouldn't give to have full luxurious locks like Garrett and Kate. They are so lucky. "Wait, how did you know I told Ms. Morvay? I didn't tell you that, did I?"

"No, I just figured because Nicky got called to the office during fifth. I have English with her."

"You do?" I undo another warm clump of hair and pet it. This is much more relaxing than attempting my Algebra 2 homework. "You didn't tell me that before."

"Yes, I did," Mia says quickly. "Anyway, I wouldn't worry about it. It'll blow over."

"I guess," I say but something is weird. "Well, Tai found my backpack in a garbage can down the hall from the bathroom. Everything's there, but I couldn't find my brush. Maybe I left it in my PE locker. You don't think she's making a voodoo doll of me, do you?"

She laughs. "No, I don't think so, but I do think you've been watching too much *Buffy.*"

I don't want to talk about Nicky anymore. "You guys going out tonight? Because after the day I had, I could really use some fun times." I also want to try out the new signs Mia's been teaching me and the signs I've been practicing with the website I found. Of course if I really had guts, I would have chatted with Devin when I saw she was online last night. But I don't and we didn't.

"Not tonight. I have to…" She trails off. "I have to take care of something. Sorry again about Nicky."

"It's not your fault. She's the psychopath, not you."

"Well, she's had it kind of rough, so…"

"Why are you defending her?" I put down my curling iron and pick up the phone. "What's up with you and Nicky, Mia?"

"Nothing," Mia retorts. "Never mind."

"Hey, are we friends or aren't we?" She's quiet except for the faint sound of screaming in the background—I'm guessing her sister's toddler is awake and very angry. I walk to the den to get online to see if maybe Devin wrote again. "Is there something I should know?"

"You're paranoid."

"You know I'll keep your secrets tighter than a pair of skinny jeans on J-Lo," I say as I flip open the laptop that isn't allowed to be moved. Her end of the line is quiet except for the baby. "That was a joke, Mia. Not a great one, but still."

She releases a small laugh, then says, "Dude, we are friends. I promise. Can we just not talk about it right now? It's complicated."

"Fine," I say but immediately get more suspicious. From my year of hanging out with professional lesbians, *it's complicated* seems to be code for *we had sex*, and if that's the case with Nicky and Mia, well, I don't even know what to say about that. But there's no way that happened, so I put it out of my mind. Now there's an awkward silence.

"Just tell Tai to let me handle it, okay?"

I secretly really like the fact that Tai has my back on this, but I say okay, even though I'm not sure I'll tell her to back off. After all, what's the danger in having two protectors from Knuckles? I can't think of one. There's more weird silence, so I see my chance. "Hey, speaking of Diego…"

She laughs. "We weren't, but go ahead."

"Any way I could beg you to go out tonight?" I whisper into the phone so my mom won't hear.

"Well…okay. My old lady says I'm grounded until I clean my room, and that's not happening anytime soon, so we'll probably have to wait until she passes out. I'll check with the crew, but I bet they'll be down."

When Mia talks about her mom passing out, I have a feeling it isn't like someone passing out from exhaustion. Then there's an explosion of yelling in Mia's room. I jump because it's so loud and close I feel it through the phone.

"Mom, I said I would in a sec!" Then more screaming, but it's muffled now by Mia's hand. "I gotta go, Abbey." She's out of breath, like she was running.

"What about tonight?" I say, even though I have a feeling Mia isn't going anywhere.

"Jesus, okay," Mia screams at her mom. "I have to go," she says to me.

"Mia?" I look at my cell's screen, but the call has ended.

I figure Mia will call back when she can. In the meantime, I log on. There's a message, and it's from Devin. I double click as fast as I can.

> *Hey Abbey,*
>   *Mia told me you were learning ASL on your own. Cool. You should Skype with me to practice. I'll be up until about midnight.*
>   *Hope to see you soon!*
>   *Devin*

I look over my shoulder. My mom's in the other room at her easel working on a new painting, so I have a little bit of privacy. It's not like Devin and I are going to cyber–make out or anything, but still.

I stare at the screen. Am I ready for this? Do I even know enough to have an actual conversation with Devin? What if I mess up and she laughs at me? What if Mia's been teaching me the wrong signs just to make me look stupid? Now my hands are sweating. I'm sure nothing's sexier than a sweaty-hand ASL conversation. I look longingly at Devin's picture and ponder my next move. Instead of taking action, however, I grab a piece of paper to make a pro-con list. I get as far as writing *pro* when a ding from my computer makes me look up. She beat me to it. The computer starts to ring like a phone.

My hair is half-curled, so I throw my head forward and mess it up in an attempt to hide its uneven texture, but I come up too fast and knock my elbow on the edge of the desk.

"You okay in there?" my mom asks.

"Nothing to see here," I yell back and close the door a little with my foot.

When I can focus again, I smile at my computer's camera and click *answer*.

"Hi, Abbey," Devin signs extra slow. Her brown hair is in two braids just like Laura from *Little House*.

"Hi," I sign back. She's sitting on her bed, and behind her is a bulletin board decorated with pictures of friends. I scan them quickly to see if any look like you-know-who girls. I can't tell. But Devin's just as cute as I remember her—God bless push-up bras. It's taking every ounce of control I have not to stare at her cleavage. "What's up?" I sign, trying to remain Triple C like Garrett has taught me: calm, cute, and classy.

"Not much," she signs.

We continue like this until I've exhausted all my getting-acquainted signs, which takes about forty-five seconds. "Wait," I sign and flip frantically through my ASL dictionary so I can ask how her classes are going.

She says, "Hey," to get my attention. "What word?" she signs, and then says out loud, "Remember, I can read your lips."

"I know," I sign, but I don't want her to think I expect her to. I find the word I'm looking for. "How was school today?" I sign, very, very slowly, speaking at the same time in case she doesn't understand what I'm signing. At this rate, it's going to be tomorrow before I get three complete sentences out.

"Are you talking to me?" my mom asks from the living room.

"My mom," I sign and point and then yell, "No, I'm talking to a friend online."

"Why don't you use your cell phone? Did you lose it?"

I look back at Devin and roll my eyes. "Sorry," I sign because that's the one sign I know I have down. "It's Devin, Mom. Remember, I told you about her. Mia's cousin?" Of course I left out the detail that I first met Devin on the night I snuck out of the house.

I hear the familiar sound of my mom cleaning off her paintbrush in her jar of water. Oh God. Here we go. "Oh, are you signing?" She leans down in front of the computer and waves. "This is so cool! How did you two figure this out?"

Devin laughs and signs *hello* to my mom.

"Devin, this is my mom," I say and then fingerspell my mom's name, "*S-U-S-A-N*."

Devin signs a reply.

"She says it's nice to meet you, Mom."

"Nice to meet you, Devin," my mom says slowly and loudly. "This is so cool," my mom says again. "You'll have to show me how to do this. Oh my gosh, your Aunt Robin will be thrilled." Unable to contain herself, my mom waves again. Devin waves back.

I'm dying of humiliation, but my mom is too transfixed to notice. "Mom, I'll show you later. Adios. So long. Farewell."

"Okay, but don't stay up much longer. Time for bed," she says, and then finally leaves.

I turn to Devin again and say, "It's like she was transplanted from the fifties or something. The TV remote still excites her."

Devin laughs, and I wish I could make her laugh with ASL, but it's kind of hard to do when I only know about forty signs.

"Anyway," I sign, "sorry."

"That's okay."

Then nothing happens for a few torturous seconds.

"She's really pretty," Devin signs.

"I guess. More embarrassing than pretty," I say because the only words I know from those two sentences are *I* and *pretty*, which I learned so if the opportunity presented itself, I could use them to compliment Devin.

Then Devin signs something that makes me blush. At least, I think she did. Regardless, I am blushing, but I need confirmation just in case my eyes are trying to deceive me. "Can you repeat that?" I sign.

"Beautiful like you," she signs extra slowly.

I sign, "Thanks." And then I look down for a second to consider my next sentence. Is this flirting or just niceness? When I look up again, Devin's looking into me, and then she does it again—that thing she did the first time we met—tilts her head to the side, smiles slyly, but instead of pushing her hair behind her ear, she grabs the tip of one of her braids and twirls it between her fingers like I do every time I get nervous.

Like now. I toss aside the clump of hair I'm twirling. The letters WWGD flash into my panicking brain. Okay, Abbey, what *would* Garrett do? I conclude that Garrett would say some encouraging words, like *What does she have to do, give you a full-frontal flash, freshie? Go for it already!*

So right about then, I decide to grow a pair. "Did Mia tell you about me?" I sign.

"Can you repeat that?" she replies, but her smile shifts from flirtatious to mischievous. She obviously knows what I'm talking about.

It's the first sign I looked up when I checked out the ASL

dictionary, so it's not like I have to look it up. I'm not sure which sign to use since there are two, so I sign both. "I'm a lesbian." I look over my shoulder, nervous to sign it with my mom so close by. I can count the number of people I've said this to on one hand, so I hope she appreciates how hard it was for me to do it now, and in a new language for that matter.

"Sure, why?"

"What do you think?"

She shrugs, "Nothing. Mia is, too." And then I think she signs that she has a lot of gay friends, but I don't ask her to repeat it.

Old Abbey would have moved the conversation on, but not the new, ovary-growing Abbey, so I sign, "And you?"

"Me what?" she signs, feigning confusion.

My brow furrows slightly because now I feel like I'm being played and no one is telling me the name of the game. But when she smiles, I smile back. I can't help it. "Are you…" I pause because I'm about as good at flirting as the forty-year-old virgin. "Are you…like me?"

She shrugs. "I don't know. We just met."

I nod. "I understand," is all I can sign because I don't know what else I could say, even if I did know the signs.

"I'm not tall like you," she signs. "I'm not blond. I play volleyball, not basketball."

"Right," I sign.

"But"—she looks up and thinks for a second—"I like chocolate. You like chocolate?"

"Yes."

"Do you like to read?"

I nod and sign, "A lot."

"Me, too." And then she reaches for a book on her desk and holds up Stephen King's latest. She kisses her fingers like an Italian, so I guess he's one of her favorite authors.

"Wait," I sign and run out to the living room to get my copy from the coffee table. My mom spots me on her way to the bathroom.

"Abbey Road, it's past your bedtime, honey."

"Okay, I'll say good-bye. Hang on." I run back to my dad's office and hold up the book, smiling like it proves something more than we both like to read horror.

"Cool," she signs.

We're staring at each other closely now, and I'm suddenly finding myself in a faraway place as I look into her smiling eyes. I haven't left the planet like this since my days with Keeta, and it's nice to get away. I think Devin's enjoying the trip, too.

Then she looks down at her phone, which must have vibrated. As she reads a text, her smile fades. "I have to go."

"You okay?"

"Yeah. I just need to go."

"I have to go, too. Thank you for helping me with my ASL," I sign slowly.

Another text comes in, and she looks more worried but looks up to finish our call. "Meet again tomorrow night?" she asks.

I nod, then say, "Maybe then we can figure out if we're alike or not."

She shrugs but smiles a little. "Maybe."

"Good night, Devin," I sign and smile back.

"Good night. See you later."

The screen goes blank. I flip through the emotions chapter of my ASL dictionary, but I don't think there's a sign that can sum up how I feel right now. I don't even think English has one. Something tells me French does, though.

In bed, I close my eyes and try to let sleep take me away, but all I can think about is how lame I was. *Are you like me?* What a stupid question. She's nothing like you, Abbey. She's perfect and you couldn't flirt your way into a blindfolded lesbian Jello fight. I roll over on my back and sigh. I watch the fan whirling above me, hope it's affixed well, and let my mind wander. First I wonder how many people have been severely injured by falling ceiling fans. Then the thought of people being injured makes me think of my dad, and I wonder if he died quickly. There are a lot of things I wonder about his death, but it never seems like the right time to ask. Then for some reason the thought of death makes me think of Keeta. Maybe it's the hot night and my loss of fluids from sweating so much, but I feel a longing for her that I thought I'd finally gotten over. What am I saying? I am so over Keeta. It's Devin I want. Devin. Devin. Ms. maybe-she-is Devin.

I close my eyes again and see Devin's smile and hazel eyes, her braids resting on her chest. Now I'm thinking of how the soft curves of her breasts peeked out of her yellow tank top, and how when she reached for the book, I could see even more, like her lacy pink bra.

I cover my head with my pillow to muffle my laughter. I may not have had sex with a girl yet, but I certainly want to, which makes me, in my opinion, one step closer to being 100 percent sure.

CHAPTER SIX

Mia never called back, and now it's been two days since I've seen her at school. She's good at living up to her name and goes MIA a lot, but this time I feel like it's different; something's not right. I tried to get her status from Devin, but she isn't writing me back either, so when I finally see Mia in the hall this morning at the start of break, I grab her backpack and yank her backward. "Caught you," I say and laugh.

But she just looks stoically at me and says, "Yeah, now what?"

I steer her to the cafeteria and we get in line for what have to be crack-laced sugar-coated cinnamon rolls—otherwise, why would I crave them worse than filet mignon? "Where've you been?"

"Around," Mia says, avoiding eye contact with me and looking over her shoulder every five seconds like she's just shoplifted some candy bars and doesn't want to get caught.

I pay for my steaming hot roll and say thank you to the lunch lady because if you don't she will systematically destroy your life. Besides, she puts up with a thousand hormonal and hungry teenagers a day, so why not be polite?

We walk to the nearest table, and that's when I notice Mia's stride is stiff and slow. "Are you okay?" I ask with my mouth full because I can't wait to sit down before taking a bite. I use my backpack to wipe crumbs and other debris off the bench and sit down. "What happened?" I ask using ASL.

She looks over her shoulder again, then turns back to me. "Like I said, I was around. Why? What did you hear?"

"Now who's paranoid?" Then I look where she's looking. At first, all I see are a dozen or so other addicts devouring their rolls, but then I catch sight of Nicky sitting with her back to us at a table with Naomi and Rachel. I scrunch up my nose like the sight of her makes the whole place stink worse than Mom's Brussels sprout surprise. Does Nicky have something to do with why Mia's been missing?

"Come on, Mia. What's going on with you?" What I also want to ask is why Devin hasn't written me back or tried to Skype with me again, but I don't want to get her mad. She's staring intently at my roll, so I reluctantly offer her a bite. She shakes her head, but now I feel bad for not offering to buy her one, too. "Dude, seriously," I push the roll over to her. "I'm full anyway," I lie.

"Well, if you're going to throw it away." She picks it up and finishes it off in two huge bites. I slide my milk in her direction and she gulps that down, too.

That's when I notice her hair isn't done in its usual carefully spiked way and the tank she's wearing is the same one she was in last time I saw her. "When was the last time you were at home?"

She shrugs, shakes her leg nervously, and bites the skin around her fingernail. "Sorry I ate your damn roll, okay?"

One benefit of being a compulsive liar last year is I can spot them faster than highlighted words on a page. "You always bite your nails when you lie." I knock her knee with mine. "Come on, Mia. Friends or not?"

She sighs. "You're such a pain in my ass."

"Yes," I agree, "but I'm a pain in the ass you should trust by now."

"Truth?" she finally says.

I can tell she needs me now, so I don't say anything sarcastic and just look at her and wait.

"I got kicked out that night we talked on the phone."

"Kicked out?" I say too loudly so she shushes me. "What do you mean?" I whisper.

"It's no big deal," she signs.

"You mean, like, kicked out of your house?" I secretly wish her problem wasn't such a big deal because I don't know how to deal with it or what to say next. "You should talk to Ms. Morvay," I say because she's my go-to grown-up for all problems.

"It's not like it's the first time," Mia says and signs, trying to help me learn ASL even now.

The bell rings and I gather my trash. "Mia, where did you go?"

"I slept on Devin's floor one night."

That explains Devin's text and maybe her distance. Does Devin not want Mia to know that we talk? "And the other?" I ask, refocusing quickly.

She shrugs again. "A friend's house."

I wish we didn't have to go to class so we could talk more, but since it's officially basketball season, I can't start ditching now. I put my backpack on and she follows me to the bins. "You could've stayed with me."

"It's cool. I'll go home after school today and babysit my sis's kid and do the dishes and buy the groceries and it'll be just like the good old days." And then she laughs and shakes her head. "Jesus, she'll probably ground me for not coming home."

I can't force myself to laugh. To Mia, that's reality. But to me, not having my mom's love is the worst possible thing that could ever happen. What if I told my mom about me and she actually kicked me out of my own house? Where would I go? Who would I call? I guess I'd call Kate because even though she's annoying as hell and judges everything I do, she's still my BFF.

Mia and I are heading to the other exit, away from Nicky. I'm relieved to not have to cross the path of Knuckles. It's been quiet and peaceful the past few days, and I'd like to keep it that way. Wait, has Nicky even been at school?

Mia peeks over her shoulder one more time, and the look on her face suddenly shifts. She sprints full speed across the cafeteria. Beyond the blur that is Mia, I see Tai heading right for Nicky. And Tai looks more pissed than I've ever seen her.

Are they both going to jump Nicky? Did they plan this? Is that why Mia was so obsessed with looking at Nicky?

Now I'm running toward the three of them. Three-on-one doesn't seem fair at all, but I'm not planning on fighting. Oddly enough, as much as I hate every part of her, I'm running to stop them from punching Nicky's face in.

By the time I get to Nicky's table, Tai has Nicky up by her shirt, and since Tai's as tall as me, Nicky's feet are barely touching the ground. "You hear me, you worthless skank? Look at her. Touch her locker. Even think about her and you will regret it. I promise you."

"Let her go, Tai," Mia says while pulling on Tai's free arm.

"Get out of here, Thurber. I got this," Tai yells.

"I said leave her alone, Tai." Mia shoves Tai.

Tai pushes Nicky down on the bench. Then with a look that would scare Mrs. Stum to tears, Tai turns to Mia. "You want to go, Thurber? Get in line, but this bitch is first," she says, pointing at Nicky, who has since stood up slightly, the look on her face showing she knows she can't run. It's all about image. If she runs, she'll be laughed at and lose all credibility. Plus, since she's completely psychotic, she's probably looking forward to the fight.

Mia doesn't back down from Tai, and now I'm thinking that Mia is just about as insane as Nicky. "Let's go, then," she says, looking up at Tai's face with no fear in her voice.

Meanwhile I'm still trying to figure out why Tai is doing this now, why Mia is defending Nicky, and if we can wrap this up so I can get to English sometime soon because that was the late bell that just rang over our heads. The risk of being tardy helps me find an ounce of bravery, so I step between them and say with a shaky voice probably no more audible than a whisper, "No one is fighting anyone. Let's just go to class and forget this happened."

Mia steps back. Tai glares at her but throws no punches. For a second things seem like they are going to be okay.

"Yeah, let's do what the dyke says," Nicky says, and like a rock hitting a beehive, her words stir everything up again.

In a flash, Tai's arm flies through the air. Her first punch hits Nicky so hard she falls back on the table. Nicky screams, "My nose!" but Tai's second punch to Nicky's gut knocks the wind out of her and shuts her up fast.

Suddenly we're surrounded by a dozen or so guys yelling, "Fight, fight, fight!" and I want to scream, *This is not a fight, you idiots! This is a mistake! Go get help!* but I don't get the chance.

Tai steps back to recharge for another round, but then Mia rams Tai, yelling, "Leave her alone!" I try to grab Mia before she has her hands on Tai, but Garrett's right—I have the reflexes of an eighty-year-old. Even though Mia is barely half Tai's height, she easily pulls Tai to the floor like this isn't her first cafeteria brawl. Maybe Nicky and Mia have more in common than I first thought.

"Chick fight!" the boys are now shouting.

"Shut up!" I scream at them, but one of them shoves me and I fall hard on my knees. Tai and Mia roll toward me, so I guess that's why I dare to try to break them apart. First I pull at Mia, who's on top of Tai. "Mia, stop!" She ignores me, but what does happen is I get an elbow to my cheek. I can't tell whose it was. "Mia!" I try to get her off Tai by pulling on her arm, but they roll away from me. That's when a Swiss Army Knife falls out of Mia's pocket.

Everyone knows a fight means suspension, but a knife means expulsion. As in, not invited back, ever. Mia can't get expelled. Her mom would—I don't even know what she'd do. Even in this moment, I want to protect Mia, so I reach for the knife, but before I can grasp it, I'm yanked up off the ground by my backpack. Ms. Morvay tosses my five-eleven frame aside like I'm an empty plastic bag, and I land in Jake's arms. Jake? Was he here the whole time? Was he one of the guys cheering them on? I push him away, but he holds on to me, like he's trying to help me or something. "Get off me, you jerk!" I yell and he lets me go.

I turn to the fight and pray that Ms. Morvay misses the knife, but I should know better. All I can do is watch as she angrily kicks it against the wall and then goes in for Mia, who has Tai's head pinned down with one hand and is about to punch her with the other.

I don't know when I started, but I'm crying. I should be pissed, not weeping like a baby, but I think it's because two of my dearest friends are currently pummeling each other and also probably because one of these dear friends nailed me in the face and it's killing me.

Ms. Morvay grabs Mia's arm midswing, throws her off Tai, and pins her to the ground on her stomach with her knee in her back. With her other hand she calls for Mr. Ikers and Mr. Sanchez on her radio. Then she points at Tai with an authoritative finger. "Don't you move an inch, Tai." The guys get her attention next. "The rest of you, get to class before I write you up!" They disperse quickly.

Before he leaves, Jake says, "Abbey, I was just trying to—"

I put my hand up to stop him from talking. I'm surprised it works.

Me, Ms. Morvay, Mia, and Tai are the only ones left. Apparently, Nicky and her dumb-ass friends fled sometime after Mia attacked Tai.

It's quiet now except for everyone breathing heavily.

Then Tai tries to make her case. "It's Nicky's fault, Ms. M., and you know it."

"I don't want to hear it, Tai." Ms. Morvay shuts her down. Mr. Ikers and Mr. Sanchez finally show up. "Take her," she says to Mr. Ikers, pointing at Tai. "Abbey, you go with Sanchez. And Sanchez, grab that weapon." She points at the knife that remained untouched the entire time. Maybe since she didn't use it, Mia won't get into trouble.

I start to walk in front of Mr. Sanchez but nearly fall down because my legs are shaking so much. The closest I've ever come to a fight is when Stef found out about me and Keeta last year, but she never threw a punch. Instead she used words to beat me up. Does this even count as a fight for me? I didn't start it, I didn't punch anyone, yet my face is throbbing, and I'm being escorted to the office like a convict. My tears quickly return. Whether or not this was my fight, no doubt about it, my mom is definitely going to get a call about it. I use the rest of the walk to the office to try to manufacture a storm of lies to get us all out of this one.

Mia and Tai are quickly put in separate offices. I'm told to sit and wait, and given strict instructions to not say a word. A few minutes later, Nicky's brought in and seated next to the principal's secretary, Evelyn. I heard over the supervisor's radio that they caught her trying to shimmy under the fence out by the baseball field. If I wasn't so afraid of Evelyn, I would have laughed in Nicky's face, but I'm afraid of most of the office staff, so I remain quiet. As soon as Mr. Ikers leaves, Nicky tries to explain how she was in no way involved in the fight, but Evelyn shuts her up with a snap of her fingers.

Ms. Morvay escorts a hard-looking woman with faded tattoos on her neck and black roots showing through her bleach-damaged hair into Principal O'Brien's office. I assume this is Mia's mom.

Twenty minutes tick slowly by, and the bell to signify the end of fourth rings. So much for acing that quiz in art. I wonder how much longer until my mom gets here. I look over at Nicky again. The front of her shirt has blood drips on it from Tai's punch to her nose. Nicky catches me staring, and without skipping a beat, she signs, "Bitch." Not only does her message make me reconfirm that she's evil, but it also forces me to acknowledge that when Mia said things were complicated between her and Nicky, there was probably sex involved. They obviously aren't enemies, and the thought that they are something more than friends makes me sick to my stomach. Somehow I manage to hold down the two bites of cinnamon roll but can't help squinting my eyes and scrunching up my face as I ponder Mia and Nicky's relationship. Doing this, however, reminds me of my own injury.

I pat my eye and cheek lightly. It feels like I've got a marble under my skin. Thanks to basketball, it isn't my first face wound, but it's definitely the first time I've gotten hurt by a friend.

There is a sudden uproar from inside O'Brien's office. After closer listening, I determine the yelling voice belongs to Mia's mom. Then O'Brien yells, "Ms. Thurber, you need to calm down." Ms. Morvay says something very forcibly, too, and then her voice crackles out of the radio on Evelyn's desk. "Officer Ellis, we need you in O'Brien's. ASAP."

Gila High's community officer, Officer Ellis, quickly walks across the lobby where we are sitting. His belt is heavy with his artillery that clanks against his hips. The thought that he might have to use any of that on Mia or anyone else around here makes me finally realize how serious this situation's getting. I should be in there, explaining how it's all my fault. I bounce my leg and twirl my hair to distract myself. Regret creeps into me and darkens my insides like a toxic haze. I should've told Ms. Morvay about Nicky sooner. I should've told Mrs. Schwartz. I should've told my mom.

Speaking of my mom. "Abbey, what happened to your face?" She looks over at Nicky. "Are you responsible for this?"

Nicky glares at my mom, and I swear my mom might murder her, but before she can, Principal O'Brien's door opens. Mia's mom's in handcuffs. "I brought her into this world. You don't get to tell me I can't slap my kid if she needs it! You don't know what a pain in the ass she is!"

"Do yourself a favor, and stop talking, Ms. Thurber," Officer Ellis says calmly as he leads her out.

In the background I see Mia. Her face is red. She's not crying, but what I see seems worse than that. She's just staring at the ground. She seems broken, and all I want to do is run to her and hug her and say how sorry I am for everything. Instead, I start to cry.

Nicky takes a different approach and is quickly out of her seat and in Mia's mom's face. "It's about time you get locked up after all the crap you put her through."

Ms. Morvay grabs Nicky and shoves her into the chair again. "Not another word."

Another cop comes into the office. I don't recognize her. She walks into O'Brien's and heads for Mia. Oh no. The knife. They aren't going to arrest her just for having it, are they? I finally stand up to protest, as if anyone will listen to a word I have to say. "It isn't her fault, Ms. Morvay. Nicky was the one who started it. Mia was just trying to protect me." I say this last part even though it's a lie. I mean, that's not at all what was going on today. It's obvious Mia was protecting Nicky, but my claim sounds better and makes more sense than the truth.

"Abbey, sit down," Evelyn demands and I obey, but I don't stop talking, as if now my words are going to change everything.

"It's my fault, Ms. Morvay. Don't let them take her."

Mia won't look at me. Her mom won't shut up. And Nicky's glaring at me like I'm the one who started it all. I hate this. I hate her. I hate myself.

My mom comes to my side. Ms. Morvay motions us into her

office, the very same office that holds all my secrets. My tears quickly dry up. What am I going to do to keep it that way?

I should be thinking about Mia. I should be worrying about where they're taking her and how I'm to blame. And what about Tai? What's going to happen to her? But all I can think about is how I'm stuck in a small room with the one woman who knows every secret about my life and another woman who wants to know what the heck is going on.

I have a feeling my mom isn't just talking about what happened today. Yep, I have a pretty good feeling my mom is talking big picture here. Like, she might finally demand the truth about what the heck is going on *with me.*

Is this it? It feels like now or never, but even Garrett couldn't prepare me for this kind of outing.

In the end, though, I get through the afternoon without having to divulge my big lesbian secret to my mom. I can't prove it, but I swear Ms. Morvay has a serious look of disappointment as we leave her office. But her judgment isn't fair at all. What would she know about it?

Chapter Seven

W hy do I have to be here? She's your friend, not mine." I've decided to spend the rest of my weekend slumped on the couch in a state of worry and irritation about Mia and Nicky and wallow in depression about my confusing crush on drop-dead gorgeous, not-gay Devin. The last thing I want to do is be a part of a stupid grown-up dinner with my mom's stupid friends and pretend to be interested in anything not regarding my life's current dilemmas.

"All you have to do is sit at the dinner table and act like you're not a spoiled brat," my mom says in an eerily calm way.

She hardly ever says mean things like that to me. But, still. Having dinner with some old lady who worked with my dad sounds like the truest form of torture. So I give it one last shot. "Dad isn't here. Why do you even care?"

Bringing him up is never a good idea, especially when we are getting into it. I regret it, too, even if I do finally get my way.

"Fine, Abbey. Do what you like." She sits in front of her easel and angrily mixes some paints on her palette.

I watch my mom for a minute as she dabs her brush in a mixture of brown and white. She is normally beautiful, but now she is frowning and hunched over her painting. Me and my attitude have turned her ugly. "Mom, I'm sorry. I'll do it."

"It's okay, Abbey. I know I shouldn't make you. It's fine." She doesn't even look at me.

"What time are they coming?"

She adds a thin line of light brown to the large wing of the falcon, and I wonder how she knows how hard to push down, when to pick up the brush, or when enough is enough. "Six," she says.

"Okay, I'll get ready," I say, and as I walk to my room, I realize she knows how to play me better than Keeta or Devin or any other girl in the world can.

❖

"Could you get that, honey?"

I look over from my mountain of homework spread out on the coffee table in front of the television. My mom has her head deep in the oven, so I have to play hostess. I am used to putting on a show, though. As the daughter of an artist, I learned at an early age how to be respectful to strangers who come over to meet with my mom and discuss her work.

"Abbey?" Mom calls again.

I stack my books neatly under the table. "Yeah, I'm going," I say as I hurry to the door and open it.

"Oh, Abbey. Look at you," says the woman on the other side of the screen door. She's a middle-aged blonde dressed in a low-cut red dress.

I like her already because, even though she comes close, she doesn't comment on how big I've gotten. I say hi and welcome her in.

"We forgot the wine in the car. Liz will be right in," she says as she enters the kitchen.

"I'm so glad you could make it, Juliana. You look amazing." My mom wipes her hands on a dish towel and they hug. "Abbey, this is a colleague of your dad's and a friend of mine. Do you remember her? Juliana, this is my daughter, Abbey. But I guess you guys just met."

"Yeah," I mumble, feeling awkward.

"Oh, Susie. She's so grown-up…and tall!"

I smile and nod my head. Minus two points from the lady in red.

"Last time I saw you was…Gosh, has it been that long, Susie?"

I assume by her incomplete sentence that the last time we met was at my dad's memorial. It's no surprise that I don't remember her at all. I don't remember much from that day.

"I can't wait to meet your wife," my mom says, changing the subject, probably for my benefit.

But wait. Rewind. Did my mom just say wife?

"That's me."

We all turn toward the voice. And there she is. Juliana's wife. Aka Ms. Morvay, and she's wearing a tight blue skirt, a shirt that would make Kate proud, and a pair of heels that make my normally Hillary

Clinton–esque counselor look like a freaking Victoria's Secret model. Then I remember how mad I am at her. She didn't have to tell anyone about the knife, but she did. And she's the one who sent Mia away to God knows where for God knows how long. And to top it off, she's been hiding this? Now I'm even more mad at her.

My mom startles me when she speaks. "Oh, what a small world," she says and walks over to Ms. Morvay and they hug. "How funny. All this time, and I didn't know."

I glare at my mom. *Or did you?*

Juliana seems to be feigning surprise, too, when she says, "Oh, you must go to Gila High, Abbey."

I can only nod my head because as mad as I am at Ms. Morvay, I'm doing a secret happy dance. She's one of the Gila High herd. That is so cool.

"I can go if this is too weird for you," Ms. Morvay says to me. "Really, I understand."

"Nonsense," My mom grabs the corkscrew from the drawer. I haven't seen her this lively in years. Maybe it's because she's going to be able to drink something besides soymilk with dinner and have civil conversations with adults, not her snotty daughter. "There's no reason that we should be uncomfortable. Right, Abbey?"

Still cemented to the tile floor with my mouth open like a taxidermied trout, I nod my head. There are no words for this moment.

"There, you see? It's fine," Mom says, then hands Juliana and Ms. Morvay each a full glass of wine. Ms. Morvay gulps down quite a bit before we move to the living room for brie, some mushroom stuff my mom made, and crackers.

For the first time ever, I envy those grown-ups and their glasses of alcohol. I want to soften this awkward situation, too. So, instead, I wash down my nervousness with ice water and crackers topped with cheese and mushroom pâté.

For the second time this week, I'm trapped in a room with the one woman who knows everything and the one who wants to know more and one more woman who has no clue about the torment little ol' me is experiencing. This is proven by all her probing questions.

"So, Abbey, what year are you now?" Juliana asks.

"Freshman. I mean, sophomore," I say and shove another mushroom-topped cracker in my mouth so I won't be able to talk. I look down the hall because I swear I might accidentally look at

Juliana's breasts since they're just hanging out there like a couple of flesh-colored honeydew melons. And don't even get me started on Ms. Morvay, who has been fidgeting in her skirt ever since we sat down.

"Do you like your classes?"

I chew and nod.

"Any surprises so far this year?"

I can think of one big surprise, but I just nod at her because my mouth is dry from the crackers and nerves.

"I mean, with your classes and teachers. Are they harder than you expected?"

"Yeah," I say cryptically. Why is she being so nosy, and why are my mom and Ms. Morvay just sitting there watching like we're at Wimbledon?

"Are you on any teams?"

"Basketball. Hopefully." I look at my mom to make sure she doesn't have any plans to ground me from my only reason to attend Gila High—or to live, for that matter. She's pouring more wine and doesn't see me.

"That's neat. Liz played basketball in high school, too."

We all look over at Ms. Morvay and she, still looking rather pale and pained, shakes her head, smiles, and barely waits for my mom to stop pouring before throwing back another few gulps of wine.

At first I can't figure out why Ms. Morvay is so freaked-out. I mean, I think it's pretty awesome she's gay. But I guess that kind of personal information could impact her job as a high school counselor, especially if Principal O'Brien doesn't know or if other kids find out.

And then things get a little too personal for me. "So, you must know Keeta Moreno then," Juliana says and then turns to Ms. Morvay. "She played at Gila, right?"

"This is great cheese, Susan." Ms. Morvay tries, I'll give her that.

"Well, Keeta's already made a name for herself at Pima. She's in my intro bio class. I go to a lot of their games since almost the whole team has been in a class of mine. Will she know you if I tell her you said hi?"

"Of course Keeta will remember Abbey," my mom chimes in. "They were great friends. You didn't tell me she was playing at Pima, Abbey."

I don't remember telling Juliana to tell anyone I said hi, and I didn't even know Keeta was playing at Pima until now. Besides, Keeta probably hasn't thought about me all summer. But I try not to be weird about the whole thing since my mom's sitting right here. "Yeah, she'll probably remember who I am. Tell her I said hi."

Then my mom gets all excited and slaps her knee like she's just solved the world's energy crisis. "I know, Abbey. We should all go to a game together. That would be fun, wouldn't it?"

Ms. Morvay starts coughing on a cracker and has to leave the room. Juliana follows to make sure she's okay. I'll have to thank Ms. Morvay later.

When they resettle, my mom says, "Oh, Juliana, I want to show you the research I found in Ryan's office. I don't know if you ever got to read it. Maybe it'll be useful, still. Abbey, you and Liz—Ms. Morvay, I mean—can enjoy some cool air out back if you like."

Hearing my dad's first name is weird. I mean, I see it a lot on the mail and stuff, but in our house, he's Dad. And I don't like Juliana looking at his things. What research? Why didn't my mom tell me? Why is she going through his stuff now?

"All right, Abbey?" my mom asks, not content with my lack of reply.

"Yeah, okay," I finally say.

Ms. Morvay and I walk outside. I dust off a couple of patio chairs and we sit. Instead of twirling my hair like usual, I tear apart some of the fallen pods from the palo verde tree and say, "So…"

Then after what seems like an eternity, she says, "I feel really guilty about not telling you about me sooner. But when Juliana said your mom invited us to dinner, I figured it would be a good time to get it out in the open. Of course, as you can see, coming out is still nerve-racking sometimes."

Her apologetic tone softens me too easily and I drop my angry front. "I know, Ms. M. It's okay. I mean, you keep a lot of secrets for me. I promise I won't tell."

This makes her laugh. "Thanks. I promise I won't tell, too."

I smile finally. "Deal."

"So, you still haven't come out to your mom?"

I shrug. "How can I? I take one look at her and don't see how I can do that to her after all she's done for me. How did you come out to your parents?"

She ignores my question. "Your mom isn't exactly a homophobe, Abbey. She and Juliana have been friends since before you were born. In fact, Juliana first introduced your dad to your mom. They were all undergrads at the U of A together." She pulls up the front of her shirt again and crosses her arms over her chest. "God, this shirt. I don't know how I let Juliana convince me to wear it."

Because you look really hot in it, but I can't tell her that so I look up at the sky. It looks like it's on fire with flaming reds and pinks flaring up across the horizon. The sun is moving slower than I do on the track jumping over hurdles, but I like that it's taking its time.

"I'm glad," I say. "I mean, I'm glad you're here."

"Well, thanks." Then it's quiet again. "About Mia, Abbey—"

"I was mad at you, but I know you had to. It's your job. At least no one was hurt with it."

She nods her head. "Sometimes my job is amazing, but sometimes it feels awful. Are you worried about Mia?"

"Yeah," I say. "Where is she?"

"Well"—Ms. Morvay sits back, giving up on hiding her body—"it's confidential. I can't share those details with anyone."

"Oh." I rest my chin on my hand and look down. "I understand."

"But since we seem unable to keep any secrets from each other, I guess you can know she won't be going back to her mom's."

"That's good, but where is she now?"

"She's in a girls' group home because her sister is in no condition to care for her, and that's all she had left after her mom."

"How long does she have to be there?" I'm relieved she's not in juvie, but a group home doesn't seem much better. I wonder if she's scared. I hate that I can't comfort her. "When can I see her?"

"She has a school board appearance on Monday. The good news is she doesn't have any prior offenses, so the police didn't charge her."

"And the bad news?" The sky is darker now and the crickets seem to loudly applaud the sun's retreat. "When can she come back to Gila?"

"She probably can't, Abbey. I'm sorry."

"But she was only protecting me. Nicky's the one who should be kicked out." I don't mean to, but my voice gets louder. "Tai only got suspended and she's the one who started the fight."

"I know. I'll try, but rules are rules, Abbey. Mia had a knife at school. Gila has a strict no-tolerance policy when it comes to these things. She'll enroll at one of the alternative schools once she gets placed in a foster home."

I stand up. "A what? You mean, she's, like, homeless now?"

"There's no one else." Ms. Morvay tries to grab my hand, but I pull away. "Not yet, anyway."

"This isn't fair! It's all your fault."

"Abbey, lower your voice," my mom commands from the doorway. "Liz, I'm so sorry. Apologize right now, Abbey."

"Apologize? Who's going to apologize to Mia?"

"Abbey, these things have a way of working out. If you'll sit down, I'll explain what's going to happen."

"You should've just left us alone," I say. "She wasn't going to use that knife, and you know it."

"Maybe we should go, honey," Juliana says, putting her hand on Ms. Morvay's shoulder.

"No, I'm the one who has to go." I don't know how I do it so quickly, but I'm out the backyard gate, strapping on my helmet, halfway down the driveway on my bike before my mom even has a chance to call after me.

But I think my mom knows me enough by now to understand I just need to ride it off. Riding my bike is sometimes the only way I can sort it all out. I don't have a destination in mind until I reach the end of my block. That's when I turn right onto Grant and head for the one person I know would understand the most.

❖

I pull up to a campus map at the entrance of ASDB. I can't find the dorms, so I rack my brain trying to remember the building that Devin told me she lives in. It's an animal, that's all I know. I search the map again. Think, Abbey. I try to remember the dumb joke I said— something about a litter box for the bathroom. That's it: Wildcat Den.

I ride my bike over to Devin's dorm and stash it in the bushes because in my hurried fury, I forgot my lock. I race up the front steps and try the door. Locked. I look for a call button of some sort, but there's nothing outside. Since I forgot my cell phone, too, this plan is falling apart quickly. I bang on the doors; no one comes. I nearly sit on the steps and cry, but then I hear laughter coming from around the corner so I walk over to see if they might be able to help me get to Devin. Remembering that they could be blind or deaf, I announce my arrival by saying and signing, "Hi."

"I recognize that voice. It's Abbey, right?" A guy stands up and walks over to me.

"Diego and Shortie? Oh my God, I'm so glad to see you guys. Did you hear about Mia? I need to see Devin. Is she here?"

"Yeah, Devin emailed us. That's so effed up," Shortie says and takes a swig from her beer bottle. "You lucked out. Dev didn't go home this weekend."

"Yeah, Mia's been dealing with some heavy stuff lately," Diego says. "And then there's that chick she's been hanging out with. She seems like bad news."

"Nicky?" I say between clenched teeth.

"That's the one," Diego says. "Don't like her. Don't know why."

"I feel the same, but I know why." I'm still trying to understand and accept the truth of why Mia protected Nicky, and it makes me sick.

"Come on. I'll let you in. Devin will be glad to see you. We'll be right back, babe." Shortie places her bottle carefully down on the cement slab they were using as a bench, then grabs my hand and pulls me around the corner.

She slides her student ID into the door and waits for the click. I thought I'd have to lead Shortie through the building, but she gets us to Devin's room on the second floor without a single misstep. She pushes a doorbell, but no sound comes from inside.

As soon as I see Devin, I can tell she's been crying, but she smiles. She's wearing a pair of SpongeBob boxers and a tank top. Could she be more adorable?

"Well, my work here is done," Shortie says and heads for the elevator.

I'm not sure what I'm supposed to say. I'm not even sure what I'm doing here. Maybe she's mad at me. I mean, I'm the reason it all happened. But when Devin pulls me in her room and hugs me close, I know I made the right choice to come over. Maybe she needs me as much as I need her.

I sit down in her desk chair and tell her what happened, leaving out the part about Ms. Morvay being gay. I try to sign at first, but then give up because my hands are shaky and my mind is racing. Instead, she reads my lips, asking me to repeat a few things now and then. By the time I've dumped the details on her, Devin seems more pissed off than me.

"I told her to stay away from Nicky." Devin starts signing quickly, I guess mostly to herself. Then she says, "My dad says she can't live with us. There's barely enough room for me when I come home. Plus, she'd be out in Green Valley. She'd die of boredom."

I frown as my last hope for Mia gets taken away.

"I can't believe she's with Nicky again," Devin signs.

"Wait, Mia and Nicky were—" I have to pause so I don't choke on the words. "They were dating before? Are you serious?"

Devin stops her pacing. "You didn't know?"

My stomach begins to ache at the thought of it. How could Mia keep this from me? That's why she wanted to handle it herself and keep Tai out of it? "No," I sign. "I didn't know."

Devin plops down on her bed. "Well, now you do. They went out last year, but Nicky got super possessive and crazy, even about Mia hanging out with me. Me? I'm her cousin. So Mia broke up with her."

My face is stuck on disgust. That's who Mia started dating last year?

"Don't try to understand it," she signs.

"So all that stuff Nicky did to me was because I was friends with Mia?" The pain in my stomach stabs again. How could Mia keep this from me? But then I get real. *Pretty sure you're keeping something from Mia, too, Abbey. Like your continued crush on her very straight cousin.*

"Nicky's stupid. I don't get it," Devin signs.

"Yeah," I agree quickly, but I soften my face finally because I do get it. Love can make you act insane—I should know.

"Anyway, at least she's out of my evil aunt's house."

I nod. "But now what? This sucks," I sign and hug my legs to my chest to see if that will help ease my stomachache. No go. I'm still hurting, but instead of admitting it, I ask, "Can I use your cell?"

Even though I'm sure my mom's anger is going to slap me through the phone, I dial home and brace myself for the worst.

Mom picks up on the first ring.

"It's me."

"Oh, thank God, Abbey. I was so worried. Where are you? Are you okay?"

I explain how I rode to Devin's dorm. She takes it a lot better than I thought she would. She even lets me stay a little longer and says she'll pick me up downstairs in half an hour. This gift of time with Devin is enough to make me giggle, but I don't want either one of them to think I'm weird, so I play it cool, thank my mom, and hang up.

"I guess she isn't going to kill me," I try to sign.

I must be close to signing that right because Devin signs, "You're lucky your mom is so nice."

I nod. I am lucky. I feel lucky being with Devin at this moment, too, and wonder how she's feeling about me being in her dorm. It's not like it's the right time for a first kiss with Devin while Mia's in lockdown somewhere, but a girl can dream.

"Want to watch TV until your mom gets here?" Devin asks.

"Sure," I sign.

She pats the bed next to her, and for a moment all my pains dissipate.

She throws a pillow at me and I put it behind my head and make myself comfortable next to her. She spells out what I guess are two names of shows, but my brain shuts down. It's certainly not the first time I've sat next to a girl on a bed. I need to relax. Just be in the moment.

She smells like fruity shampoo and coconut lotion, and the way she's hunched down with the computer on her lap makes her breasts even more prominent. She fingerspells the titles again, and now that I can see my choices on the screen I understand what she's fingerspelling.

One Tree Hill or *Pretty Little Liars*? If she is gay, she must really be into femmes.

I shrug because I'm not really that into either, but at this point, I'd watch ten hours of *Real Housewives* if she wanted to.

My unenthusiastic response causes her to search for something else. "Hey, have you seen *Anyone But Me*?" She points to the screen.

I shake my head, but I'm definitely intrigued. The picture for it is two girls, one looking sort of longingly at the other.

"So good." She clicks for the show to start. The slow Wi-Fi at her school takes a while, so we're just sitting here. Side by side. Waiting. Almost touching.

I focus on her keyboard. Then on her bedspread. Then on her desk. Basically anywhere but her eyes. I'm sure if she looks at me she'll know everything I'm thinking. The show finally loads, but no sound comes on during the intro commercial, not that I care.

"Sorry, I forgot. Do you want the sound on?" Devin asks as if she can read my mind, only reaffirming my fear that she can tell what else is happening in there.

"No, it's fine."

"Okay." She turns her attention back to the screen. "I can't believe you haven't seen this show."

By the time the opening scene pops up, I can't concentrate. I decide that if I don't kiss Devin in the next five seconds, I'm going to die. My gut churns at the thought of it, but I'm sure that's just my excited nerves. After all, it's been a long time since I kissed a girl. I shake my head slightly to get Keeta out of there. Will I remember how to kiss? I got plenty of practice kissing Keeta, but what if it's not as easy this time? What if our mouths don't match up? What if I'm totally off base here and she *is* straight and I kiss her and she gets mad and tells Mia and Mia never talks to me again?

There sure are a lot of what-ifs when it comes to Devin.

Instead of leaning toward her or sending her a glance that says *take me now*, I begin to sweat. First it hits my hands, then my feet, and then my upper lip, which I wipe quickly with the sleeve of my shirt. This is stupid. What's my problem? *Just kiss her, Abbey.*

I press my hands on my shorts to dry them off just in case things go beyond kissing, but at this point I'm officially sweating everywhere like I just stepped out of a sauna.

She looks my way now and must notice my flushed state. She pauses the show, which I've missed entirely, but what's frozen on the screen makes my eyes pop out: two really hot girls holding hands in a park. If that's not a sign, I don't know what is.

"You okay? Is it too hot in here?" Devin asks with a smile on her face that I remember seeing the first night we met.

"Maybe it's the laptop," I sign, and then wave my hand in front of my face. "I'm fine."

Now she looks concerned and unconvinced. "You sure?"

I sign yes about five times because it's an easy one, and I really want to be okay. I close my eyes when another wave of nausea hits my body. I'm not okay. This is insane.

Devin leans over and turns on the small fan that sits on her desk. As she does this, her tank top rides up, revealing her back and the top of her underwear. This does the opposite of cooling me down.

When she returns, she leans on her elbow facing me. Her stomach is exposed and her cleavage is closer than ever to my face. "Better?" she asks as the tiny fan oscillates next to us.

The fan's breeze feels like someone blowing softly in my face. Goose bumps hit my body and I shiver. Her gaze is lingering. This is it, now or never, I tell myself. But all I can do is say, "Yeah. Thanks." Opportunity number two, missed. I look away to hide my humiliation as pain returns to my stomach.

After closing the laptop, Devin sits crossed-legged in front of me. She leans forward, but instead of kissing me, she presses the inside of her wrist to my forehead. "You're on fire."

On fire for you, I think to myself. But as I sit up to make my move,

I feel dizzy, and the pain feels like a knife stabbing me and slowly turning. The smell of her coconut lotion no longer intoxicates me with feelings of swooning. Instead, I feel like throwing up. Like, for reals. Like, right at this very moment. Oh my God. This is happening.

The look of panic on my face must be easy to read because Devin jumps off the bed, lands on the other side of her room in one leap, grabs her trash can, and shoves it under my head.

And me? Well, I let it rip.

CHAPTER EIGHT

After a night on my bathroom floor and a whole day in bed, I can now sit up without dry heaving. Yes, thanks to my mom's bacteria-laced mushroom pâté, not only did I lose all of Sunday and most of today, I also lost the contents of my stomach in Devin's *Glee* trash can and all chances of ever kissing her.

As it turns out, though, I wasn't the only victim that night. Juliana and Ms. Morvay got sick, too. I was going to make some crack about how my mom was trying to systematically kill off all the lesbians but decided that was a pretty lame way to come out. Definitely not Garrett approved. But if there's one way to get a mom to forgive you for acting out at a dinner party, this is it. She feels horrible, like, more horrible than ever, and I'm taking full advantage. In fact, she's off on a quest for orange Popsicles, Gatorade, and a strawberry Eegee's slushie. And even though I'm feeling almost all better, I'm thinking about pushing for all of Tuesday off, too.

With the house to myself, I slowly walk doubled-over in pain to the laptop. I type in my first search: *How to get over throwing up in front of your crush*, but nothing useful comes up. I try: *How to be more attractive after throwing up in front of someone you like*, but again get no good hits. Devin did text me a couple of times, but I couldn't bring myself to write back. I don't see how I can recover from this incident.

I'm just about to log off when I hear a ding. Oh, Mylanta. It's her. *Are you feeling better? Wanna Skype?*

Double ha. There's no way in hell Devin, or anyone not living in my home, can see the state of my hair or face. And thank Silicon Valley there's no smell-o-net yet. I stare at the box where my reply should go, but I'm still so embarrassed. Maybe she knows something about Mia, though.

Come on. Stop avoiding me. I've got three little sisters. I've seen tons of puke. That was nothing.

The thought of her watching me vomit makes me cringe, but it's not the throwing up that I'm most embarrassed about; it's the moaning and writhing around on her floor afterward that makes me feel like we can never meet face-to-face again. I must've looked and sounded like nearly dead roadkill. There's no going back to being cute or sexy after that, if I was ever there in the first place.

Are you going to make me come over there?

Nope. Definitely not. *I'm here.*

Was it the flu?

No, my mom poisoned me with bad mushrooms. Lol. I don't know why I add the lol. Stupid.

Oh, man. She must feel terrible. Have you heard from Mia?

I'm glad to move on to Mia. The further I can get from thinking that anything could ever happen between Devin and me, the better off I'll be. *I haven't been to school. I know nothing. You?*

She had her hearing today—she got expelled. Now she's waiting for a foster home to open up. I wish she could just stay in my room like she always did before. This sucks. I hate not knowing where she is.

The guilt returns, quickly replacing my embarrassment, but all I type is, *Yeah,* because I don't know how to make it better. I always seem to make things worse. *I'm so sorry, Dev.*

I wish you were here.

The words wash over me, relieving me like a hot shower that I desperately need. But she's probably just being nice, so I don't get too excited. *Me? You wouldn't be missing her if it wasn't for me. I should've confronted Nicky myself or something.*

Actually, I'd be wishing you were here even if Mia was okay. Then she adds a winky face. What is this? A smiley face is for friends, but a winky face usually means something a little more.

What the hell does she want from me? I wish she'd just give it to me straight or bi or lez…or whatever! I take a deep breath and contemplate my next message.

When can I see you again? she types before I get a chance to respond.

Now what do I say? On one of my shoulders, Garrett is sitting with devil horns on her head, whispering, *She wants you, Abbey. Go for it.* But on the other shoulder is know-it-all Kate, telling me, *She's straight, Abbey, and you probably are, too. Stop bothering the poor thing. Why don't you go out with that nice boy, Jake?*

Devin types, *Why are you being so shy?*

I think about my options and flick both Kate and Garrett away and go out on my own. _I'm not being shy. Just confused, I guess._

About?

You.

The word sits at the bottom of our conversation for a good thirty seconds. I'm convinced that I screwed it all up again.

What's so confusing? I miss you and wish you were here. I've already seen that entire series four times, and if you don't get what I mean, then never mind.

The corners of my mouth turn up and my two-day frown finally breaks. I make her wait longer than I should. _Okay, okay. I get what you mean._ And add, _I miss you, too._ And then I get all brave and type a winky face.

Good, but don't tell Mia.

I'm not sure if she means about liking me, or about her liking any girl, but if there's one thing I can usually do right, it's keep a secret. After all, Mia had her secrets from me, so I guess now I have mine, too. _I promise. I won't tell a soul._

❖

"You mean, she could live with us?" I say before taking a bite of the Top Ramen my mom just put in front of me. It's been days since I recovered, but I really like Top Ramen and Gatorade, so I request it for another night. "Like, for forever?" I say slowly because I feel torn, like that happy/sad drama face. On the one side, I'm smiling like nuts because it's Mia and she's one of my best friends and that means she wouldn't have to be in some freakish foster-care situation. But on the other side, I'm crying a little. I mean, I don't know what exactly we are, but Devin and I sort of declared like for one another the other night, and now Mia's going to be living here and be around twenty-four seven. And if she's not here, she'll probably be at Devin's. How are we ever going to have that secret first kiss with Mia around?

"Well, there are a few legal hurdles to jump, but the chances of the court saying no to Mia staying with us are pretty slim. It would just be until some other good option becomes available. I've already been through foster-care certification, I work at home, I have a steady income, and we have plenty of room. But it's up to you. I just thought, well, I know how close you two are."

"You hardly even know her, though. You would do that for her?"

My mom turns on the water at the sink and waits for it to heat up. "Well, I know what she means to you, and that she was protecting you from that bully. If she's your friend, then she must be a good person, and why not let her be in a home with someone who already cares about her."

These last words from my mom remind me of what is true. Mia is really important to me. And, if I recall my freshman year correctly, the last time I put my girl lust before a friendship, things got really bad, really fast. Mia's safety and care are more important than whatever it is that may or may not happen between me and Devin.

I push my chair away from the table and walk to her at the sink. "You're the best mom ever." I hug her and rest my head against her shoulder.

"Oh, now I'm the best mom ever. We'll see what tomorrow brings." She hugs me back.

"Yeah, no guarantees." I keep my hold on her because I don't want her to ever stop loving me and a little bit because I don't want her to see the panic on my face. There's no hiding that Mia's gay. My mom is no fool. Plus, Mia isn't closeted with anyone. What if she thinks we're a couple? Wait, she wouldn't let her live here if she thought that, would she?

"What is it, Abbey?" my mom asks when we part.

"Nothing, just tired," I lie.

She shakes her head and laughs. "You're twirling."

I quickly drop my clump of hair and make up something. "Why are you already cleared to be a foster parent?"

She leans against the counter. "Abbey Road, first I want you to know you are the greatest gift I have ever been given."

"M'kay," I say, but now I'm really nervous.

"After you were born, there were some complications. Our doctor said I probably couldn't have any more children."

"Oh, sorry," I say, the guilt practically drowning me. "You wanted more?"

"Just one more, maybe two. So when you were about four, we decided to look into fostering with the hope of adopting. But your dad's job at the U of A was just taking off and so was my commission work. We got certified but put it off and put it off and then…well."

I'm frowning, but not because I'm mad. I guess I've always wondered what it would be like to have a brother or sister. I mean, Kate's sister, Jenn, is a total pain in her ass, but she's also there when it matters most. A lot of times I wish I had something like that, even if it was just someone to gang up on my mom and take a stand against her cooking once in a while. "And you got stuck with me of all kids," I say, feeling even worse about the secret I've been keeping from her.

"Yeah, but you're pretty handy to have around," she says and smiles. Her blue eyes are glassy with tears that she won't let fall because she's had years of practice holding them in. She pats my head. "Plus, I love you madly, and you keep my mind sharp while trying to figure out why you do the things you do. Living with you is like playing a twenty-four hour brain game."

"Ha-ha."

"So, what should we do about helping Mia out, honey?"

Though I'm still mad about the whole Mia-secretly-dating-Nicky thing, it's Mia. Plus, if Mia's here, maybe Devin will be here more, too. I can make it work. I'm sure of it. "Of course. Let's do this."

❖

It's my mom's idea to invite Devin over for dinner, so me, Mia, and Devin pile into the backseat of our blue Volvo. I try to follow along with what they're signing but miss most of it. I don't care, though. I'm just glad to be with them and that things look like they're going to be okay for once.

When we arrive back home, there are a few of Mia's things stacked in the closet. Earlier that day, Ms. Morvay drove over to her house, and with permission from the court took whatever Mia's sister bagged up. I told her not to forget Mia's silk-screening materials. I was pleased to see they had made it, along with some clothes, books, and a few stuffed animals that looked like they had been loved very well by Mia. I'm glad, too, that Ms. Morvay unpacked some of Mia's things. I can't imagine coming home to find all my stuff in Hefty bags.

After admiring my dad's antique desk and the new comforter my mom bought, Mia sits down and looks around. I'm not sure, but I don't think she's ever had her own room.

"Ms. Brooks," Mia says quietly.

"Call me Susan."

That makes Mia smile for the first time since we picked her up. "I really don't know how to thank you. I—"

"Oh, Mia, you don't have to thank me." She touches Mia's shoulder. "I'm just so sorry this whole thing had to happen at all."

I nod, hoping that Mia can tell I forgive her for Nicky.

"I'm not," Devin signs. "I'm glad you're finally out of there."

"Yeah. Me, too, I guess," Mia says. You'd think she'd be totally relieved.

I feel like Mia and Devin need some time alone, so I excuse myself to do homework. My mom takes the hint and heads down the hall to the kitchen and starts preparing dinner for "her girls."

Alone in my room, I plop down in my desk chair and sigh. I do have homework, a whole lot of it, but I'm not really in the mood. Instead, I unzip my guitar from its case and hold it in my lap. Images of my dad are the first to pour into my mind, but Keeta soon follows. I close my eyes and play the movie I always play in my head when I accidentally think of her: the first time we met and she called me Amara, the first time I heard her singing in the guitar shop, that first kiss behind the oleander bushes at school, the winter nights in her room, where I quickly lost track of the hours while we kissed and talked and kissed some more. It's funny how I don't think of the reason we broke up. My ease in forgiving her is baffling. I always thought I was a stickler for integrity and faithfulness. I guess when you've been in love, though, you learn to let go of the bad memories and train yourself to keep the good ones close.

The loud knock at my door startles me. I figure it's my mom, so I mumble, "Come in." When no one enters, I say it louder, but with the tone that my mom has been getting sort of sick of lately.

The next knock is louder, like someone kicking the door. I put my guitar on the bed and walk over to open the door. "What? Oh, hey. Sorry, Devin."

Devin has her hands full with the tray of food, so she can't sign. Instead she looks down at the tray, and I open the door all the way for her. She carefully puts the tray in the center of the bed, then places the glasses of milk onto my bedside table.

"Wow, what is this stuff?" she signs, looking at the pile of veggies and tofu decorated with some sort of orange noodles and chopped peanuts.

"Well, it's nut, plant, or fungus. They seem to be the only choices around here lately," I say, pulling my desk chair over. "Where's Mia?" I sign.

"Sleeping." Devin tries a bite. "This is good."

"You don't have to lie, Devin. My mom can't see you."

She looks at me and rolls her eyes. After readying another bite she leans forward and feeds me a forkful. She watches as I chew.

"Wow," I sign.

"I told you." She lets out one of her loud laughs that always make me feel like life should be taken less seriously.

"How you girls doing?" my mom says, peeking her head in the room.

"Mom, what is this stuff?" I don't mean for it to come out that way—I'm just happy to be enjoying food again. "I mean, it's really good."

Devin nods and smiles as she chews on another mouthful.

"Oh, I just wanted to try something new. It's called pad Thai."

"Well, I'm loving it, Mom. Thanks. Is Mia still sleeping?" I sign and say. It's hard, but I'm getting better at it.

"Yeah, honey. She's had a rough time. Let's just give her a while to adjust and rest. Oh, Devin, I can drive you home in about an hour, okay?" My mom signs *drive* and *okay* which makes me realize that I better be careful about teaching her too many signs. I wouldn't want her to eavesdrop on my conversations with Devin and Mia.

Devin nods. "Thanks."

❖

Even though her campus is really safe, I volunteer to walk Devin to her room. Besides, I want to say good night and, barring any unforeseen bouts of vomiting, maybe something else.

As we walk up the stairs, Devin signs, "Your mom is really cool."

"Yeah, she's cool," I sign. "I hope Mia likes it at my house."

"You kidding? It's like La Paloma Resort compared to her old place."

We're in front of her door now, so I feel the need to announce it. "Here we are."

Devin looks at her door and signs. "Yep. Here we are."

I shove my hands in my pockets, unintentionally shutting down my ability to communicate with her. *Just do it, Abbey. Kiss her! What are you so afraid of?*

But while I'm trying to figure out what exactly my problem is, Devin pulls me into her room, shuts the door behind us, and presses me against it. When I feel her soft lips against mine, I jump slightly, but then quickly relax against the door. Thank God someone had the nerve to do it. My hands come out of hiding and I pull her closer to me. I can feel her heart beating against my chest. She must be on tiptoe, which makes me smile.

She pulls away. "What's so funny?"

I shake my head because I can't find words. "I'm just really happy."

"Was that okay?"

"Your kiss?"

She nods.

"Perfection," I sign and touch her cheek.

"You're the first girl I've ever kissed."

"Wow. Really?" And I don't mean to, but suddenly I'm comparing it to the first time I kissed Keeta. "So, you've kissed boys?"

"Of course," she signs, like I'm crazy for even asking. "Haven't you?"

I shake my head. "Never."

"Shut up. Even Mia's kissed a boy."

I don't mean to, but I scrunch up my face because ew. "Well, I'm glad to be your first girl."

"Me, too." She kisses me again and I'm pretty sure my legs are going to buckle, so I hold on to the doorknob. I wonder how many boys she's kissed. Has she done more than that? Who cares, Abbey. Just enjoy this.

Then my phone sings Salt-N-Pepa's "Shoop," which was my mom's choice for a ringtone. What a mood wrecker. I hold up the phone. "My mom."

She pouts but opens the door for me then looks around before she signs, "Text me later?"

"Yes. For sure." I want to kiss her one last time, but she looks nervous and is keeping her distance.

"And you won't tell Mia, right?"

"I promise," I sign slowly so she'll know I mean it. I turn and take the stairs three at a time so my mom won't get suspicious.

"Everything okay, Abbey? What took you so long?"

"Sorry. We had to help her roommate with a spider situation." It surprises me how quickly I come up with the lies, but I guess after last year, I'm a pro. This realization doesn't make me feel good, but the smell of Devin's lip gloss on my lips does. I guess the mystery of Devin is solved, and now I have one huge secret to keep from Mia. How am I going to pull this off? Up until now, I only had my mom to keep secrets from in my house. But I'm resolved. I can totally do this.

To test my secret keeping abilities, I knock on Mia's door before heading to my room.

"You up, Mia?"

"Yeah, come in."

She's in her bed, which is littered with Kleenex.

"Hey. You okay?"

"Totally. Allergies. Sorry about the mess." She gathers up the tissues and shoves them in the front pouch of her sweatshirt.

I know about Mia and her allergies. And I know she's really only affected by the exploding blossoms of the acacia trees, which aren't around in late fall, but I play along.

"Do you want some medicine? I think my mom has some Benadryl or something."

"Nah, thanks, though."

I stand above her and feel protective all of a sudden, like her mother should have. "Is your bed comfortable?"

"Yeah, thanks."

"Do you have enough pillows?"

She nods. "More than enough. Devin get home okay?"

I fight the urge to smile and I'm successful. Score one for me. "Yeah, she did. She's really glad you're here. Me, too, Mia."

Mia nods. "Thanks, Abs."

"Can I do anything for you?" I'm thinking she might want a glass of water or some leftovers.

But I guess Mia is thinking bigger. "Promise me you won't hurt her, Abbey."

"What do you mean?" I should know better than to play stupid with Mia. I don't know how, but she knows. Then I think about how Devin's going to think I told her and dump me—resulting in the world's shortest lesbian relationship in history.

"She's all I have left," Mia says.

"Mia, we're not—"

"She doesn't know I know. But I see the way she looks at you. I used to look at you that way, too, remember?" I do remember, but I thought she'd forgotten.

"Are you going to say something? She didn't want..." I don't want to hurt Mia's feelings, so I shut myself up. "She wanted to tell you herself. She made me promise not to tell. I'm sorry."

How is it I'm apologizing to her already? I mean, she's the one who was seeing Nicky behind my back, and she hasn't apologized yet.

"I need you to promise me, Abbey. I don't care how crazy you think I am for asking you to."

Of all people, Mia should know that love is a messed-up thing with surprises that aren't always fun. But I do it anyway. "I won't hurt her, Mia. I promise. Okay?"

"Thanks. And thanks for all this." She gestures to the bed and all the toiletries my mom bought for her. "I mean it."

"You'd do the same for me."

She nods and looks away. I know Mia doesn't like to show her feelings, so I say good night and close the door behind me.

So much for keeping Devin a secret.

Chapter Nine

Fifteen and seven-eighths of a year is too young to die. I have my whole life ahead of me. So why, oh why, is Coach Riley trying to kill me?

"Come on, ladies. Push it. Let's go," he bellows.

"Push it real good," Kate says under her breath, and I smile but don't laugh. To laugh would result in my immediate demise. It's our twentieth set of suicide lines today. Only forty minutes of practice have gone by. I'm about to black out and/or quit. I'm hoping for the first.

Kate's breathing hard, too. Her normally well-manicured look is sadly disheveled and dripping with sweat. On our next set of lines, she doesn't even make eye contact as we pass each other at half court. It's like if we thought about anything besides putting one foot in front of the other, we'd totally fall apart.

Finally, Coach blows his whistle. "Two minute water break, ladies."

Like someone turned off the team's power switch, we all collapse exactly where we are. Our team manager does her best to quench our thirsts with water bottles in the two minutes we are given. After I get a squirt, I roll and face Kate. I tried to tell her about Devin in PE, but Kate consumed our locker-room chat with updates on her bad seat dilemma in physics. And since she seems incapable of speaking at the moment, I see my chance.

"I kissed her." I whisper because there are some new girls on the JV team, and I haven't yet assessed their level of homophobia.

Kate turns to look at me, her breathing still labored. "You're going to have to be"—she wipes her face off with a towel—"more specific."

I roll my eyes. Just because of last year's somewhat scandalous behavior of some of us you-know-who girls, Kate claims to never be able to keep track of who is into whom. "Devin. You know, Mia's cousin."

"Oh, right. The deaf one. And?"

I'm irritated by the way Kate refers to Devin, but I let it go this time. "I really like her."

"Time's up, ladies. Let's go," Coach yells from the baseline.

I sigh and push myself up. Kate holds her arms above her, and I give her a pull. "And I'm her first," I whisper to her as we join the rest of our team.

This makes Kate scan me up and down and act impressed for the first time, maybe ever. "Watch out, now."

I shove her. "It's not like that. She—" Then I realize we're surrounded by our teammates. "D actually kissed me."

She laughs. "Well, that makes a lot more sense."

Coach begins to divide us into teams. Kate and I are sent to the same team, me as center, and Kate as a forward. It's no guarantee that we're starting in the game in two weeks because he keeps switching things up, but it'd make sense to have us together.

As I take my position on the block, I regret telling her that last part—about Devin being the one who kissed me. Maybe she'd take me more seriously if I was the one making the moves. Like, maybe she'll finally stop thinking I'll grow out of it and go back to being the old Abbey. But maybe I'm the one who hasn't quite believed it. If I was so sure, so confident in who I am, I would have been the one to kiss Devin first. Then right in the middle of my identity crisis, Riley's voice screams its way into my ear, making me jump out of my skin. "Brooks! Look alive!"

"Sorry, Coach." I put my doubts on hold for a later time. I look across the key and see Kate shake her head at me, as if to say, *There goes Abbey again with her ridiculous girl drama.* Maybe playing on the same team as her won't be as cool as I thought it would be.

At the end of practice, Coach has us line up against the green mat attached to the brick wall on the far side of the gym. I think he's going to tell us what a great job we've done and how impressed he is, but no. Instead he makes us finish up the day with wall squats. The twelve of us moan loudly, but this only makes him add another minute to our time. Just when I'm about to cry, the whistle blows one last time. Practice is finally over.

After we clean up in our separate changing areas, Kate meets me out front where I'm lying on the steps, and we wait for my mom. She's getting her license next month, though. So soon enough, she'll be able to drive us around.

"Hey," she says, standing over me.

I roll toward her and grunt.

"That was fun, huh?"

"Yeah, loads."

"I think I ran my ass off."

"No kidding."

"No, I mean literally. I may have to sue Coach. My ass is one of my best attributes, you know." She turns so I can check it out. "I'm sure my mom will represent me." She smiles.

I smile, too. Straight or gay, we are best friends forever with the bracelets to prove it. "Yeah, I'm sure she will."

She plops down next to me on the steps. "So, is it weird with Mia living with you guys? I mean, does she still like you and stuff?"

I slowly push myself to a seated position. "Nah, we're just friends. It's totally cool. I'm just glad my mom let her. I mean, it's my fault she got kicked out in the first place."

"Um, no it's not. It's Nicky's fault. What a B. At least she's staying away from you now. I guess Tai and Mia showed her."

"Yeah." I don't bother telling her the truth about Mia and Nicky. Then I realize Nicky might even be worse to me than before with Mia living with me. Why didn't I think of that earlier? But so far, things are back to normal. Then I laugh a little to myself. Normal. Ha. That'll be the day.

As soon as we pull into our gravel driveway, I bolt to the bathroom to jump into a hot shower. Devin's taking the four thirty bus from the west side. That means I only have thirty minutes to defunk and clean up. Mia's already home watching a VH-1 '80s video marathon. I run by like I'm the Flash, but apparently, she still sees me.

"What's the rush?" she says as I run by.

Before I answer, I've already slammed the bathroom door. Within seconds I'm getting undressed in front of the desert animals my mom painted on the bathroom wall last year. "No rush. Just hot and sweaty," I yell through the bathroom door.

"I bet," Mia says with a knowing tone, which I don't appreciate since my mom's in the kitchen.

Just like before with Keeta, it's getting sort of hard to hide that Devin and I are sort of dating, and I don't need Mia to make it more obvious. Plus, I don't know what to expect from Mia. How's she going to keep on pretending she doesn't know? And why is she pretending? Why doesn't she just tell Devin she knows? Ugh, I really hate secrets.

"Devin's here!" my mom calls down the hall. Even though I took a shower, I'm back to sweating again as I frantically run around my room, trying on various outfits I think might flatter my bony boy-like frame, but it's hopeless. I give up and slip on my favorite cutoffs and Ani tank top. My hair is still wet, so I put it back in a bun and walk down the hall.

There's no sign of Mia, so I assume she's napping off her four-hour school day as usual. I take one last look at my teeth in the hall mirror before rounding the corner to the kitchen. As much trouble as I have finding clothes to make me look halfway decent, Devin seems to have no trouble finding something to flatter her sexy curves. She's not what someone would call skinny—she's way better, like the love child of Marilyn Monroe and Sofia Vergara. Her clothes hug her tight, but not in a slutty girl sort of way. And the pink shirt she's wearing tonight is so low cut that I can't even look at her because surely my mom will see my gaze linger on Devin's chest too long. To keep my eyes busy, I open the fridge and hide in there. "You want something to drink?" I sign above the door.

"Water," Devin has to say out loud since I'm refusing to look her way.

"Okay, the money's by the phone," my mom says. "There's enough for breadsticks, too. I'll be home by nine. Don't make a mess, honey."

"Okay, Mom," I say to the condiments lined up along the fridge's door.

"Abbey, you're contributing to global warming."

"I'm looking for something." I shuffle some stuff around.

"Well, hurry up." Then I think she signs something to Devin because I hear Devin's laugh.

I pop up from behind the fridge because I want to make sure my mom isn't embarrassing me with her bad signing. "'Bye, Mom. You don't want to be late for your students."

"Yeah, yeah. I'm leaving," she says and shuts the front door behind her.

I wait until the car starts and she's headed down the street before looking at Devin the way I have wanted to since she arrived. We haven't been real-time face-to-face since we last kissed, so my usual script of doubt runs through my mind: it was a mistake, she regrets the whole thing, and I'm such an idiot for thinking she's into me. Plus

I'm nervous that I'm going to mess up my signs. Though I'm getting to know her quite well from our nightly chats online, it's harder to be funny, flirty, and cool in the flesh, in a language that's new to me, without my dictionary right by my side.

"Hi," I sign and reach for her hand, but she pulls back. Uh-oh. She looks over her shoulder, then back at me. "Mia?" she asks.

"Oh, she's sleeping."

"Like always," she signs, then looks down and traces her shoe along the kitchen tile's grout line.

Things are feeling strained, and I don't want them to. "Wow, that shirt"—I smile and heat rises in my face—"it's nice."

"I thought you might like it." She takes a step closer. "I've missed you."

"Me, too." I want to be the one who kisses her this time, but she seems so nervous. If only she knew Mia knew. If only the whole world knew everything and everyone was okay with it all. If only.

Devin runs her hand through her curls and looks around my kitchen, then back at me. She has the most incredible eyes, and her light brown hair framing her face makes them stand out even more. "Mia sleeps pretty hard," she signs finally.

I nod. "True." I listen to the kitchen clock tick a slower rhythm than my heart. I wonder what she's thinking and if it's the same as me.

Another wave of doubt tries to wash over me, but I push it back. Before she can stop me, I gently pull her to me. There's no resistance this time. And when our lips meet and our bodies touch, all doubt disappears. The sweet taste of her lip gloss takes me back to that first kiss, and the softness of her tongue against mine makes my muscles weak. I want to fall to the floor and take her there with me, but I manage to stay upright by leaning against the cool granite counter. She presses into me even more, and the weight of her body against mine makes me breathe heavily. My hands are in her hair, then on her shoulders, then they make their way down to the small of her back. I pull up the back of her shirt a little. Her skin feels so smooth. She kisses me harder. The world around us disappears. We are weightless and floating on clouds. I swear I can see stars behind my eyelids. I bite her bottom lip softly, and she moans louder than I think she means to, and then her body tenses and she pulls back.

My eyes open. I hit the gravity-stricken planet hard when I see her face. She looks startled. Almost angry. Oh my God. I blew it. "I'm sorry," I sign quickly.

"No, it's okay."

"What's wrong?" But before Devin can answer, I hear Mia's door open. "Mia," I spell quickly.

Devin sits quickly at the table, straightens out her shirt, and pretends to be blowing her nose into a Kleenex she pulls out of the box by the phone.

Mia walks by the kitchen, nods at Devin, then me, and falls onto the couch. "What's for dinner?" she signs above her head.

"Pizza," I say without taking my eyes off Devin. My lips are throbbing, along with other parts of me, and it feels like there's a big neon sign flashing *We were just making out!* hanging over our heads. Devin, in the meantime, has lost all color and looks like she might cry. "It's okay," I sign to reassure her, but she just shakes her head and signs that she has to go to the bathroom. I point down the hall.

"What kind of pizza do you like?" I ask Mia.

"Black olive and mushroom."

The mention of mushrooms brings back bad memories. "What about Devin? What does she like?"

"Same, same," Mia sings.

"Great. Black olive and"—I gag slightly—"mushroom it is."

Devin enters, sits down next to Mia, and stretches out her legs. I guess that leaves the floor for me.

By eight thirty we are stuffed. I'm curled up on the living room floor under a blanket while Mia and Devin enjoy the couch. We've had our fill of trash TV, so we agree to watch a movie. Mia wins the coin toss and wants to watch *D.E.B.S.*, but I play the not-out-to-my-mom card and Devin picks *Bridesmaids*. As the movie starts, I replay my kitchen make-out session with Devin over and over and over again in my mind. Like my fingertips have a memory, I can still feel the softness of her hair and body. I close my eyes and nearly let out a contented sigh of happiness until Mia's and Devin's laughter slaps me back to reality. But then I quickly get distracted by what Devin said before—about kissing a boy—and I wonder if she's a virgin.

I had my chance to not be a virgin, but I chickened out. And it seems like the worst part about pre-sex life is freaking out about getting the sex stuff all wrong. Devin said I was her first girl, but that doesn't mean she's a virgin. She certainly doesn't kiss like one, whatever that means. Then I wonder how many boyfriends she's had. The thought of Devin with a guy makes me want to gag worse than mushrooms. In fact, I shudder at the thought of Garrett with a guy, too. And Kate? Ugh.

Gross. Does this make me a homosexist? I laugh a little at my new title, but they don't notice because my laughter falls in line with theirs.

And what about Mia? She seems to have one of those lives people write stories about. Besides Garrett, she'd be the perfect one to ask about what happens when you lose your virginity to a girl, but since I'm currently dating her dearest cousin, I don't think that'd go over well. Yeah. Maybe I should ask someone else. Not that I'm going to need that information anytime soon. Devin and I just started dating, and I'm still into taking things slow. But after the way she acted tonight, I have no idea what to think. And it's as if Mia doesn't want to give us a second alone.

"Hey, girls," my mom says as she unloads her bags on the kitchen table. It's past nine and she's late. I wonder why, but I don't ask, hoping to model how not to be nosy.

"Hey, Mom. How was class?"

"Great. I saw Juliana tonight. She's teaching Environmental Bio across the quad from me. Oh, and Keeta was there," she says.

I don't think I'll ever get used to Keeta's name being said in my house, especially in present company. Mia is far from a fan, and Devin is far from informed. "Oh yeah? That's cool."

"She told me to say hi to you," my mom says, like it's no big deal. Like I'm not going to pay for this friendly gesture after Devin leaves.

I sit up and start to collect our plates and glasses. "Cool," I say to my mom as I pass her on the way to the sink. I quickly glance at the spot on the counter that will be forever known as Second Base. "The pizza was good. Thanks, Mom."

"Thank you, Mrs. Brooks," Devin signs.

"You're welcome," my mom signs.

Mia adds, "Yeah, it was just what I needed. Now I can sleep for the next two days," and then yawns, which spreads to the rest of us faster than germs at Golf N' Stuff. It gets quiet except for the commercial blaring on the TV.

"I'll get my shoes on so we can take Devin home," I finally say. "Her curfew is ten, so we have to hurry."

"Well, if you want to, Devin, you can stay," my mom says.

Panic hits my heart for some reason. I can tell Mia's shocked, too.

Devin looks at me and then at Mia. She signs something to Mia.

Mia tells my mom, "She has to call her parents who have to call the school."

"Great. Abbey, get something for Devin to wear to bed."

I smile. "Okay." I muffle my gleeful giggles as I walk quickly down the hall to my bedroom. We don't have a sofa bed or anything, and I don't like the idea of my girlfriend—if that's what we are—sleeping on the floor, so I offer her my bed and take the couch. After everyone goes to bed, I sneak down the hall and slink into my room like a cat. I don't want to scare Devin by sneaking up on her, so I turn on the overhead light for a second so she can see it's me.

But snuggled up to Devin is a peacefully sleeping Mia. Devin puts her finger up to her lips, blows a kiss my way, and signs, "Good night." I blow a kiss back and turn off the light. I guess Mia needs Devin more than I realized. I guess Devin really is all Mia has left. Unless, of course, Mia is just being a brat. I'll stick with the first theory to give her the benefit of the doubt.

CHAPTER TEN

"Abbey! Come on! I'm open!" Ashley yells at me. Who does this freshman think she is?

Coach Riley's whistle screams in my ear and I stop dribbling. "What? I was trying to run it through."

He sighs heavily, closes his eyes, and tips his head forward as if in prayer, a move he does a lot in the preseason. He finally says, "Abbey, if you run it through and it works, then pass the dang ball. Got it?"

I bounce pass the ball back to Eva and roll my eyes, careful not to let him see. "Yeah, I get it."

"What's wrong with you, Abs?" Kate whispers as we set up the offense again.

"Nothing. I'm just tired." I think she believes me. But for once I'm not lying. Everything is pretty much totally okay. I mean, Devin and I are still talking and signing online, Mia seems to be fine with keeping her knowledge of it secret from all necessary people, Kate's in love and happily distracted, it looks like I'm starting in next week's game, and my mom seems too consumed to notice I'm chatting with Devin every chance I get. Even Nicky has been leaving me alone. But I guess there's one problem.

As my teammates and I run another set of suicides at the end of practice, I think about what's really been distracting me today. As excited as I am to be with Devin, I'm worried. Last time I fell for a girl, things kind of unraveled in my life. Have I learned from my mistakes? Will this time be different? Well, one thing's for sure, Devin won't treat me like Keeta did, so either way, it's going to be better. I just have to balance it all better than last year. No problem, I tell myself, though I can see right through my own lack of confidence.

I towel off my face at the end of practice and walk to the locker room. Why am I so worried? I'm a totally different person now even if everyone else around me doesn't see it. I'm caught up in my thoughts so I don't notice Garrett until I reach my locker in the varsity locker room, a perk of having friends in high places.

"Dude, I haven't seen you this spaced out in a long time. You okay?" She pulls her practice clothes from her bag and strips off her shirt. "What, are you in love again?" She laughs.

Since Garrett's playing varsity this year, I haven't seen her as much. She hasn't even met Devin yet, though I did show her Devin's Facebook page.

"Well, I think I'm getting there," I say.

"Aww, my little gaybie's growing up. Is it that deaf chick?"

"Devin," I say, trying not to let my irritation show.

"Right," Garrett says. "So, what are we talking? Still just flirting, Sandra Dee?" She bats her eyes at me.

I shake my head. "More than that." I smile big.

"Ooh, kissing?"

"Yes, and a little more."

Garrett raises one eyebrow. "You didn't go deep-sea diving, did you?"

My usual look of confusion prompts her to clarify.

"You know, have a beaver playdate, hike her rubyfruit jungle, go cherry picking?" With the last one she makes a gesture with her fingers that I'm 100 percent sure is not an actual sign in ASL.

"No, G. We didn't do any of that."

She fakes a yawn. "Boring."

I don't want her to think I'm totally incapable of naughtiness, so I say, "Well, I slipped my hands down her pants a little. She has a great butt," which is not quite a lie. I mean, I was just about to do that before Devin pulled away when we were in the kitchen.

Finally, Garrett seems slightly impressed. "Good for you, freshie."

I clear my throat, but really, what's the point? I might as well embrace this nickname and move on.

"Very hot," she says.

"You talking about me again, babe?" Tai asks as she walks into the locker room. "What's up, Abbey?"

"Abbey has a new cow in her life. They did more than kiss but haven't rung each other's bells yet."

"Sweet," Tai says, quickly stripping down to her bra and underwear. "So, how long you two been dating?"

I really didn't expect the neon bra, not to mention *sexy* written on the butt of Tai's boy shorts, so I quickly get flustered and look down at my shoes. "Uh, a couple of weeks, I guess."

"Don't, Tai," Garrett yells. I look up and see Garrett grab her deodorant out of Tai's hand. "Get your own."

Tai puts her hands on her hips and pouts. "Why don't you love me anymore?"

"Oh my God," Garrett says and tosses the Secret back to Tai. "You are such a child."

At first I thought it would be cool to play on the same team as your girlfriend, but I'm beginning to see the benefit of seeing someone at an entirely different school. Distance does make the heart grow fonder, for sure.

That's why I'm so excited for Friday night. Devin has a standing invitation to spend Friday nights at our house. Her parents okayed it after talking with my mom last week. All the grown-ups thought it would be best for Mia and Devin to have time together, which seems like it would benefit me, too. But if Mia has her way, Devin and I won't have a second alone. I'm beginning to wonder if Mia really is okay with me dating Devin.

Tai walks over to Garrett, still nearly naked, and hugs her from behind. She whispers in her ear, but Garrett doesn't melt like I imagine I would if Tai did that to me. Instead Garrett uses her butt to push Tai away. "Get dressed. You're freaking Abbey out."

Tai turns to me. "Baby D, am I freaking you out?"

I try not to look freaked-out as I keep eye contact and shake my head. But the truth is, Tai's so gorgeous, and her long legs and arms, defined muscles, and dark brown skin are just the beginning. I've never seen a girl with a six pack, at least not in person, and her smile is perfect—sweet and friendly all the time.

"Wait, are you guys"—I lower my voice—"lesbians?" I whisper, trying to ease the tension. "Ewwww."

Instead of laughing, Garrett throws Tai's practice clothes at her. "Get out of here. I need to talk to Abbey in private."

"Fine. I'll just go find some freshmen to freak out. They're more fun anyway."

After Tai leaves, I sit cross-legged on the large table in the middle of the room. "What do you want to talk to me about?" I'm excited because she never needs my help with anything. Maybe this is my moment to shine, to be here for her for once.

Garrett finishes braiding her hair and ties the end off. "Oh, nothing. I just needed some space. I'm suffocating. She's here, she's home, she's constantly getting me out of class. I'm sick of it. Anyway, back to you. This girl is Mia's cousin, right?"

"Yeah, but Mia doesn't know, so you can't tell anyone else, okay?" The truth is too much to explain right now.

"Nice. Ballsy of you," Garrett says and nods as she puts on her shoes. "You do have good taste, I'll give you that. Always bad judgment, but pretty good taste."

"All right. No more Abbey bashing allowed. Coach Riley already met the daily quota."

But, once again, I turn to Garrett for help. "Hey, what are you doing this Saturday night?"

Garrett slams her locker shut and stretches her quads. "Um, I dunno, but at this point I'll do anything to get out of the house, even go out with a skinny cow like you, especially if there's drinking involved."

My smile fades.

"Sorry, I forgot who I was talking to. Why? What do you want to do?"

"I was wondering if we could hang out. You know, talk."

"You need girl advice, huh?" she asks, smiling slyly.

I hate how transparent I am around her. Or around everyone, so I try to lie. "It's no big deal. I just thought we could chill at a coffee shop, and…" But I can't think of what else to say.

"And talk about girls?"

I throw my sweat-soaked towel at her. "Yes, okay. I'm hopeless without you. Is that what you want to hear?"

She successfully dodges it. "I'll pick you up at six thirty. But do me a favor back."

"Sure."

"Don't tell, Tai, okay? She'll want to come, and I just can't stand the thought of it."

"Yeah, okay," I agree and like that day at the court with Jordan, I feel bad for agreeing to lie to Tai, but it is what it is.

❖

Even though it's almost Halloween, my pool is still warm, so Mia, Devin, and I decide to take a quick dip since it might be one of our last chances to swim past five without getting goose bumps. Mia doesn't like wearing bathing suits, so she opts for the sports bra and shorts combo. I have two suits in my dresser: a two piece and a one piece. I give Devin her pick, and of course she chooses the one piece, leaving me with the skimpy two piece that I bought last summer only because Kate wouldn't take no for an answer. I swear I see Devin hide a giggle as she saunters down to the bathroom to change.

Both Mia and Devin make catcalls at me when I drop my towel on the chair and walk over to the pool steps. I don't look horrible in the green-and-black polka-dotted suit, but it certainly isn't my style. I get in quickly and try to hide under the clear blue water.

The moon is sliced in half and hanging above our heads. Its light, combined with the pool light below, makes Devin's eyes seem to glow like amber. I catch her gaze as she swims backward toward the deep end of the pool. I'm instantly transfixed but keep careful track of Mia so I don't slip up.

Mia is doing handstands underwater, so I take advantage of the opportunity. "You look really beautiful," I sign to Devin, who is now leaning against the wall, her breasts rising and sinking with each breath. She smiles, then sinks down and disappears underwater.

Mia finally comes up for air. "Hey," she says, and then goes under again to push her hair back. "Where's D?"

That's when I see that Devin is zooming across the pool's floor, heading right for me.

"You better run," Mia says. "She's coming at you."

I turn and try to push my legs through the heavy water. I don't get two feet before I'm pounced on from behind. She grabs my waist and, in one swift movement, flings me over her shoulder.

"Oh, you are so dead!" I dive underwater and tickle her right above her knees. I get her good, but to keep her from screaming, I pull her down in the water. She holds her finger to her lips, and that's all the reminder I need that I need to pull back and continue to pretend that Mia doesn't know.

When we come up for air, Mia's drying off by the patio table. "Hey, you cold or something? Get back in here," I say.

"Nah, I'm beat. Long week at school." She wraps the towel tightly around her body, then shimmies out of her soaked shorts and sports bra and drapes them over the lounge chair. "I'll see you guys in the morning. Sleep well." Then she adds, "You're welcome, Abbey," when her back is turned and she's sure Devin can't see her mouth.

I smile, but I feel suddenly nauseous with nervousness.

Devin slips underwater again, and when she resurfaces she's in front of me. "Do you think she's coming back?" she signs.

I look at the house. The light in the bathroom is off and there's no sign of life. I shake my head and sign, "She's in her room. Probably already asleep."

Devin smiles and wraps her legs around me so she doesn't have to hold on. "I hope so," she signs, and then leans in to kiss my ear softly.

I run my hands slowly up her legs and pull her closer. I feel the water rush away as our bodies come together. I like this feeling of weightlessness and how we float there as one.

We kiss for a long time, but I keep it PG because I never had the nerve to ask her why she suddenly pulled away last time we were like this, so I feel like I should hold back and let her take the lead. But then her bathing suit's shoulder strap seductively slips off her shoulder, and I think that deserves attention. I leave her lips, kiss her neck, and then kiss her bare shoulder.

After a few more minutes of kissing we decide we're getting too pruney to stay in the pool, so we walk over to the hammock in the corner of the yard and ungracefully get settled in it. The large towel we have draped over us is damp, but the body heat underneath keeps us plenty warm. I feel her breath on my chest as she lies close, relaxed and heavy. She's running her fingers up and down my bare stomach, making it quiver. It's been a long time since anyone touched me like this. Then she lifts up her head and smiles. "What are you thinking about?" she asks.

Seconds earlier, I was thinking about how two thin layers of spandex were all that separated me from lying naked with a beautiful girl in my hammock. I tell her a different and better truth. "About how I want to hold you in my arms until the sun replaces the moon," I try to sign, hoping she gets the general idea.

She smiles and all is right in the world.

I look up at the desert night sky. It's a map my dad taught me how to read without the help of technology. After locating all my favorite constellations, I tap her shoulder. "What's your sign?"

She giggles. "Why are you asking me now? You already know I like you."

"Just tell me."

"*P-I-S-C-E-S*," she fingerspells.

"Yikes," I sign.

She slaps my leg. "Shut up."

"That explains why you're so stubborn."

She pouts.

"Sorry." I sit up so she can see me more easily. "I can show you where your sign is if you want."

"Really? Cool."

"Okay, it's an easy one. And it's one of my favorites." I look up and realize pointing out stars to someone who has to look at me for directions on where to look is going to be hard. I decide to start with a large star and work my way out from there. I point at Andromeda and tell her to look for its brightest star. After we locate that, it's just a few stars southeast to Pisces. "There you are," I sign. Then I trace the V of Pisces and the small circle in the sky where it comes to an end. "Do you see it?"

She nods.

I look at her looking up and feel proud of remembering.

We stare up at it for a few seconds, and then I tap her arm again to get her attention. "You know, you're beautiful, up there and down here."

She runs her fingers through her wet hair and looks down. "Stop lying, Abbey." Then she looks up again. "Where's yours?"

I look up and search the sky. My dad and I used to race to see who could find it first. It's a long complicated arrangement of stars and hard to decipher. Thinking of my dad again is hard, and all of a sudden I feel protective of what we shared. "I can't find it," I finally sign, even though it's a lie. I don't know why I do it. Maybe it's starting to feel like we're getting too close. "You look tired. We should probably go to bed."

"Yeah, okay, but first..." She leans in quickly to kiss me, but because I didn't expect her to move, our weight makes the hammock sway backward, and down we go.

She screams loudly as we tumble out, and I fall on her. Now we have literally fallen head over heels for each other. This thought makes me laugh even though I'm pretty sure I'm bleeding somewhere. "You okay?" I sign.

She's laughing, too, and nods.

Then I hear the back door open and slap my hand over Devin's mouth. "Mia," I sign.

Her eyes nearly pop out of her head, but I'm feeling a sense of relief. Maybe we can all stop the charade finally. But when I hear my mom's voice, my eyes get wide, too.

"Abbey? Are you okay? Where are you? Mia?"

"My mom," I sign and Devin covers her own mouth with both her hands.

I jump up off the lawn. "Hey, Mom!"

"Jesus, Abbey, you scared me. What are you doing? Are you okay?"

"Yep. I was just helping Devin up." I grab hold of Devin's hands and pull her off the ground. "She was swinging on the hammock while I was swimming and then, oops, she fell out. She's okay." I turn to Devin. "You're okay, right?"

Devin nods and grabs the towel to wrap around her. I can tell she's freaking out, but she doesn't know she has nothing to worry about. After all, she hasn't seen one of my greatest skills in action: lying to my mom.

"Oh," my mom says, but the way she says it makes my heart race. It wasn't like, *Oh, I see. Well, that makes sense.* It was more like, *Oh. Oh, my. Oh, I see what's going on here.*

"Well," she says slowly. "It's late and you girls need to come inside now."

"Yep. Okay. Sorry if we woke you up."

"Just get inside and go to bed," she says. "Abbey, I already made up the couch for you." It's obvious this last part was said very intentionally.

We head to the back door, neither one of us looking at the other or at my mom.

Scared doesn't even begin to describe how I feel.

CHAPTER ELEVEN

If I have to endure Mia's confusing glares much longer, I'll twirl my hair into a giant mass of Rastafarian dreads. It's like all of a sudden she's mad about Devin and me. After I told her what happened last night, how my mom found us after we fell out of the hammock, things shifted. Instead of laughing like I thought she would, she just shrugged and said, "Close call."

So I whisper to her, "Why are you being like this?"

She flips through the channels. "Why are you so paranoid?"

"I'm not." I look at my watch, then go to the bathroom to check my hair again. Finally I hear Garrett honking outside and grab my wallet.

"'Bye, honey," my mom says from behind her easel. "Have fun. See you at around nine?"

"Yeah," I say right before I slam the door shut and run to the car. "Thank God you're here. Punch it."

The idea of having a sister is getting a little old. I mean, if having a sister means someone is always on your case about stuff that isn't their business, then no, thanks. I'd rather be alone.

I look over at Garrett. Even though she's wearing a zip-up hoodie, I can't help but notice her cleavage. "Uh, hello. How much do you charge?"

"What? You think it's too much?" she says, looking down at her chest.

"The opposite. Did Tai see you leaving the house like that?"

"So what if she did? Besides, she's not the boss of me," she says as she speeds up to fly through a yellow light. "I mean, she's always doing whatever she wants. Half the time I think she's lying about where she is, you know? That reminds me, if she asks, we went to the U of A library to study."

"Really, G? You don't find that a little hypocritical?"

"Says the girl who hates cheaters, but happily cheated with Keeta last year?" She looks over at me and smirks. "Tell me I'm wrong."

I roll my eyes. "Whatever."

Garrett swerves into a parking spot, and now I'm bummed out. I was hoping she'd stick with the itinerary so I could binge on fries and a mocha shake at the Ugly Mug. Of course, I wouldn't have to depend on others to drive me around if I'd continue my driving lessons with my mom. But, after that disastrous start, neither one of us seems eager to try again.

We walk down Fourth Avenue, then head into a bookstore called Hermione's. "Where are you taking me, G?" I finally ask. "I thought we were getting coffee?"

"Stop being such a baby. Besides, it's about time you know about this place. I mean, if you're committing to being a cow, which it seems you are, you have to know where the rest of your herd hangs out."

Twinkling Christmas lights illuminate a doorway in the back of the bookstore. The sign above the entry says *Sappho's*. "How do I look?" Garrett asks while pulling down on her shirt, revealing the top of her bra.

"Cute color," I say, giving up on reprimanding. Might as well compliment her.

"I know, right?" She opens the door for both of us. "Brace yourself and try not to stare."

I follow Garrett and her boobs and wonder about her own intentions tonight. Is she here just to hang out with me, or is she here to do some scamming of her own?

After we order our coffee drinks, Garrett selects our seats and we get settled. She smiles big at me. "Well, what do you think?"

I take it all in. It's like every lesbian in Tucson has descended upon this little café: big and tall, short and skinny, white and brown, middle-aged and baby dykes in training—they're all here. A women's soccer game plays on the TV on the opposite wall. At the counter, the super-butch lesbian who took our order dries coffee cups and nods her head to the music playing through speakers. I recognize it, which makes me feel proud. I immediately want to call Mia to tell her they're playing her favorite Ani song. I also want to stand up and yell, *Hello, my people!* But instead I act as calm as possible. "It's cool."

My gaping mouth must show my shock because then Garrett says,

"It's like lezzie-palooza, huh? It's always like a freaking Lilith Fair concert in here. A damn cattle ranch. Dykestock, baby."

"I didn't know something like this existed in Tucson. Why didn't you take me here before?" I ask as two twentysomething cows walk to a table near us.

"Well, there's one ugly reason why," Garrett says under her breath.

"Hey, G," the tall one in the Mercury jersey says. "You staying out of trouble?"

Garrett simultaneously rolls her eyes, tosses her hair over her shoulder, and pushes her breasts to attention. "Whatever, Sadie," Garrett says and flips her off.

"You wish, honey," Sadie whispers, and then sits down with, I assume, her girlfriend because they immediately hold hands.

"Friend of yours?" I whisper.

"No one you need to know. One of my regrets, that's all."

I'm still so impressed with Garrett's mysterious and exciting life, which really just means she's had sex with girls and I find that mysterious and exciting. Garrett likes to call me a virginarian or, when she's being especially mean, Abstinent Abbey. It's not that I don't want to. I do, but how does someone ever get the nerve to get naked in front of someone? Then again, I guess you don't have to be naked to have sex. Then a gaggle of college girls walk in. I guess they're on a U of A team since they all have some Wildcat gear on. I'm tall, but these girls aren't just tall; they're strong. One girl in particular sort of scares me. Then I think about having sex with her and I shudder. She'd break me like a pretzel stick.

Garrett sees the big one, too. "Man, check out that butch," she says behind her hand. "Damn, someone get that dyke a bike." I laugh even though I don't get it. I guess I'm destined to be a clueless baby D forever. Our drinks are ready and the girl calls Garrett's name. As she leaves to get our drinks she says, "We seriously have to get you to a gay pride parade this year, freshie."

On her way back to our table, Garrett looks toward the girl that she flipped off earlier. "What, Sadie? You playing a game of Sneer the Queer, or something? Stop effing staring at me."

Sadie laughs. "You haven't changed a bit, G. Does Tai even know you're here?"

"Screw you," Garrett says, but then turns toward me. "Crap."

"What? Do you think she'll tell?"

She glances over her shoulder slightly. "Nah. I doubt she even has Tai's number."

We watch the game for a few minutes, then Garrett leans over to me and whispers, "I sort of made out with Jordan last night."

"You what with who?"

"Remember, the guy we played at Gila. He called and wanted to play one-on-one." She puts air quotes around the last part of her sentence, though she didn't need to for my benefit. I may be stupid when it comes to flirting, but I do know that a game of one-on-one is just an excuse to bump up against someone you like.

"What about Tai? What about being—"

"I'm bi, Abbey, and you need to let go of whatever biphobic thing you've got going on. Being bi is real, so get over it. Besides, I'm too young to be tied down like this. It was hot, in case you were wondering."

I feel stupid after her lecture, but just say, "I wasn't wondering, but good for you, I guess." I look back at the screen partly because I'm embarrassed and because I can't process this news.

Garrett leans back and sighs. "He was kind of small though," she says and holds up the salt shaker in her hand. "That was disappointing."

I don't normally ask the stupid questions I'm thinking, but this one can't be stopped. "Wait, what does making out with a guy mean to you? How would you know what his, you know, looks like?"

She shrugs. "His shorts were thin."

I grimace at the thought of her with him and feel worse about Tai being in the dark. "G, have you talked to Tai about how you feel? Maybe she feels the same way. I know I'm not the expert here, but it only seems fair to Tai."

"Are you kidding? She tells me every night how she never wants to live without me. How she feels like she would die if we ever broke up."

I don't mean to, but I frown again. It sounds like Garrett can't break up with Tai even if she wanted to. It's like she's trapped. That can't be good for either of them.

"Never mind, I shouldn't have told you. You'll keep my secret, though, right?"

I'm feeling guilty for being here for some reason, so instead of looking around at all the very attractive girls, I'm trying to get invested in the game.

"Hello, Abbey?" Garrett flicks my nose. "Confirmation needed."

"I'll keep it tighter than my chastity belt, 'kay?"

She laughs loudly and the women sitting around us turn to look. "You kill me, Abs. You really do." One of the U of A girls walks past us to the bathroom. "I have the sudden urge to pee," Garrett says. "Don't leave. I'll be right back."

"Where would I go?" I say, but I'm ready to leave. I feel like a total outcast in here, so I avoid eye contact with all patrons, shred a napkin, and question my ability to be anything but a nervous, naive, and awkward person.

"What did I miss?" Garrett says when she finally returns and plops down next to me, a wide grin on her face.

I hide the napkin bits in my hand. "Nothing." Maybe now we can get down to the reason I wanted to hang out with her: me and my girl-on-girl questions. But she looks like she's going to implode, so I forget about my needs and ask, "What's with the smiling? Good time in the bathroom?"

"You could say that."

"Are you going to elaborate?"

"Okay, that totally hot ten over there dished over her digits."

I look over my shoulder. "Who? What?"

"After I did my business, I was washing my hands and kind of made eye contact with her. I asked her name and if she played basketball at U of A. She does. She's a freshman."

"Yeah?" How does she do it? And can she teach me?

"And she was all, *You look really familiar. What's your name?* So I was all, *Garrett, but most people call me G*, and she was all…oh my God, she has the sexiest voice, Abbey." She closes her eyes to emphasis the swoon.

Before she opens them again, I'm elbowing her hard in her side. "Tai is here," I whisper behind a menu, hiding myself but leaving Garrett in the open.

For the first time since I've known Tai, she looks distraught as she approaches us. "I thought you two were at the library."

Garrett nervously laughs and just says, "Whatever," which would piss me off as much as it seems to piss off Tai. And suddenly that roomy café feels like a four-by-four foot cell with limited air. Out of the corner of my eye, I see Sadie smiling smugly. She must have had something to do with Tai's sudden appearance. Some people, I swear.

I know Garrett well enough to know that a dramatic scene in this place would kill her, so when Tai says through clenched teeth, "We need to talk. Outside," Garrett obeys quickly.

I'm incapable of sitting alone, so I sneak out the door a few seconds after them and wait what I think is a safe distance away.

"You didn't think I would find out? That's your excuse? Are you kidding me?" Tai says.

"Tai, honey, listen…" Garrett says quietly. It looks like Garrett is trying to get Tai to stay, but Tai storms off, not looking at me as she passes. Garrett is left leaning against the wall and starts to cry. Wasn't she just bragging about making out with Jordan and giggling about getting a girl's number? I guess it's different when you're the one playing with the power switch.

For the first time ever, Garrett reminds me of me. What is it about love that we are willing to hurt so much for? And what makes us jump back in after we are decimated and destroyed? How can we believe that each time it will be different? I have no answers. Instead I walk to her, put my arm around her, and steer us toward her car.

❖

"You went to bed in a hurry last night," Mia says, then stuffs her mouth with a spoonful of Twix, a cereal my mom would never let me have.

"I was tired." I glare at her sitting smugly across from me in her usual sweatshirt and boxers, then decide things are getting too personal around here, and I don't like being accountable to someone—I mean someone who knows more about what I'm up to than my mom.

Mia shakes her head and eats another spoonful of cereal. "I'm not even going to ask."

"Good, don't." I pick up the box of Twix, but as I tip the box farther and farther, nothing pours out. "Nice," I say and get up to get the box of healthy cereal from the cupboard. I try to drown my floating Os with my spoon, but they keep on popping up. "Long story."

Mia finishes off her slurping and then says, "You better tell me or I'm going to assume the worst, and you do not want me to do that."

I could always talk to Mia before, about everything. But ever since I started seeing Devin, it's been getting more weird and, now, too dangerous. I don't say anything and don't look up, but I can feel her staring hard at me.

"Okay, whatever. Be a liar."

My mouth opens to convince her I'm not lying, but nothing comes out. I don't have anything to hide, but I'm struggling with which secrets I'm keeping from whom. Maybe that's why I'm so tired.

"The truth will set you free, Abs."

I get up and pour my cereal in the sink even though I'm not done. I sit on the kitchen counter and bounce a rhythmic beat against the cupboards. After a minute of that, I sigh and start the tale. I should stop myself, but I tell her everything—kind of. I do tell how cool Sappho's was, but not about how many hot girls there were. Mostly, I focus on Tai and Garrett.

"How about you? You get any numbers?"

"No. I'm not exactly looking, as you know." Is she jealous because she's protective of Devin or jealous because of something else? Sometimes I wonder.

Mia sees me staring at her quizzically and rolls her eyes. "Whatever."

"Whatever what?" I say back, trying to get her to explain, but my mom walks in to refill her coffee mug and interrupts us.

"Abbey, how many times have I told you not to sit up there? Get down. You're too big for climbing on counters."

"Okay, okay," I say and slide off the countertop, missing the days when my mom found me more adorable and less annoying.

"What are you girls up to today?" she asks as she rummages through the fridge for the cream. "I mean, of course, after you clean the bathroom, vacuum, dust, and water the backyard."

My mom is really getting into having two kids to use as maids around the house. In fact, I don't think she's done any cleaning since Mia moved in. It doesn't help that Mia is a neat freak and actually likes cleaning. Or maybe she just feels obliged because my mom took her in.

"Dibs on the backyard!" I raise my hand.

"Abbey, you did that last week. It's your turn to clean the bathroom," she says after gulping down some coffee.

"I don't mind doing it, Susan," Mia says and smiles at me.

I smile back, but being as in touch with my feelings as she is, I'm sure Mia reads what I'm really saying on the inside.

"No, no, Mia. You've done too much. You water, and Abbey will clean the bathroom."

"Whatever you say goes," Mia says.

And that's when I emphatically decide that sisters are totally overrated.

CHAPTER TWELVE

Even though things didn't get patched up between Garrett and Tai, Garrett has a renewed sassy attitude today to match her low-cut T-shirt and practically painted-on jeans. I guess they ended the way she wanted or she's really good at faking it. On the other hand, when I saw Tai in the hall this morning, she totally ignored me and looked angry. I wanted to console her and headed toward her, but her quick one-eighty away from me was a clear enough hint that she didn't want to talk to me.

Meanwhile, Garrett's got a sway in her hips that she claimed was going to bring all the girls and boys to the yard. I didn't argue with her there.

While I change for practice, she lies on the table in the varsity locker room, killing time until her practice starts. "We are over like *How I Met Your Mother*," she says, then feigns death.

"Yeah, I get it. So now what?"

"She moved out on Sunday, back to her dad's house." As much as I am glad for her and her newfound freedom, I feel bad for Tai. They were like the Ellen and Portia of Gila, and I think everyone around here thought they'd last. How can there be any hope for the rest of us if G and Tai didn't make it?

I turn around and face the lockers while conducting the magic bra switch without revealing a bare breast, then pull on my workout tank. "Don't you think you'll miss her?" I ask as I tie my shorts.

"Are you kidding? No more sharing showers, my bed, or underwear. Do you know how irritating it is to have your favorite underwear ruined by your girlfriend's insanely heavy flow?"

Kate walks in just in time to hear about Tai's period, and I swear I see her consider walking back out. Instead she says, "Five minutes, Abbey. Hurry up. You know we'll pay if we're late." She looks at herself in the full-length mirror and evens out her socks. "Sorry about you and Tai, Garrett. That sucks."

Garrett shrugs. "Thanks, but I'm fine."

"Yeah, some things are for the best, I guess, huh?" Kate says, like her relationship with Dumbass Derrick last year has made her a wise woman.

I hide my eye roll from them both, hand Garrett my brush and hairband, then take a seat between her legs and she sits up and starts to French braid my hair. "What about playing ball? Isn't it going to be weird to share the court with Tai?"

"Nah. You know how it is," Garrett says as she quickly weaves my hair. "On the court, it's all business. I think she'll be cool. I am."

Kate and I exchange a glance. Without saying a word, I know we're both thinking the same thing.

Garrett wraps the band around the end of my braid and pushes me off the table. "That'll cost you Hot Cheetos and a Gatorade. I'm freaking starving. I can't make it until after practice."

"Sorry, G. I'm broke. My mom is being extra stingy since Mia moved in."

Garrett looks over to Kate, and although no services were given to Kate, she digs into her bag and tosses over some cash for the vending machine. "Get me a melon one while you're at it."

I look up at the clock and we only have one minute left. "Crap. Let's jet, Kate."

As Garrett follows us out to the gym, I hear her whisper to Kate, "Hey, I've been meaning to ask you, is Jordan in your physics class?"

"You mean Jordan Jones?" Kate says and laughs for some reason. "Yes. Why?"

"Just wondering. Wait, you don't like him, do you?"

"He's good eye candy, but I've got my eyes on his best friend, Miguel. Why, do *you* like him?"

There's a hint of excitement in Kate's voice. She's always held out hope for Garrett since she's bi. Not that Kate's a total homophobe, but she still thinks life would be a lot easier for us if we weren't so lesbian. Sometimes I secretly agree.

"Don't tell anyone, but we kind of hooked up." Garrett looks bashfully away, but I can tell it's fake. She's not embarrassed by anything.

Then, as if a switch flipped in Kate's body, she grabs Garrett and squeals. "OMG, are you serious? What if you end up with Jordan and

I end up with Miguel? We could go on double dates and go to prom together and…"

And just like that, I feel like I have disappeared. So I tug on Kate's ponytail. "Hey, Gossip Girl, we're going to be late," I say and tap my wrist.

"Yeah, yeah, Abs," Kate says, waving me off. "G, you totally need to call me tonight."

I could leave her behind, but it feels like if I do, she wouldn't even care, and that feels worse to me than anything Coach could do to us. "He's coming, Kate." I pull on her shirt this time and start to drag her toward the edge of the court.

"Promise you'll call me, G," Kate says to Garrett again as I pull her along.

"Okay," Garrett says. I think she's just as shocked as me by Kate's enthusiasm. And then she crosses her heart. "I will."

Even though we're in a full sprint to the court, Coach Riley blows his whistle before we make it to the baseline. "Thanks to Ms. Brooks and Ms. Townsend, it looks like you all will be running a little extra today."

The scowls from my teammates are like daggers, but they can stare all they like, I don't care. I've got my own problems. First I lose Mia to that stupid alternative high school, then I can't be friends with Tai because I lost her in the divorce and Garrett not-so-subtly threatened me if I ever hung out with Tai behind her back, and now Garrett is abandoning me altogether.

Suddenly, I feel like a herd of one.

After another grueling practice, plus the extra wall squats, suicides, and push-ups, I stumble into my house and head right for the laptop, which is now in the living room, giving me even less privacy than when it was in my dad's office, aka Mia's room. I know I need to shower. I know I need to eat. I know I need to get my homework done, but all I can think about is seeing Devin. I click on her name and wait. I texted that I was getting home late, but she never texted back. Maybe she went to dinner early? The computer rings, and I know when I see her face, I'll feel relaxed for the first time all day. And tonight I'm finally going to do it. I'm going to ask the big question: Devin, will you be my girlfriend?

That is, if she ever answers.

❖

I'm about two episodes deep into *I Didn't Know I Was Pregnant*, and my mom, who has been at her easel all afternoon, has done her best not to show her concern. She finally breaks her silence when I change it to *My Teen Is Pregnant and So Am I.*

"Uh, Abbey Road," she says quietly, "is there something you want to tell me?"

"Ha-ha, Mom," I say. "Very funny." If only I were pregnant. Somehow that seems like an easier thing to tell my mom. Ever since that night when she found Devin and me, I've been avoiding talking to her, and it seems like she's done the same to me. Today we were alone for the first time in a long time, but instead of coming clean, I spent almost all day avoiding her in my room until she forced me off my bed so she could wash my sheets. Now I'm piled out on the couch, waiting for life to happen. Devin's out of town, Mia's sleeping yet again, and Garrett and Kate are at the mall doing whatever girls who like guys do together—yet another mystery to me. I sigh heavily.

"Why don't you call Kate? She hasn't been over lately."

"Busy." I grunt, then flip back to the other show. It's another toilet-born baby. Gross. I flip it back.

"What about Garrett? What's she up to?"

My mom sure knows how to rub it in without knowing she's rubbing it in. Plus, there's no point in calling them because after the mall Kate and Garrett are going to be at Kate's getting ready for their double date with Jordan and Miguel. The last text update I got was of them getting their toes painted in Cherry Popsicle Red. After that, I turned off my cell. What's the point?

"Maybe you guys can go to the park to play basketball or something," my mom continues after adding another few lines to her painting because she can't talk and paint at the same time.

"I have cramps," I say because it seems to be the only thing that gets grown-ups to leave you alone.

"Well, that's a relief," my mom says and laughs at her joke, then leans in again toward her canvas. "Homework done?" she says a minute later.

Clearly I have exhausted my time limit being a pile on the couch. If I don't move, she'll drive me insane with questions and suggestions. I turn off the TV and make a silent decision to go play basketball by myself because there's nothing like playing a sport by yourself to help you feel less dissed by all your so-called friends.

After changing into my workout clothes, I announce my intentions.

"I'm going to practice free throws at Columbus Park. Be back in like an hour."

"Sounds good, honey. I'll have dinner ready by then."

"Whatever," I say under my breath before slipping in my earbuds. She doesn't deserve my snarkiness, but I can't seem to help myself.

❖

"Sorry," I say, out of breath, as I slam the kitchen door behind me. It's ten past seven and I'm late for dinner. "I couldn't call because I forgot my phone here." I take my usual chair at the dining table and start to serve myself some of the lukewarm pasta that does not look like normal pasta, covered in sauce that does not look like normal sauce. "Looks good, Mom."

"Mia made it," my mom says. "Isn't that great?"

I fight back the urge to simultaneously spit out the bite in my mouth and gag. "Yeah, that's cool. Thanks, Mia."

She nods at me then continues the conversation they were having before I rushed in.

"So anyway, then"—Mia says between bites of her salad—"Mr. Johnson said art is everything. Art can be a stop sign, a milk carton, a painting, a pile of chairs. So as an artist, I'm curious about what you think. I mean, I kind of bragged about living with a real artist, and I promised him I'd ask you and report back to class tomorrow."

"Oh, my first official interview," my mom says and smiles wide. "Do you need some paper to write down what I'm going to say?"

"Nope." Mia taps her forehead. "I have a great memory. I can recall everything said, done"—Mia looks over at me—"or promised."

I glare back at her. What's that supposed to mean? Anyway, I'm just being paranoid, so I let it go and quickly eat my meal and change my mind about coming out to my mom tonight. Tomorrow would be better. Or maybe next weekend before Devin comes over. Wait, if I tell my mom, would she let me have Devin over anymore? Maybe honesty isn't the best policy.

I've been pushing the last few bites of my dinner around on my plate distracted by my inner conflict when my mom's voice interrupts me. "Abbey, did you hear me?"

"Huh?" I look up and she's at the sink. Mia's clearing the table like the kiss ass that she is. "What?"

"You're on dishes tonight since Mia made dinner."

"Sucker," Mia says under her breath.

"But, Mom," I whine, "I have tons to do." My argument is so weak I'm almost embarrassed.

"Tons?" my mom questions. "If you had tons, how did you manage to watch five hours of TV and play basketball?"

"Fine, fine," I say to get her to stop. "I'll do them right after I shower."

She tosses the dish towel at me. "You'll do them now."

Yep, not coming out tonight. That's for sure.

After dishes—and I swear, Mia used an exorbitant number of pots and pans for one meal—I collapse on my bed with my cell phone in my hand. Devin hasn't texted all day. I'm sure she's busy posing for pictures and stuff, but it wouldn't kill her to send a quick hello. Besides it's almost ten. Aren't weddings over by now? So in a needy gesture, I send another text: *Hey, it's me. Just saying hi. Hope you had a fun time.* Then I wait. And wait. After three minutes of torture, I decide to shower.

I check my phone on the way to the bathroom. Nothing. Could Mia have told Devin? Told her what? This is stupid.

I spend way too long in the shower, so now my body temp has increased and I'm getting all sweaty again. After I slip on my tank and shorts, I open the shutters and spin open my window. That's when I hear giggling. One laugh I know, the other sounds eerily familiar. I press my head against my screen and look toward Mia's window. What the hell?

With the help of the porch light, I see two legs kicking in the air. They definitely belong to a girl, and she's trying to get into Mia's window and failing miserably. It brings me back to my days with Keeta, and I almost laugh it off, but then I see her shoes: a pair of black Cons with hot pink patches. I will never forget those shoes since they were all I saw of Nicky that day she caught me in the bathroom.

After she gets through the window, Mia shuts it quickly, and I'm left standing here with questions swarming my brain. How can she do this? Didn't she say they were through? How can she betray my mom like this? After everything we've done for her. But mostly I'm pissed off and wondering how she dares to bring that bitch into my house.

Before I know it, I'm out my door and standing with clenched fists at Mia's. I reach for the door handle, but the thought of seeing them in an embrace makes me sick to my stomach. Instead I pound on her door and wait.

She doesn't come. What, does she think I'll go away?

I figure my warning has separated them, so I grab the handle and bust in like the FBI. I catch the same view of Nicky, but this time she's struggling to get out of Mia's room. "What the hell, Mia?" I point at Nicky. "In my house?"

By now Nicky has given up and is out of the window, standing behind Mia as if she's afraid of me.

"Shhh," is Mia's only reaction. She shuts the door quickly. "Chill the eff out."

"Chill out?" I yell. "I thought you guys were through. You promised me. How could you do this?"

Mia points to the door. "You're going to wake up your mom, Abbey. Is that what you want?"

I look at Nicky and then Mia. "I want you both out of my house."

"What in the world is going on?" my mom asks from the doorway. "Why are you yelling, Abbey?" My mom has her hands on her hips and looks a bit crazed from being woken up by my screaming, but then she finally sees Nicky, who she saw that day in the office but was never introduced to. "And who are you?"

For some reason, the minute my mom shows up, a huge lump settles in my throat, but I swallow it so I can out Mia and Nicky. "Mom, meet Nicky. You know, the girl who destroyed my locker and stole my backpack. You know, the reason Mia got expelled."

Nicky, who looks paler than ever, says, "Uh, I should go," and takes a step toward the door, but my mom doesn't budge. "Or, I can stay." Nicky sits on the bed's edge.

"Someone needs to tell me what's going on," my mom demands.

"Well, you see—" Nicky starts.

"Not you," my mom says, and Nicky shuts her mouth.

Instead of explaining to my mom, I continue to tell Mia how I feel. "I just can't believe you would do this after all we've been through. What kind of friend are you? We did everything for you."

"Abbey, look, just let me—"

"How long have you been lying to me? And taking advantage of my mom like this? How can you do that to her?"

"Are you kidding me?" Mia yells back. "How can *I* do that to her? You need to stop yourself before—"

"What's that supposed to mean?" I ask, even though I know exactly what she's getting at, but she wouldn't dare. "How can you bring that trash into our house?"

"Look, girls. Let's just calm down," my mom says, trying to stop us both from saying anything else we're going to regret, but it's too late. The next thing comes out before I can stop it.

"Just because your mom hates you doesn't mean you can treat mine like crap."

"Abbey!" my mom says, "That's enough."

And I guess it really is because Mia comes right at me. I step back and my mom steps forward, grabbing Mia by the arm. It's enough to stop Mia from coming closer. "She doesn't mean that, Mia," my mom says softly.

"No, she's right," Mia says, her voice cracking. "My mom totally hates me." Then angry tears start to stream down her face. "But at least I'm not the one keeping secrets from a really amazing mom. Unless, of course, you've finally told her you're gayer than—" She quickly covers her mouth, and her wide eyes look from me to my mom. "Oh, shit," she whispers into her hand.

I can't breathe. I feel like every bone in my body is broken. I can't speak, either, so I don't deny it. The pain is nearly unbearable. I didn't think the way Keeta betrayed me last year could be topped, but I was wrong. I can't look at my mom, so I look away from Mia and down at the carpet and bite my lip. I don't want Nicky to see me cry. I don't want to see the shame in my mom's face. I want to die.

My mom finally takes control again. "How did you get here, Nicky?"

Nicky clears her throat. "Uh, I drove, Mrs. Brooks."

"Well, I suggest you drive yourself home now. Thank you."

She grabs her coat and slinks out of the room and out the front door. For the first and probably last time in my life, I wish I could trade places with her.

After Nicky leaves, my mom sends me to my room and orders Mia to stay in hers. I guess she figures we all need a moment to gather ourselves. And maybe she needs one more than me or Mia.

My room feels different now. Sitting here waiting for my mom, I feel shameful of every Tegan and Sara and Marilyn Monroe poster. This wasn't how it was supposed to go. At all. Even Garrett couldn't have predicted this outcome.

I grab my phone. Garrett'll know what I should do. She'll have the advice she always has that makes everything better. She's probably still out with Kate on the double date, but maybe she'll check.

G, my mom knows. Can you talk? I push send and wait.

There's no reply. To make matters worse, as if that's possible, I still haven't heard from Devin all day and it's past eleven. She can't still be at the reception. I text her again. *Dev, can you call me, please. Major things happening over here. I need you.*

As soon as I send the text, there's a knock on my door. "Abbey, can I come in?" my mom whispers.

I nod even though she can't see me because the sound of her voice makes me start to cry and I can't talk.

"I'm coming in, Abbey," my mom cautions, as if I have anything else to hide.

By the time she sits down next to me, I am three tissues into my breakdown.

"My Abbey Road," she says and pulls me to her. She rocks me back and forth like she used to when I wasn't an almost six-foot-tall liar. "You know I love you so much."

I let out another sob.

"Shhh…" She pushes my wet hair away from my face and lifts my chin. I finally look her in the eyes. They're filled with tears, too. "I love you and I always will. No matter what."

"I don't deserve it." I am cry yelling, but not because I'm angry. I think it's because now that she knows the truth, she'll know all the lies. I feel so ashamed. "I'm sorry." I fold into myself and she holds me again.

She lets me empty my tear reserves and then says, "Let's try this again, Abbey. Just you and me."

I wipe my face on my sleeve. "What do you mean?"

"Well, I have a feeling that wasn't the way you expected, you know, things to go."

I clear my throat. Is she going to force me to say it? "Yeah, not really."

"Just so you know, Mia feels terrible. She started to pack her things to leave, but I talked her into staying. Are you okay with that?"

I nod even though I don't know how I feel about Mia right now. I guess deep down, I don't hate her enough to send her out into the streets.

My mom scoots back from me and turns to face me. "So, is there something you want to tell me, Abbey Road?"

The nickname makes me cry again, but I try the trick Garrett taught me, and I'm able to stop the tears. I'll be sure to tell her the role she played in my coming-out moment. Now I'm looking down at my hands because even though my mom knows, and she says she loves me, and it's already been done, saying the words feels impossible.

"Go ahead, honey."

My phone signals that I have a text and we both jump. I glance over at it and see Devin's name illuminated on the screen. Her timing is incredible. It's all I can do to not reply. Instead, I turn the phone over, which feels like I just cut an important part of my body off.

I look back down at my hands and wonder why this is so hard. *She's here. She loves you. Just say it.* "Okay, so…"

She nods to encourage me.

"Mom." I look up and she's smiling, which makes my next words a whole lot easier. "Mom, I'm not fond of your tofu casserole."

"Abbey!" She laughs and hits me with my Wildcat pillow.

"No, really. I'm sorry. I hope we can move forward, though."

"You're impossible, you know that?" She's still smiling and that's all I need.

"And while I'm making confessions, I might as well let you know I like girls, you know, in a more-than-friend kind of way." All those words seem easier than saying one three-letter word to my mom. Or the more awkward one: lesbian. For now, I think it's good enough that she knows I'm a you-know-who girl.

She hugs me tight, and then says, "I think that's wonderful and you're wonderful, Abbey. And you know your dad would be so proud of you, too, don't you?"

Why did she have to go there? My smile falls and a new round of tears rush down my face. "How do you know, Mom?"

She rubs my back and lets me cry a little more, then she says, "You were his light and you still are. I know he'd be the first in line to march in a gay pride parade with a big sign telling the world how much he loves you. And thank you for telling me." She hugs me again. "I love you, and I really appreciate that you trust me enough to tell me this."

I try to pull back, but her arms have me trapped like a giant claw. "I love you, too."

She finally releases me and asks, "How did I do?"

I laugh. "What do you mean? Have you been rehearsing your reaction?"

"Well, a little. The ladies at the PFLAG meeting helped me out." She clasps her hands like she's excited. "I can't wait to tell them!" She's beaming with pride, but I'm a little confused, so she says, "PFLAG stands for Parents, Friends, and Family of Lesbians and Gays."

"Duh, Mom," I say because I've known about them since last year and have been plotting how I might leave a flyer around for her to find but was too chicken. Now that I know she was going there behind my back, I'm kind of irked. "You mean you've been talking to people about me?"

She touches my knee. "Honey, it's totally confidential. I never even used your name. Please don't be upset. I just needed some support."

I lean against the wall to give us some more distance. "Why? Were you freaked-out about me?"

Devin texts again, or maybe it's Garrett. I ignore my phone, but like a drug addict, I feel it pulling at me, and now I feel like I'm only half-present in the conversation—the most important conversation I can have with my mom. I put a pillow over the phone to get myself back on track. "How long have you known?" I don't know why it matters, but now that I know she's been talking about me with strangers, I feel like I have the right to know.

"Abbey, that's not important. The important thing is I love you and accept you as you are, and you don't have to keep secrets from me anymore."

My face gets hot after she mentions secrets. She must know everything. About Keeta and Stef and why I almost flunked out of high school last year. I'm so embarrassed that I get angry with her to hide it. "Why didn't you tell me you knew?"

"I wanted you to come to me when you were ready. I wanted to respect your journey."

"My journey?" Saying it out loud makes us both giggle a little and forces me to lighten up. "What have these ladies been filling your head with?"

"I just didn't want to push you away any more than you already were. I thought I was doing the right thing. I'm new to this, too."

Her vulnerability makes me forgive her instantly. "Speaking of secrets, I feel like I need to make some more confessions." I pull my knees up to my chest. "Do you want to hear them?"

"Only if you want to tell me. And only if they're not about my lasagna."

I take a deep breath and start with the obvious. "Well, Keeta and I were sort of dating last year."

She nods, but then realizes she might want to fake being surprised so I won't feel bad. "Oh, really. Are you guys still dating?"

If only she could handle the whole truth, or if I could dare tell her we never really were girlfriends, according to Keeta. "No, that's over," I say and feel proud.

"Okay," she says. "Any more confessions?"

Oh, so many, but there's no way I can tell her about the nights Keeta sneaked into my room after lights-out, how much I ditched class to spend time with her, or how I found Garrett in Keeta's bedroom, which is why it all came to an end. But I do feel like I should tell her a last truth. "Well, there is one more thing."

"What's that, honey?" She reaches over and holds my hand. I can tell she already knows. My confession is only for me, so I can feel better about coming clean.

Another text comes in. I abandon control, toss the pillow aside, and pick the phone up. My mom and I both look at it. Devin's pic pops up, and out of the corner of my eye I see my mom smile a little.

"You can answer it," she says and gets up. "You don't want to worry her." She kisses me on the forehead and taps my nose with her finger.

I breathe a sigh of relief, but then realize that another person knows about Devin when Devin didn't want anyone to know. "Mom?"

She stops at the door.

"No one knows about her. Not even Mia," I say, quickly reverting to lying. I have no shame. "And we haven't done anything here when she spent the night, just so you know."

"Okay, I believe you. But we need to talk about that, about Devin spending the night here."

I roll my eyes. "Mom, we won't…" I can't face the rest of that sentence.

"Well, we still need to talk. Tomorrow. 'Night, sweetie. I love you."

"Love you, too, Mom."

She shuts the door behind her.

"Mom?" I call to her.

She quickly peeks her head back in. "Yes?"

"Thanks for loving me."

She smiles and looks like she's about to cry again. "Easiest thing I ever had to do, Abbey Road."

CHAPTER THIRTEEN

How can so much go so wrong in such a short amount of time? This is what I'm thinking about while Mrs. Stum rambles on. Instead of filling in my worksheet, I'm sketching jagged cliffs in the margins and wishing I could jump off them.

This is due to the long list of tragedies that happened this morning. First, when my mom got up this morning, she went to wake Mia up, but Mia was gone. She never slept in her bed last night. Her note said she was at a friend's house, she was safe, and that she already called her caseworker, so don't worry. Then, before I left the house, my mom told me we needed to talk when I got home from practice. I'm predicting new rules, embarrassing questions, and no love life. After that, I got in the car this morning with Garrett and Kate, and they talked the whole time about their date with the dumb boys and never bothered to ask me how my coming-out went. I'm surprised they even remembered to pick me up.

I jump when I hear my name. Jake's name follows, then Daphne's and Eric. What just happened?

I look over my shoulder at Jake to try and get clarification on why we've been named together. He points to the handout I've been decimating with doodles. Oh no, group project. Not that I have anything against Jake, but whenever there's a group project assigned, I end up doing all the work. At least Daphne's in my group. Maybe this time will be different. Still, I add this to my list of tragedies.

I walk like a zombie to PE because I didn't sleep last night. Instead I spent all night worrying about my mom knowing about me. Plus, I can't concentrate on anything not knowing where Mia slept last night. No way she went home, and Devin's still out of town, so she couldn't have crashed there. I begin to strip down in front of my graffiti-scarred locker. I still can't believe Nicky was in my house. How can Mia be friends, or whatever, with her? I would never do that to a friend. Then I quickly check myself and get real. Yes, I would. When I'm in love, I seem willing to betray any friend.

"Abs, think fast," Kate says as she passes a basketball at me.

I react too slowly, and the ball hits me in the right boob. "Ow. Why'd you do that?"

She sits down on the bench. "Sorry, I thought you'd catch it. Schwartz is starting her basketball unit today. Cool, huh? It's like free practice time."

I pull my hair back into a ponytail and nod.

"What's up with you today? You hardly said a word in the car." She looks over her shoulder. "Girl trouble?"

I shrug because I'm not sure what to say. Things with me and Devin are...okay, I guess. I did finally get to text with her last night, but it was brief and PG because she was sharing a bed with her mom in the hotel room. So I didn't get to tell her anything, not even about Nicky and Mia or how much I missed her. Or the big news, that I'm out to my mom, but something tells me she might get freaked-out about that last bit.

"Come on, Abbey. What's up? It's me, your BFF." She seems so sincere. It makes me suspicious.

Mrs. Schwartz yells her usual threat into the locker room, so I grab my shoes and slip them on without tying them so we can get out to our numbers before we're marked tardy. On our way out, I whisper to Kate, "I did it."

Kate's obviously thinking sex by the look on her face, so I quickly elaborate. "I told my mom, about, you know."

She grabs me and shakes me. "Shut up! How did it go? Good? I bet it was good. Your mom is so rad."

I haven't seen her this excited since last year when I had an almost date with Jake. "Well, it was a complicated coming-out evening, but it ended good."

"Yeah?" Kate says, actually interested in what I'm saying. "Well, give me the details."

"Okay, first—"

Mrs. Schwartz notices my shoes. "Ms. Brooks, are you trying to get yourself killed? Tie those laces and get on your number. I've got a full pack of detention slips that I vow to work through before Wednesday."

I take three dramatic steps to my number and bend down to tie my shoes. While Mrs. Schwartz writes up three girls for tardies, I whisper to Kate, "Mia ran away last night."

Behind her arm, as she pretends to stretch, Kate asks, "Where do you think she went? Not home, I hope."

I shake my head. "I think I have an idea of where she is." I look over my shoulder to see if I can spot Nicky on her number. I should have known; she's absent. "At Nicky's."

"Are you serious? That's messed up."

I cover my mouth with the collar of my shirt and whisper, "I think I'll go over to Nicky's to get her." This is not yet a well-developed plan, and by the look on Kate's face I can tell she thinks it a bad one. "What? It's not like she'll do anything to me with Mia right there."

"And if Mia isn't there?" Kate asks. "Have you thought about what—"

We're supposed to be numbering off for teams, and it's her turn to say her number but she doesn't know which one to say. Mrs. Schwartz has her hands on her hips, which is one irritated gesture away from a detention. "My Lord, Coach Riley sure does have his hands full with you two."

"Sorry, Mrs. Schwartz. Five?" Kate says, and it's a lucky guess.

Kate and I are on separate teams, so we won't get to talk until after class. But by the time we're done changing, she's got an excuse about rushing off to see if she can catch Miguel. "Text me in your next class, though," she says as she bolts out the door.

I'm headed toward English in a hurry, too, because I had to swing by my locker to get *Julius Caesar* before Mr. Kotofski has a cow. I round the corner fast and smack right into someone. "Sorry," I say, and then, "Oh, hey," when I realize who it is.

The shock of the impact must have temporarily disabled her effort to ignore me because Tai actually smiles when she realizes it's me. "We have to stop meeting like this." She laughs and rubs her shoulder. "How you been?"

I laugh nervously because I'm afraid Garrett will see us talking, which is stupid. "Oh, you know, the usual."

She leans against the wall and smiles. "Uh-oh. Who's the lucky girl now? Still that chick from ASDB?"

"I think so," I say, because sometimes it's so hard to tell. "You doing okay?"

She runs her hand over her short hair. "Yeah, you know. I'm

hanging in there. Nothing like finding out your ex-girlfriend is dating the MVP of the boys' basketball team."

I make a face. "Oh, you know about that?"

"Are you new here, baby D? Everyone knows about it. But that's the past. I'm just trying to keep my head down and graduate. Speaking of which, how're your grades?"

I like how she thinks I need her to look out for me. "Well, I haven't been suspended or failed any classes"—the bell rings above our heads—"yet, anyway. You still got the hook-up with those passes?" I smile and flutter my eyes at her. "For your ol' pal, Abbey?"

"Hmm. I could never resist those blue eyes of yours. Come on." She takes my hand and we run to the girls' bathroom. Like sneaking out of my house, sneaking around campus feels exciting, but I don't let myself laugh until we're both safely hidden in the large stall on the end.

"Shhh." She puts one hand over my mouth and uses the other to dig into her backpack pocket. "I know I've got some in here somewhere. Hang on." She empties the pocket's contents into my hands. "You keep lookout."

Instead of watching for feet under the door, I look at the pile of goods accumulating in my palms: ChapStick, Altoids, tampon, coins, a plastic fork, three vocab cards—I'm guessing from Government—and then an official school printout catches my attention. It has Nicky's full name on it: Nicole Ann Brown. "What's this?" My hands are full so I can't point to it; I just nod my head to the pile and she sees what I see.

Tai looks up from her archeological dig. "Oh yeah, I forgot I had that. I told you I was going to print out her schedule and address, didn't I? Guess I didn't need it, though. That blow to her nose felt so good. She hasn't messed with you since, has she?" She takes her backpack contents from my hands and stuffs them back in the pocket after she finally finds the pad of passes.

"No, not exactly." I can tell Tai is about to demand the whole story, so I spill everything about how Mia outed me to my mom, and how Nicky was there to see the whole thing, and how Mia has disappeared.

"So you really think she's at Nicky's?" Tai asks.

I nod. "Part of me wants to just go over there and knock on Nicky's door to get Mia back, but like Kate said, what if Mia's not there and it's just me and Nicky, face-to-face, no one there to stop her from killing me."

I'm trying to be subtle, but Tai can see right through my game.

"So when should I pick you up?" she asks while handing me my pass to English.

"Well, if you really don't mind…"

"Abbey, I'm not going to let you go over there without me. So, when you wanna do this? After varsity practice?"

"You're my hero, Tai." I hug her, and like I did that day she saved me from Nicky, I feel myself relax into her. She holds me close, too. I've missed her more than I realized. Then, because her arms make me feel like I'm safe to say anything, I whisper, "I don't know how she could let you go," even though it's a thought I didn't expect to ever say to Tai.

"I could say the same about you and K."

I smile into her neck and feel the urge to hug her closer. I fight it, though, and instead we part.

She clears her throat as if to gather herself. "Right. Well, you better get to class before Mr. K. misses you too much. See you at your house at, say, seven thirty?"

"Yeah." I should probably bring Devin, too, but I think it'll be easier if it's just us two. "Thanks again for this." I hold the pass up and back my way out of the stall. "See you later."

"*Hasta*, baby D. Be good."

"I'm always good," I say over my shoulder and, for some reason, smile the whole way to English.

❖

"Holy rainbow flag, I thought I'd never get out of there," I say and slam Tai's Jeep door closed. "Thanks for not leaving." Tai's been patiently waiting for twenty minutes while my mom and I finished our big talk about Devin needing to make alternative plans for the weekend and her new open-door rule if I have her, or any one else I'm dating, over to our house.

"No sweat," Tai says, shifts the car, and accelerates down my street.

I can't tell if she's mad, so I keep talking. "Is it always like this when you first come out? So many new rules and so much awkwardness. I already miss sneaking around."

Tai laughs quietly. "Yeah, I bet you do."

I shove her, then say, "Thanks for doing this. It's really cool considering how, you know, Mia and you aren't exactly best buds." Tai speeds up to make a yellow light and by the time we zoom through the intersection, the light's definitely already red. My hands start to sweat. "You're cool with doing this, right? You're not going to beat up Mia, are you?"

She nods as she looks in her rearview mirror. "Sorry, just in a hurry. I have a thing I need to get to by nine."

"A thing? You mean a date?"

She shrugs.

I'm relieved she's not mad at me but weirdly disappointed about her plans. I choose to show neither emotion. "Cool, with who?"

"No one you know," she says. "I'm sure of it," she adds cryptically. "You know what you're going to say to Nicky or Mia?"

I make a face. "That would've been a good thing to think about, huh?"

She laughs. "Maybe, but you seem to be good on your feet, so I'm sure you'll be fine."

Five minutes later we're slowly rolling down Hawthorne Street. "I can't believe she lives in this neighborhood," I say as I search for the house number. "I kind of imagined her in more of a Stone and Grant sort of hood."

"There it is." Tai nods at a ginormous two-story white stucco house. The Spanish-tile roof makes it look like a mission or fancy hotel. The flowering and landscaped yard puts our ragtag collection of cacti and dirt to shame, and perfectly manicured palm trees stand on guard along the path that leads to a giant custom wooden door like the ones I've seen on those real-estate TV shows. In the driveway are three BMWs, one so new it doesn't even have a plate yet.

"Damn," Tai says as she turns off the car. "Maybe it'd be worth being her friend after all."

"Are you sure this is her address?" For some reason, I felt a lot braver when I thought she was white trash.

She flips on the dome light and looks at the printout. "Yep. This is it. Come on. Let's do this."

I swallow hard and force myself out of Tai's Jeep. I push the glowing doorbell and a symphony of bells plays inside. We both giggle. Then someone yells, "Nicole, honey, could you get that?"

Seconds later the massive door opens and before us stands a version of Nicky I have never seen before. Nicky quickly looks over her shoulder, then closes the door so whoever is inside can't see us. "What the hell are you doing here?" she whispers.

I'm still trying to get over how she looks. No dark eyeliner, no cigarette smoke lingering around her like an ashtray is hidden on her body. And what's that she's wearing? Pink U of A sweats?"

Since I'm stunned to silence, Tai steps in to save the day. "We want to talk to Mia."

"What makes you think she's here?"

I finally find my voice. "Just go get her and make this easier on yourself." I point to Tai as if to say *before this chick kicks your ass*.

To send the message home, Tai says, "Nice Beemers. Shame if something were to happen to them."

Nicky scowls, and then yells, "Friends of mine," to her mom who wants to know who's at the door. When she looks back at the two of us, she looks pained. "Mia can't come out here."

I step closer to her, and surprisingly, she steps back. "If you don't send her out right now, I will just have to tell your mom everything about your scandalous double life." I know it's mean, but I'm dealing with Nicky here, so my threat seems fair.

"Jesus," Nicky whispers. "Calm down. It's just…my parents don't know Mia's here."

I cross my arms over my chest and tilt my head. "Do whatever you need to do, but we aren't leaving without seeing her."

Nicky rubs her forehead. "Okay, but can you guys handle being normal until we get to my room?"

Tai looks at her watch. "Can we get this over with?"

Nicky opens the door wider and we walk into the foyer. A crystal chandelier illuminates the space, and Tai can't help but let out a whistle when she sees the giant staircase. Nicky's mom is reading on the couch and her dad is watching TV, and I am in shock that these two seemingly normal-looking adults spawned such an evil child.

"Mom and Dad, these are my friends, Abbey and Tai." It's the first time I've heard Nicky use my actual name.

I fight the urge to compliment her on saying it without vomiting. Instead I say and wave hi to her parents. Tai smiles and says, "Really nice to meet you. You have a beautiful home," because she's always a charmer, even with parents.

They seem so pleased to have two nice teenagers in their house for once, but when I remember that we're not actually friends of Nicky's, I feel bad for giving them false hope. After her mom insists on serving us some homemade cookies and fancy sodas in glass bottles, Nicky leads us up the stairs to her room.

Stale smoke combined with a toxic air freshener lingers in the air, and Tai and I both cough. The room reflects the Nicky I know: dark, mean, sharp, and dangerous. Her bed sits on the floor and clothes are piled like gopher mounds around the room. But what's this? A Tegan and Sara poster? It's the very same one I have in my room. Ani, too? This discovery is refreshing and creepy at the same time, and I feel compelled to remove mine as soon as I get home. There's a lot more going on in her room—swimming trophies and ribbons from horse shows—but there's no sign of Mia, so I get nervous. Is this a trap?

Then Nicky points to a door. "She's in the closet."

I raise my eyebrows because Mia's the most out person I know, and I don't think she's ever been in the closet, like ever.

I stand my ground, still convinced that Nicky's going to shove me in there and torture me for the next thirty years. But because Tai's in a bit of a hurry, she marches over and swings the door open.

"What the hell?" I say because I can't believe what I see.

Mia can't seem to believe we're there either, so there's a stare-off as we all try to figure out what to say next. Mia finally breaks the silence and holds up her plate. "Nacho?"

I scowl. "No, I don't want a freaking nacho, Mia. Why did you leave like that?"

Mia looks down at her makeshift bed made from layers of blankets and pillows and pulls at the feathers that are poking out of the down comforter.

"I'm waiting," I say, channeling my mom, but I can tell Mia's about to cry and that's why she won't look up or speak. We aren't getting anywhere like this, so I march into the closet that's bigger than my kitchen and dining room combined. Before shutting the door behind me, I turn to Tai. "Please don't kill her. I'll be right back."

Tai shrugs. "No promises."

Nicky swallows loudly and looks like a frantic Chihuahua as I close the door.

Back in the Taj Mahal of closets, I take a seat in front of Mia. She still won't look at me, so I flick her hard on the forehead.

"Ouch," she says, rubbing her forehead. "What did you do that for?"

"Distraction."

"From?"

I know better than to mention she was about to cry, so I say, "Just wanted to make sure you were sober. You know, not being held here drugged, against your will." The corner of her mouth makes the subtlest movement up. It's close to an actual smile, so I say, "Never thought I'd see the day when you were in the closet." I get a half smile and that's better, but she's still holding back. "Come on, Mia, look at me."

She glances up for a second but quickly looks down again.

So I do what any good friend would do. I clap my hands on either side of her face, squish her cheeks together, and force her to look me in the eyes. "I forgive you, Mia. I do." She hasn't asked for forgiveness, but I know her and this is how this needs to go. Besides, Tai may or may not be murdering Nicky on the other side of the closet door, so I need to speed things up. "Now, grab your bag. We're going home." I stand up and reach out my hand. "Come on."

She doesn't take it. Instead she shakes her head and says, "I can't."

"Yes, you can." I quickly fling open the closet door to show her how untrapped she is and see Tai with Nicky's fancy earphones on, bopping her head to some tunes. I'm glad they're playing nice, but I don't like the idea of them becoming friends at all. I close the door again. "You're free to go, see?"

"I'm not going back to your house, Abs. Not after what I did to you. To your mom. No way."

"What you did? Geez, Mia, you made it finally happen. I mean, at first I was pretty pissed, but now it's done. No more secrets, and she's totally cool with it. Kind of. I mean, mostly. It's a little weird, but other than that, it's good. Besides, I miss you."

"You don't get it," she whisper yells into her hands, which are hiding her face. "I can't go back. I lied to you about Nicky. I outed you to your mom. I messed up so bad. Why are you even here right now?" I can hear she's crying, but she won't let me see it.

If there's one thing I learned last year, it's that whatever mistake a friend of mine makes, I'm sure to make the very same mistake, times a million. And I learned to forgive quickly when the friend is worth it. Mia's worth it to me, so I tell her so. "You're one of my best friends, Mia. You get me, and I know I'd want you to forgive me if I messed up, too." I think about Devin and hope I won't give Mia a reason to have to forgive me.

She finally looks up at me. "I would. You know I would. I'm sorry I kept things from you."

Laughter comes from the other side of the door. I hear both Nicky and Tai, so I know it's not Tai laughing maniacally while smothering Nicky with a pillow. "So, you and Nicky?"

Mia shrugs. "I don't know. I guess we're dating again."

"Well, is it serious? Should I start looking for venues and an Ani cover band?"

Mia finally laughs. I take this as a sign that we can pack up and head out, so I grab her bag.

"Abbey," she holds on to the strap, and even though I pull hard at it, she won't let go. "It's because we're friends I don't want to go back home with you. It'll ruin us. I don't want that."

"Is this about the dishes? I'll do them twice next week. I promise. Now let's skedaddle before Tai makes a move on your"—I have to pause a second so I can say it without grimacing—"girlfriend."

"Abs, I'm going to stay with Ms. Morvay."

"Ms. M.? But how? Why? When?" I drop her bag and plop down on her bedroll. "She knows you're here and not with us?" Damn, Ms. M. sure can hold secrets. I hate and love that about her.

"No, not exactly." By the confused look on my face, Mia knows I need more info. "Before I moved in with you guys, before I got suspended, before a lot of stuff got out, she said I was welcome at her house anytime."

Speaking of secrets, there's no way Ms. Morvay would invite Mia there unless she already knew she was gay. So that must mean Mia's known for a while and she never told me. I'm always the last to know, I guess.

"They were working on becoming foster parents before this all went down," Mia continues. "The paperwork just cleared, that's why I'm going now."

"So, you think that Ms. Morvay's still cool with it. I mean, considering…" I hope Mia will fill in the blank.

"Considering I ran away here? Yeah, I think she'll be okay. She'll probably make me promise to never do it again. You know how she is with making you promise stuff."

"Right," I say. "And it'll be cool to live with her and her…" Come on, Mia. Spill it.

"Her two black Labs? I know. I love dogs." Then she smiles slightly. She knows I know, but she's not letting me know she knows. What a punk. "Have you met her dogs?" she asks, then winks.

I gather this is the closest we're going to get to affirming what we both know, so I say, "Yep, beautiful dogs. Very friendly." The smell of her cold nachos and Nicky's shoes starts to make me feel sick, so I say, "Now what? I mean, my mom had to call your caseworker. I begged her not to, but she's a rule follower and she was really scared when you weren't there."

"I know, Ms. M. worked it out." She reaches out and touches my hand. "I'm really sorry about what I did, Abs."

I nod my head. "Well, at least it's all out now. You. Me. Nicky. Everything."

There's a knock on the door and Nicky peeks her head in. "My parentals have gone to bed. Ready?"

"They go to bed early," I say and look at my watch. How is it already past nine? "Crap, Tai's date." I stand up quickly and walk past Nicky, making sure I don't let any part of her touch me, not even my hoodie. "Tai?" I look around frantically and then ask, "Where is she?" in a way that makes it seem like I think Nicky has captured her, too.

"She took off like ten minutes ago," Nicky says.

I throw my hands up in the air. "Great. Just great. Now what?" I'm nearly five miles from home. I could take a bus, but that sounds about as safe as walking along Speedway by myself. I guess I'd better call my mom. Of course, that'll take some explaining since I said I was getting pizza with Tai, and with our newfound honesty, I don't feel like getting caught in another lie. Maybe Garrett's home?

"I told Tai I'd take you home," Nicky says.

I shake my head. "That's okay. I'll walk." I decide a possible kidnapping suits me better than getting in a car with Nicky. If this situation doesn't force me to learn how to drive, I don't know what will.

"She was going to take me to Ms. M.'s anyway," Mia says as she adjusts her bag on her shoulder. "This is perfect."

"Oh yes, perfect is the word I was looking for," I say and roll my eyes.

Nicky cracks her bedroom door open, surveys the hall, and motions us to follow her down the stairs. Along the way, I quickly glance at the family portraits proudly displayed. In every one, Nicky is dressed like a preppy overachiever, and she's smiling as if she's a totally normal girl, a girl who does normal things. Talk about a two-faced liar. Her brother is in most of them, but then disappears as we descend the stairs. That must be so hard.

We get into the oldest BMW, which isn't old at all, just not brand-spanking-new. I sit behind Mia and try not to find the leather seats comfortable or enjoy the fact that Nicky has a mix of all my favorite chick singers playing on her fancy stereo. Until Nicky apologizes, I have no reason to be cordial. Just because she and Mia are—*barf*—

dating, doesn't mean I have to like it. I'm frowning even more as we turn down my street because I hate that Nicky knows how to get to my house. That's one thing I'm still mad at Mia about. How could she let that into my home? Gross.

Thanks to Mia's suggestion, Nicky parks a couple of houses down the street, so my mom doesn't know it was Nicky who took me home and get upset. When I walk up to my house I see my mom is standing at the kitchen sink, probably rinsing out paint palettes. She looks older than I want her to. How can she keep aging when I feel like I'm still a little girl? It doesn't seem fair. Then again, it's all so unfair right now: Mia dating Nicky, Garrett leaving Tai, Kate and Garrett becoming BFFs, and how the closer I try to get to Devin, the further away she feels.

"Have a good time, honey?" my mom asks as I storm by, fuming from all the unfairness.

"Awesome," I say over my shoulder. "Gotta pee," I lie and close the bathroom door. I run the water so she can't hear me crying because if she asked me what was wrong, I wouldn't even know where to begin. Instead, I lean against the back of the toilet and silently weep.

CHAPTER FOURTEEN

Halloween stopped being fun for me at around fifth grade when people started saying, *Aren't you too big for trick-or-treating?* Yes, I was too big for it, but not too old for it.

But now that I'm in high school, the focus of Halloween has shifted. Now apparently it's all about drinking and dressing up as a slutty whatever. Last year around this time, Kate and I weren't even talking, so I stayed home and did my usual Keeta swooning and handed out candy. But this year, Kate and I are definitely talking and she definitely wants to go to a party, and I don't mean an innocent apple-bobbing one. I didn't agree to join her, but that means very little to Kate, which is why we are at Party City wandering the aisles of costumes. At least she wants to spend time with me, and these days, I'll take what I can get.

"I think Miguel will like it," Kate says as she contemplates a Sexy Referee costume. "But the Sassy Care Bear is super cute, too."

The only redeeming thing about the Care Bear costume is that it has a rainbow on it, but I don't tell her that. I just shrug and pretend to look at a Tavern Wench costume.

"Ew. No," Kate says as she walks past me, shaking her head. "What about this one? You'd look adorbs in this."

The label says *NBA Lakers costume*, but from where I'm standing it looks like a couple of sweatbands, bootie shorts, and a tank top so small even our tiny teammate, five-foot-one Fabiola, wouldn't be able to squeeze into it. "This isn't a costume, Kate. This is a cry for help." I take it from her and hang it up next to the Sexy Ketchup Bottle.

"Come on, you've got a great body, Abs, and I mean that in the most sincere, nonlesbian way possible."

I laugh. "You're high. I do not have the kind of body that would look good in any of these."

She ignores me and grabs a purple *Teletubbies* costume off the rack. "How about this? It's totally gay, right?"

A woman one rack down looks over at us and scoffs.

Kate notices her glare and clarifies. "No, I mean actually gay. Like, not in a mean way." Then she looks over at me and whispers, "Wasn't the purple one gay?"

I shrug and then smile inside because her face is redder than the Naughty Devil costume.

Kate glances back toward the woman who is now shaking her head in disgust. Kate can't handle judgment, especially by people she doesn't know, so she says, "Listen lady, my best friend is gay." She points at me, outing me to the whole aisle. "And I have a friend who's bi."

"Whatever," the woman says and walks away.

But Kate doesn't back down, not when her image is on the line. "I'm not a homophobe!" Several people turn around to look at her. One middle-aged man claps.

"You handled that well," I say and let out a small laugh.

"Thanks for nothing," she whisper yells at me. "Just for that, you're trying this on, and this one, and"—she holds up the Fantasy Unicorn—"oh yes, this one."

I begin to back up, but what I know for sure about Kate is when it comes to me and fitting rooms, she always wins. Before I can make my getaway, she has one hand like a cuff around my wrist and is dragging me to my doom.

"Excuse me," she announces to no one in particular, "me and my gay friend have some costumes to try on."

❖

My mom is frowning. Not like she's sad, but more like she's confused. "How exactly is this a unicorn costume?" She fluffs up my tiny tutu with the pencil in her hand.

I glance down at the low-cut white minidress, tiny iridescent petticoat, fishnet stockings, and white high heels. "Well, that's what the label said, and look…" I bend forward to show her my horn and glittery ears. "See? Unicorn."

The crease between her eyebrows deepens. "Uh-huh. I see."

After trying it on, Kate made me come out of the dressing room and stand in front of the three-sided mirror, and a guy walked past and whistled. I found his gesture rude and disgusting, naturally, but then, especially after I saw what I looked like, I kind of liked the attention. Not in a bisexual way, but more of a maybe-I'm-not-so-bad-looking kind of way. Maybe I could pull this costume off, after all.

Meanwhile, my mom is rubbing her neck with one hand and her lower back with the other like she just survived a car accident. "And where exactly do you think you're going dressed like this?"

"A party?" I say, and I then try to retract my apprehension. "Miguel, Kate's boyfriend, is having a Halloween party at his house."

My mom squints.

"It's more like a get together or gathering of a few friends. Totally supervised and totally PG. Parents will be there. No biggie." Lies, lies, lies.

Now her hands are on her hips and confusion has shifted to sass. "Well, you aren't leaving this house dressed like a"—she pauses and mimes air quotes—"unicorn."

"But, Mom—"

"Nope. Not happening." She walks to the kitchen to turn off the teakettle that is screaming for attention. "Figure out another costume."

I wobble over to the kitchen to argue my case. "She's going to be here in ten minutes. How am I supposed to find another costume?"

My mom pours the hot water into her cup and quietly dips and re-dips her teabag. "You're a smart, creative girl, honey. You'll figure something out."

"I'll be sixteen in two weeks, Mom."

"Yes, and you shouldn't even be dating yet, but I let that one go."

She's got me there, but I continue. "Everyone else wears costumes like this." I can't believe I'm playing that card about this slutty outfit, but I was really hoping to surprise Devin. You know, after I sneak off and leave Miguel's party to go hang out at ASDB's party, which is only three blocks from Miguel's house, which is also the only reason I agreed to go with Kate at all.

"Figure it out, Abbey Road." My mom finds my argument as lame as I do.

I kick off my slutty shoes and storm down the hall to my room. I pick up my cell phone to check for a text from Devin. None from her, but Kate's text doesn't help matters: *Can't wait to see you in that costume, punk ass.* So much for my first Halloween party. I guess it's back to sitting at home with my mom, watching, God help me, *It's the*

Great Pumpkin, Charlie Brown again while drowning my loneliness in Kit Kats and Tootsie Rolls.

I take off the costume and stand in front of my open closet. The U of A sweatshirt I permanently borrowed from Keeta last year catches my eye like it always does. I grab it and look over my shoulder at my Wilbur pillow on my bed. Wildcat fan? Stupid, but it's my only option. I quickly dress in my same clothes from today and pull on the sweatshirt. Kate honks outside as my mom knocks at my door.

"Everyone needs to just hold on," I yell, then grab my cell and some cash from my wallet, and throw open the door. I'm greeted by my mom who's standing in my way with her arms outstretched. "Starving artist," she announces as she models her costume, which consists of a palette in one hand, a paintbrush in the other, one of her paint-stained aprons tied around her waist, and a sign hanging around her neck that reads: *Will paint for food.*

The smile on her face is even more ridiculous than her costume, so it's pretty impossible to stay mad at her. "Not bad, right?"

I hate to admit it, but it's better than mine. "Yeah. Pretty good."

"Good." She takes the apron off and ties it onto me, then hands me the other props. Kate honks again.

"Mom, I gotta go."

"No, wait." She runs to her easel and opens up a couple of jars filled with her own mixed paints, then dabs a couple of brushes into them.

My phone vibrates in my pocket. Kate has the patience of a hungry baby, and if I don't get out there right now, not only will she throw a tantrum, but she'll leave me behind for sure. I start to turn to walk out, but before I can stop her, my mom is decorating my face with random lines of paint.

"There, now you look the part."

"Thanks, Mom." Awesome. Not.

"Love you, honey. Be safe. And you remember your curfew?"

"Eleven fifteen," I say over my shoulder and throw her a peace sign for some reason.

"Make good choices!" she calls out the door, channeling the mom from *Freaky Friday*. You would think I was an untrustworthy daughter who lied to her constantly or something. Oh, wait.

"What the freaking frack, Abs?" Kate says out the window as I approach. "I knew you'd chicken out. Didn't I tell you she would?" she says to Garrett.

I crawl into the backseat and place my props beside me to put on my seat belt, but I forget that my face is still wet and accidentally get paint on the strap and smear paint across my cheek. I almost scream about how much I hate my mom, but instead I sigh, click the buckle in place, and silently pout.

"So much for showing off your legs for days," Kate says as we pull away. "You disappoint me, Abbey. You really do."

Garrett adjusts her boobs in her very low-cut Wonder Woman costume. "Well, at least she won't lose her girls while reaching for a chip. Are my areolas showing?" she asks Kate and turns for inspection as we idle at a red light.

"It's not like Jordan will mind if they are," I mumble from the back. No one hears me.

Kate pulls down her Naughty Red Riding Hood petticoat and pulls up her thigh-high stockings. "Geez, turn up the heat. I'm kind of freezing my ass off over here."

I laugh to myself and remind myself that my mom's not so bad after all.

❖

After we arrive, Kate and Garrett make a beeline to a Ping-Pong table lined with cups on both ends. I fake drink from the red cup filled with stinky beer that Kate insisted I carry around, and I try not to get too annoyed when people ask what I'm supposed to be. To say I'm a fish out of water at this party is the greatest understatement of the century, so I decide to go hide in the bathroom. But after waiting outside the door for ten minutes, I resolve that whatever's taking so long in there, I don't want to be around when the door opens.

As I graze the snack table I repeatedly look out the window at Garrett outside. Since she's my driver and Kate can't drive a stick, I made her promise not to drink tonight. She did promise, but I'm still checking up on her. If there's one thing I don't mess around with, it's drunk driving. Not after losing my dad because some jerk got behind the wheel after drinking too much. She's sipping a Diet Coke. Maybe she can be trusted after all.

Instead of sneaking off to ASDB without telling anyone where I'm going—which was my original plan until I realized if something happened to me, my mom would die if no one knew where I was—I empty my red cup in the sink and attempt to locate Kate to tell her where I'm going. I walk into the backyard, which is apparently couples territory because everyone is paired up like animals boarding Noah's ark. Without another person attached to my side, maneuvering around the lovebirds is easy, and I finally find Kate sitting in Miguel's lap at the patio table.

"Abbey, babbly, wabbly," Kate shouts and throws up her hands as if my arrival is worth celebrating. "Look, Miguel. It's Abbey, or Big Bird. So hard to tell." She cracks herself up.

"So," I say as I stand in front of her, "you're drunk." I'm pretty sure this is her first time, but who knows what she's kept from me. I watch her and reconsider my plan. Maybe I shouldn't leave her. "Kate, it's only been like thirty minutes. How much have you had to drink?"

She looks into her cup and then at Miguel. "Like only fro or frix beers, right, honey?" She's holding up three fingers.

I squint at her. "Well, which is it? Fro or frix?"

This makes her laugh so hard she spills some of her drink on the grass.

Miguel takes her cup from her. "When was the last time she ate?" he asks, seeming a little irritated.

"Look, I'm invisible," Kate says as she hides under her red cloak. "You can't see me." She starts laughing so hard that she falls forward, off Miguel's lap and onto the ground. Then she cracks up some more.

Like Miguel, I'm not laughing at all. She is beyond trashed. Was she drinking before she got me? Either way, there goes my night because if I leave, who knows what'll happen to her.

"I've gotta check on the food. Abbey, can you"—Miguel motions to Kate on the ground like she's a mess that needs to be mopped up— "do something with her?"

"Yeah, fine." I look down at Kate and sigh. Halloween is back to sucking. It's been over two weeks since Devin and I have seen each other, and thanks to my mom's new rules, the time we spent together was public and lame. All I wanted to do was make out with her behind a bush or something, for crying out loud. And now this?

Kate is resting on her back now, and her cheap costume is breaking up like it's made of Fruit Roll-Ups. If she flops around too much more, this party's going to take a new turn, and she's going to make quite a name for herself.

I quickly text, *Kate's drunk. Can't leave her,* and hope Devin reads between the lines. You know, that I miss her like crazy. Kate's on the move, so I slip my phone in my pocket and run after her before she makes it to the pool.

Once I have my grip on her, I guide her to Garrett, who appears to be dominating the beer-pong game. "G, Kate's trashed. We need to go."

Kate hears her name and attempts to make her case. "No, no, no. I only had this many and that means I can drive in two hours." She rubs her eyes. "I just need to rest for a second." She falls to the ground and leans against my legs like I'm a tree.

I look to Garrett for help. She's the older role model here. She'll know what to do. But instead of worried, she looks relaxed and very unconcerned. "Just let her sleep, Abs. She'll be fine in a few hours and then we'll head out."

I look closely at Garrett. What's up with her? Her eyes seem far away and unfamiliar. "Garrett, are you drinking, too? Jesus." I grab her Diet Coke and smell it like I've seen teachers and parents do in the movies. It smells toxic, but just like Diet Coke should smell.

"Dude, Abbey. Hang on. It's my turn." As the partygoers standing around the table yell her name, Garrett skillfully bounces a Ping-Pong ball in a distant cup causing more cheers. Of course, she is the best at this, too. "Drink, Cassidy!" Garrett says and points to a girl I've never met. Then Garrett turns back to me. "I told you I wasn't going to drink and I'm not drinking, 'kay?"

I'm about to crack the case about Garrett's behavior, but then I hear a moan coming from the ground. Kate better not puke on my shoes.

"I'm cold, Abbey," Kate whines. I can see why she might be chilly. The buttons of Kate's top have all popped off. The lacy hot-pink bra I'm sure she was hoping only Miguel would see is now on display. Even though I'm cold, I strip off my Keeta sweatshirt and attempt to dress her quickly, but she's flopping around like a giant Raggedy Ann doll.

"We need to take her to my house, Garrett. Now." My stern voice shocks me but doesn't seem to affect Garrett at all.

"Ask Mikey or Paul. You'll take them, right guys?" she says to a couple of dudes who are working the keg.

Mikey, the tall one who's in the middle of drinking from the nozzle, gives Garrett a thumbs-up. Meanwhile, the one I assume is Paul is making out with a girl and can't respond because he has his tongue down her throat; the girl's wearing the very same slutty unicorn costume I almost wore. Well, that would have been embarrassing.

"Problem solved," Garrett says confidently. "Now if you two will excuse me, I need some chips and Oreos before I die." She walks away, leaving us in the hands of two drunk guys who've already forgotten the favor they agreed to.

"I love you, Abbey," Kate calls from the ground. "You're so wonderful. I love you so much. You're, like, my favorite person in the whole world. Don't leave me. Let's stay together forever."

I lean down and hoist her up. "Okay, Kate. Come on." I wrap her arm around me. "Let's go find a place for you to rest."

"As long as you come, too, my bestie-westie. You're going to lie down with me, too, right?"

I can tell by the looks of some people we pass along the way that Kate's loudly expressed affection and desire to lie down with me are causing rumors to fly like tortillas at graduation. I try to get her to shut up by covering her mouth, but she licks my hand. I remove it and wipe it on my pants.

"Yay, me and my Abbey are going to sleep together. Slumber party," she shouts and throws a fist up in the air. We're covering pretty good ground and are very close to the front door when she bumps into Miguel in the living room. When she realizes it's him, she grabs his shirt and leans into him closely, like she's about to kiss him, but then says, "Me and my bestie are going to sleep together and you're not invited. Girls only!" And then she laughs. "Get it? Because she's a lesbian!" she yells over the music, cracking herself up again. Now all eyes are on us, and anyone at that party who was the least bit unsure about my sexuality can stop wondering now, and Kate isn't doing herself any favors to squash the ever-present rumor that she's a you-know-who girl, too.

I don't even know what to say, so I roll my eyes, point to Kate, say, "Lightweight," and force out a laugh. I just want to get her out of there as fast as possible—hopefully, before she makes things worse.

"Why aren't you laughing, honey?" Kate says to Miguel. "Are you mad at me? I was just joking. I love you."

"Okay, Kate," I say and try to pull her along, but she won't release Miguel.

"Don't be mad. He's mad at me, huh, Abbey?"

Miguel peels her hand off his shirt and drops it like it's contaminated. "Should've known better than to date a sophomore." Then he turns to me. "Make sure she doesn't puke in my mom's rosemary bush. She uses that to cook."

"Got it." I drag Kate away before he sees her cry. What an ass.

I prop weeping Kate up on the front porch bench and take out my cell phone. It's only nine o'clock. Maybe if we just wait it out, Kate will sober up and Garrett will go back to normal, too, and we can all leave together as if nothing ever happened. Yeah, and maybe Tucson won't reach 100 degrees next summer.

I scroll through my contacts for a possible alternative ride home and see what I already knew: my options are limited. My mom has been telling me for years that I can always call her, no matter what, and she'll come get me. She even detailed a scenario much like this one, but I feel compelled to prove to her that I would never get myself in a situation like this, that I am responsible. I want to avoid involving her at all costs.

What about Tai? No, she's always bailing me out of everything, and I'm sure the last thing she wants is to see Garrett tonight. I pause briefly on Keeta's name. Does she even have a car? She didn't when we were together, but maybe now that she's in college? Wait, what am I even saying? No, absolutely not.

Mia. Maybe she could borrow Ms. M.'s car? One slight hang-up: Mia doesn't have her license either. Who else has a car? I twirl my hair to think. What if? No, she's a worse option than Keeta. I shiver because Kate has my sweatshirt and because the thought of asking Nicky for help is giving me the chills.

Meanwhile, back on the bench, Kate is stirring again. "Abbey? I don't feel good."

I look up from my phone and see she's fallen over and is lying with her face smooshed against the wooden slats of the sun-battered bench.

"Crap," I say and push send on my cell phone even though it makes my stomach cringe. Cradling my phone between my shoulder and ear, I help Kate up and direct her to the large blooming rosemary bush next to the front door. The strong smell of the herb makes her dry heave. I rub her back and whisper, "Let it all out, Kate." And boy, does she ever.

Chapter Fifteen

Is she going to puke?" Nicky asks out her car window as Kate and I make our way to her BMW, Kate's head flopping around with each step.

"She's empty. Don't worry," I say snottily even though Nicky is doing me a huge favor. Checking myself, I say, "Thanks for coming."

Mia helps me strap Kate into the backseat. I walk around to the other side of the car, but before getting in, I ask, "Are you sure you're sober?"

"Abbey, we told you. We're not partying tonight. Chill out," says Mia.

"Yeah, you really need to learn to trust people," Nicky chimes in.

"Trust?" I question them both. I look at Kate who is fast asleep and then at Mia. She wouldn't lie to me about this. She knows about my dad. I do trust her. Trusting Nicky is definitely questionable, but if Mia says I can trust her, too, I will.

"I know I can do some effed-up things, Abbey, but I don't mess around like that. Get in," Nicky says and starts the car.

I open the door and crawl in.

"Where to?" Nicky asks as she pulls away from Miguel's house.

The quiet in the car is comforting, so I say, "Can we just drive around for a little bit?"

"We have to be back at Ms. M.'s by midnight," Mia says as she turns on the radio, "but I'm game for whatever. Should we get drunk ass some coffee or something?"

I paid attention in my eighth grade health class, so I know coffee doesn't do much more than make a drunk person a hyperactive drunk person. But, then again, I haven't exactly eaten, and it would be a good waste of time. "Yeah, sure. But can we swing by ASDB first?"

Nicky flips a U-turn. "Booty call?"

I look at Mia, furious. "Thanks for keeping that a secret. No one's supposed to know, remember?"

Mia throws her hands up and shrugs. "She got it out of me. Sorry."

"Girlfriend privileges, Abbey. You gotta know that rule by now," Nicky says.

Girlfriends. Yuck. "Just don't say anything to anyone else, please. You, too, Mia. Blabbermouth."

Mia smiles sheepishly. "Swear," she says and zips her mouth shut.

"In the vault," Nicky says and makes a hard right.

Kate topples into my lap. I push her back to a seated position, but she falls again, onto my leg. I give up and pet her hair away from her face. This is the most intimate we've ever been, and she'll never remember it. I love her, too, but can't tell her that anymore without her thinking it's something more. Yet she can tell the whole world. Maybe there's something to be said about being drunk and blurting out whatever you're actually feeling.

My argument for drunkenness is interrupted when Nicky slams on the brakes. Kate flops forward but is stopped by her seat belt and rolls back into my lap.

"Coyote," Nicky announces, then accelerates again.

The sooner we get to ASDB, the better. I need to get out of this car, away from drunk Kate, and into Devin's arms. That's when I'll feel like everything's okay. And it's been way too long. We pull up to the front of ASDB and my door is open before Nicky puts the car into park. She mumbles something about how I must be eager to get laid, but I ignore her, slam the door shut, and bolt across campus to find the school's Halloween party.

The loud music helps guide me to the cafeteria. Half of the cafeteria lights are on, which I guess makes sense. I mean, if people are signing, you need to see their hands. I'm relieved because that means finding Devin will be that much easier. I scan the food tables, but she's not there. I check out the dance floor, but it's too thick with students dancing to see her.

I get on tiptoe, and that's when I spot her. I instantly smile.

She told me she was going to dress up as a witch, but her witch costume doesn't consist of hairy warts and a long, loose, tattered black robe. Nope, she's dressed up as the sexiest witch I've ever seen, and as she bounces to the beat, her pushed-up cleavage follows along. I wave to try to get her attention, but she doesn't see me. For some reason, I don't dare walk onto the dance floor. It's like I'm standing on the edge of an ocean, and I don't know how to swim. I've never actually been to a school dance, and I've never actually danced in front of anyone. Plus, I feel really out of place and like everyone can tell I shouldn't be here.

While contemplating my next move, I watch a guy make a decisive move of his own. He looks older than both of us and has been dancing somewhat near Devin, then gets closer and closer and finally so close that his hips are moving to the same beat as Devin's. And she doesn't seem to mind at all.

I need to get in there, so I leap in and hope I don't drown in the waves of arms and stomping feet. I'm only a few sweaty bodies away when I look up again to try to get Devin's attention.

But Devin is turned away from me now and facing the guy. With no chance of being seen by the teachers on the perimeter, their legs quickly become intertwined, and their bodies press together like they're having vertical sex. His hands are on Devin's butt, and he pulls her in even closer. Again, Devin doesn't seem to mind.

My smile fades, and I consider letting the tide of bodies push me back to shore. I'll sneak away and pretend I never saw them. I'll pretend I'm not hurt, that I'm totally okay with someone else touching Devin, but I'm not, so I don't. I defiantly hold my spot because I'm the new Abbey, the out Abbey who has nothing to lose and the confidence of a bona fide you-know-who girl. So instead of cowering away, I push on and tap Devin's shoulder.

She doesn't respond, but the guy notices me and pulls away to get Devin's attention. He signs something to Devin and Devin turns around.

"What are you doing here?" she shouts, instead of signing, as if she wants to purposely out me as hearing. "I thought you were with Kate."

I sign, "I'm surprising you." I fake a smile, then sign, "Surprise."

Everyone around us starts to jump, like the song demands they do, so now I'm being bashed by dancers who seem to have no control of their body parts.

"Okay," Devin signs as we get pushed together, but instead of grinding we push back from one another to create space, the space that seems to be growing between us, especially now.

An elbow smacks me in the back of my head and makes my head hit Devin's. We both rub our foreheads and nod at a really sweaty guy who seems hopped up on Red Bull and Mountain Dew. He signs that he's sorry, then bounces away. Then another guy bounces on my foot, and I've about reached my max of bodily and emotional abuse. It's obvious she's not happy to see me.

"I'll text you later," I sign and turn away.

She grabs my hand, but her grip isn't strong enough to keep me there, and I'm not sure she even tried very hard. If she wants me, she can come get me.

At the gym's entrance I look back. She's dancing again, which tells me everything I need to know.

❖

"What's the plan?" Mia asks. We're parked a couple of houses down from my house. It's eleven o'clock, so I've got fifteen minutes to figure out what to do with Kate.

"Why don't you just walk her right in there? Tell your mom she's really tired. Took allergy pills or something," Nicky suggests.

I stare at Nicky with a straight face. "What kind of moronic parent would fall for that?"

Nicky shrugs. "You'd be surprised what parents believe when they want to believe it."

She makes a good point.

"What if we pull a Keeta?" Mia asks.

I look at Kate, who is more awake but still wobbly. "I don't know. Do you think we could get her up there?"

Mia reveals her bare arm and flexes. "I've been working out."

Nicky laughs and rolls her eyes because Mia's arms are super skinny, and she'd probably lose to me in an arm-wrestling match, which isn't saying much.

"Okay," I say because I haven't been caught yet, sneaking anyone in or out of my window.

Mia and I pull Kate out of the car, but before we all start walking to my house, Nicky says, "Hey, wait, Abbey."

I leave Kate in Mia's charge and turn around to face Nicky. "What," I snap because I'm stressed out and just potentially lost another girlfriend and am not in the mood for more trouble.

"I just…" Nicky looks down and taps the toe of her left Converse on the gravel.

"Kind of in a hurry here."

"I'm sorry. There. Okay? What I did to you was really messed up."

I don't have the energy to hate her anymore, so I say, "Thanks," and leave it at that. It doesn't mean we're going to hang out anytime soon, but at least I don't have to carry around that anger anymore.

I walk into my house and greet my mom who is watching *The Daily Show*. My role is to make small talk and distract her while Nicky and Mia walk Kate to my window.

"Hi, Abbey Road," my mom says when she sees me. "How was the party? Where's your sweatshirt? Aren't you cold?"

I had been cold up to the point where I walked away from Devin. After that, I felt like my face was on fire. "I let Kate borrow it. Her costume broke," I say, letting out a small piece of truth. "How was your night? Lots of trick-or-treaters?"

"Yep. And you were right about those costumes." She shakes her head. "What has the world come to? I mean, whatever happened to scary witches and ghosts and goblins and—"

"I know, I know," I say before my mom gets on a good-ol'-days tangent. I figure Nicky and Mia have had plenty of time to scurry across the driveway to my window. "It's a shame. Well, I'm off to bed." I lean over and kiss her cheek. When I do, I swear I hear her trying to smell my breath. "'Night, Mom."

"'Night, my little Abbey Roo. Love you."

Her sweet farewell only reminds me of my upcoming deceit and makes me feel awful; how quickly I've digressed. Maybe I should just tell her about Kate. I mean, it's not like I drank. I stop halfway down the hall and look over my shoulder. Maybe I should just tell her. I open my mouth, then slam it shut and head to my room. Why isn't the right choice ever the easiest?

After closing my bedroom door behind me, I hurry to my window and fling open the shutters. Operation Kate needs to be deployed, and quickly.

I clear any breakables from the landing area and remove the window screen. "Okay, boost her in."

"Abbey!" Kate yells when she sees me. Then she says, "Peek-a-boob!" and lifts the sweatshirt over her head, revealing her bra for the second time that night.

I grab at the sweatshirt and yank it down while simultaneously shushing her, but she won't stop laughing.

"Be quiet or we're going to get caught," Mia explains in a whisper.

"Oh, are we whispering now? Okay. I can whisper, too." She salutes Mia. "Aye, aye, Captain."

Nicky and Mia bend down to get a good grip on Kate, but her body keeps on folding underneath her.

"Come on, Kate," Mia pleads, "jump in."

Kate jumps, but instead of jumping into the window's opening, she jumps straight up with her arms down at her side. "Whee," she whispers.

Exasperated, Mia and Nicky stand up and put their hands on their hips. "This is a stupid plan," Nicky declares. "Why don't we just go through the front door after your mom goes to bed. That's how I got this one in my house." She points at Mia.

I look over my shoulder. Can I rely on my mom to stay in bed? No, too risky. "One more time. Kate, jump into my room when they pick you up, okay?"

Kate nods and seems to be concentrating. "I can totally get in this window." She pushes Mia and Nicky away. "Step back, muff munchers."

Mia raises an eyebrow. "Excuse me?"

"She did not just call us that," Nicky says.

"Who's she been hanging out with these days?" Mia asks me.

Only Garrett would teach Kate something like that, but before I can answer them, Kate leaps into the open window and consequently knocks her head hard against mine.

I manage to trap my scream in my mouth by biting my own hand, but Kate forgets our whispering game and lets out a blood curdling *owwwww* as she dangles half-in and half-out of the window. I rush to my door to try and lock it, but I'm too late.

"Abbey!" my mom says frantically as she flings the door open, nearly taking off my nose. "What…" She gets a glimpse of Kate, then looks back at me, waiting for an explanation.

Before I can speak, Kate recovers from her injury and waves. "Hi, Abbey's mom. It's me, Kate."

"I can see that," my mom says. "What are you doing in the window?"

Again, I attempt to explain, but my mom says, "Not another word, young lady," and walks over to Kate. I worry for a second about Nicky and Mia getting caught, but if I know them, they're already halfway to the car. For once, I wish I were with them.

"I'm," Kate starts, but then laughs. "I'm…I'm…stuck, Ms. Susan," Kate declares.

"Yes. Yes, you are," my mom says quietly, which is definitely a dangerous sign. The softer her voice gets, the angrier she is inside. "Why are you stuck in Abbey's window?"

Kate tosses up her arms. "I really don't know, but can you help me, please? It kind of hurts." Kate struggles to wriggle farther into the room.

My mom turns to me. "How much has she had to drink?"

I'm twirling away on my ponytail, trying to figure out how much trouble I'm in, so I don't answer right away.

My mom takes two steps to reach me and holds me by the shoulders. "Have you been drinking, too?"

I drop my hair and look her in the eyes so she'll know I'm not lying. "No, Mom, I swear. I promise. I'm sorry. I shouldn't have tried to sneak her in. I just didn't want her to get into trouble."

"Oh no," Kate says, "are we in trouble?" And then the *sorry*s start pouring out of her along with another round of tears. "I'm so sorry Abbey. I ruined everything." She drops her head. "I'm a terrible person. I'm so sorry." Then because her head is dangling and the snot is running in her nose instead of out of her nose, she snorts, which makes her laugh. I nearly laugh, too, but contain myself.

"Abbey, go outside and get her down. Quickly," my mom orders. "Be careful of the ocotillo."

Kate continues to apologize as I run down the hall and out my front door. I look for Mia and Nicky, but just as I predicted, her car is gone.

My mom eases Kate back out of the window, and I catch her on the other side. Kate starts to cry again, but at least she's stopped saying how sorry she is. I swear, I never thought someone apologizing would ever be annoying. I was wrong.

My mom's already on the phone with Kate's mom by the time we stumble through my front door. I place Kate on the couch and watch as she slowly tips over. She falls asleep right away.

"How did you get here?" Mom asks while still on the phone. "Where's Garrett?"

"Mia and"—I hesitate because as much as I dislike and distrust Nicky, multiply that times a thousand for my mom—"Nicky."

My mom glares at me. "Were they drinking?"

"No, I swear, Mom. I checked."

Kate suddenly sits up and declares, "I smell like potatoes," and then leans back, only to topple over again. The smell of the rosemary on her face must be confusing her.

"Okay, I'll see you soon." After my mom hangs up the phone, she walks over and stands in front of me. I wait for her to say how disappointed she is in me and how she thought she could trust me and what a waste of human flesh I am. I hold back my tears and wait.

But she just looks at me carefully and finally says, "You're a good friend, Abbey. Kate's lucky to have you." She pulls me in for a hug, and it's the best feeling in the whole world.

For the first time tonight, I think everything's going to be okay.

"Of course, you know you're grounded, right?"

And there goes that. "But, Mom, I didn't even drink." She's still hugging me tight even though my arms are dangling beside me. "I'm the hero, remember?"

"You should have called me, Abbey."

"I know." I hug her again. "I'm sorry." And I am. I'm sorry for everything.

Chapter Sixteen

On Monday morning I stalk the halls before first period, hoping to find Kate before chem. Since she's grounded, her mom dropped her off and will pick her up after school. And after Garrett failed to pick me up this morning, I came to the conclusion that carpool is officially over until further notice. Kate finally makes it to her locker, and even though I greet her with a hey and a smile, she extracts her physics book from the bottom of the pile, slams her locker shut, and brushes by me as if I'm a ghost.

Her long stride is an even match for me so I easily keep up. "Hey, why are you ignoring me? You're the one that screwed up."

"How could you do that to me, Abbey?"

"What are you talking about? You should be thanking me. I saved you from making a total ass of yourself." She doesn't respond and is now walking quickly in the opposite direction of my class, but I feel like I have to explain. "Kate—".

"Saved me?" She takes a quick left down the stairs. "I'm grounded for life, and my mom took away my cell phone. My life is over thanks to you."

I grab the sleeve of her sweater so she'll slow down and listen. She finally stops for a second at the bottom of the stairs. "Do you have any idea how drunk you were? And how half-naked you were?" I whisper. "Who knows where you would have ended up."

She glares at me then takes off again. I follow, but then she stops suddenly, making me put my brakes on, too. A freshman who was tailing me too closely slams into me. I glare at her even though she apologizes quickly.

"That's the point of being drunk. Thanks a lot for ruining everything. Oh, and by the way, Miguel text-dumped me, so there you go. You got what you wanted."

"What I wanted?" Is she for real? "Kate, listen—" But I don't know why I'm defending myself, so I stop talking. She storms off, leaving me alone with unnecessary guilt and shock. The first bell rings over my head, and I bolt to class. For the first time all year, I'm looking forward to getting my brain scrambled by equations I don't understand. It's got to be better than thinking about Kate, or Devin, or Garrett, or any of this BS.

There's an air of relaxation in the room, so I look around suspiciously. That's when I see the sub at the front. "Oh, glorious day, Mrs. Dumb is absent," I say to Jake as I take my seat.

"Yep, better protect your eyes. Things might get out of control in here."

I laugh, then focus my attention on what the sub is saying about our group projects. "So that means you're to work on your projects the entire period." I would've preferred a movie, but at least maybe I'll be distracted by Jake's funny comments and drawings.

Jake, Daphne, Eric, and I choose to convene at a lab table in the front of the room. The logical starting point would be to pick our topic, but instead, Daphne unpacks some green folders, hands one to each of us, and declares, in an unbossy tone, that our first order of business is to choose our team name. "To build community," she declares after she can sense the rest of her group is a little confused.

Daphne used to be an invisible wallflower in middle school. I sort of remember her being around, but if you asked me what she sounded like or dressed like, I couldn't tell you. Did she ever talk at all? Maybe not. That's why Kate vetoed Sara's suggestion to have Daphne join our Geek Pack. Too mousy, Kate said. But now Daphne has certainly bloomed into her name and self. Unlike Kate, she didn't take the fake-up approach that most girls try out in high school. Instead, she grew in confidence and poise.

She clears her throat to ease the awkwardness of our silence. "So far, I've come up with JADE, which is an acronym of our initials." No one has a reaction. "Or how about Team Up and Atom? What about you guys? Any ideas?"

Her pen is poised over a notebook that she's already dedicated to the project. She'd have made an excellent addition to our club. Too bad.

Jake lets out a delayed chuckle. "Up and Atom. That's clever." Then he looks at her with a slight tilt to his head like he's seeing her in a new light. "That one works for me."

He reminds me of how Devin looked at me that first night

we went out, but instead of feeling that usual warm feeling surge throughout my body when I think about her, I feel depressed. We haven't talked or texted since I stormed away from her at the dance. I keep waiting for her to reach out and apologize, but she's kept her distance. Now what?

"The Mighty Ions?" Eric suggests. Daphne records his idea because she's a fair leader and isn't a smarty-pants know-it-all brat who thinks only her ideas are good, like someone else I know. If she wasn't getting googly-eyed looks from Jake at the moment, I might even like to be her friend. But right now, his attention is making me jealous and miserable, and this combination of feelings usually expresses itself as hostility.

"Abbey, do you have any ideas you'd like to contribute?" Daphne asks me.

I want to say that I don't give two moles what the hell we name ourselves, but instead I shake my head so as not to lash out and look like a crazy person.

We anonymously vote—she even brought tiny Post-its for us to write on—and it's decided: we are now the Up and Atoms. For the next forty-five minutes, I sit back and let them do all the work and act like the loser group member I've always hated.

By practice, I'm less angry and more exhausted and worried. I decided around lunch that there was no way I could lose Devin already, or ever. What was I so crazy upset about anyway? Dancing with a stupid guy? So I break down and text her.

Hey, I'm sorry about the other night. I was just really looking forward to seeing you and then Kate ruined that and I was just angry and then I saw you with that guy, which is stupid. I mean you like girls, right? Well, you like me anyway. I mean right? Unless you kiss other girls you don't like. At any rate, I like you. A lot. And I'm so, so sorry again.

I stare at my phone and reread what has to be the lamest, wordiest, most unnecessary apology ever. If Garrett read it, she'd be ashamed of me. Way too desperate. So I delete words until I'm left with: *Hey, I'm sorry about the other night. I like you. A lot. And I'm so sorry again.* I scrunch up my face in disgust. Still stupid and still too much. Am I really sorry for anything? Shouldn't she be the one apologizing? Come on, Abbey. Grow some ovaries. I delete the entire message and type, *I hope everything's okay. Do we need to talk?* I send it but immediately regret it. Did that sound like I want to break up? Because I don't. It sounds like I'm angry, but I'm not. Not really. Why did I send that? I suck at life.

❖

"Can a hangover last more than one day?" Kate asks me, as if I am the drunk expert, and more importantly, as if she hadn't acted like a total bitch to me earlier.

"I don't know, why don't you ask Garrett." I say this first part with a heavy dose of irritation, but then exhaust my ability to stay angry anymore at anyone and say, "She probably knows about that stuff."

Kate shrugs. "I think she's mad at me or something. I keep calling her cell, but it just goes to voice mail. Have you talked to her?"

I bend over to stretch my hammies. "Nope, grounded from my phone and computer all weekend, remember?"

"Thanks to me, huh?" She frowns. "Sorry."

Before I question her quick shift from hate to gratitude, Coach Riley walks into the gym. So instead of speaking, I shove Kate and shake my finger at her as if to say, *You're welcome, but don't ever pull that crap on me again.* I think she gets what I mean.

Coach drops the bag of basketballs at the baseline and orders us to run. Then after our extra laps and our shorter session of stretching, he divides us up into teams. Unlike Mrs. Schwartz, Coach Riley always puts Kate and me on the same team: me as center, Kate at the block. Not today, though. As we walk onto the court to take our usual positions, he yells, "Brooks, stay. Townsend, take center." Kate walks slowly to my usual spot. When our eyes meet, she shrugs. I look to our point guard for info, but she looks just as confused. What's he doing? We've got a game this week. Why is he changing everything now?

He marches to the other end of the court, so the rest of us follow like a line of baby geese following their abusive mama goose. "Set up Gila Gold," he demands. I don't move because I have no idea what he wants me to do. I glance over my shoulder and look longingly at Kate and the rest of the starters. I know I've been distracted a bit during practice lately, but I thought I was giving it 110 percent when it came to basketball. My grades are good and I haven't ditched once, so why am I getting demoted?

"Galvan, take center. Mendez, block. The rest of you know where to go."

My teammates scramble on the court, but there are still no orders for me to join.

Three of us players are left standing on the sideline. Me and the usual two, Bella and Shanti. They're sophomores, too, but didn't play last year and have some catching up to do.

When Coach is satisfied with the placement of everyone, he says, "Bella and Shanti, sub in after ten minutes. Brooks, in my office. Now." His green workout pants *swish, swish* as he quickly walks across the courts.

To say Coach's office is kind of messy would be like saying Brittney Griner is a little tall and a tiny bit gay. As controlling as he is about his team, the guy could use a little help in here. He doesn't make an effort to clear off one of his many chairs piled high with college brochures, team uniform catalogs, and various coffee-stained papers, so instead of sitting, I stand in front of his desk. "We have a situation, Brooks," he says but doesn't yell. It's almost as if he's—no, he can't be. Is he sad?

I swallow loudly. As far as I know, I'm the only gay one left on the JV team. Is this about that? Did he find out about my make-out sessions with Keeta in the back of the bus? But that was last year, why would he care now? And why would he care about me being gay? It doesn't mean anything when I'm on the court.

"Your pal Taisha has decided to screw up our entire program." He tosses his clipboard on the pile of sports magazines on his desk. It slides off and its fall is broken by the mound of uniforms on the floor.

"Tai?" Now I'm really confused. "What did she do?" I dare to ask even though I know Coach likes to do most of the talking.

"I'm getting to that, Brooks." He leans back in his chair and stares at me. "You like playing on my team?" he asks, squinting into me, as if trying to detect a lie.

"Yes, sir. A lot," I whisper and shift my weight. I want to ask what that has to do with Tai but know I have to be patient.

"Well, you have a choice to make then. Tai quit the varsity team today. Coach Alvarez"—he makes a face because Garrett told me he hates her for being so young and having the varsity position instead of him—"needs a second-string center. She wants you to move up. She needs to know by tomorrow."

"Tai quit? But why?" I accidently say out loud.

He ignores my questions, stands up, and I get the hint that he wants me out of his office now, so I turn to the door. "Tomorrow by sixth period," he says.

I leave his office more confused than ever.

I don't say a word about Coach's news to my mom as she drives me home after practice. I'm still in shock and can't deal with my mom's million questions about something I'm not sure about. I can't get ahold of Tai after practice, so I try Garrett. If anyone knows what happened, it's G. But I get no answer. I leave a manic message comprised of excited squeals about the possibilities of being bumped up and questions of concern about why Tai quit. I know Garrett doesn't want much to do with Tai lately, but she can at least fill me in on the details.

At dinner, though, my mom can tell something is wrong. "Abbey, you haven't even touched your scalloped potatoes. They're your favorite. What's wrong? Are you feeling sick? PMS?"

I shake my head and laugh a little inside. Every time I'm the least bit moody or depressed or have a shift in appetite, my mom asks if it's PMS. According to her, I'm nearly about to get my period twenty-nine days a month. Maybe I should start marking it on her calendar.

"What?" she asks. "Did I say something funny?"

I take a big bite of my potatoes to buy time. But this news is almost good, so why am I scared? If I play varsity as a sophomore, then by senior year, I'll have that much more experience, that much more play time at the higher level. Maybe I'd be good enough for a scholarship. Ha. Maybe I need to focus on getting my grades up if I want a scholarship.

"Well," I start and almost take another bite, but place down my fork instead, "Coach Alvarez, you know, the varsity coach, wants me to move up to her team."

"I thought you already told them you wanted to stay on JV."

"I did, I mean, I do. But things have changed. There's an opening."

"How did that happen?"

No point in hiding the truth. For once, the truth won't get me in trouble. "Tai quit."

She frowns and chews her food. After a big gulp of milk, she says, "That's too bad. Things get too hard between her and Garrett on the court?"

I'm shocked she went there. I shouldn't be—I did tell her they were together, and I did tell her they broke up, but I didn't expect my mom to be so aware of what their breakup would mean. "Maybe?" I say, ashamed that I didn't go to that conclusion first. Duh.

"Well, will playing for the varsity impact your grades? What about Kate?"

As in tune as she is with Garrett and Tai, she is way out of touch with Kate and me. Even if I did save Kate from making an even bigger fool of herself at Miguel's party, it doesn't mean we're solid. It just means that I am, and always will be, codependent and pathetic. "Well, she was bummed out." I avoid the grade question because I don't anticipate it will impact my grades, but how the heck should I know. No promises.

"Well, as long as I don't get any bad progress reports from Ms. Morvay, it's okay with me."

"Not those again, Mom," I whine. "Come on."

"I guess you have a lot to think about, don't you?" she says, ignoring my plea. She starts to clear the table. "I'll do dishes tonight, honey. You get to your homework."

Back in my room, I lay out the night's load of homework. I don't know if they do it on purpose, but it seems like every teacher assigns homework on the same nights and none on the other nights. In front of me are my chem book, my *Animal Farm* novel, my sketchbook, and my algebra book. I could approach it alphabetically, by level of difficulty, or by the amount of distaste or love I have for the subject. The last option seems best, so I grab my sketchbook because I like my art class the least. I like Ms. Chafouleas, I just suck at drawing and can't seem to mature past my fifth-grade talents in this area.

Our assignment is to sketch an interesting object that represents who we are, so that's why my basketball is sitting in front of me. It's been ten minutes, but all I've managed to do is draw a circle, which I didn't even sketch freehand but still looks lopsided. Thankfully my phone alerts me of a text.

I smile when I see it's Devin. I can't wait to tell her I'm sorry for being so immature and how I got bumped up to varsity, but then the corners of my mouth drop as soon as I read what she sent. *Yeah, we should talk.*

As much as I hate being grounded, I feel thankful this time. Unlike Kate, I'd rather be dumped in a text message than face-to-face because I'd rather ugly cry in private than let someone see how much they hurt me. *I can't go anywhere*, I write back. *Grounded because of last weekend.* Then because I don't want her to think it was something I did, I add, *Kate got me in trouble.*

Yeah. Mia told me. Well, can I come over?

I twirl a bit of hair and contemplate my next text. The answer isn't no because I'm sure if I told my mom that I needed to see Devin, she'd be okay with that, but I'd rather put off being dumped as long as possible—maybe until she changes her mind? Before I respond, though, I get a call from Garrett. I consider ignoring it, but I'll go to any lengths at this point to avoid being brokenhearted.

"Hey, G."

"Don't hey-G me, little miss."

"What's your problem?"

Devin's next text pops up on my phone. *Abbey, are you there?*

I decide to grow a pair and deal with Devin, so I say, "G, I'm texting with Devin. Can I call you back?"

"Oh, hot lesbian sexting? Are you sending pics, too?"

"You couldn't be more off base."

"She's dumping you, huh? That sucks."

"How come you assume she's dumping me? Why can't I be dumping her? Is that so crazy?"

"Hmm, how can I put this nicely?"

I sigh.

"Abs, you're like a really sad and tragic, but sweet, starving stray cat."

"Oh, please, do go on."

"The minute anyone feeds the slightest amount of attention to you, you follow them around and dedicate yourself to them completely. Even once they stop feeding you or petting you, you still hang on with the hope that they might, someday, just once more, do it again. You see what I mean?"

I rest my head on my basketball and sigh because it's hard to deny what she's saying. But I really like Devin and not just because she liked me back. At least, I don't think that's why.

"But there are worse kinds of cats to be, Abs." My lack of verbal response must cue her to try and make me feel better. "I mean, at least you're not afraid of human contact like some people we know. And at least you don't go around howling for sex in alleys like some other people we know." She clears her throat and says "Keeta" under her breath, but I'm thinking the description sounds more like Garrett.

In the meantime, it seems Devin has grown irritated with me because her next text reads, *Okay, whatever. I guess text me when or if you want to talk again.*

"G, I really need to go."

"Fine, fine. See you at practice, freshie. Can't wait to break you in."

I type in a response to Devin as fast as my fingers will allow. *Sorry. Garrett called and was all upset and needed to talk.* Only a slight stretch of the truth. *I'm so, so, so, so sorry about everything. I miss you so much. Sorry, again*, but before I push send, an image of a scraggly emaciated dirty cat pops into my head. Am I as pathetic as Garrett says? If not, why am I the one always apologizing? What did I do? Was I the one who was grinding my you-know-what on some guy's you-know-where on the dance floor? I delete the last two sentences and a couple of *so*s and send the rest in an attempt to be less homeless-sad-kitty-like. One brief sorry is enough. Or it should be.

I wait and I wait for a response. Then I do a little homework and wait some more. I take my phone to the bathroom when I brush my teeth. I put it next to my pillow when I go to bed. I stare at it until my eyes water and my lids get heavy. What does Garrett know? I should have sent a million sorrys.

❖

Sometime while I slept, I got this message from Devin: *Abbey, I really liked spending time with you, but I think maybe we need to move on. I'm just not really sure who I am or what I want and I don't want to involve you in my confusion. It's not fair to you. You're a beautiful girl and I hope we can still hang out without it being weird. Thanks. And, please, I know it's asking a lot, but can you keep this all from Mia. I just can't deal with that part of it.*

After reading her message, I call Mia as I wait for Garrett to pick me up before school, assuming we're back on since we talked last night.

"She broke up with me," I say to Mia without having to fight back any tears. Maybe that's a sign I should pay attention to.

"Yeah, I figured she would," is Mia's reply.

I throw up my hand for no one to see. Do all my friends think I'm a loser or something? "Well, thanks for that. Was it because I'm hearing?" I wonder if it was too annoying to communicate with me.

"No." Then she shoves what I assume is a huge bite of cereal into her mouth because her next sentence is completely unclear. I give her time to chew. "It's because you're a girl, Abbey. I told you. She's not gay. She heard me talking about you and, I don't know, got curious about being with a girl."

"Well, I hope she writes a good report on the experience." I try to joke, even though Mia's words sting a little. I was just a curiosity? Ouch. "Well, just so we're clear, I didn't break her heart. So I'm off the hook from a beating from you, right?"

She laughs and takes another bite.

While she eats I accidently let a thought escape my mouth. "I'll never be the heartbreaker, huh? Garrett's right, I'm destined to be dumped."

I hear three loud gulps in the phone, then Mia lets out an airy burp. "Sorry. Abs, I gotta go, but how long until you're not grounded anymore? Can we hang out tonight?"

"I'll see," I say, a little disappointed that she didn't even try to dispute my comment. "I'm going to tell my mom I got dumped, so hopefully she'll feel sorry for me and let me see you."

She laughs. "Good plan. Nice to see you're using your outness to your advantage." I hear a distant honk. "Hold on. I'm coming," she yells away from the phone. "Ms. M. is in a hurry. Gotta jet. And, Abbey..."

"Yeah?" I don't mean to, but I begin to slip into self-deprecating sadness.

"You're more of a heartbreaker than you'll ever know." And then the line is silent.

CHAPTER SEVENTEEN

"Happy birthday!" my mom sings as I hobble into the kitchen. She comes at me with arms open wide for a big birthday bear hug, but instead of allowing her to hug me, I put up my hand and say, "No touching, please. Pain. All over." After last's night's practice, I'm feeling muscles in places no human being should. Riley has got nothing on Coach Alvarez's postgame punishments, which were on the edge of child endangerment on the court last night. I haven't even played in a game yet and it's only November and I hurt this much? Maybe I'm not ready for the big-girl league.

I ease myself down into my seat and let out a high-pitched thank you as my muscles contract.

"Oh, honey." She pours my milk for me since I'm in no condition to lift a gallon by myself and rushes to the stove to attend to the giant A-shaped pancake on the griddle. "It's been two weeks, Abbey Road. Shouldn't your muscles have adjusted yet? Maybe she's working you girls too hard."

All I can do is grunt in agreement.

"Sixteen," my mom says to herself. "It doesn't seem possible."

So far, sixteen feels the same as fifteen. The only major difference is I'm a few inches taller, my feet are bigger, and like Katy Perry, I've kissed a girl or two. This last thought makes me think about Devin, and now I'm feeling sad. What's worse is Mia told me Devin has a boyfriend now. What is it with all these lesbians in my life falling for guys? Will I end up like them, too?

"Why the serious face?" Mom asks as she places my pancake in front of me, along with my traditional birthday-morning present.

I unwrap the book and smile. It's not her usual genre, something from the canon of classics. It's a totally gay book. "*Ash*? Cool."

"The lady at Hermione's Books said it's one of the best. A retelling of *Cinderella*, but with a twist. Have you already read it?"

"Not yet." She looks so pleased with herself for buying me some lesbian fiction, so I add, "Looks good."

"I'm glad."

"Thanks," I say and put it down. "So, tonight…"

"Golden Buddha?" she smiles as she flips my pancake.

The reality of what turning sixteen would look like is failing to meet my high expectations. In my wonderful world of make-believe, where I'm not a gangly dork, I'd be celebrated by all my close friends, then ride off into the sunset in the car I somehow managed to learn how to drive, with a girl I managed to keep sitting beside me. But no. My reality is a dinner for two at the Golden Buddha. Kate did ask if she and Garrett could take me out, but it's a Tuesday, a school night, and I'm still kind of trying to stay on top of things so my mom doesn't regret letting me be on the varsity team.

"Can Mia come?" I ask with hesitation because Kate's the only one that's been allowed to infiltrate our birthday dinner.

"Of course! The more, the merrier." She doesn't ask about Kate and I'm grateful.

I polish off my cereal. "Thanks again for the book, Mom." I give her a hug and make my way slowly to my bedroom.

❖

"Dig in, ladies. This ain't a pride picnic!" Coach yells at Garrett and me as we sprint full speed down the court to run a fast-break drill for what has to be the hundredth time. Garrett looks like she's about to give birth as she passes me the ball once I'm in position to make a layup. I don't screw it up, thank God.

Instead of being pleased, Coach Alvarez puts her hand over her eyes and raises her other arm. "Can someone, anyone, tell me what they did wrong?"

I look at my new teammates. Birch and Willow, a pair of twins apparently named by tree-loving hippie parents, are bent over in pain from their own drills that the assistant coach has been putting them through, so they don't volunteer an answer. The other potential starters, Carly, Jessica, and Sabrina, all shrug. Everyone else is on another court working on defense drills. The only one who dares to raise her hand is Garrett.

"Not," she takes a breath, "fast enough."

"Thank God," Coach says. "I'm not surrounded by morons, after all. Faster, get it?"

We both nod our heads.

"*Bueno*. Water break."

We all walk to the bleachers, grab water bottles, and collapse. When I am absolutely positive Coach is out of earshot, I ask, "Hey, G. Is Coach a yestergay or something?"

"And here I didn't think you ever listened to my vocabulary lessons," she says and laughs.

"Well, what is she? She seems so cow-like and even teases us about it, but she's living with Mr. Fred. So what the hell?"

Garrett sprays another stream of water down her throat. "She's totally trying to play the straight game. I don't buy it, though. I mean, have you ever considered that Mr. Fred is gay, too, and they're just trying to fool us all? She's hot, though. I'd do her."

"Scandalous," I whisper and look over at Coach A. She's super young-looking. She must be in college still.

"Hey, she's only four or five years older than me. You dated Keeta and she's three years older. How's it any different?"

I shrug. "Just seems wrong." But Garrett makes a compelling argument. She's not that much older than us.

"Speaking of scandalous, what mishaps will my sweet-slutty-sixteen Abbey have tonight? Dolphin ankle tattoo? All night session of *Little House on the Prairie*?"

"Dinner with Mom and Mia. Nothing big."

Coach blows her whistle, and we all rise and run to her on command like a pack of dogs. "All right, ladies, some changes have to be made to our starting lineup since your teammate Jessica here decided to sprain her ankle." We all look at Jess on the bleachers. I feel her pain because I was there last year. "Eyes, ladies." We look back to Coach. "We've got a game against Saguaro on Friday and as you all know, those cows don't play nice."

I look around at my teammates. No one else seems disturbed that she is being so blatantly…I don't know, would you call it homophobic if she's mostly right about that team?

"Virgin Mary, take point." Garrett runs to the top of the key with a ball. "Wonder Twins, take the wings." Birch and Willow run on the court, too. Coach reviews her roster and looks at the remaining players on the baseline and frowns. "Carlita, this block." Carly, who's the opposite of small in every which way, takes the block. She'll definitely give The Fridge, my nemesis from last year, a run for her money. "And…" Coach slowly looks down the lineup, then pauses at me and squints, as if she's trying to look into my soul.

I want to grin at her with an innocent, sheepish no-teeth smile, as if to say, *Who me? No, no, I'm too new and fragile to play on Friday.* But, for some reason, I squint back at her instead.

She makes a contorted face as if she's doubtful, a face I've seen directed at me on many occasions. "I don't know," she says to no one. "They could eat her alive." Then she shrugs as if that's the least of her worries. "Okay, Grumpy Gills, get on the court," she says and points at me.

Cursed again, I scream in my head but do as I'm told and take the block opposite Carly. As far as nicknames go, Grumpy Gills is a step down from last year's nickname, which was Crutch. I've got to work extra hard to make sure I get an upgrade as soon as possible.

❖

"Hey," Mia says as she sits next to me in the usual booth my mom and I request for my birthday. "Ms. M. and Juliana say happy birthday."

One look at her and I'm smiling because she dressed up for me. Sure, she's still wearing Doc Martens and shorts, but they're new shorts and, instead of a tank top, she's wearing a short-sleeve button-down shirt. I don't compliment her, though, because I know she'll just swat it back like a shot being rejected on the court. Instead I say, "And you? What do you say?"

"Me?" She smiles big and winks slightly. I don't know if she does it on purpose. She must. Either way, it always makes my stomach flitter for a second. "Oh, I just say, what's for dinner? I'm starving." She picks up a menu and nudges me over as if she needs more room.

I shove her back and roll my eyes. That'll be the extent of her affection for the evening, but I know she cares.

After we order, my mom takes a present out of her purse. "Present time," she says and places the box in front of me.

"Oh. Me, too." Mia takes a card out of her jacket pocket and places it on the table.

I open Mia's envelope. Inside is a mix-CD of new songs from all our favorite chick singers. "This is really cool, Mia. Thanks." I read over the lists of songs and am reminded of the first CD she ever gave me. Mia single-handedly broke me of my top-forty habit, and I'm reminded of how grateful I am to her for it. I look over at her, but she's looking down. Even if she has no money to her name, she always gives me the best gifts. She really is a good friend. "Thanks, buddy. I really like it."

"No big deal. I had them downloaded already. Whatever." She winks again. My stomach flutters again. I wonder for a second what that's all about, but only for a second because my mom interrupts.

"My turn! Open it." She's way more giddy than I've seen her, so I get nervous. What if I hate it?

I take a deep breath and smile. "Okay, okay," and quickly unwrap the present. Inside a small box is a key ring. A key ring with a car key on it. A key that's seen better days. It's the key to my mom's blue Volvo station wagon. "What does this mean?"

"It's yours now, Abbey," she says and smiles widely. "Now all you have to do is learn how to drive it."

I still haven't said thank you, and I realize I might be sounding a little ungrateful. "Seriously? This is crazy. And, um, cool," I say, which is a half lie. This *is* all crazy, but not a bit cool. Once again, my mom has manipulated me into the driver's seat. Mia is smiling slyly. "You knew, didn't you?" I ask her.

"Well, every girl needs a good driving CD." Mia and my mom high-five.

"Aren't you excited, Abbey?" my mom asks. "Now you can take driving lessons in your own car, and you can start driving yourself to school. No more waiting for rides."

My head is spinning. The possibilities are kind of exciting. I could get a summer job. I would never have to ride Suntran again, ever. I could take a girl on a date. This last realization makes me smile. Then I think about how the back of the Volvo folds down to allow two people to sleep in it, which leads me to think about my previous conclusion about how the only place to have sex with privacy is in the backseat of a car, and how my mom just gave me keys to a sex mobile. Is she insane or just stupidly trustworthy? At least I won't get knocked up. There's one major benefit of being a lesbian. Maybe that's how she feels about it, too. "This is cool, Mom," I say before my manic train of thought begins to show on my face. "You're the best. But what about you?"

"Well, I guess I'll just have to go and get my own car. Wait, what's this?" She pulls a key chain with a shiny VW emblem on it. "I already did."

"Well, happy birthday to you, too, I guess."

She smiles. "Yep. Happy birthday to me, too."

Chapter Eighteen

"Push!" Coach yells from the sideline.

Garrett hurls the ball downcourt to my open hand. It's too far ahead of me and goes out of bounds, but not before number twelve from Saguaro's team gets a finger on it.

"Blue ball," the ref announces and the small crowd of Saguaro fans cheer, "Blue balls!" back into the gym and then laugh.

I'm gasping like a dying fish as I line up for our inbound play. Carly pushes her way in front of me, faces me, and gives me a nod right before Willow smacks the ball to signal our play. I fake left, then bolt right, Carly rolls toward the key, then quickly runs across the paint to screen for me. I'm open for half a second, which is all it takes for Willow to bounce pass the ball into me. I pump fake, my defender lands on me, but I manage to push my way through her beefy arms to draw a foul.

"Two shots. Line up, ladies."

It's only the first half of my first varsity game of my short basketball career, and I know for sure if I don't die on the court tonight, I'm in for life. There's something about the contact, the sweat, pushing my body to the extreme, and the constant decision making that makes me forget everything that isn't basketball: my most recent failure to complete a driving lesson with my mom, my humiliating performance on my Algebra 2 test, and even the fact that I wore a new pair of pants without taking off the *8 Long* sticker, which earned me a new nickname in chemistry. This shiny polyester uniform is my superhero costume, and I need it now more than ever.

I swish my first shot. Thank God.

Garrett and Birch slap my butt, and unlike before, I'm not fazed by the assault to my rear. I line myself up for the next shot, but as I release the ball someone screams, "Brick!" which succeeds in throwing me off along with my shot. The ball hits the back of the basket and bounces up in a high arc, which gives me time to grab my own rebound.

I jump, but just when I think the ball's all mine, I stop midair as if I've hit a wall. A wall named The Fridge. We wrestle for the rebound. I hold on for dear life, but because she weighs about fifty pounds more than I do and can probably bench-press me, I'm flung off to the sideline. Whistles blow and a jump ball is called. "Blue ball!" the crowd jeers again.

That I'm on the ground again doesn't surprise me. What does surprise me, though, is the hand that's offered. I look up and see The Fridge standing over me, massive and imposing as an ox.

"Got a promotion, huh?" she says as I take her hand, which makes me think she's either a somewhat-nice person after all, or a psychotic bitch trying to get into my head. I go with the latter, but before I can line up again for the inbound play, a whistle blows and I'm subbed out of the game.

I sit on the bench, watching my teammates hustling. Garrett makes a three, so we all stand up to cheer. We're up by ten. Birch snags a pass across court and finds Willow's open hand. Up by twelve. The two of them don't show any emotions after the fast break, but nod knowingly at each other and set up for defense. Must be a twin thing. Saguaro's girls are getting frustrated. I see The Fridge make some familiar moves on Carly, but Carly's just as big and plays just as dirty. While the two of them engage in secret warfare, the ball makes its way to Garrett again, at the top of the key. The swish of the three echoes through the gym and forces the Saguaro coach to call a time-out.

I scurry to the huddle. "Grumpy Gills and Teenage Witch, check in for the Wonder Twins." Sabrina and I report our subbing to the score table, and before the buzzer goes off, Coach has some encouraging words. "And for the love of Hillary Clinton, don't screw up this lead. Got it?"

We all nod, yell, "Offense," and head back out on the court.

And then turnover, after turnover, after foul, after foul, we, especially me, do the opposite of what Coach wants and screw everything up.

I'm not sure what part of the evening was the worst: the look of satisfaction on The Fridge's face as we slapped hands after the game, that I contributed to our surprising loss by fouling like a crazy person who can't control her appendages, or the postgame lecture from Coach Alvarez, whose words are still ringing in my ears.

I get home, and I call Mia. She's not much for my basketball game play-by-plays but is usually willing to listen. I especially need to unload how I bricked six shots in a row and then fouled out, thanks to The Fridge and her wicked ways.

"Well, you'll get them next time," Mia says, which is what she always says when we lose, but this time she follows up with, "I'm sure you did better than you think," which is sweet.

I remember life is not all about me and ask, "How are things with Ms. M., anyway. Is it totally cool living with real live lesbians?"

"They aren't making pornos every night, if that's what you think."

I let out an "ew," and then cover my eyes. "Thanks for the visuals," I yell because the last thing I need in my head are images of Ms. M. and her wife together.

"They're really pretty boring actually. I don't know why everyone gets all upset about the lesbian lifestyle, whatever that means. As far as I can tell, it includes walking dogs, cleaning litter boxes, grocery shopping, and binge watching Showtime. Total snoozeville over here."

I change the subject. "How are things with my pal Psycho Nicky?"

"We broke up."

Now I feel like an ass, so I say so. "Well, I feel like an ass. Sorry. When?"

"Last week," she says, but I can't tell if she wants to say more about it.

I risk dejection and ask, "Why? What happened?"

She sighs, and I wait. Then she finally says, "I don't know. Ms. M. tried to be cool at first, but then said she didn't want her over, and she's not out to her parents, like, at all. So we couldn't really be together. We kind of grew apart, I guess. It's cool, though. I mean, after what she did to you. Sorry about all that."

She says it's cool, but I can tell she's sad, which makes me sad, but instead I say, "What doesn't kill us makes us less afraid to die."

"Huh?"

"Never mind—just another uplifting Coachism. Speaking of psychotic, Coach A. takes the cake."

"Because she's a closeted cow," Mia says and laughs. "Even Ms. M. says so. Anyway, I gotta go start my homework before Ms. M.'s missus gets all upset and naggy. She's seriously committed to the strict-cop role. It's like a freaking episode of *The Fosters* over here."

"Wanna hang out soon? I mean, since our social calendars seem to have opened up."

"Yeah, I guess we're both single again. At the same time. Kind of like last year, huh?"

Last year feels like eons ago and it went by like a blip, not like ten long months of torture, elation, sadness, and recovery. "So, what're you saying? You stalking me again?"

"Hmm," she says, and I can feel her sly smile through the phone, "maybe I am."

❖

Going from seven to seven, five days a week, is slowly killing me. I have no social life, but more importantly, my homework is barely getting done. So tonight it's all about getting caught up. Me and Willie Shakes are going to spend the evening together. Yes, just as soon as I finish this one episode of *Untold Stories of the ER*, I'm going to hit the books.

In the middle of the fourth consecutive episode, I've made myself a new promise: after *this* episode, I will stay up late and get caught up. Then my cell rings.

"What're you doing?" Mia asks without saying hello.

"Nothing. Homework."

"Liar. Turn off the TV and talk to me."

I mute the TV so I can read the subtitles. I must see if the guy who shoved a glass pot pipe in his butt survives. "What's up?" I say sleepily. It's only nine thirty, but it might as well be two in the morning.

"I met someone," she says, excitement in her voice. "At school. I thought I was the only one, but I guess not. Her name is Maddy—it's short for Madeline. Isn't that cute?"

"Yeah, cute," I say, trying to hide my…I don't know, maybe it's jealousy, with boredom. "What's she look like?"

"Dude, she's drop-dead. Long blond hair, blue eyes, long legs. And she's funny. Super funny. And smart. You know she *chose* to go to alt ed? She's, like, the only one there who didn't screw up. She was just sick of high-school drama. You wouldn't know anything about that, huh, Abs."

"Sounds like you two should run away and get gay-ried. Congrats." My sarcasm may not be doing a perfect job of hiding the truth, but I'm too tired to care. The truth is, I like Mia being available to me, even if we're just friends. Immature and twisted, I know.

"Don't be a hater, Abbey. I want you to meet her. What are you doing this Saturday?"

I contemplate my plans. The list is short: Saturday morning practice, laundry, and homework, but before I can answer, she decides for me.

"Meet us at Ugly Mug Saturday night. Her friend's playing at the open mic."

How can that guy say he doesn't know how the pipe got there?

"You didn't turn off the TV, did you?"

I click it off finally. "Yes, nag."

"Okay, Saturday?"

"Yeah, yeah. I'll be there. 'Bye."

"Okay, 'bye."

And with that nothing-but-friends farewell, we hang up.

CHAPTER NINETEEN

Maybe there's no such thing as happiness. Especially when your name is Abbey Brooks. Today, I've awoken to the worst cramps known to woman. My mom forces me to drink her concoction of baking soda, lemon juice, and warm water, but there's no improvement. "I'm dying. Bleeding out," I whine from the bathroom floor as I lie in the fetal position.

"Well, dying might be a little extreme, Abbey," my mom says. "How about a heating pad? I think we still have one." She starts to dig through the contents of the bathroom cupboard causing a bottle of peroxide to fall on my head.

"Ow," I scream, but mostly from anger, not pain. "Watch what you're doing up there."

I open my eyes because her lack of response makes me nervous. Sure enough, her hand is firmly on her hip and she's looking down at me. "Excuse me? I'm just trying to help here."

"Sorry," I whisper. Garrett honks outside. "Crap, what time is it?"

"Seventy thirty. Should I call the attendance office? Are you going to stay home?"

"No." I grab the side of the tub and push myself up to a kneeling position. "I have to go. It's a game day. Can you take me in a little bit?"

"Okay, I'll tell Garrett and Kate. Hurry up and shower. You don't want to miss too much chemistry."

I moan as I turn the knobs on. "No, wouldn't want to miss a second of that."

❖

Of course my tardy note gets thoroughly scrutinized by Mrs. Stum. "Ill? Then why are you here now? Suddenly you're better?"

I grimace as I shift from one foot to the other. "Not exactly, but hopefully."

"Well, hopefully you won't contaminate the rest of us with your germs," she says unsympathetically. "Today's the last chance you and your group will have for planning. Nice of you to come late and contagious." She tears up the pass in her usual fashion and sends me on my way.

I hobble to the table where Daphne's holding another well-organized meeting. "Sorry I'm late," I mumble.

I receive an agenda from her upon my arrival. "We're on item three," she says and subtly scoots away from me.

"I'm not contagious. I promise." I look at her with a grimace on my face.

She knowingly nods while Jake and Eric remain clueless.

Item three is the delegation of presentation parts. And even though she did most of the research and put together most of the presentation—Jake drew a really cool illustration for the introduction slide—she doesn't seem to mind letting us take some of the credit. "Now, the question is, do we want to meet one last time to rehearse before Monday?"

The answer in Daphne's head is a resounding yes. So to make up for my lack of previous effort, I offer my house. Besides, it'll be good for my mom to see me putting effort into school.

"Fabulous, Abbey. I'm volunteering all day Saturday at the SPCA, so is Sunday okay for you guys? Shall we take a vote?" She starts to dig into her backpack for her ballots.

Jake, who has been silently admiring her from across the table, smiles and gently says, "We're all game. Right, Team Up and Atom? Sunday?"

We all nod.

"Okay, awesome. How does lunchtime sound? We can each bring an item to share. I'll bring crustless egg-salad sandwiches." She claps with pleasure. Oddly, it's at that moment that I see how she and Jake are perfect for each other. For some reason this ruins my day more.

To avoid the Kate-and-Garrett show after school before we depart for our game, I hide in the library and get caught up on homework since I know I won't get to it while waiting for my game. Eventually, however, I have to face the music and get in line to board the bus.

"You," Kate says, pointing at me as I approach, "need to give me some Gatorade."

"Me, too," Garrett yells over her shoulder. She's arranging her bag and pillow. It used to be that the back of the bus was reserved for the lesbians that coupled up on the teams. Now, it's just for varsity players. No more blankets hiding hands, just bags of food and pillows for comfort. I'll admit it was very awkward knowing they were back there doing who knows what, but when it was my turn to be back there with Keeta…well, I loved every minute of it, and the farther the school, the better. I try to keep her off my mind as we settle in on the very same seat Keeta and I shared last year. Not that we did anything more than kiss and hold hands, but just kissing can be pretty damn amazing with the right girl. Not that I'm thinking about that, though. Nope.

It's only a forty-minute journey through the desert to Sahuarita High, but with Kate in front of me and Garrett next to me, I'm destined to be annoyed the whole ride there.

"Hey, Abbey," Kate says after downing half of my Gatorade, "there's this guy on the varsity team. His name's David. He's pretty cute, and tall, and kind of nerdy. He's probably just your type."

"Well, I'm guessing I'm not his type."

Kate frowns. "Why not? I mean, he's tall. You're tall. He's smart, and you used to be." She and Garrett laugh.

"I don't know, maybe I'm just too lesbian. You know, because I'm a lesbian."

Garrett wrinkles her nose as if she's doubtful. "How do you know? Maybe you're bi like me."

The thought has crossed my mind from time to time. I mean, how do I know if I'm completely gay? "I'm just not into them, G." I hope that's the end of it because as annoying conversations go, I wasn't expecting one so personal.

"You're just not trying hard enough," Garrett says, as if we're discussing my inability to draw a horse, not like guys.

My stomach tenses like she just punched me. Instead of cowering away as usual, I look at her in amazement.

"What?" she snaps. No one questions Garrett, especially not me.

But that was before. Before she cheated on and then dumped Tai. As far as I'm concerned, she's not my gay hero anymore. "When did my being a lesbian become a problem for you?" Then I turn to Kate. "And when did it become a problem for you again?"

Kate looks down. "It's not, I just thought…"

But I'm mostly angry with Garrett. She should know better. "I know you're going through some sort of identity shift. But that's your issue, not mine, so lay off."

Garrett's sitting at the end of the seat I'm on, so instead of changing seats like I want to, I turn to the window. My stomach starts to hurt, but I think it's only because the cramps are returning.

I've never told Garrett off like that. Maybe no one has. She doesn't say a word, picks up her bag, and moves to sit in front of Kate. Just as well. I need to return to my fetal position anyway, so I spread out in the backseat. It's never been this empty on an away game. Leave it to Abbey to clear it out.

The first quarter of the game flies by. We're like a well-oiled machine, and even though Garrett isn't exactly talking to me at the moment, she doesn't let it get in the way of her drive to win. When I'm open, she passes to me, a little harder than usual, but still. We're up by ten, and I'm at the line for the fifth time because their center is suffering from tall-girl issues, like over-the-back fouls.

After I make the second shot, the buzzer goes off, and Willow subs in for Carly and Jessica subs in for me. I take the chair next to Coach because it's the only empty one. The good news is she only sits for a few seconds at a time, so I should be fairly safe from her verbal attacks, but lately she's been a little nicer, especially to me for some reason.

"Garrett, call the play," Coach yells. "What are you doing?" She slams her clipboard down on her chair. It bounces off and falls to the floor. I get up quickly and squat to pick it up. I sense the need to look down at my shorts at this moment, and that's when I see it.

This is not happening, I scream in my head and hurry back to my chair. Even though my shorts have a stain, the chair is clean. How long has it been there? Did Garrett see and not tell me? Would she be that mean?

Coach yells at Garrett to take a time-out and the buzzer goes off. The rest of my teammates on the bench stand up to offer their seats to those coming off the court. Except me. No, I will not be rising at this time. Instead I lean forward, careful to keep my lower region from making contact with the chair.

Of course, Coach notices. "Brooks. Get your butt up. Actually, go sub in for Birch. Play forward."

I don't move. I just stare ahead like I didn't hear her.

"Is there a problem, Double G?" Coach asks. Her foot taps the court while she waits.

I look down at the floor and then up at Coach. "Um…"

The rest of my teammates seem to clue in and try to defend me. "She got sick on the drive here, Coach," Willow says.

"Yeah, I'm good to go, Coach," Birch adds. "I don't need a sub."

"Am I talking to any of you right now?" Coach's face is turning a deep shade of red, even more red than Coach Riley's when we mess up a play. "Get up, check in, and get your butt and head in the game, Brooks."

I fight back the tears welling up in my eyes. "I can't Coach. I'm…"

"You're what?" she whisper yells through clenched teeth. "We know you can't be pregnant."

Birch's and Willow's mouths drop open on that one. I have a feeling Coach scares them more than even me.

I can't say it, so I stand and show Coach my shorts. The rest of my teammates let out sympathetic moans. Not Coach, though.

"Don't you guys know how to deal with this by now? Do I need to dedicate a practice to how calendars and feminine products work?"

I don't think it'll help trying to explain to her that I'm indeed aware how tampons work, but mine is failing me now. The buzzer sounds, signaling either the end or the worsening of my humiliation. She won't make me go out there, will she?

"Birch, you stay in. Red Badge of Humiliation, get out of here and change."

Sophie tosses me my warm-up jacket and I tie it around my waist before shamefully running to the locker room.

I want to die, and this time, I mean it.

❖

I tell Mia about the incident, but she seems unconcerned. "It's not like you were on a hot date or anything. I mean, who do you know in Sahuarita anyway?"

"That's not the point." We're waiting for Maddy to pick us up from Ms. Morvay's, which I guess is Mia's place, too, for now. Mia was right about them: Ms. Morvay and her wife are pretty ordinary. So far tonight I've witnessed Ms. Morvay clean up the dinner dishes and her wife laugh at Internet cat videos, which she made us watch. Hot.

When Maddy rings the doorbell, Mia jumps up to answer as if it's Ani DiFranco at the door. They hug and Mia invites her in.

I've heard that everyone has a doppelgänger out there in the world, waiting to meet up with its partner at any moment. I never really thought that was true until now. Maddy's just as Mia described: tall—like me, blond hair—like me, which is long—like mine, and blue eyes…yup. But the kicker is when she speaks. She even sounds like me.

They're holding hands and can barely keep their eyes off each other. To keep myself from making a face, I look over at Ms. Morvay, who's lounging on the couch reading. She looks up just then, too, and smiles. I fake a smile and then look down.

"You look great," Mia whispers to Maddy.

"No, you look great," Maddy whispers back.

Mia giggles. "We look great together, I guess."

I clear my throat. I haven't yet been introduced, not that anyone had noticed.

"Oh, dude, sorry," Mia says to me. "Abbey, this is *the* Maddy."

I nearly laugh as Maddy extends her hand. Abbey and Maddy? No one else finds that a weird coincidence?

"Nice to meet you finally, Abbey. Mia talks about you all the time," Maddy says politely, like I would.

"Yeah, you, too. Glad to meet…" But before I can finish, they're gazing into each other's eyes again.

My God, this is going to be a long night.

❖

By the time our group has finished practicing Daphne's presentation, Daphne and Jake exchange over twenty flirtatious glances, I eat more than my share of the little egg-salad sandwiches, and it's a quarter to three. I'm rushing them out the door, but my mom has her own agenda. She may have married a scientist, but his left-brain skills never penetrated or influenced her right brain, so she's asking a million questions about our topic.

"Well, you see, Mrs. Brooks, if you compare the—" Daphne starts.

"Mom," I say, trying not to show too much irritation, so I won't get a lecture from her after they leave, "I can explain it later, okay? Daphne, Jake, Eric—you guys rock. See you Monday, bright and early." I gently push them out the door. They carpooled, so Jake rushes ahead to open the passenger door for Daphne. It's cute but makes me want to scratch my eyes out. What is wrong with me?

CHAPTER TWENTY

It's three o'clock on the fifth day of my winter break. I haven't showered, and I'm elbow deep into a bag of salt-and-vinegar chips when the phone rings. I ignore it because Buffy and Spike are about to kiss, and even though it's so wrong, there's just something so right about it. I can totally relate.

"Abbey!" my mom calls from the laundry room. "Could you get that? I'm expecting a call from my client."

I moan my disapproval.

"Abbey," she says again, but this time her voice is more high-pitched and quite a bit more irritated.

I don't bother seeing who it is because anyone I care about would have called my cell. "Brooks residence," I say in my best secretary voice. "Abbey Brooks speaking."

"Wow, very professional," Mia says.

I pull my eyes off the TV screen for the first time in a week. "Do you need to talk to my mom about something?" Why else would she be calling the landline?

"Nah, just thought I'd call you to say hi. Your cell phone is off or something."

"I guess I need to charge it. Well, hi."

My mom walks in with her arms full of hot clothes and dumps them on me. "Fold these," she demands. I guess she's getting a little fed up with my lazefest. "Then dishes."

Yep, definitely fed up. But the warmth of the clothes makes me relax deeper into the couch. "How's Maddy?" I ask, even though I know Mia's been stuck like tree sap to my evil twin. With Garrett changing teams and Tai gone off the face of the planet, I swear a country singer needs to write me a song called "Where Have All the Lesbians Gone?"

Just as she's about to respond, my mom grabs the phone out of my hand. "Hello, this is Abbey's mom."

"Mom." I shove the clothes off me and try to get the phone from her.

"Who is this?…Hi, Mia, I'm going to ask that Abbey call you back later, okay?…Great. You have a good day, too." She hangs up and puts the phone in her pocket. "Wow, looks like your afternoon just opened up. Those clothes aren't going to fold themselves, my Abbey Roo."

"Don't call me that after you totally humiliated me."

"I asked you to do the dishes four hours ago, this laundry yesterday, and to sweep the back patio last week. Get up, get moving, and get it done." The phone rings in her pocket. Before I can retaliate, she answers, "Brooks residence, Susan Brooks speaking," and all I can do is storm off to the kitchen and angrily turn the water on and wait for the sink to fill.

When I'm angry at her like this, I think about my dad. Like, if he were here, nothing would ever go wrong and everything would be perfect—all unicorns and glitter all the time. It's easy to imagine him in this perfect light because I don't remember ever feeling angry at him. Except after he died, of course. But then again, he never had to find out about me. He never had to feel disappointed, and I never lied to him because I never had anything to lie to him about. Maybe if he knew me now, he'd feel embarrassed or disappointed. Maybe I'm lucky I'll never have to know.

I'm deep in my thoughts when my mom touches my back.

"What?" I ask, looking out the window so she won't notice I'm about to cry. I turn on the water again to rinse the dishes I have piled up on the other side of the sink.

"Sorry I snapped at you and embarrassed you on the phone."

I shrug. "It's okay. Sorry I've been so lazy."

"Hey," she turns off the water and forces me to turn around. "You're not lazy. I know you work hard at school and at practice. I just need a little help around here, okay?"

I nod, but for some reason my lip quivers.

"Oh, Abbey," she says sweetly and pulls me in for a hug. "I'm sorry."

I feel bad letting her think the tears are about our fight and not about my dad, but I don't tell her so because I don't want her to cry, too. Instead I hug her with my wet hands and silently vow to be a better daughter.

She releases me finally and then sits at the table. I turn around to continue my chore.

"So, that was a new client," she says.

"Yeah?"

"He's opening up a restaurant and wants me to paint a mural in the lobby. It sounds like a really amazing opportunity and a lucrative one."

"Sweet, Mom. Congratulations. When will you start?"

"Well, I'll send some initial sketches this week, and I imagine I'll be able to start painting next week. But there's one problem. Well, not really a problem, exactly."

I dry off my hands and turn around. "He wants you to use scratch-and-sniff paints?"

"Not quite." She laughs. "But that's a genius idea. Actually, it's that his restaurant isn't exactly in Tucson."

The salt-and-vinegar chips I ate earlier have left my mouth dryer than the Rillito riverbed in May, so I make my way to the fridge and fight the urge to drink the lemonade right from the bottle since my mom is watching. "Well, where exactly is it?" I ask, pouring some in a glass like a civilized person.

"Mesa," she says.

"That's a long commute. You'll have to leave really, really early every morning. That sucks."

"Actually, he's offered to pay for me to stay in a hotel nearby. Isn't that cool?"

"I guess so," I say and nothing more. In all my years of living, I haven't been away from my mom for more than a day. As much as she annoys and nags me, the thought of her being more than a bike-ride away makes me really scared. I guess she can tell.

"Sweetie, I'll only be gone a week. I promise. And you can stay with Mia or Kate so you won't be alone."

I make a face. Neither one seems like a good option at the time, but I don't want my mom to worry about me, so I say, "Why can't I just stay here?"

Mom raises her eyebrows. "No, honey. I don't think so. I'd feel much better if you weren't alone."

The thought of being alone sounds amazing. I'd hardly have to wear clothes and I could eat breakfast for dinner. Then a thought pops into my head—a dirty one that involves me and someone else and having the house to ourselves. "Mom, it's not like I'm going to have parties or anything," I say to give it one last shot even though I know she won't waver.

"No. Not yet, honey."

"Okay, fine. So, what do you know about this guy? I mean, what if he's a killer or rapist or Republican?"

"Now, now, Abbey. Some of my best clients are Republicans."

"I'm just saying, you're going up there and…who knows?" Am I being a little paranoid? Perhaps. Do I care? No.

"Abbey, he's a friend of your Aunt Sara. She knows him very well."

"Sure, but how well do you really know Aunt Sara?" She throws a banana at me and I guess I deserve it. "All right. I guess you can go."

"Thanks, *Mom*," she says. "I promise not to stay out past eleven fifteen, okay?"

I smile, but inside I've got a thousand thoughts running through my manic mind: A week with no mom? What if I get sick? Who'll take care of me? What if I need a ride? What if I run out of shampoo? What if I can't find my lucky socks? That's right about when I realize that my mom is right. I need to start taking care of myself and my needs a little more around here.

Back in my room, I'm thinking about who to stay with. At Kate's house, I'd have to endure nightly makeovers and magazine articles that inform me of ways to make him scream for more and how to increase my eyelash volume. No, thanks. Besides, Ms. Morvay is cool, and I'm sure she wouldn't mind one more little lezzie roaming her home. So after I tell my mom my choice, she calls to ask. She gets a quick *Absolutely!* from the Mrs. and Mrs., and that's that.

After saying good night to my mom, who surprisingly made it to eleven o'clock, I head to my room to start on my New Year's resolutions.

1. Pass all my classes with Bs or better

I should aim for all As, but I'm a realist.

2. More weightlifting

A necessity if I'm going to face The Fridge and live to tell.

3. Get my license

The carrot of freedom is the driving force behind this goal. That, and sex.

4. Improve my free throw percentage by 10 percent
5. Be a better daughter

This should be really easy, or really hard. Depends on the day.

6. No more lying

I make a face after writing that one. Can you be sixteen and not lie, ever? I don't see how. Instead of erasing it, though, I add: *as much to my mom*, which seems more attainable.

There's one last resolution I want to add, but I'm too shy to write it down, which is pure irony. I take a deep breath and convince myself this list's for my eyes only, so I might as well go for gold. If not here, then where?

7. Stop being such a prude and go for it.

Of course, I'm talking about sex. No need to write it out, though.

Writing that one down gives me a little more courage and gumption, so I add one last thing to my list:

8. Take control of my life and be bold!

Satisfied, I store my list deep in my bedside drawer, and then turn on the TV to watch the ball drop. Not exactly a big, brave, bold move, but I'm tired from all that thinking.

❖

On my last day of winter break, I kiss my mom good-bye in the car before she drives away to Mesa. "Be good and help with the dishes and don't leave messes and don't watch that trash TV."

"Okay, okay." I'll miss her, but not all of her.

"And be polite, and don't forget to charge your phone so I can call you if I need to."

I'm loading up my shoulders with my bags. "Okay, okay."

"And—"

"Mom, you're going to hit traffic if you don't get on the road."

As she pulls away, I feel a sense of relief and a sense of emptiness. Luckily Mia is there to help me feel better. She opens the door and bows. "Your Majesty."

I curtsy back, enter the foyer, and drop my bags at her feet. "Thank you. That will be all."

"I hope you're happy," she says, picking up my things. "I had to clean my room and vacuum the house because for some insane reason, they consider you a guest."

"Aw, did you have to hide all your dildos, too?" I whisper.

She scowls. "Yes, very inconvenient."

I stop walking. "I was kidding."

"Oh yeah, me, too," she says and laughs.

Juliana descends upon us. "Abbey, we're so excited to have you here." She hugs me like we're related. It's sweet, but I'm glad Ms. Morvay isn't getting up to hug me because we've never done that before, and I like our professional distance.

Since Ms. Morvay and Juliana are convinced we're best buds and not bed buddies, I get to stay in Mia's room. I try to insist on taking the blow-up mattress on the floor, but they all insist more that I don't. So I'm up in Mia's comfy bed, but feeling sleepless. Partly due to Mia's sneezing fit from allergies, but then there's other stuff keeping me up, too. Girl stuff.

"Abbey?" Mia's voice sounds like it's right next to me, but when I open my eyes expecting her face, I can see she's still in her bed. "You awake?"

"Yes, unfortunately." I'd finally fallen asleep briefly because Ms. Morvay made Mia chug some Benadryl. "Isn't that stuff supposed to knock you out?" I say grumpily because we have a game tomorrow and it's past midnight and unlike some people around here, my school starts at seven forty-five, not nine.

"It's not hydrocodone," she says.

"What do you want, Mia?"

"Sorry," she whispers. "Never mind."

"Mia, what?"

"I was just thinking about that night at your house. I'm really sorry again."

I don't have to ask her to clarify. I know exactly which night. "We're cool. I mean, it was bound to come out, so to speak, sooner or later. I know you didn't mean it." She didn't, but I'm wondering now if I'm too quick to forgive. Not just Mia, but everyone. "Go to sleep, please."

But Mia continues. "Abbey, you're, like…"

She stops. I don't know if she's fallen asleep or trying to think of what she's going to say next, but I feel awake now, so I fill in her blank. "Annoying and ever present, like a stain on your favorite tank top?"

She chuckles. "No."

"Um, I'm the Tegan to your Sara?"

She turns over and sneezes in my direction. "Yes, that last one, but not in the sisterly way, more like the best-frienderly way. Is that a word?"

"We can make it one." I'm smiling now. I've always felt close to Mia, too, but still consider Kate to be my BFF. Maybe that's just out of habit, though. Can you have more than one best friend? I'm not sure if she means any of this or if she's just spewing drug-induced sentiments, but I say, "Me, too."

"Yeah?" The digital clock's light-up numbers help me see her smile. "You mean that?"

I nod. "I think you know me more than anyone. You know the good and pretty much all the bad of who I am. I don't think anyone else has a complete picture."

"That's true. Same for you, Abs. No one knows me quite like you."

"What about Maddy?" I ask, not even making a face when I say her name. "Or Devin? I mean, she's known you all your life."

She nods. "It's different with you, though. I mean, Dev kind of has to like me. We're family. And Maddy's, well, great."

Her tone sounds less than happy, which makes me feel satisfied, which in turn makes me feel petty, so I say, "You're lucky to have each other."

"Yeah, but, I don't know."

"What don't you know? You guys totally get along, and she seems perfect for you." I roll my eyes because I know she can't see me. "And as far as I can tell, you really like her."

"Yeah, I guess," Mia says. "She's smart and funny and pretty, but…"

"But…?" I say, propping my head on my hand. I'm never going to be able to get back to sleep now, so I might as well get totally involved in this conversation. "What's your deal? Are you impossible to please or something?"

"It's just that…" Mia says, and then finally adds, "she's no Abbey Brooks."

"So, I'm not pretty, smart, or funny? Thanks."

"That's not what I meant."

"Well, she might as well be me. You haven't noticed how she looks just like me, you weirdo?"

"That's what Ms. M. said, too. I don't see it, though. I mean, come on, you're so, well…It doesn't really matter. Good night, Abs." I hear her turn away from me, then the music from her iPod playing in her ears.

"So what?" I ask, but she doesn't answer. I could turn the light on and investigate further. I could yank the music out of her ears and demand an answer. Suddenly I feel like it's hot like the middle of July and push all the covers off me. Maybe I should've stayed with Kate. Things like this never happen when we hang out.

Chapter Twenty-one

I'm on the bus heading to Saguaro High for the match of the year: The Fridge vs. Abbey Brooks, Round 2. The last time we met, her team came out the victors, but with the help of my own adrenaline and the Diet Coke I gulped down at lunch, I am totally amped for this game. First of all, and perhaps most importantly, I don't have my period. Secondly, Coach A. has stopped calling me Red Badge of Humiliation and even Grumpy Gills. In fact, she hasn't called me a single name ever since I saw her talking to Tai a few days ago in her office, which is probably a coincidence. Tai is a good protector, but no one can make Coach A. change her evils ways. At any rate, I'm feeling good, ankle is good, and I'm ready.

"Two shots," the ref says as I walk to the top of the key and wait for the ball. As my teammates line up, I lock eyes with The Fridge who scowls at me because she's frustrated and angry. This is her fourth foul, and the fourth quarter just started.

I sink the first one.

"Let's keep it clean out there, ladies," says the ref like she always does, hoping we might all be a little more polite or something to each other. She's our favorite ref, though, and all the cows in our league thinks she's a total RILF. I'm briefly distracted by her tight black polyester pants but quickly give myself an internal smack across the face and prepare for my next shot. In my head, I repeat my usual mantra: Bounce, bounce, bounce. Pause. Bend knees. Power. Release. Wrist. Score.

The ball swishes through the net.

We're up by three and it stays that way for the next seven and a half minutes. I feel like we totally have this game, but as Garrett smacks my butt on her way by, she reminds me it's not over until the buzzer goes off.

We're running a man-on-man defense, so naturally my man is The Fridge. I take my position beside her, protecting the key like a rabid guard dog. Like always, she stomps on my feet trying to trip me up, but I'm moving my feet like I'm on an advanced level of *Dance Dance Revolution*. As the ball is passed around quickly, I track it and her the whole time, which is how I see the lob from the other wing. I pivot away from The Fridge, and thinking I have the calves of Lisa Leslie, I leap into the air to intercept it. Meanwhile, back on the ground and reality, The Fridge taps into a secret source of grace, sneaks her way past me, grabs the ball right as I think I'm about to touch it, takes a dribble in toward the net, and shoots. On my way down, my elbow lands on her head. I hear the whistle of my foul being called, then watch as her shot circles the rim of the hoop and finally falls in as the buzzer goes off.

I mouth an expletive because I know if I yell it, a technical could be called, and then I'll really pay in practice tomorrow.

My screwup is like bleeding in my shorts times a thousand because this affects everyone, not just me. I shouldn't have left my position. I got cocky. Coach says there's no room on the court for cock. I thought she was just being sexist until now.

"One shot, ladies. Line up."

The Fridge looks extremely focused, and as she readies for the shot, her features soften. She's big, but she's more muscle bulk than chubby. Maybe one of her resolutions was to lift more, too. After she makes her shot, we jog back to our bench to get ready for the next five minutes of overtime.

"What the hell was that, Brooks?" So much for being off Coach's radar.

I say I'm sorry, but she's moved on and doesn't hear me.

As she scribbles out our play on the whiteboard, her hands are shaking. "After the screen, cut, Willow. Do you hear me?"

Willow nods from behind a damp towel. She's been playing the entire game but still has incredible stamina. It must run in the family because Birch is the same way.

"Garrett, I want you in and out, in and out, in and out, in and out," Coach shouts, feverishly drawing heavy arrows on the board.

From behind her towel, Garrett whispers, "That's what she said," and because I'm in mid-swig of my water, I choke on it instead of doing something foolish like laughing.

Coach glares at us both, but then goes back to the board. "Abbey, I

want you on number thirteen like a sunburn on a white girl at Breakers
Water Park. Got it?"

I nod, fully recovered from my lapse of seriousness. "Yes, Coach."
The buzzer goes off. "Hands in," Garrett yells. "Gila on three."
We shout our cheer and walk onto the court to take our positions.

Luckily, I reach the jump ball first and tap it to Garrett. We run
Blue for our offense, which is really just a fast-paced play that requires
me to run up and down the key a lot. In practice, it's a piece of cake,
but out here on the court, I'm being trailed by an angry appliance who
doesn't mind getting friendly if she needs to. This is proven when she
rams her hips into me, hoping to stop me from getting position on the
block.

Last year, I would have backed off, and I don't know if it's my
advancement in girl-on-girl action off the court, but instead I back right
into her like she's a comfy lounge chair. I even use my arm to pull her
closer when she tries to step away. As a result of my way too familiar
response, I confuse her and manage to push her under the basket long
enough to get a bounce pass from Sabrina, turn, and drop shot the ball
in for two.

On the way down to the other end of the court, she runs alongside
me as I run backward. "It looks like someone's finally ready to play
with the big girls."

I roll my eyes. "Bring it."

She laughs like a nemesis would. "Oh, I will."

We shove for position, then she bolts out to the three-point line. I
get caught up in a screen, but I'm not too worried. She's a giant like me,
not an outside shooter. No way she'll make it.

Swish. The RILF raises both her hands confirming The Fridge's
three pointer.

I swear again under my breath and run downcourt, but they're
bringing out a full-court press, so I put the brakes on and cut across
to help Garrett get the ball in. I've lost track of The Fridge completely
until, as I'm about to receive the long lob from Garrett, she snatches it
midair, hurls it to her teammate, and it's another two-point play.

Garrett is beyond pissed. Coach is screaming unintelligible words.
Even Willow and Birch are shaking their heads.

Sabrina is the only one who'll make eye contact with me. "Don't
let her get into your head, Abbey. Play smart. Come on!" She smacks
my butt hard, and it's what I need to shake off what just happened.

We break the press this time and it's three on two. Willow and Birch pass it twice between them, then pass it to me. It's high, but I grab it, do a spin move around The Fridge, and put it in for two.

And then the whistle blows.

I want to collapse at the hip to try and catch my breath like everyone else, but I'm trying to hear the call. The refs are conferring on the baseline. I have no idea what they could be deliberating. Was there a foul away from the ball? Whatever it is, those two points better count.

The non-RILF ref blows her whistle. "Pushing, White. Thirteen. That's five. You're out," she says to The Fridge.

"Are you kidding me?" she responds loudly.

My look of confusion matches the rest of the players on the court. Garrett walks over as if she can tell I'm having a crisis of integrity.

"She wasn't even near me, G. You saw the shot," I whisper to her.

She shrugs and uses the bottom of her jersey to wipe the sweat dripping down her face. "Lucky break, Abs."

"But—" I start to say, but the ref interrupts.

"One shot, twenty-one. Let's go."

The Fridge finally walks off the court, lucky to not get a T thrown into the mix. As I receive the ball from the ref, I hear her complaining to her coach. I'm feeling relieved and guilty all at the same time, a familiar combination for me lately.

I have to shake it off, though. My team needs this shot. I need this shot to redeem myself. Visualize it going in, I tell myself. Please, for the love of gummy bears, *make it*, I beg myself.

Naturally, I miss, but Garrett gets the rebound and makes her jump shot. We win by one. And even though it wasn't pretty, we're now in line for league champs. During our good-job hand slaps, The Fridge doesn't look me in the eyes. I'm somewhat relieved, but I was hoping she might, so I could quickly apologize with a sympathetic glance. Maybe it's just as well.

After changing and a quick splash down in the sinks, we slowly head out to the busses. The freshmen girls added another *L* to their record, but JV pulled off a win, too, so overall the mood is jovial and spirited. I guess that's why I don't notice that I forgot my gym bag until Garrett points it out.

"Oh, crap. Tell Coach I'll be right there," I yell over my shoulder as I sprint to the locker room. I think I hear Garrett say *maybe* and hope she's joking.

The first door is locked and so is the second one I try. "Come on," I yell at the door as I repeatedly push down on the bar. "Please?"

The door suddenly opens, but not because I have special powers—because a human on the other side just happened to be coming out.

"Thanks," I yell as I run in. I round the row of lockers to where I think I left it, but it's gone. I look around quickly, and then start opening lockers but only find a candy wrapper and some white Velcro shoes leftover from the '90s. Defeated, I rest my head on the last locker. "Shit," I say, finally letting out a swear word.

"Looking for this?"

Before I turn around, I yell another *shit* in my head. Of all the girls, on all the teams, she had to be the one to find my bag? I turn around to match the voice with the face. Yep, it's The Fridge. But I have to admit, out of her uniform, in normal street clothes, with her brown hair down and washed, she looks a lot less scary, almost friendly.

"I was just about to run it out to your bus."

"Really?" I ask. "Not out to the Dumpster?"

"You don't think I'm like that all the time, do you?" She holds my bag out for me to take. "I mean, it would be really unfair of me to assume you were a conniving saboteur all the time." Then she laughs, and so do I. She's got a great smile, nice teeth, and her chubby cheeks make her look sweet. Not to mention, she's got a good vocabulary.

I approach her slowly, like she could turn on me at any second. What happens, though, is the closer I get, the better she smells and the nicer she looks. Wait, what am I doing? We hate her, remember? But as I stand in front of her and reach out to take my bag, she doesn't growl or punch me. In fact, something entirely different happens. We stare at each other in a strangely intimate way. Like the way people in the movies do when they are about to…Have I lost my mind?

I clear my throat and look at the locker-room door as if someone has entered. She looks, too, but no one's there.

I take my bag from her, careful to not let any part of me touch her. "Thanks, and good game. Sorry about that cheap foul."

She shrugs and puts her hands in the pockets of her khaki shorts. "I had it coming, I guess. Your feet okay?"

"Yeah," I say, and then there's three seconds of silence that feel like a million. "Well"—I point to the door—"I better. My bus."

She smiles and nods. "Yeah. Good luck against Palo Verde. Watch number ten for the pump fake."

I walk backward toward the exit. "Thanks—" I realize I don't know her real name. "See you."

She smirks and says, "Violet. But my friends call me Vi."

The girly name shocks me almost as much as my sudden desire to kiss her. I've lost the ability to speak, so I smile, wave good-bye, and push myself through the door. It closes and locks behind me, and I lean against it to catch my breath for the hundredth time tonight. What was that and where did it come from? Am I crazy, or did she want to kiss me, too? I decide on crazy, and I'm about to push myself away from the door, but, like a magnet, it's forcing me to stay. She *so* wanted to kiss me, too. My New Year's Eve resolution list pops into my head, most specifically the last one: take control of my life and be bold.

I bite my bottom lip. What if this isn't what it seems? What if I go in there, and she tells everyone I tried to come on to her and they all laugh. Yeah, Abbey, like you've never had to get over anything humiliating before? I guess Garrett's right; once you've bled out in front of everyone, you're pretty set on reaching your embarrassing-moment-of-the-year quota. Besides, I know I'm wrong about a lot of things, but the look a girl gets right when she's about to kiss you… that's something I think I know pretty well now.

I turn around and yank on the door to get back into the locker room, but, duh, it's locked. I knock on it, in a normal way at first, but when Vi doesn't come, I pound more urgently. A nagging in my head reminds me that I'm going to be in so much trouble for making my teammates wait. Coach is going to kill me tomorrow in practice, but it suddenly seems worth it.

I let my head fall against the door momentarily, then I push myself free from its pull and mope away. As usual, Abbey Brooks makes her move too late. Who do I think I am, anyway? Kissing a girl I hardly even know, my enemy no less. I need my head checked. Obviously, I'm suffering from a slight concussion or maybe dehydration.

I'm halfway across the court when I hear, "You forget something else?"

I stop in my tracks, turn around, and smile wide. I jog over to her, and in those few seconds I imagine pushing her against the door and, before she has a chance to ask what I'm doing, I kiss her like it's the last New Year's Eve on earth. At first, she'd be too stunned and just stand there, but once our tongues met, she'd grab me and pull me into her. The kiss would be so deep and long we'd drop to the floor and…

But instead of any of that happening, when I get to her I stand close enough to smell her shampoo—I think it's Pantene—and say, "Violet what?"

"Really? All that pounding to find out my last name?" she says, leaning against the door frame. "You could've just looked it up on the school's webpage."

I know I'm blushing. "Right. Sorry." This interaction is the opposite of what I imagined. Somehow, I must turn things around.

"Anything else?" she asks quietly.

Her breathy whisper sends a chill down my body and I'm speechless. I really should've been more organized about this bold move of mine. Daphne would have had an agenda or at least a flowchart of things to say. But before I have a chance to surely make an ass out of myself by spewing nonsense at her, Garrett yells from the gym entrance, "Abbey Brooks. We will leave your sorry sophomore ass! Let's go!"

I don't look over my shoulder. Maybe there's a chance I can still salvage this moment. I look at Vi with desperate eyes. Read my mind, dammit.

Instead, Vi nods her head toward Garrett. "You guys together or something?"

I roll my eyes. "God, no. She's just…bossy."

"Well, you better go before she grounds you." She crosses her arms, increasing her cleavage.

I almost defend Garrett, but before I can, she yells, "Abbey! I mean it!"

"She really does sound like she means it, and you don't want to piss off Garrett Church. Even I know that." She laughs. I'd laugh, too, if I wasn't so nervous.

I can still salvage this moment. It's not too late. Ask for her number, Abbey. Tell her she smells good. Touch her soft hair. But instead of any of that, I turn around and run to Garrett without saying another word to Violet.

"Hustle, freshie!" Garrett yells as I jog toward her.

Because my body and brain feel disconnected, I do as I'm told. I'm concentrating so hard on not falling as I run away, that I don't even look over my shoulder one last time to see if Violet's still there. I'm so pathetic.

When I reach Garret, she asks, "What the hell was that about? She want to kick your ass or something?"

"Yeah," I quickly lie. "Good thing you got me when you did."

"Well, Coach is pissed," she says and starts to walk quickly toward the bus.

I settle in the backseat all alone again. As the bus rumbles away from Saguaro, I can't get Vi's face out of my head. I don't know exactly what that was, but it was something. And I don't know how, but I'm going to find a way to see her again. No more waiting for life to come to me. Next time, I'm taking charge. Sigh. Next time.

CHAPTER TWENTY-TWO

My mom, who couldn't stand the smell of my ripe uniform any longer, has braved the task of unpacking my gym bag. "This is disgusting, Abbey. How can you live like this?" She tosses a half-eaten and moldy PB and J in a Ziploc and a mostly empty bag of gummy bears into the kitchen garbage along with gum wrappers and an unopened but smooshed Luna bar.

"Hey, that's still good," I say and grab it from the can and open it up. "See, just a little flattened." I take a bite and she rolls her eyes.

"What about this? Is this for school?" She unfolds my permission form for my art class field trip. "This was due last week, Abbey." She grabs a pen from my bag and signs it. "This is why I can't leave you home alone. Everything would fall apart without me."

I don't argue with her there. But is it so bad that I still need her once in a while?

After taking out my uniform and socks, she gives my bag one final shake over the trash can. A folded piece of paper falls out. "What about this?"

I may be unorganized and messy and a little forgetful, but I do know that whatever she's holding was not placed in my bag by me, so I grab it from her before she has a chance to open it. "That's private," I say. Even though I'm out, she certainly doesn't need to read a secret letter from a fellow you-know-who girl, if that's what this is.

"Well, if you don't want me to see your things, maybe you could do this yourself," she says as she carries my clothes to the laundry room. "Dinner in five minutes."

I walk the note to my room, close the door, and feel compelled to lock it. It's been about a week since my last game—I hope to God that whatever this is, it wasn't urgent.

I take in a breath and unfold it. It's a list of some sort.

Ten Things I Know About You From Looking Inside This Bag:

1. *You like gummy bears, but not the orange ones.*
2. *You prefer a low poly/cotton sock.*
3. *You're either a good writer or a good bullshitter. Nice job on that Animal Farm essay—poor Boxer!*
4. *You're a doodler.*
5. *You hoard pens. I counted fifteen in one pocket. You obviously have a problem.*
6. *Trident Original Flavor is your favorite gum. Four out of five dentists would agree with your choice.*
7. *Your permission form for your field trip is due tomorrow. Better get on that.*
8. *You sweat...a lot.*
9. *You like lists. I see that number three on your to-do list is to practice free throws. Good job. It's working.*
10. *You eat a lot but never finish anything. What's up with that?*

If you'd like to dispute any of my conclusions, please feel free.
Violet

She included her phone number in her sign-off.

"Abbey Road," my mom calls from the kitchen, interrupting me midswoon.

At first I'm mad that Vi went through my stuff, but then forgive her because she did have to figure out who it belonged to. Then I'm relieved this was just a stupid to-do list and my secret New Year's list is safely in my bedside drawer. And then I cringe at the thought of her touching my sweaty uniform. How incredibly unsexy. But how did she know, even before we had our interaction in the locker room, that there was maybe something between us? What if she was wrong? How come everyone else is so much braver than me? There are so many possible answers to this last question, but dinner's waiting and Mom's waiting, so there's no time to contemplate it now. What I do know for sure, though, is I'll be making a phone call after dinner. I can at least be that brave, can't I?

I blow out a long whistle when I see the gourmet spread: lemon chicken, mixed-green salad, and a dish filled with tiny pasta-like things my mom keeps calling *king-wa* or something. "Wow, what's the special occasion?" I ask nervously because I'm suddenly feeling like bad news is coming my way.

"I just love you, Abbey Road."

I look at her. "And?"

"And I feel bad for having to go up to Mesa again and for missing your last game. Now, tell me everything. How did you do against that girl who gave you the black eye last year? Is she still scary?"

"Hey," I say with a full mouth of food, pointing my fork at my mom. "She wasn't scary, per se. She's just really tough to beat."

"Well, did you beat her this time?"

Mom's not eating. Why isn't she eating? I nod. "Yeah, we won. She fouled out, though."

She moves her salad around with her fork. "That's good, honey."

I put down my fork, "Mom, what's wrong?"

She takes a long drink of milk, borrowing one of my best moves for avoiding answering or buying time to formulate an answer.

"Spill it," I say with arms crossed.

"It's not a problem," she says, and a goofy smile spreads across her face. "More like…"

Oh, gross, I recognize that look. "You met someone?"

Her mouth drops open, but she has no immediate reply.

"Is it that guy who hired you? Was there even a mural?" I am acting indignant, but seriously, even if she did lie, am I really one to throw stones in my glass house? Then my stomach sinks. "We're not moving, are we?"

She reaches for my hand. I let her touch it, but if she says yes, I'm running away to Ms. Morvay's and staying there forever. "Mom? Just tell me."

"We're not moving, Abbey. I promise."

"Then what?" I grab a lock of my hair and twirl. "Are you in love?" I feel sick. It's not that I want my mom to stay alone forever, I just thought…Well, I never imagined she'd be with anyone else, ever.

"I'm not sure if I'm in love. I like him, though, and I'd like to spend some more time with him. If"—she looks down at the tablecloth and traces its design with her finger—"if that's okay with you."

Does she mean if I say no, she'll never talk to him again? I let out a heavy sigh. Come on, Abbey. You of all people. You're really going to be the one to tell your mom she can't be happy, are you? "We're not moving?" I confirm before giving my okay.

She shakes her head, "I promise. Everything I love is here in

Tucson. I just want to see where it can go with him. Maybe it'll be nowhere. Sometimes you just have to take a leap and see what might be below."

I wasn't even going to bring up my recent girl situation, but I can see she's feeling sensitive and open-minded, so to help my case, I say, "Mom, I get it. You should see him if that's what you want."

She relaxes for the first time tonight. "Really? You sure?"

I nod. "In fact, there's something I need to ask you."

Since she made her confession already, she begins to eat like she hasn't had food in days. "Okay, hit me."

I recall the last time I told my mom I was going on a date, circa freshman year, when Jake asked me to an all-ages concert. She put the giant DENIED stamp on it because she forgot to inform me that I wouldn't be able to date until I was sixteen, which was actually fine by me because I was a totally closeted lesbo. "Well," I start, "as you know, I'm sixteen now."

She raises one eyebrow. "Uh-huh. A sixteen-year-old who still doesn't know how to drive."

"Mom. Seriously. Let it go."

She shrugs. "I won't, but do go on."

"So that means that I can, um, you know…" Oh God, why is this so hard? Secret's out—just say it. "So, you know, I can, date, right?"

She frowns and says nothing.

Or maybe we're not ready. "Mom, that was the deal, right? You and—" It feels suddenly weird talking about him after her confession. I swallow that down and push on. "You guys said sixteen." I begin to panic. Finally, I'm trying to be upright and honest with her about a girl, but it feels like it's not going so well.

She finally looks at me. She's got tears in her eyes. "Yes, honey. That's the deal."

"Why are you crying, then? Did I say something wrong?"

She clears her throat to stop the tears from falling. "No. I'm just really glad you finally feel like you can talk to me about this. I'm just so"—tears fall, but she talks through them—"I'm just so proud of you, Abbey Road."

Oh no. I hate when she's proud of me because inevitably I do something soon after to make her feel very much *un*proud. "For what? I haven't even asked her out yet," I accidentally say, then laugh to ease the weirdness.

She laughs, too, and then blows her nose. "Sorry, I don't know what's wrong with me. So, who is this lucky"—she pauses—"girl?"

I take a big gulp of milk—my turn to gather myself. When I polish off the glass, I give my mom the details. "Her name is Vi," then add "olet" because just plain Vi sounds too sexy, and I'm trying to ask for permission to date her, so I want to keep it PG. "She plays for Saguaro." I leave out the part about her being the mean one because I don't want my mom to think I'm into some abusive stuff or anything. Wait. Am I?

My mom is still feeling proud, I can tell by the ridiculous smile on her face. "Did she ask you or did you ask her? When did all this happen? I can't believe it. My little girl," she says, propping her head in her hands like we're going to have some girl-talk moment or something. It's all I can do to not run away. "How did it happen? Tell me everything." Then she reels it in slightly. "I mean, whatever you want to share."

"Um," I start, already wanting to stop this conversation, but I have to press through it if we're going to be real with each other. "We haven't exactly asked each other anything. But I'm going to soon." I smile because it just hit me that I've never actually been on a date. I mean, not besides playing ball in the park or watching Keeta work, which really might be the saddest excuse for a date ever. "I mean, if that's okay with you."

Her smile gets even wider, if that's possible. "Of course. Can I meet her? How long has she had her license? Is she responsible? You'll take your cell phone with you just in case, right?"

Everything I dreaded about telling my mom comes out in this series of questions, but if I'm going to keep the resolutions I made, I need to keep the ones about being honest and open with her. "Mom, slow down. This just happened. I mean nothing's happened. I have to call her. And," this last part is harder to say than I thought, "if we actually go out, you can meet her if it makes you feel better." She starts to tear up again, so I attempt to end this longversation about my possible first date and turn the tables on her. "So, will I get to meet…" Did she say his name yet? If so, I've already forgotten.

"Mark," she whispers and gets that dreamy look in her eyes.

She's got it bad. This is not good.

"Not yet, honey. I want to get to know him better before introducing you."

Seems like a double standard, but I guess I understand. "Does this

Mark guy have a last name?" I may not be able to meet him, but I am definitely Googling this idiot as soon as I leave the table.

"Mark Forrester. His restaurant is called Starfish. Amazing food. I'd be embarrassed to serve him this sad attempt."

At the risk of making her cry again, I ask one more thing. Not to be mean, but because I really need to know the answer. "You're not going to forget about Dad, are you?"

She pushes away from the table and walks over to me and pulls me into her. "Never, honey. I promise you." She kisses my head.

I hug her close and swallow down my own tears this time.

❖

After dinner and dishes and a bath and last minute homework and Googling Mark Forrester and folding laundry and an episode of *The Soup*, I face the fact that I can't avoid calling Vi any longer. It's not that I don't want to talk to her, it's just, well, what if it's all awkward and weird and I say stupid things? Who am I kidding? I'm Abbey Brooks. I'll say stupid things. But what if we don't have anything to say to each other? What if it's Devin all over again and she rejects me? What if it's like Keeta all over again and she shatters my heart? The only other option is to stay single for the rest of my life to avoid all pain, but that sounds cat-infested and lonely and, frankly, I like kissing girls too much to consider that option.

I read her note for the hundredth time. What if she forgot she wrote it? What if she's mad at me? What if...what if I call her and find out?

That's right about when some of Garrett's lesbian lore makes its way into my brain. Way back when, before I was sure I was a you-know-who girl but majorly crushing on Keeta, Garrett informed me that Keeta and Tai had a few exes on the Saguaro team. More specifically, one of the big girls that we all liked to call The Fridge. If my memory serves me correctly, Vi was Tai's first.

Part of me is like, *Well, it's a small town and what do you expect? There are only so many girls under the age of eighteen available for dating.* But the other part of me is wondering if I could kiss one of Tai's exes. Then the thought makes me somehow find Vi a little less attractive, which makes me feel a lot more shallow. And if there's one kind of people I can't stand it's the shallow ones.

So instead of calling Vi, I call Tai. Not to ask for permission exactly, but to hopefully ask for advice. We cover the obligatory *Heys* and *What's ups* pretty quickly, so before I'm ready, there's nothing else to say but what I called her to say.

"You want to get to it, baby D? I'm kind of on my way out."

Of course she is. It's a Saturday night. Girls like Tai don't sit at home on Saturday nights. "Yeah, so I got this note in my bag."

"You have exactly three and a half minutes, Brooks."

"Violet—from the Saguaro team. You know her?"

"You could say that. What did her note say?"

It would be too hard to explain, so I just say, "She wants to get together."

"Aw, my little Abbey has a stalker. That's sweet. So why are you calling me?"

I remember Tai's ticking clock, so I say it quickly. "G told me you guys once, you know, dated or whatever, and so I just wondered if, one, it was okay if I call her, and two, you know if maybe you could, I don't know, tell me anything interesting about her?" That run-on sentence hopefully covered everything.

"I would hardly call it dating. We basically kissed and groped each other up at a middle-school summer basketball camp. We were pretty inexperienced back then." She laughs, probably remembering the awkwardness of not knowing what you're doing. I know it oh-so well. "She's all yours, D, but just so you know, she's gotten around since junior high."

"Haven't we all," I say, trying not to sound defensive.

"All right, well, you give her a call. I gotta go."

"Have fun with…" I wait for her to fill in the blank.

"Yep, see ya," she says and hangs up. So mysterious. I wonder why.

With my blessing from Tai and my new nervousness after hearing about Vi's vast cow experience, I ready myself to call Vi by getting a postdinner snack and playing my favorite Ani mix in the background.

Before pushing send, I remind myself to just be me. But then I remember who I am and change my encouraging words to *Just don't act like a complete and total nerd, Abbey*. My thumb tries to fight me, but I win/lose the battle and make the call.

She answers on the first ring. "Hello."

And here we go. "Hey, Violet, Vi, it's me, Abbey, Abs." I move the phone away from my mouth so I can let out the breath I had apparently been holding in.

"Abbey Abs from Gila High?"

"That's me," I say, already smiling.

"The Abbey Brooks who needs to add *Don't forget gym bag* to her to-do list?"

"Right again."

"Hmm, I didn't think I was going to hear from you. You're either a total slob who didn't clean out her bag until now, or a really calculating girl who thinks about things forever before acting on them."

Instead of saying yes to both, I say, "Don't think you're off the hook for going through my stuff. Nice list, by the way—almost one hundred percent accurate."

"What? You're crazy. I was so spot-on."

"Nope. You missed one." I roll onto my back and hold her note above me. "The most important one."

"Really? Which one?" I hear meowing on her end of the line. "No, Mufasa. Stop it," she whispers.

"Mufasa? That's cute. Do you have a Simba, too?"

"Maybe. Anyway, which one did I miss?"

"I actually love the orange gummy bears most. I eat the other ones first and save the good ones for last."

"Oh, I see. You're into delayed gratification? Good to know." Obviously, she's not new to flirting.

"So," we say at the same time.

"You first," she says.

"No, you go," I say and wait.

"Um," she starts, "God, I don't know why I'm so nervous. I'm getting all Abbey over here and sweating like crazy." She laughs and I smile on my end. I like that she's willing to show her vulnerable side even if it is at my expense.

The word *bold* flashes into my mind, and for once I don't second-guess what I'm about to say. "Vi, do you want to go out with me sometime?"

"Dude," she says, pretending to be mad. "You totally stole my line. I was getting there."

"Well, I guess I beat you again." I roll onto my stomach and laugh. I am in full-on flirt mode, and it feels comfortable and easy with her.

"Ouch. That one hurt."

"You mean, like someone purposefully stomping on your feet?"

"Something like that," she says and laughs. "I'll let you off the hook if you let me try again."

"Okay, hit me," I say, channeling a little Garrett confidence.

"Abbey?" she starts.

"Yes?" Even though I know what's coming, I'm on the edge of squealing with excitement.

"Do you want to go out with me this weekend?"

"Gee, I don't know."

"Damn, you really are a brat. On and off the court, huh?" Mufasa meows loudly into the phone again. "Even my cat thinks so."

"Tell Mufasa to pull in the claws. Yes, I'd like to go out with you this weekend, Vi."

"Really? Cool? I wasn't sure if you were just one of those, you know…"

"What?" I hope I haven't earned a slutty reputation or anything.

"You know, an SGT."

I've never heard that term before, so instead of agreeing to something I'm not sure of being, I ask for clarification.

"You know, a straight-girl tease," she explains. "You never can tell. There are a lot of them in our league."

I enthusiastically agree I'm not one and try to move us back in the date direction. "So, about this…" Do I call it a date? Does that sound too pushy? Maybe she just wants to hang out. "Um, what do you want to do on Saturday?" Suddenly I feel queasy. My first date. Holy milestone, Batgirl.

"Hmm, I've got a few ideas. You'll see. Is it okay if I drive?"

I'm oddly impressed that she has her license and access to a car. Then thinking about being with her in a car reminds me of my sex theory—that the only place to have sex without being caught is in a car. Now I'm wondering if I'm ready to have sex. I shake my head to get myself back to the present day and answer her question. "Yeah, sure." I don't tell her I can't even drive yet because I'm afraid I'll sound too immature. She's a junior after all. "What time should I expect you?" Now I sound like I'm making an appointment with a plumber.

"Is seven okay? I have to work until six."

"Yeah, sure," I say again. I'm not sure I'm showing enough excitement because I'm trying so hard to be cool, so I add, "I'm looking forward to seeing you again, Vi," because it's the truth. Then saying her name makes my stomach do flips and my palms sweat.

She sighs softly into the phone. "Me, too, Abbey. Like, really."

Then I ruin the mood by saying, "So, my mom is going to want to meet you. You know, before we go out. Is that okay?"

"Uh, okay. So I guess you're out to her?"

"Yeah, and she's totally cool with it." I smile and doodle hearts on the cover of my English notebook. "Where do you work?"

"At my dad's office. He's in real estate. You've probably seen his signs."

"Oh my God, Todd Bowersocks is your dad? His face is on the bus stop next to my house. I didn't draw the moustache or devil horns, by the way."

She laughs. "I told him not to use the head shot. Hang on," she calls to someone away from the phone. "Hey, I gotta jet. My little sister is crying and my mom insists I'm the only one who can read the story right."

Each detail of her life is making me like her more: the job, the cat, the car, the little sister. She's nothing like that girl we all know on the court—she's really sweet. More than ever, I'm glad I called. And more than ever, I'm glad I took a chance at love, or at least *like*, again.

"Okay, see you Saturday," I say. "Wait, I need to give you my address."

"Would it sound less creepy if I say I didn't use my dad's real-estate program to find your address and Google Earth your house? Because I can lie if you need me to."

And she's funny. It just keeps getting better. "No lying please. I've had my fill. See you Saturday."

"It's a date," she says, clearing up my confusion. "'Bye, Abbey Abs."

"'Bye, Violet Vi."

"'Bye," she says again.

"'Bye," I say one more time and hang up.

I drop the phone to my side, roll over, and smile into my pillow, then use it to muffle a high-pitched squeal.

I pick up the phone to call someone to share the news about my first date but can't figure out who. Plus, there's something really nice about not having any outside input. There's something mature feeling about going it alone this time. Well, not quite totally alone.

"Mom!" I yell from my bed.

A few seconds later, she pushes open the door, "What, honey. You okay?"

I sit up and hug my pillow close to me. "We're going out on Saturday," I say and smile big.

"Oh, that's great, Abbey." I can tell she's happy, but she seems nervous, too.

"It's still okay, right? I'll be back by eleven fifteen, I promise."

She smiles. "Good. And I get to meet her?" she asks, but it's obvious that a command has been stated, not a question. Classic Mom move.

I make a face. Not because I'm embarrassed by either of them, but because it's just weird. Being gay still feels so private. "Um," I say to buy time, "maybe?" I try just for the heck of it.

She raises her eyebrows. "You know, if this was a boy, your dad and I wouldn't let you leave the house without meeting the guy who was going to be driving our daughter around town for the night."

She makes a compelling argument, but still. "I know, but…"

She tilts her head and sighs.

And I've lost this battle. "Okay, okay. God. She'll be here at seven. You're not going to do anything embarrassing like call me Abbey Roo or anything, right?"

She laughs. "I'll be as normal as possible."

I toss my pillow aside and fall back onto my bed. "Great. I'm doomed."

"'Night, Abbey," she says, turning off the light and closing the door.

It's only ten and I'm so far from being tired, so I turn on my bedside lamp and walk over to my closet. What does a girl wear on her first date, anyway? I scan my clothes and frown. There's nothing in here that says *date*. Nothing. Kate's right—my clothes scream *I like to be comfortable*, which seems the antithesis of date worthy. This will never do.

And suddenly, when I least expect it, I miss and need Kate more than ever.

CHAPTER TWENTY-THREE

Is it possible to look forward to something so much the anticipation kills you before it even happens? Must be, because I can't contain my excitement any longer. That's why I decide I'm going to tell Kate about my date with Vi and actually solicit her fashion expertise. She and Garrett weren't at their usual after-school spot, so I'm waiting for them in the varsity locker room, sprawled out on the giant table, doodling on the margins of my chem worksheet and thinking a lot about Vi.

Garrett and Kate enter the locker room, and my mood quickly darkens like the two of them are clouds that just blocked my sun. "Hey," I say to be friendly, even though I'm jealous that they were off doing something without me.

"Hey, loser, what're you doing in here by yourself?" Garrett asks as she starts to strip off her clothes. Kate, who used to hide in the bathroom to change whenever a lesbian was nearby, joins in the strip show. I guess she's over it finally. Or maybe it's because she doesn't think of Garrett as gay anymore and doesn't think about me in general.

I pack up my homework. "Nothing. Where'd you guys go after school? I looked for you by the flagpole." It's not like we have a standing meeting time or place, but I can usually find them hanging out with some of the guys' team.

Kate who is standing in her leopard-print push-up bra, giggles for no reason.

I look at her then back at Garrett waiting for an explanation.

"Oh, you know, around," Garrett says.

Kate laughs harder and nearly falls over trying to get out of her jeans. I can understand her difficulty, seeing how they are skintight. I accidentally catch a glimpse of her matching thong and look away quickly. She plops down on the bench and falls over laughing. "My pants!" she cries out between hysterical outbursts.

Garrett rolls her eyes. "I should've known better."

"What's that supposed to mean?" I ask, but Garrett just shrugs.

I scoot off the table and walk over to Kate, who's slumped over. "What's wrong with you?" I push her up to a seated position and look into her eyes. I don't know what I'm looking for. "What did you guys do? Where were you?"

Garrett waves her hand in my direction without looking our way, while standing in her sports bra and underwear, inspecting her body in the full-length mirror. "She's fine. It was just a little brownie," she says, and then leaves to the bathroom stalls.

Though I've never done drugs, I know enough about them. Eating a brownie is not what we used to do at our innocent pre-high-school slumber parties.

"Kate, look at me. How many brownies did you eat?" I know how much Kate loves brownies and have never known her to eat just one.

Garrett walks back in with a full bottle of water and dumps it on Kate, who then screams.

"What the hell, Garrett?" I yell because my shoes and pants get wet, too.

"That should do it," Garrett says, satisfied. She gets dressed quickly and says, "See you in the weight room, Abs." Then she leaves me, once again, to deal with the wasted pile that is Kate.

Kate starts shaking. "I'm freezing." She attempts to take off her jeans again, but now that they're wet, they're even more stuck to her body. She tugs on the bottom but slips off the bench and knocks her head on the lockers. "Ow! Abbey, help!"

I look down at her. On so many levels, this does not look good: Kate in her bra with her pants half-off, high on God knows what, and me, one of Gila's notorious lesbos, standing above her. Just like before, I can't leave her like this. I bend down, grab the waist of her pants, and yank them hard. She slides across the wet floor.

"Whee!" she squeals and laughs. This all seems familiar.

By now her teammates are starting to enter the locker room. A few stop on their way through and stare at us in disbelief. I ignore them and don't look forward to the rumors that are going to circulate tomorrow.

"Hold on to the bench, Kate," I direct, and she hugs the metal leg of the bench while I yank again, finally freeing her legs. In the meantime, Garrett has returned.

"Forgot my towel," she says without making much eye contact. "If she ralphs, make sure it's in the trash can."

"Seriously, Garrett?"

She closes her locker. "What? She's your bestie. It's not my fault she always goes overboard. Besides, it was a couple of hours ago, she'll probably be fine soon."

I don't even know what to make of Garrett's nonchalant attitude about Kate's state. Did she get her trashed on purpose, just so Kate would make a fool of herself? "Was it just pot brownies?"

Garrett shrugs. "Think so. Her boyfriend is the one who brought them, so I'm not sure."

"Boyfriend? What boyfriend?" I ask Kate. "I thought you and Miguel broke up." Obviously, it's been a while since we talked.

"Ryder is my boyfriend. I love him. He's so"—she burps—"so hot and sexy and—" She pauses again, but this time doesn't just burp. Lucky for me, she misses my shoes.

I march over to Garrett and grab the towel from her hands. "What the hell is wrong with you? What kind of friend are you?"

"She's a big girl, Abbey. She can take care of herself," Garrett says but finally has a look of concern when she hears Kate dry heaving. "Keep the towel. See you in the weight room." She leaves again.

And in walks Coach Alvarez.

"Abbey, why aren't you in the weight—" Then she looks at Kate, then the floor, then at me.

And that's about when I lose it. My bottom lip starts to quiver and the tears fall even though crying in front of Coach A. is as pointless as crying in front of Stalin. But I can't seem to stop. I am at a loss of what to say or do. I need help.

"Alcohol or drugs?" Coach A. asks as she yanks paper towels from the dispenser. She pushes me aside and covers up the vomit, then wipes Kate's face with Garrett's towel like she's a toddler.

"A brownie," I say quietly, and then worry that she'll think I did it, too. "I wasn't with her, though, so I don't know for sure."

Coach kneels in front of Kate. "Kate, what else did you eat or drink?"

Kate says, "Special lemonade," and then tries to lie down again.

"Who was she with?" Coach asks me.

I shake my head. "I don't know," I say, protecting Garrett. Why do I still feel so loyal to her? What will it take? "I just got here and she was like this."

"He's going to be so mad at me," Kate says and starts to cry.

Coach A. rolls her eyes. "Oh, great, another crier."

At this comment, I wipe the tears off my face and try to pull myself together.

"Abbey, you stay here with her. I'll go call her mom."

"Okay." Then I notice the girls huddled in the doorway. "Don't you guys have practice?"

They slowly disperse, but I can hear them talking about Kate as they walk through the locker room. They predict she's going to get kicked off the team. I have a feeling their prediction is right. That'll be one less thing Kate and I have in common.

She's curled up now on the wooden bench, and as I look down at her, sleeping off her drunken high, I wonder how much longer the thinning thread of our history can keep us tethered together. It's fraying quickly, and I'm getting tired of trying to mend it. I mean, why should I pretend to accept and like the person she's becoming? And then I wonder if that's what she's doing with me, too.

❖

On game day I'm always nervous, but this game day feels especially diarrhea inducing. The only things keeping us from making it to the playoffs are the fourteen girls on the Palo Verde team. They have the biggest team in our league, not only in numbers, but in size. But what we lack in height, we definitely make up for in scrappiness. Sure, we don't have the fancy uniforms or matching shoes, but when it comes to hustle, we're number one.

"Get your asses down the court, ladies," Coach A. says to us in our huddle. "I've got an eighteen-year-old cat with three legs that can move faster than you tonight."

Garrett hands me a water bottle and I down as much as I can before Willow grabs it and finishes it off. We're down by eight with only five minutes left in the game. I've only scored four points, but thank God for Garrett. She's scored twenty, seven of them in the last five minutes, which is why they decided to double-team her.

"Now, I'm no math major, but if there are two girls on Garrett," Coach says, "that must mean one of you is open, right?"

My team nods, but not me. I'm distracted by the small hickey that is peeking out from under Coach's polo collar. A hickey? Really? That seems so high school.

"Birch, you're going to run baseline, screen for Will. Will, you're going to fake and roll. And Abbey"—I look attentively at her board instead of her neck—"if I see you standing still one more time, you're benched the rest of the game. After Birch gets her screen, she's coming up for you. Got it?"

"Yes, Coach."

"And look weak side, ladies. We're not going to win this unless you hustle like I know you can."

Wow, that was a near compliment.

"Defense on three," Garrett yells.

Back on the court, I line up to ready myself for rebounding the free throw. The girl next to me is PV's center. She's tall like me, but she's super, super skinny and hasn't stood a chance against my aggressive butt-bumping move under the basket. Plus, I can tell she's really straight and very uncomfortable with the girl-on-girl contact, which, of course, makes me do it more. Palo Verde's number ten shoots and misses. I get position and nab the ball, then send it downcourt into Jessica's open hand. Two points. As they try to pass it in, we snag it. Two more points. Then on a shot from the top of the key, I'm fouled, but it goes in. I make my free throw. Three more points. Down by one.

The Palo Verde girls are frazzled and their coach is pissed. There are no more time-outs for either of us, so we get to settle this gladiator style—to the death—which is about how I feel after another full-speed fast break, and they score. Someone please foul someone, I beg in my head.

Unfortunately, my wish comes true, but it's me who fouls. With only ten seconds left in the game, I have no choice but to wrap my arms around number twelve as she stalls at half court. It's our only chance of getting the ball back before time runs out, and I'm the closest one to her. It's my fifth foul, so I'm out of the game.

Like the rest of my teammates, I stand on the sideline, cheering on our team. Ten seconds left. A lot can happen in ten seconds.

The ball is slapped and the PV girls run their inbound play. My teammates are hustling hard and covering every girl. Eight seconds. Birch is jumping up and down wildly in front of the girl trying to pass it in. No one is open and Birch is making it impossible to see. Five seconds. The PV girl finally tries to lob the ball over Birch, who gets a piece of it, so it falls short. Three seconds. Willow grabs it, Garrett bolts down court. One second. Garrett hurls the ball as the buzzer goes off. Zero.

The crowd holds its breath and watches as the ball descends, hits the back of the rim, bounces high into the air, comes down again, hits the side of the basket, then the other side, and then sinks in. If it counts, that's a three pointer from *waaaay* downtown.

Before we even dare to celebrate, we look at the refs. They are conferring. I glance at Coach A., who's wringing a towel in her hands and is going to lose her mind if they even dare to question the validity of the shot. Meanwhile, my teammates and I are linked together, holding hands, arms, legs, ponytails—whatever we can grab. No one is saying a word.

One of the refs walks over to the scorekeeper's table and, as if she is enjoying torturing us, waits a few seconds for dramatic effect, then throws her hands into the air. "Three points."

Me and the gaggle of Gila High players run on the court to hug and high-five. We're thoroughly caught up in the excitement until Coach reminds us to get a grip and show some sportsmanship. As we line up to high-five Palo Verde's players, I see that some of them are crying. My smile fades quickly when I realize that for some of these girls who are seniors, this game will be the last they ever play in high school. The *good game* I say to each player tonight shifts from robotic and obligatory to heartfelt and meaningful. I can't imagine this experience ever ending for me. I'm going to cry like a baby when my time comes.

❖

To top off my great week, I have my date with Vi tonight. Since Kate never returned my calls, I forget about shopping for new date clothes and settle on baggy jeans, an ironic T-shirt covered by my navy hoodie, and my red Converse.

When I walk out to the kitchen to get a drink of water, though, my mom says, "That's what you're wearing?"

I was already on the edge of sanity, so this comment pushes me right over, which is why I throw my arms up and scream, "Thanks, Mom! Thanks a lot!" and march down the hall back to my room.

As I'm standing in front of my closet cursing Kate, my mom, and even Vi for asking me out and forcing me to care about how I look, my mom peeks in.

"Abbey, I didn't mean to…" she says from a safe distance.

"Whatever, Mom. It's clear I have no idea what I'm doing here." I violently slide each hanger down the rod. "No, no, no, no. There's nothing in here. I'm going to cancel." I grab my cell from my back pocket.

"Honey." She takes my phone and tries to calm me with a soothing voice. "What about…" She pulls a pink top that still has the tags attached. It's one Kate said was a must-have that I always thought was a little too tight and frilly for school. "This is pretty."

I shrug. "Maybe."

"And these jeans seem a little more dressy," she says as she takes down a dark pair from the stack on the shelf. "And"—she moves a pile of dirty clothes off my shoes—"these flats?"

"Not bad," I admit.

"Very cute," my mom affirms. "Two thumbs up."

I don't know if I'm annoyed or embarrassed that my mom helped me pick out my first-date outfit, but either way, I want her out of my face until Vi gets here. "Okay, thanks. See you later." I push her toward the door. "And no more mushy mom faces tonight. It's just a date."

Mostly I want her out because I don't think I want her to know that I bothered matching my underwear and bra as a just-in-case measure. There are some things we just aren't ready to share.

Ten minutes later, I hear Vi's car pull up. I half expect her to knock on my window instead of the front door and laugh to myself. Geez, Abbey, maybe it's time to set your standards higher.

Before she has a chance to ring the bell, I open the front door. I know it seems overeager, but I just want one second to look at her before my mom possibly ruins everything.

"Hey," she says as she gets out of her car. It's a red Honda Accord. Funny, I pictured her getting out of a big truck or something. "You look great."

"Thanks," I lean against the doorjamb and try to look casual. "You, too."

She's wearing a dark pair of jeans, a tight black shirt, and a leather jacket over that, pulling off a hot James Dean/Brandi Carlile look. Her hair is down and frames her face perfectly. She's wearing eye makeup that's subtle, yet makes her eyes seem even more beautiful. At that moment two things pop into my head: 1. Thank God my mom didn't let me wear the hoodie, and 2. Her T-shirt is the luckiest piece of clothing right about now.

She walks up the driveway and gives me a hug. I breathe in her perfume and Pantene and try not to melt in her arms. Like Tai's hugs, hers engulfs me completely. When we part, I notice she has a small and sweet-smelling bouquet of lilies. If the date ended right now, it would still definitely qualify as the best date ever. "These are for your mom," she says, pointing to the flowers.

"Oh, wow. You're good," I say as we enter the house. "Thanks for agreeing to meet her. She's kind of old-fashioned sometimes."

But Vi shrugs and smiles. "I think it's sweet."

My mom, who was hovering in the living room instead of waiting for us in the kitchen, walks in with her hand extended. "Violet. So nice to meet you."

Vi shakes her hand and says, "You, too, Mrs. Brooks. Thanks for letting me take Abbey out tonight." Then, almost forgetting the flowers, she says, "Oh, these are for you."

My mom is smiling so big that she looks like the one who's going on this date. Her approval and excitement make me happy, and I feel less freaked-out about the whole situation, but still, time is ticking. "Well, we better go, Mom."

"Home by eleven fifteen, Abbey," she says to me but also makes eye contact with Vi.

Vi nods and I roll my eyes. "Yeah, yeah. Promise." Then I turn to Vi. "Ready?"

We walk out to her car and Vi opens my door for me. After I'm in and Vi shuts my door, I look out the window and see my mom in the kitchen window. She's still smiling, and I can tell it's taking all her willpower not to give me a two thumbs up. And honestly, it's all I can do not to give them to her, too.

Our first stop is dinner. I'm expecting Eegee's or a taqueria, but instead we park in back of a small restaurant on Fourth Avenue I've never even noticed before, called Maya Quetzal. We are offered a seat in the window, but Vi prefers the table in the back. I wonder why but forget all about it as we share the most delicious Guatemalan food. It's here that I find out she is one of two daughters, that she's a junior at Saguaro and has been playing basketball since seventh grade. And, most importantly, she is not out to her parents, which explains the clandestine nature of our dinner, I think.

"What about you," she asks. "When did you come out?"

"Not too long ago," I say and tell my terrible tale of how it finally happened. She covers her mouth to hide her smile and says, "No way," all the way through. I can understand, though. I guess now that I have perspective, it's a pretty tragically funny story.

She takes another bite of the cheesy rice stuff and says, "I've visualized doing it, like, a thousand times, you know? You have to try this stuff." She spoons a bite and feeds it to me.

I try my best to look sexy as I take the bite. I fail when some of it dribbles onto the tablecloth. "Oops," I say and stop myself from eating it off the table like I would if I were at home. "I totally get what you mean. I think it was the hardest night of my life. But it was also one of the best."

"What about your dad? He know?"

Though I am enjoying myself, for some reason I don't feel like sharing all parts of my life yet. Maybe after Devin, I'm being extra-cautious. "No," I say, somewhat truthfully.

"Yeah, dads seem harder. My dad is super involved in my life, but I feel like this would destroy him. Why is that?"

It's awesome being the expert at something for once, so I try hard to give her some good advice. "He loves you, I'm sure. And even if he's shocked at first, he'll come around, I bet."

The bill comes shortly after, and as I reach for my wallet, she snags the slip from the table. "For someone as pretty as you are, you'd think you'd know how to act when someone takes you on a date."

I'm sure I'm now a shade of red that matches the salsa because not only am I not acting properly girly on this date, but mostly, she called me pretty.

Then I drop a little truth bomb on her. "This is my first date, actually."

She tilts her head and looks carefully at me. "Liar."

"No, really."

"Are you telling me Keeta never took you out on a date? Seriously?"

I unintentionally make a face at the mention of Keeta. Unfortunately, she notices.

"Sorry, I didn't mean to upset you. She told me you guys had dated."

"You two are friends?"

"We talk once in a while online, that's all."

I swallow down some worry and say, "Yeah, well," and nothing more. I don't want this night ruined, especially not by Keeta, so I add, "That's over, anyway."

"Sorry, I didn't know you thought it was a secret." She leaves a tip on the table. "Don't be mad. That's all she said. Swear."

As long as Vi doesn't know how much I cried over Keeta, we're good. "I'm not mad," I say and put on my coat, which Vi helps me slip on. "We dated. No big deal," I say nonchalantly. "We've both moved on."

Vi smiles. "Yeah, you mentioned that."

Back in the car, I ask her my own line of questions. "What about you? I know of at least one person you've been with."

"See, no secrets in this world," she says and laughs. "You're talking about Taisha, I suppose. Man, that was years ago. Talk about awkward."

I shrug. "I don't know, she's not a bad catch."

She looks over at me. "I guess." Then she pulls out into traffic and steers us to our next destination, a secret she's been keeping from me all night. "Dude, we were such baby dykes in junior high. Then she ended up with Garrett. How's that going, anyway?"

"They broke up, but I'm still friends with both of them." I feel the need to say that, just in case she thought about saying anything disparaging. Then I let out a sigh of relief when her story aligns with Tai's. If she had slept with Tai, I'd definitely be in the middle of what Garrett calls the Six Degrees of Lezifornication—lesbians who are connected by who they slept with.

Vi must be thinking the same sort of thing because she looks over at me and says, "You and Tai ever, you know, hang out?"

I make a sound that's supposed to indicate what a joke that is, but maybe I overdo it because then she says, "So that's a no, but you wish? I get that. She's pretty hot."

"We're just friends and that's all we'll ever be," I say, and I mean it. "She's the only one I have left who hasn't stabbed me in the back somehow, and I'd like to keep it that way."

"Okay. I get it," she says and turns into The Loft parking lot. "Well, we're here. It's Flashback Movie Night. Have you seen *But I'm a Cheerleader*?"

"Oh my God. I love that movie. It's playing? Here in Tucson? Who knew."

"Well, no spoilers—I've never seen it. I heard it was good."

I nod to try to convey coolness, but inside I'm dancing. A movie, sitting next to Vi, in the dark, side by side. Will she try to hold my hand or put her arm around me? Do the ol' reach-in-the-popcorn-bucket-at-the-same-time move?

She pays for my ticket and popcorn and leads us into the theater. "Mind if we sit back here?"

I'm totally a middle of the theater, middle row kind of girl, but I nod because I think she's still afraid of being caught. At any rate, the privacy won't be so bad. Maybe it'll mean I'll have a better chance of being kissed.

❖

I can't tell if ten minutes or ten seconds have gone by, but when we come up for air, my vision is fuzzy and my lips are throbbing. "Wow," I accidentally whisper out loud.

"Yeah," Vi says, still pressing her body against mine as we lean against her car. "That was, um, unexpected," she says and laughs lightly, "but really nice. Glad you had the guts to do it."

"There was no way I was letting you leave without a kiss," I say and lean in to kiss her again. New Year's Resolution number eight—check!

After an hour and a half of intimate hand-holding in the theater, I think we both had enough desire boiling inside to set off a dormant volcano. So instead of pulling into the driveway, she parked on the street, giving us a little bit of privacy behind the tree in my front yard. Of course, I chickened out kissing her in the car, but when she came around and opened the door for me, I got out, shut the door behind me, and pulled her to me for a kiss I couldn't hold in any longer.

She moans quietly when I nibble on her earlobe, but then pulls back and whispers, "You sure don't kiss like a sophomore."

In my head, I'm saying, *I know, huh! Go Abbey, go Abbey!* I'm like a professional. But instead of congratulating myself publically, I say, "I hope that's okay." And then I look down, feeling shy because she's looking at me so closely. And then for some reason I say, "I've never kissed a girl who's as tall as me," which is true, but not exactly romantic or necessary to share in this moment.

She laughs and whispers, "How much more time do we have?" in my ear, then kisses my neck. My legs nearly buckle.

I open my eyes long enough to look at my watch, and my stomach sinks when I see the time. "It's eleven twelve."

She leans away to look at me again. "Time sure flies when I'm with you."

I look in her eyes, too. Are they green or brown or both? I forgot to double-check at dinner. "Well, I better…" I point to my house. "My mom." Total mood killer, bringing up my mom. I subtract all cool points from earlier.

"Right." She lets go of me finally, and I take a step away from her car because I should be sure I can stand on my own before I overdo it with walking. She runs her hands through her hair because it got a little messed up during the kissing. "Well, I've never been kissed by my mortal enemy before"—she reaches out for my hand, pulls me close again, and whispers—"so I guess there's a first for everything."

"Yeah, there's that, too," I say and pull her in again for a quick good-bye kiss. The willpower it takes for me to stop kissing her is greater than anything I have experienced in my entire life. It's more than it takes to jump into my unheated pool in March, more than it takes to eat an entire serving of my mom's tofu lasagna, and even more than it takes to sit through any conversation with Kate without rolling my eyes. "Curfew," I say and gently push her away.

I look at her as long as possible as I walk backward but have to finally turn around so I won't fall and ruin the moment. I unlock my front door and close it quietly behind me. Before I'm surely given the third degree by my mom, I take a second to smile my cheesiest happy-Abbey smile.

Best. Date. Ever.

CHAPTER TWENTY-FOUR

Forty minutes into my chem test, and I'm plugging along pretty mediocrely, but I'm okay with mediocrity when it comes to this class. If I get a B or higher on this test, I'll still have a B in the class, and I will never have to see Mrs. Stum's name on my schedule ever again.

Finally, I reach the last question:

35. Molecules in a solid are arranged as follows:
    A. Spaced out and free to slide over each other
    B. Very spaced out and free to move from one to another
    C. Packed together and can only vibrate
    D. None of the above

Free to slide over each other naturally makes me think of Vi, and I quickly melt into a daydream. Mrs. Stum, who can sense teen lust and/or distraction like some sort of creepy drug dog, clears her throat, and I figuratively slap myself and refocus. But then I reread option B and imagine moving my lips from one part of Vi's body to another. Letter C is the kicker and makes me laugh out loud because it says *vibrate* and my mind is in the gutter at this point, earning me a long and lethal glare from Mrs. Stum and a verbal reminder that there is absolutely no talking during the exam.

I move through the rest of my morning classes with minimal confidence, too. Then the bell rings for lunch, and I realize my options for lunchtime companionship, which were already dwindling after Mia left, are now at an all-time low. Now that Kate has been kicked off the team and is still not speaking to me, Garrett is too busy trying to win the Hetero of the Year Award, and my other teammates seem to only be on-court friends, I am left to eat alone.

"Well, this is a sad case," Tai says as she straddles the bench and pops one of my fries into her mouth. "Thank God I'm here."

I've missed her like crazy, but I don't want her to know, for some reason. "Where the hell have you been lately?"

She laughs. "Sorry, Mom. I didn't think you cared."

I don't respond but raise my eyebrows to show I expect an answer.

"Senioritis, I guess. I've been having a bit of an attendance problem."

"You better not mess up your chances at Grand Canyon University, Tai," I say with my mouth full. "You're smarter than that."

She frowns and rests her chin on her hand. "Yeah, I know. I guess I've been distracted."

I push my fries over to her and she takes a few. "How's it going with your stepmom?"

She shrugs. "Oh, you know. According to her, I'm going to die alone and burn in hell."

The empty guest room at my house seems like a better place for Tai to finish her senior year. Would that be weird? Would Garrett allow it? I put that idea aside for now. "She actually says that to you?"

She smiles, but it's a sad smile. The kind of smile I use when I'm crying inside. "Among other things, but it's cool. I mean, just a few more months and I'll be done with this place for good."

"Yeah," I say, trying to stay positive. Then it hits me, just a few more months and I'm going to be a junior. A junior who can't drive, hasn't had sex, and can barely dress herself. Awesome.

Tai flicks my earlobe. "You nervous about the game or something? You're a little more spaced-out than usual."

I haven't really been thinking much about our game this Friday, but I say, "Well, I wouldn't have to be if you were still on the team. My season would have ended last week. So thanks for this."

"Whatever—you love it. Besides, you'll get more action playing varsity. JV girls are all still stuck in their awkward I-don't-know-if-I-am phase. What a drag. Older women are where it's at."

Her mention of getting action takes me quickly back to the end of my date with Vi, and like Mrs. Stum, Tai seems to have the ability to tell where my mind has gone. "But why am I telling you this?" she teases. "You've probably proven my theory true." She elbows me and whispers, "Huh, you little heifer?"

I scrunch up my face as I attempt to lie. "Don't get all excited. I don't have anything to report." It's not quite a lie, but I want to keep my kisses with Vi a little more private than with Keeta—then maybe the whole world won't know my business this time.

Tai looks at me, seems to contemplate saying something else on the topic of girls, but doesn't. Instead she says, "Well, I gotta go," and gets up.

"Where? We've still got twenty minutes left of lunch."

"Um, I need to get some makeup assignments."

"If you say so." I'm totally joking, but the look on her face says I'm onto something. Is she dating someone new? Is that where she's been?

Before she leaves, she grabs my head and kisses the top of it, which startles me and makes me nervously look around to make sure no one saw. What am I so scared of? My reaction makes her laugh, but I look up at her with a confused look on my face. "What was that for?"

"You're something else, Abbey," she says, and then messes up my hair like she's my big sister. "See you later, baby D. Be good."

"I'm always good," I say loudly enough for her to hear over the din of the other students talking.

"That's what I hear," she says and turns around laughing.

I wonder if Vi is worse at keeping secrets than I am.

❖

When I open my locker at the end of school Friday, the note falls out and drops in the mysterious puddle that I have been very strategic in avoiding all day. "Great," I say to no one and pick it up. There's no writing on the outside, so I unfold it, trying to avoid the damp parts. "This better be worth it."

> *Abbey,*
> *I know I've been a total bitch, but will you please, please meet me in the locker room after school? Please? I need your help.*
> *Kate*

The first thing that comes to mind is *hell, no*. But, if there's one thing I know about Kate, it's that she never asks for help with anything, so this must be pretty major if she's in need of mine. I close my locker and toss the note in the garbage can on my way to the locker room. First, we'll see if she's even there.

"Hey," she says when I walk into the varsity locker room.

"Hey," I say and nod to Willow and Birch, who are already changed for the game.

"We were just leaving," Birch says and grabs both her and her sister's bags. "Come on, Will."

"Wow, I sure can clear a room," I say to lighten the mood.

"I think it's me," Kate says. "I really made an ass out of myself last time I was in here."

"Well, if you call crying in your own pile of throw up as you sit pretty in your matching leopard-print thong and bra, then…maybe a little." I smile and she does, too. Will it be as easy as making fun of her to get us back on the train to Friendship Town? Do I even want to go there with her?

"Abbey," she starts to say but is choked up by tears. After she wipes them away, she finishes. "I, um, can't do this by myself."

I walk closer to her but still can't bring myself to hold her close like I would've done in the past. "Do what?"

She opens her backpack, takes out a box, and puts it on the bench.

"First Response Pregnancy Test? Are you kidding me, Kate?"

Her mascara is a wreck, and so is she. "I know. It's so Lifetime," she says and cries into her hands.

Carly and Sabrina walk in, so I quickly hide the box in my shirt. "Hey," I say to them.

"Hey," they say back.

"PMS," I say and point to Kate.

They nod, and then leave as quickly as they came in.

I can't stand to see her like this, so I reluctantly sit down next to her. "Are you late?"

She shrugs. "I think so. Like a few days. I swear, Abbey, if it's negative, I'm changing everything. No more partying. No more Ryder. I was so drunk I don't even remember…" She looks away. "It's not how I thought my first time would be, that's for sure."

The next words feel too heavy to say, like pushing a boulder out of my mouth with my tongue. "Did he rape you?"

"No." But then she rubs her forehead and says, "I don't know. I mean, I wanted to do it, but I was really drunk, Abbey. I don't remember if there was a condom." She looks over at me. "I don't even know if he, you know, came inside of me."

I'm so grossed out that I nearly take my own turn at barfing on the bench we're sitting on. But, instead, I hold it together for Kate's sake.

"Well, there's one way to find out." I take the box out from under my shirt. "Shall we?"

"I can't pee with you standing out there," Kate says from inside the stall. "Turn the water on or something."

I run the water until I hear her flush. She exits the stall holding the stick as far from her as possible. "Okay, start timing it."

I look at my watch. I have my playoff game, the game of my lifetime thus far, in less than an hour. And instead of meditating about sinking free throws and warming up with my team, I'm looking at a plastic stick soaked in Kate's pee. Suddenly, I'm angry. She *would* do this now, today of all days. It finally hits me: it's always going to be like this.

"How much longer?" she asks, with her free hand covering her eyes like she's waiting for a birthday surprise.

"Thirty seconds." Then, to be mean, I add, "Thirty seconds and we'll see if you ruined your life or not."

She uncovers her eyes and the look she gives me puts Mrs. Stum's to shame. But Kate's has pain intermingled in it, and that makes me feel bad instead of scared.

"Sorry," I whisper. "Time's up."

We both lean in closer to the stick and inspect it. One line. She's not pregnant.

"Oh, thank God," she says and laughs.

She hugs me, but instead of embracing her, I say, "Ew. Pee."

She tosses the stick in the garbage and washes her hands. "Thank you for being here, Abbey. I didn't know where else to turn."

"Yeah, well"—I pull a chunk of my ponytail to twirl—"I hope you learned something from this." I cringe at how much I sound like my mom, but maybe she needs to hear it, so I go on. "You said you'd change if you weren't."

"I will. I am." She looks in the mirror to fix her makeup. "I'm going to go to Ryder's house to break up with him right now." Then she hugs me again. My arms remain by my side. "You're the best, Abbey. I'll be back for your game to cheer you on. I promise."

She grabs her bag and leaves the bathroom with her usual sassiness and confidence. And me? I'm left standing there with my usual post-Kate emptiness and loneliness.

I shake off Kate's near miss and change for my game. Like always, when I slip on my jersey, I think of Keeta. As long as I'm wearing the very same jersey she wore, I'll always feel that connection. Maybe that's not good, though. Maybe I should grab a different number next year.

I'm caught up in this consideration when Tori runs in and yells, "Coach says you'll sit this game out if you don't get on the court in the next forty seconds. Hurry the hell up, Abbey!"

I stuff my clothes and bag in my locker and slam it shut, forgetting to grab a hair band. I have no time to fight with the lock, so I run out onto the court with my hair flowing behind me like a Disney princess instead of a ballplayer ready to kick ass.

I ask every girl I see if she has a spare band, but no one does. I try to keep it back by tying it into a knot, but it doesn't stay up for more than a few steps. Then as I stand in line waiting for my chance to shoot a layup, I hear a *psst* from the sideline.

I look over and I see Vi. I haven't seen her since our date, and she looks even more kissable than before. She takes down her hair and winks just enough for me to see and no one else. Seeing her here in my gym, especially in her street clothes instead of a uniform, feels so out of context that I think I'm dreaming, so I don't say anything as she subtly hands the band to me like we're dealing drugs. "Good luck," she whispers.

I bend over to put my hair into a ponytail just as the ball is passed to me—it misses me entirely but nails Coach. Her coffee splatters all over her good-luck shirt. I run over to help her clean it up, but she shoos me away with her hand and I obey.

When the Flowing Wells players run onto the court, their fans cheer louder than anything we've ever heard in our gym before. The Caballeros are number one in our league, so it's easy to understand their massive following. To make myself feel worse, I look up at our stands to see how we compare to the packed bleachers on the visitors' side. Besides a few parents, our crowd mostly consists of the players on our freshman and JV teams. But then my eyes land on two people I didn't expect to see sitting together: Tai and Vi. I'm nervous to see them talking but also curious as to why Tai is even here. It seems pretty gutsy that she came to the game, considering how she left the team and all. A few seats over is my mom. Next to my mom are Juliana and Ms. Morvay, and Mia is sitting with Devin next to them. It's like the entire cast of my dysfunctional life decided to show up here on the same night. The only one missing is Kate. Figures she didn't make it back. Her absence feels like our final good-bye.

Right about then is when I feel Garrett's elbow stab me in my ribs. It's all I need to look away from the stands and pay attention to my team again.

But Garrett is less confident, so she takes hold of my shoulders and says, "Look, I'm sure I don't have to tell you this, but this game is kinda important, so if you could get your mind off your V until it's over, that'd be real swell." Then she shoves me onto the court toward the center circle, where I'm greeted by the tallest girl I have ever seen in my life.

I'd like to say we were the David team that took down the Goliath that is Flowing Wells. And I'd like to say I scored an all-time high of thirty points and pulled down just as many boards. I'd like to say we're league champs and going to the playoffs, but all of that would be a bunch of lies and I'm trying to cut back. The truth may set some people free, but mine just makes me feel like crawling in a dark place and hiding forever.

To start with, in my very last game of the season, I scored three, that's right, *three* points. Number twenty-five, who from this point forward will be referred to as The Wall, was impossible to shoot over, dribble around, and, most importantly, defend. I fouled out in the third quarter.

So instead of going out with a bang, we went out with the clang of the ball bouncing off the rim, over, and over, and over, and over again.

I keep it together through the high fives and the postgame debrief with my team and Coach, but when I finally get a second alone in the bathroom stall, I let the tears quietly flow. At least, I think I'm being quiet as I stand in there, sobbing away.

"Baby D? You okay in there?" Tai says from above me.

I grab a bunch of toilet paper, blow my nose, and try to fake happiness. "Yeah, just, um, allergies," I say without looking up.

"You guys tried your best. Seriously. They just had a better game, that's all."

I blow again. "Yeah."

"Come on out of there before you get a disease. They haven't cleaned these bathrooms since Coach was a student here."

I cover my head with my hood. "I don't want to. I'm too embarrassed."

"Why? Because you lost? Because you only scored three points? Or is it because your girlfriend saw you choke?"

I don't deny any of Tai's theories. I'm too tired and depressed.

"I give up. You try," Tai says to someone.

I look up just in time to see Garrett's face peeking over the stall wall and then disappearing.

"Oh my God, what is this? Is my mom out there, too?" I feel stupid and hope to God Vi isn't part of this extraction team. "I'm coming out." I blow my nose one last time. "Put down the Jaws of Life."

I push the door open slowly, but as soon as I exit the stall I am tackled by Kate's sister Jenn, Garrett, Tai, and Tori.

"Grab her legs," Carly directs.

"I can't! They're everywhere," Tori says and laughs.

I try to kick the groping hands off me but lose the battle when Tai and Garrett use their strength to torture me instead of protect me like they used to do.

"Oh, we got a wiggly one tonight!" Jenn says as they make their way past the lockers, toward the showers that no one ever uses. "Good thing I'm here to help."

"Let me go! I'm serious!" I yell and try to squirm my way loose, but my lack of muscle and sibling-fighting skills are really hindering my escape.

"Uh-oh, you guys," Garrett says, "she's serious!"

They all laugh.

"Sorry, baby D," Tai says. "Tradition is tradition. Youngest player on the team gets a good soak at the end of the season."

"Willow, get the water," Garrett demands, but Willow, being the nice person she is, hesitates. I'll remember her kindness when I later retaliate against my captors. Garrett hands my arm over to Tori, marches over to the shower knobs, and turns on the cold water.

"I hate you all!" I yell, but part of me wants to laugh, too. Part of me, deep down, is excited to be part of a tradition. That is, until the freezing water hits me, and I let out a blood-curdling scream. They hold me under the stream until I start to choke.

"Okay, that's enough," Coach A. says.

They drop me onto the tile floor.

"Oh, and, Abbey?" Coach says in a tone I don't recognize because it's nearly friendly.

My lips are shivering, but I manage to say, "Y-y-yes, C-c-coach."

She half smiles and says, "Good season, newbie," and tosses me a towel. "Looking forward to working with you again next year."

Still exhilarated from their successful capture, my so-called friends high-five one another.

I look up at them. "You guys are assholes."

They agree.

Jenn takes off, claiming that she needs to kick her sister's ass before heading back to NAU. I hope she's able to beat or talk some sense into Kate. Before Tai leaves, she assures me she didn't let on that she knew Vi was obviously there to watch me, not because she was just interested in the game. When that secret is revealed, Garrett kicks my foot and tells me I'm in big trouble for keeping Vi a secret, and that she expects a full report this weekend. Then she runs after Tai.

My anger subsides as I watch each member of this crew of misfits leave. It's like no matter what's passed between us, we're all bound together by basketball. Win or lose, I guess it makes it all worth it. Willow, Tori, Sabrina, and Birch help me up and make sure I'm okay, then leave, too.

Now I'm alone. Wet, slightly bruised, still disappointed in myself, and alone.

The good news is the cold shower cleaned the salty sweat from my hair and face, so if I get to see Vi, I won't be so gross.

After I change and cautiously exit the locker room, I'm greeted by my mom, Ms. Morvay, and Mia. Thankfully, Juliana had to take Devin back to school. And I'm glad Devin's not there because I'm not sure if my little soul could have taken another awkward moment.

Speaking of awkward, my mom says, "Violet said she'd call you later, sweetie."

Mia makes a face. "Who's Violet? Sounds like a pal of Strawberry Shortcake."

"She's just a friend I met on another team," I say, hoping my mom will have a tad more kindness than Tai and keep her mouth shut. Out of the corner of my eye, I swear I see Ms. Morvay crack a smile.

"Hmm," Mia says before my mom can say anything, "I didn't approve of any new friends."

"Well, I guess you can write me up for defiance," I say as we walk across the gym one last time. "You can add it to my long list of screwups."

Sensing I need more than her usual dose of sarcasm, Mia drapes her arm around me. "Well, I guess I'll let it pass this time, Brooks, but don't let it happen again. And of course, I expect to meet this new friend of yours."

I rest my head on the top of hers and say, "Yes ma'am," but I'm thinking, not yet. I need her to myself just a little bit longer.

❖

The last time I celebrated Valentine's Day, I ended up collapsed on the front steps of Gila in a pathetic mound of heart-wrenching drama and snot. So naturally, as this Valentine's Day arrives, I'm feeling a great sense of dread and fear. True, things with Vi are going well, so I shouldn't have to worry. Since our first date, we went out again and we had an epic game of mini-golf, and perhaps more importantly, we had an epic game of how-far-can-we-go-without-taking-our-clothes-off in the backseat of her Honda. Which leads me to the title of my new dilemma—Lesbian Sex: What exactly qualifies as sex and how exactly is it done?

Normally when I am met with a question I can't answer, I am happy to Google it. However, since I share a computer with my mother, in a very public space in the house, I have to be very, very careful. And I've come to learn that Googling anything lesbian will result in naked-lady pics and porn sites. I even once tried searching for something as innocent as *books for lesbian teenagers*, and boy, did I get an eyeful. At any rate, I need answers and they aren't going to be found on my laptop or given to me in health class because the closest thing Mr. Fred came to discussing lesbian sex was when he said, "Clean hands are an important part of a healthy sexual experience. No glove, no love for those of you…uh, who go that way." And even though I'm out to my mom, I'd rather tweeze out my nose hairs one by one or reread *Lord of the Flies* than talk to her about S-E-X with girls. No, thank you.

Garrett is my usual go-to on all things NC-17, but she's been distant lately, especially since our season ended. We're definitely back on friendly terms, but whenever I call, she seems like she's in a big hurry to get off the phone. I temporarily consider calling in that late-night teen sex advice line, Dr. Drew. But, knowing my luck, someone else in Tucson would be listening and I'd be outed once more as the girl who likes girls but doesn't know what to do with them. My only hope is Mia, but I haven't exactly told her about Vi, and something about talking to Mia about sex makes me feel weird. In an act of desperation, I almost call her, but then fall back on my bed, suddenly exhausted. I think I need a vacation from my brain.

I close my eyes and think about Vi to try to make myself feel better, and it works instantly. I'm not as nervous about going all the way with her as I was with Keeta. I think it's that everything isn't so new and unfamiliar this time. Well, almost everything, which brings me back to sex. Keeta and I came close a few times, but I repeatedly chickened out. I regretted it then and I regret it now.

My phone buzzes in my hand. It's Vi.

"Hey, I was just thinking about you," I say, out of breath for some reason.

"Well, by all means, continue. I didn't mean to interrupt you. I know how frustrating that can be."

"You're a dirty girl," I say and let out a throaty seductive laugh like a lifetime smoker, then whisper, "Very naughty."

"Speaking of naughty, what are you doing Friday? It's Valentine's Day, in case you didn't know."

"Hmm. Friday's when I normally vacuum the house, wash the walls, braid my hair, and sing to the birds outside my window. So, you know…" Playing hard to get might be a little overdone, but it's the only move I feel confident making.

"Well, I have two tickets to the James Bond premiere that say otherwise. I'll pick you up at seven. We're going to be eating out, too, so come hungry." She laughs a little after this last part and adds, "I mean, if you're into that."

And with that, my need to call Mia has just tripled.

After I hang up with Vi, I push aside my feeling of weirdness and call Mia. "Can you talk?" I say with a hint of desperation in my voice. "Are you alone?"

"And hello to you, too. I'm fine, thanks."

"Sorry, I just need some advice, sort of, and you're my only hope."

"If this is about sex, I'm going to need to call you back after dinner. I can't pontificate on lady parts with an empty stomach."

"Um, call me back after you eat then."

"Whoa, I was joking, but I guess you're not."

"If it's too weird, I understand."

"Weird, why would it be weird? It's not like you and I are ever going to do it together, so there's no worry in giving away my trade secrets or anything."

I don't say anything to that. I don't know why.

"I mean, right?" she asks.

"Right," I finally say and regret calling her about this. I should've followed my gut. "Shoot, my mom's calling me," I lie. "I have to go set the table."

"Yeah, me, too."

She doesn't call me back that night and I don't call her either.

❖

"Well, you and Vi have French-kissed, right?" Garrett whispers.

"Yes," I confirm.

"Is she good at it? What are we talking about here—slobbery, sucky, or slick?"

"Very slick and wonderful," I say, then look over my shoulder. I'm supposed to be looking for a book on World War I, but instead, when I saw Garrett working on an essay in the library computer lab, I broke free from my class and cornered her with the sex question because it's already Valentine's Day, and I'm running out of time.

"Okay, well, then imagine how good that kiss from her would feel if, you know, she took a trip to Belize on you."

"What the hell are you talking about, G?"

"Belize, Abbey. You know?" She looks down at her lap.

I rub my head. "Please just help me."

"Okay, I see we need to start at the beginning." She types *World Map Western Hemisphere* into the search bar and chooses the first map that pops up. "First of all, imagine this is your body."

"Okay," I say, but I'm doubtful of the direction this conversation is going.

"Your head is Canada, your feet are…let's say, Argentina. Your boobs are somewhere around Utah. Have you gotten action in Utah yet?"

"Yeah," I say, remembering my last make-out session with Vi.

"Over or under the bra?"

"A little of both."

"Uh-huh. I see. Was there kissing or just groping?"

"Why do you need to know that?"

"No reason, it's just been a while for me."

I shove her. "Finish your stupid analogy, G. I'm going to get in trouble."

"So, if Utah is your mountain range"—she looks at my chest—"well, your little hilly area, then the top of Mexico is your stomach, which is a nice place to kiss, too."

"Uh-huh," I say, "I think I know where you're going."

"Then where is Belize?" she asks.

I move in closer and find it. "There," I say proudly and put my finger on the screen. "But it's so small."

Garrett looks at me like she's finally reached her point of exasperation.

"Oh, I get it," I say and remove my finger.

"It may be small, but it's definitely worth the visit. It can get a little wet down there, though. Lots of water means unexpected swells, tropical storms and stuff."

I have nothing to say to that.

"You've gone exploring around there yourself, right?"

One of my classmates walks behind us, and I try to hide the screen like we're looking at a giant vagina and not a map. "I don't see why that matters."

"Well, you can't expect to just jump on a plane to her Belize if you haven't even spent any time in your own. You know, you gotta learn the language. Understand the traffic laws. Just saying."

"I've been there, okay," I snap. "Not as much as everyone else, probably, but I've been." I'm starting to sweat. I regret this whole thing. Why does my drive to find answers override my drive to not make myself look like a total moron?

Garrett laughs again. "We need to get you drunk, Abbey. Maybe that'll loosen you up a little. Sure helped with Kate."

If she only knew where that got Kate. "Are we almost done here?"

"Well, be sure you've tidied up the place. You know what I mean?"

I nod, feeling more nervous than when we started this geography lesson. I have one last question, though. "If she"—I clear my throat—"visits me, should I repay the visit right away?"

Garrett tilts her head. "Depends. Vi's a tough nut to crack. Sometimes the butchies don't let you touch them."

"Why not?" So far, things have been pretty equal, but maybe that's where she'll draw the line. Come to think of it, Keeta never really let me touch her. She was always the one making the moves, but I thought it was because I didn't know what I was doing.

"I can't explain it. Anyway, Vi isn't like a capital *B* butch. She's like, in between, huh? Like a femme butch. A futch?" She laughs.

I shrug. "She's just, I don't know. She's paid for everything on our dates. She opens my door for me. Does that make her a butch?" I wonder why everyone has to fall in a certain category. I don't even know what I am, for crying out loud. I did take an online survey once, though, to try and figure it out. My results were completely unhelpful: 55 percent femme. What does that even mean? I'm the one who wears the skort in the relationship?

Garrett looks at her watch. "Look, freshie. I gotta wrap up this little sex-ed sesh here. This essay is due in thirty minutes and this forged pass expires in twenty."

I look at the map on the screen one last time as if I need to memorize where all the parts are before my big test tonight. "Okay, thanks, G."

Before I go, though, Garrett says, "Abbey, remember last year when you were all caught up in Keeta and worried about every little thing and consumed with confusion?"

I nod.

"Well, knock it the eff off. You're a certified, card-carrying member of the herd now. Stop overthinking everything and have some fun. I promise you won't get knocked up and, God help us all, you might even enjoy yourself. Got it?"

"Yeah," I say and let out a sigh of relief. "You're right. Thanks again, G."

She's already turned away from me and typing quickly, but mumbles, "Meanwhile, I'll be a one-woman show again tonight. Jesus, things are definitely ass-backwards around here."

I leave the library that day resolved to reach two new goals: 1. Return after sixth period to actually check out a book on World War I, and 2. Increase my familiarity with Belize. Before I do, though, I need to replace my overstuffed suitcase of inhibitions with some confidence and maybe some snorkeling gear and see where the night takes me.

CHAPTER TWENTY-FIVE

G rounded? But it's Valentine's Day," I whine into the phone.
Vi sighs on the other end. "I know. I'm sorry."

"What did you do?" I kick off the new shoes I bought. Just as well, they were uncomfortably tight. Much like this new bra, which I squirm out of, too. "Are your parents super strict or something?"

"Not normally, but I guess I screwed up this time."

I know I'm going to sound childish, but I say it anyway. "But I made you a card. It's got sparkles on it and everything."

She laughs. "Sparkles and everything? Wow. Can you save it? I'll be ungrounded next weekend."

"A whole week? Now you have to tell me what you did."

"Abbey," my mom says on the other side of the door.

"Hang on, Vi." I cover the phone and say, "Enter," to my mom.

My mouth drops open. She looks ten years younger. Who knew my mom had legs and, ew, cleavage. My mood shifts and I express my unhappiness that she's going out with Mr. Big Shot again by acting like a baby. "Well, my date is grounded, so I'll just be here alone. On Valentine's Day. Again. But you have fun."

She looks at her watch. "I'm sorry, I have to go. We're meeting there at six. Don't wait up. Love you." She blows me a kiss and closes the door behind her.

I turn my attention back to Vi. "Sorry. Anyway. What was it, shoplifting? Ditching class? Bad grades?" I can't imagine she could do anything of the sort. She seems so well put together whenever I see her, much more than me. At least I'm out to my mom, though. I reward myself points for that.

"No, nothing like that. I forgot to give my dad a message from a client."

"Uh, that seems a little bit of a harsh punishment."

"Not when you're the number one real estate agent in Southern Arizona. Anyway, I blame you."

"Me? What did I do?"

"You're distracting me, Abbey. I'm off my game because of you."

I'm smiling big, making a total fool of myself, but no one is here to see, so I don't care. "Oh yeah? How am I so distracting?"

"Well, first of all, your lips," she whispers, which immediately causes a flood in Belize. "And I've been thinking a lot about how I might be able to get you alone with me so I can—shoot, I gotta go."

Then the line goes dead. "Hello? Vi?" Nothing.

I look at my phone. It's not me, so it must be at her end. "Vi?" I say again, but she doesn't respond. Something tells me I shouldn't call back. She must have gotten caught on the phone or something. Maybe she was grounded from that, too. That's probably all, Abbey. Don't start getting all weird. She'll call back when she can.

In the meantime, it's still flooding over here in Belize. I've got the house to myself, so maybe it's time I pay my semi-annual visit.

❖

One week without Vi is going to kill me. Of course, this whole thing would be a nonissue if I could just learn how to drive. Then I could surprise her at school one day. Maybe it's time I bite the bullet and just do it. I walk into the living room to announce my brave intentions before dinner, but my mom's on the phone with Mark again. It's gag-inducing to watch the way she laughs and flirts. I mean, seriously, get a room.

When she finally says good-bye to her man, I'm on my second Luna bar and washing that down with milk straight from the carton. She catches me midgulp, but I just shrug as if to say, this is what happens when you neglect your daughter.

"When you're done with that, we need to talk."

To delay a talk, I continue to drink until I get brain freeze and have to stop. I press my hand against my forehead. "Owww."

"That's what you get," she says and sits down at the table and points to the seat across from her.

The last time we had one of these talks, I got in big, big trouble for failing my classes. This time, though, as far as I'm aware, I'm not failing anything. Still I ask, "What did I do?"

"Why do you always assume the worst? You didn't do anything. I just want to talk to you. Why is that so scary?"

I cross my arms and glare at her. I'm not buying it. "Go on then. Talk."

She grabs a lock of her long blond hair and starts to twirl it, which is totally my move. Or has it been hers and I unknowingly inherited it? "Well," she finally starts, "things are really going well with Mark."

My worry deepens. "That's cool," I lie.

"I'd really like it if we could talk about him without that homicidal look on your face."

I roll my eyes. "Sorry."

"I'm going to drive up there to visit him this weekend, okay?"

I look down and fiddle with the placemat. "Yeah, I guess. But"—I look up at her to ensure absolute comprehension of what I'm going to say next—"I am not moving there."

"I'm just visiting. We're just dating, long distance. I'm sure you can relate to how hard it is to be away from someone you like."

I don't like having this in common with my mom, but I can't deny it, so I nod.

"You'll stay with Mia again, okay? I already talked to Juliana and Liz."

The mention of Mia makes my cheeks heat up with embarrassment. But to hide my redness, I rub my face as if I am tired. "Yeah, okay. Sure," I say, but what I really mean is, triple crap with cherries on top. Then I finally remember my reason for coming out here. "I was going to ask you to give me another driving lesson this weekend."

"This weekend? Really, Abbey, now you're being childish."

"Mom, I was. I swear," I yell because I can't stand it when she thinks I'm lying when I'm finally not.

"Well, I'm sorry. Rain check, I guess."

I shrug and have a feeling this is the first rain check of many to come.

❖

Four days have passed and I haven't heard from Vi. No texts, no calls, no posts online. I'm not going to lie, I'm freaking out a little. To ease my worries, I call Tai for some possible reassurance or enlightenment.

"You okay, baby D?"

How can she tell I need help? I even tried to hide the desperation in my voice when I said hello. "Yeah, just calling to say hey."

"Really? Well, hey."

"Hey," I say again.

"Yeah, we've covered that."

Like most of what I do, I regret this, too. Why can't I think before I act? "What're you doing?"

"Hiding in my room, like always. And you? What mess can I help you out of today?"

"What makes you think I'm in a mess?"

"I've known you for two years, Abbey, and if there's one thing you are, it's consistent. So, things with Vi not going well?"

I give up on the masquerade and fess up. "She's grounded and I haven't heard from her. What's up with that? Is she really in trouble or is she avoiding me?"

"Dude, yeah. Her dad is, like, psychotically strict. She once got pulled from two games because she was late picking up her little sister by like five minutes. He's an asshat."

"Okay. So she's not avoiding me?"

"Probably not, Abs. But if you're worried, drive over to Saguaro and surprise her."

"How? It would take me three transfers to get there on Suntran."

"Well, they do make these things called cars. You are familiar?"

"I still don't have my license."

"Didn't you complete driver's ed?"

"Yep."

"Pass your written test?"

"Uh-huh."

"So what the hell are you waiting for?"

"Someone besides my mom to teach me, I guess."

"Why? What's wrong with your mom? She's cool."

"Nothing's wrong with her, but something happens to me when I'm behind the wheel and she's there. I freak out. I think"—I haven't admitted this to anyone before—"I think I'm scared I'll accidentally kill her. And then I'll have no one."

"Would she let someone else teach you?"

"She won't pay for those driving classes. She thinks they're a waste of money."

"I'll do it."

At first I'm excited at the idea, but then come to my senses. "Thanks, but I don't think my mom would go for it. She's paranoid."

"I'm eighteen with a perfect driving record. We can use your Volvo. Why don't you ask her?"

"I don't know."

"Or spend the rest of your life riding Suntran and bumming rides from your mom. Sounds like a celibate future."

She really knows how to sell it. "Well, it can't hurt to ask. Okay. I will. Thanks, Tai."

"In the meantime, want a ride to Vi's? I know where she lives."

I really do want to see her but think I'll wait a little longer—it can only help us, to miss each other more. "Nah, I better not. Sounds like she'll get in trouble if I do."

"Probably a good call. Okay, lemme know about your mom. I'll be here in hell's waiting room in the meantime," she says and chuckles.

"Tai?" I haven't checked in with my mom about this either, but I'm just going to say it anyway. "You know you can come stay with us if you need to. We have the space."

"You're sweet, baby D, but I think I can make it. Seventy-one more days. No sweat."

"Well, if you change your mind."

"You're the first one I'll call."

Shockingly, after my mom gave me the third degree about whether or not Tai and I were friends or more than that and I finally convinced her that, yes indeed, we are just friends, she said yes to both requests, which leads me to believe that I have been approaching this whole Mark thing from the wrong angle. She's clearly unaffected by my pouting and snarky behavior, but what seems to work is tapping into her guilt. She must really feel terrible about seeing this guy and dumping me at Ms. Morvay's. This is an excellent revelation.

As she hugs me good-bye on Saturday morning, I reassure her that I will call her each night and behave myself. "You behave, too, Mom," I tease and she turns a shade of red I am definitely familiar with.

Tai's picking me up for my second driving lesson at two, and Mia seems disappointed we won't be spending the afternoon together, but I remind her she'll be sick of me soon enough. She agrees. Besides, she has afternoon plans with my twin, so what does she care?

For whatever reason, I feel much more relaxed in the car with

Tai than I do with my mom. Not that her life isn't worth the same as my mom's—it's just that, I don't know, Tai speaks my language better than my mom. For example, instead of bracing the passenger-side door when she sees a curve or pressing her foot hard into the floor when I approach a stop sign, Tai says stuff like, "You got this," and, "Nice stop. Like a boss."

Today, Tai takes a detour from our usual route to the nearby empty strip mall parking lot and announces, "It's time."

"I'm not ready," I say, recalling how I slammed into the pedestrians in the driver's ed simulator and hit two garbage cans on the last driving excursion I took with my mom. "Maybe next time."

"Nah. You're ready. We'll start off in a really chill neighborhood. Wide streets."

"What if..." I say, looking at her as she adeptly navigates the roads of East Tucson. "Are those new earrings? Pretty."

Tai touches the stones in her ear. "Yeah, thanks."

"Who gave you those?"

"Someone."

"Why are you being so secretive about this girl? If I don't know her, then tell me who it is."

Tai looks in the rearview mirror to change lanes. "You'll meet her when I'm ready for you to meet her. In the meantime, stop being so nosy and let's get you that license."

I drop it even though I really don't want to. Tai, like Mia, will only reveal what she wants, when she wants. Talk about stubborn. So I change our topic back to a safe, boring one—me. "You really think I'm ready?"

She pulls over and unbuckles her seat belt. She looks over at me very seriously and says, "I know you're ready. I wouldn't say so if I didn't believe it, 'kay?"

We switch spots and buckle in.

Because we're almost the same height, I don't have to adjust much. The car's still running, but I forget and turn the ignition key anyway. The sound makes me jump. "Sorry!"

She laughs. "It's okay. You got this."

I put the car into drive and remind myself that the gas is on the right—push the right for flight. I release my foot from the brake, the car moves forward, and I steer us into the road.

We go like this for a few seconds until Tai says, "Yeah, uh, you'll need to accelerate sometime soon, Abbey, at least to fifteen miles per hour."

I grip the wheel. "Okay, okay." I press the accelerator and feel the engine respond. At first it's scary but then I ease into it. Not bad. Not bad at all.

"Which way?" I ask Tai as we're at a stop sign, idling.

"You're the one driving," she says and looks out the window.

As I decide which way to go, I feel like laughing. For the first time in my life, I'm behind the wheel, literally and figuratively. For the first time ever, I get to decide which way to go. Suddenly, I want to see Vi and have my way with her. Who knew driving would be such a turn-on?

I push the blinker down and accidently hit the curb as I turn right.

"Oh my God," I say and slam on the brakes, but all Tai does is say, "Curb check. Curb in place."

I recover, make a left, then another right and a left, and conclude I'd make a great postal worker. But when I see a traffic light in the distance I pull over and press my foot firmly on the brake.

"What're you doing?" Tai asks.

"I can't go that way. Busy street."

"Abbey, if you only take the side streets, you'll never get anywhere—at least, not in any timely manner. You're ready. Go for it." She puts her hand on my leg. "Time to live in the fast lane."

I look in her eyes and almost trust her. "You really think so?"

"Never been more sure about anything in my life. I swear."

I look forward, my eyes on the prize. "Okay, but maybe not the fast lane…at least not today."

She laughs. "You call the shots."

I take a deep breath, push down on the accelerator, and head toward the stoplight.

❖

"I have two words for you—*terri* and *fying*," I say to my mom when she asks how my most recent driving lesson with Tai went. "She was trying to kill me."

My mom, who I can tell is trying to stay neutral, looks over at Tai who is calmly sipping the tea my mom offered her. "What happened?" Mom asks Tai.

"Oh, she's just freaking out because we accidentally got on the freeway for about three hundred feet. She's fine. She did great tonight."

"The freeway?" my mom repeats. "That's very advanced."

"You want to explain how it happened, or should I?" Tai asks me, but what she really means is that I better fess up to the whole thing and how it was my fault.

"It's hard to remember right and left and gas and brake and mirrors and…" I stop because I realize I'm not making a great argument for myself, for ever driving alone in the car. "I went left when Tai said turn right. I guess it wasn't so bad."

Instead of getting upset, my mom says, "Tai, thank you so much for teaching Abbey how to drive. I've certainly tried and failed."

"No problem, Ms. B. She's a fast learner. Well, I better go," Tai says and takes her cup to the sink. "Thanks for this."

My mom walks to her wallet and takes out a twenty. "Here, for your time."

But Tai refuses. "I would have just been driving myself around tonight anyway."

What I know and mom doesn't is Tai would do anything to avoid being at home with her parents, which makes me remember our spare room and how empty it is. "Mom, can Tai stay for dinner?"

"Abbey, that's okay," Tai says as she backs away toward the kitchen door. "My parents are expecting me."

That's a big lie, I'm sure, so I say, "Come on, let us repay you somehow. My mom will feel terrible if you don't. Huh, Mom?"

"Yes, please stay," my mom says, picking up on my urgency. "I can talk to your parents if you want me to."

"No," Tai says louder than we all expected. "I mean, it's cool. I'll text them. They'll be fine with it."

"Great, I'll get started on dinner then. You like lasagna?"

Oh no—not the tofu one again. I nearly protest, but then my mom takes out a package of meat and I breathe a sigh of relief.

"Sounds great," Tai says.

Tai and I collapse in front of the TV. I instinctively turn to *Say Yes to the Dress*, but Tai groans. "Really?"

"Fine. What do you want to watch?"

She grabs the remote from my hand and turns it to PBS. "*Masterpiece Theatre* is on."

"I'll give it ten minutes, but after that, it's back to my show."

She shakes my hand. "Deal."

An hour later the credits roll on *Masterpiece Theatre* and I'm a believer. And once again, Tai shows a side of her I never knew before.

❖

I'm smiling on the inside and out as I get ready for my date with Vi. I think tonight will be the night. I mean, if she's still into me. Then I let that thought grow faster than an annoying weed and start to panic. *She's taking me out to break up with me. This is it. It's over.* Of course it couldn't last. I mean, look at me. I take in the full-length image of my grasshopper-esque body. Who would ever want this? I turn around to see how my butt looks in my jeans. Not bad, I guess. Maybe she just likes my butt?

My phone beeps. *Can't wait to see you, Abbey. I'll be over in twenty. Hope you're as excited as I am.*

I let out a sigh and some self-hate. See, dumbass. She likes you.

When Vi rings my doorbell I prance down the hall like I'm a six-year-old playing ponies. "I'll get it," I sing. I'm breathy and feel flushed when I swing open the door, but my breathing returns to normal when I see Vi and what appears to be a very small version of her.

"Hey," she says and points at the kid. "Change of plans."

My Belize quickly dries up like a desert. "Yeah. I should say so."

❖

"Turns out Vi was in trouble again," I explain to Tai as I deftly change lanes. "Sunday drive much?" I say as we pass the slow-moving car. Sunrise Boulevard is my favorite, and it's irritating when the retirees get in my way. "We spent the evening at that bouncy-house place surrounded by a bunch of sweaty, smelly kids. I swear I think I picked up five hundred viruses. If I don't get sick, it'll be a miracle." I slow for a red light. Tai isn't saying much, so I keep on filling the empty space. "I mean, it's as if the universe is trying to keep us from being together. Or is it her dad? Do you think he knows and is sabotaging our dates?"

I look over at Tai for a confirmation of some sort, but she seems uninterested. "Pedestrian," she says and points at a lady crossing the road.

"Thanks." I slow down. "Anyway, I don't know how much longer I can go without seeing her. I mean, really seeing her. You know what I mean? Sorry, is it weird talking about her with you?"

Tai shakes her head. "Better get out of this lane. Construction."

Instead of following her directions, I take a right and turn off the busy road. I pull over, put the Volvo into park, turn off the engine, and let the silence wash over us for the first time tonight.

"What's going on?" I turn toward her. "You having girl troubles? Parents woes?"

"No and yes."

"Look, I talked to my mom. She said it was totally okay if you stay with us."

Tai looks at me. "You did? She did?" Then she shakes her head. "It's too much trouble."

"It's not. Come on. It'll be fun. We can do each other's hair and nails and choreograph dances to the *Grease* soundtrack."

I get a little chuckle out of her.

"I'll even let you watch PBS whenever you want. Do you think your dad will let you?"

At this she turns to look at me. "He was more than eager to drop me off at Garrett's last year. But maybe now that I'm eighteen, it's really up to me. It would just be until I graduate. Then I'll have a place to go." She seems happier, but still needs reassurance. "You sure?"

"Girl, please. My mom loves it. You should have seen the way she doted on Mia. I swear, she wants to build on to the house just so more of my friends can move in. You all make me look bad, I'll tell you that."

She dusts off the dash with the sleeve of her sweatshirt. "What about Vi? Won't that be weird?"

"Not unless it'll be too weird for you. I mean, we usually go out, so…"

We sit quietly contemplating the situation, then she says, "I'll stay out of your way. I just need to finish school."

"Sure," is all I say because I can tell how hard it is for her to accept help.

"Okay," she says, and the air feels lighter.

I turn the key. "I think I need a drink."

She raises her eyebrows. "Uh, I don't think…"

I laugh. "Relax. I mean a mocha shake from the Ugly Mug."

"But that's all the way across town."

I pull out onto Sunrise again. "Not unless I take the freeway. Like you said, I'm never going to get anywhere unless I take the fast lane, right?"

"I guess so."

"Well, I'm ready to go places. Are you?" I push down my blinker and merge onto the freeway ramp.

She looks nervous but nods her head.

"Okay, then"—I look over my shoulder and accelerate—"let's go."

Chapter Twenty-six

Does she have a different girl over every night?" Garrett asks as she takes another nacho off my plate. "Probably, huh. She's such a player."

I knew having Tai stay with us would be weird for Garrett, but I figured she'd moved on already. Clearly, I was wrong. Tai has moved on, but there's no way I'm going to be the one to tell Garrett this news.

"I mean, she *is* drop-dead gorgeous. Who wouldn't want to do her? You better not even think about it for a second, freshie."

She's looking at me like she's going to murder me, so I quickly respond, "We're just friends. That's all we'll ever be. I promise." Has the thought crossed my mind? Sure. Have I maybe taken a little mind vacation with Tai? Possibly. Would I ever admit that to Garrett or Tai? Never.

"What, she's not good enough for you?" Garrett asks, revealing a sort of protective jealousy that I've never seen from her before. Interesting.

I say nothing because there's no safe response. If I agree that she's good enough for me, I'll have to spend the next ten minutes reassuring Garrett, again, that Tai and I are not secret lovers. If I disagree, I'll have to spend the next ten minutes reassuring her that I do think Tai is a great catch—which will then lead to why I'm not sleeping with her. Seriously, with only ten minutes left of lunch, I'm just trying to enjoy my cold nachos, a little bit of sun on my face, and the fact that in less than six hours, I'll get to be in Vi's arms—finally.

"You're awfully quiet," Garrett comments. "What are you hiding?"

"G," I say after pulling my nachos back toward me, "I thought you and Tai were done. I mean, I thought you and girls were done."

She grabs my soda, but after realizing there's only a sip left, puts it down again. "Bi-sex-ual, Abbey. Do I need to explain the concept again? Would an illustration help?"

I roll my eyes. I get it, but I don't. I mean, boys and girls are so, so, so different. How can she like both? I don't dare ask that, though. "Well, at any rate, you broke up with Tai and you seemed really happy. Are you regretting it or something?"

She bites on a chip and part of it falls into her cleavage. "Crap." She goes in after it, exposing her bra without a care in the world. That's when Kate walks by, holding Ryder's hand. Like her spirit, her makeup is darker. Like her life, her clothes are disheveled.

Our eyes meet. She smiles and waves. Out of instinct, I do the same, but my smile is clearly fake. At least, it is to me. Who knows what she can see anymore.

Garrett turns around to see who I'm waving at. "Oh," she says, retracting her hand from her blouse with the piece of chip in her hand, "success." She holds it up like it's a chunk of gold, then pops it in her mouth, ignoring Kate altogether. I want to ask about their relationship breakdown, but the bell's going to ring. No time for storytelling if I'm going to avoid a tardy. Then I remember I didn't finish the reading for history. "G, what do you know about the industrialization period and its impact on women?"

Instead of helping me, Garrett asks, "Speaking of women, you and Vi do any traveling yet?"

I run my ponytail between my fingers.

I guess my twirl speaks louder than words because then she yells, "Seriously?" which causes the drama kids to stop their improv skit and look over. "Jesus—you guys really into taking it slow or trying for the world record in longest foreplay?"

"There have been extenuating circumstances."

"If it were me—"

"You'd have already earned enough frequent-flyer miles for a free trip?"

She laughs. "Good one, Abbey. Exactly. I mean, she's pretty hot when she's not trying to break you in half on the court."

"Well, we're not you."

Thankfully, Garrett doesn't take offense to my snide remark. "Hope you don't end up in another Devin situation. That would suck. I'll have to start calling you Abbey the Great Unfinisher."

The bell rings. "Thanks, G. That's sweet."

But instead of scurrying to World Civ, I fall back onto the grass. It's March and things are starting to grow back, so the lawn feels fresh and soft. "I don't want to go."

Garrett is easily persuaded. "Then let's not." She digs into her bag and pulls out a pad of passes, probably leftover from her days with Tai.

The temptation is great. But the worry of getting caught, getting grounded, and then missing yet another chance to see Vi is enough to refuse. I push myself up and wipe the grass off my clothes and hair. "Can't risk it, G."

She sighs. "All right, but one of these days, Abbey, we're going to have some fun—whether you like it or not."

I doubt I'll ever be interested in the kind of fun Garrett's interested in, but say, "Yeah, someday," and head off to class for some G-rated Abbey fun.

❖

With my metaphoric passport in my purse, I hop into Vi's Honda. Finally, it's just the two of us and we have a whole night without interruptions. My mom told me to have fun and Tai told me not to get pregnant. I plan on adhering to both bits of advice.

"You look really good," she says after I shut my door. She's seems like she wants to kiss me, but there's something stopping her. Maybe we've grown apart after all this time. Maybe she's going to break up with me. Maybe I should make a move and see what happens.

Instead, I say, "Thanks," and pull up my top a little bit to reveal a tad less boobage. Garrett suggested something with easy access, and I can't believe I listened to her.

We pull out of my driveway and make our way to the end of my street. At the stop sign, Vi turns to me and says, "Can I kiss you now?"

"Please, now," I say as I lean toward her. When we meet in the middle, the softness of her lips warms me up from my head to my toes to the point where I'm sure the windows are already fogged up. She's a terrific kisser. I could kiss her forever. I could kiss her until the sun comes up. I could kiss her until next basketball season. I could kiss her until I graduate. I could kiss Ms. Violet Bowersocks until—

Until my mean, love-hating old neighbor Mr. Nelson honks behind us. We part and laugh. "Oops," I say and sit back and secretly squeeze my legs together. If that was just a kiss to start us off, I don't know if I'm going to be able to make it through the night without wanting more. Like an addict, one little taste of her, and it's all I can think about.

❖

"Wait, are you telling me she did you right there in the movie theater?" Garrett asks, laughing at how I'm trying to cover her mouth so the entire cafeteria doesn't hear. "You mean you finally gave a passport stamp away?"

"G, shut up." I shove my half-eaten roll in her mouth. "It wasn't like that."

She spits out the roll. "Ew, stale. Well, did you?"

"It's just that—" I start, but then realize that two girls the next table over are leaning in close to us. I whisper to Garrett, "Let's go to the quad," and pick up my tray.

We find a spot on the quad away from the rest of the ever-present ears of my classmates.

Garrett tucks her shirt under her bra and rolls up her sleeves because she's never one to miss an opportunity to start on her tan. "Did you have an O or not, freshie? And don't hold back. I'm looking at one month with no action over here. Consider this your gift to me after all I've done for you."

"You mean, all you've done *to* me."

"You say tomato, I say spill it."

I put my hair up into a bun and contemplate my next words. I can't wait until the day when I'm the authority on all things lesbian. That way, maybe I can stop having these embarrassing conversations with Garrett.

"Over or under the pants?" Garrett asks, getting impatient with my pondering.

I clear my throat and whisper, "Over."

She rolls her eyes.

I undo my bun and attempt to French-braid my hair the way Garrett showed me.

"Jesus, Henrietta Hairdresser, just tell me. I won't laugh."

I drop my hair. "It was kind of, I mean, it felt almost like it, but then someone walked by, and she pulled away and it sort of…"

"Fizzled?"

I start pulling at the grass since she won't let me play with my hair. "Yeah. Fizzled. So does that mean…"

"Yeah, sorry to break it to you—that's a delayed flight, Abs. No one left the ground, so no one gets a stamp. Bummer. What about after the movie?"

I shrug. "I don't know. I got all weird after the lights came on. Like everyone knew what we were doing. She drove me home. We kissed good-bye and that was all."

Garrett knocks her leg against mine. "Abbey, you gotta cut yourself some slack. It'll happen when it's supposed to," she says, offering a slight amount of sympathy. Just enough to get me to open up even more.

"I'm just worried that the same thing will happen with Vi that happened with Keeta."

Garrett puts up her right hand. "Dude, I swear I will not shag your girl again."

I manage to laugh a little. "That's not what I meant, but I appreciate that."

"And do you?" she asks, sitting up and looking at me carefully.

"Do I what?"

"Swear you won't sleep with my Tai."

I could argue that she isn't her girlfriend and that Garrett tossed her aside like a pair of last year's basketball shoes, but I don't. "Yeah, I swear."

"Swear on your guitar? On your Beatles paraphernalia? On your mom?"

I throw the pile of grass in Garrett's face, partly because you don't bring my mom's life into any promise and partly because she's acting so pathetic, like me, and it's not becoming. "You need to stop yourself. For the hundredth time, we're just friends and that's all. I have a girlfriend, and you have…whatever you have, and Tai has"—I almost slip up—"her mind on graduating and going to GCU next year, so don't you think it's time to move on?" I think I make a fairly compelling argument and compliment myself for being so mature and for giving such good advice.

Garrett feels different, however. "What the hell do you know about me and Tai, anyway? Just keep your giant-ass mitts off her, okay?"

I'm quickly scared off my high horse and go back to the dynamic we're used to. "Yeah, okay, G. I promise."

"Good." She's satisfied but still irritated.

The bell rings. We part ways quickly and quietly. At this rate, I'm not going to have any friends left by the end of the year.

❖

"Where is it?" I say to myself as I get ready to go out with Vi. I frantically search through my purse again. "Mom!" I yell.

No response.

I yell again, but louder and more panicked than before. This makes her run into the bathroom like a good mom should have on my first bellow. "What? What's wrong?"

"I can't find my cell. Have you seen it?"

She looks at me with dagger eyes that could take down an army of the undead. "I'm on the phone, Abbey." She holds up the phone as proof.

"Sorry," I whisper. "I'll ask Tai."

"Good idea," she says and heads back to the living room.

When I know she's a safe distance, I mock her. "Good idea."

"I heard that, Abbey Brooks," she yells from the other room.

Dang, she's good. I walk to Tai's door and knock. "Hey, Tai, have you seen my phone?" I say into her door.

She cracks it open just far enough so one eye and part of her nose stick out. "It's on top of the fridge."

"Really? How did it get there?"

"You put it up there while you were gathering condiments for your predinner sandwich."

"I did? Weird. You okay? What's with this?" I kick the door slightly and smile. "You got a girl in there or something?" I ask and giggle. "You know the rules."

She opens the door fully to let me see what's in there, and I think to shut me up before I say too much. Garrett salutes me, but then says, "Beat it." She must have come over when I was in the shower.

Tai looks sheepishly down again as if she's ashamed.

"All right, well, you two have a good night. Later." I softly hit Tai's arm as if to say, *Stay strong, sister*. I'm not sure it translates, though.

❖

Vi said she had something special planned for tonight. I love how she surprises me. I love how thoughtful and fun she is. I love so much about her, but I'm not sure if I'm in love with her. Is that weird? I feel like I fell for Keeta really quickly, but Garrett says that's just because it was my first girl. I think it's partly that, but partly because it was Keeta. It was different all over, I guess.

"You okay, Abbey?" Vi asks after taking a big gulp from her Slurpee. "You seem, I don't know, tired?" She takes my hand in hers. She has wonderful hands. I love them, too.

"Yeah, I'm totally fine. Just a long week, I guess. Where the heck are we going?" We've been heading down Speedway for miles and she's passed all my guesses.

"You'll see," she says and smiles. She takes another drink and offers me some, but I shake my head because it won't go well with my minty gum. "I'm taking you someplace where I can have you all to myself," she says and then looks over at me and winks.

"Oh?" I swallow down a lump of nervousness and hope she doesn't notice my hand sweat. "Cool."

She lets go of my hand and runs her fingers through my hair, like she knows my greatest weakness. I'm all hers.

We ride Speedway until it turns into Gates Pass. The houses are fewer and fewer and farther and farther apart, and the dark night feels wider without all the neon signs and stoplights. By now I'm fully confused about where we're headed, but I don't ask because Vi has her music turned up and is singing along to a song I don't know. She seems really happy, so I stay quiet and enjoy the ride.

After a steep climb up a narrow road, we encounter twists and turns that remind me of the roller coasters at Six Flags, except we're not safely secured to a track. On one side of us is a dark drop-off into the Sonoran desert and on the other is a rocky mountainside.

"Vi," I plead loudly over her music as I grip the handle above my door. "Can you slow down a bit?"

"What?" she says, taking her eyes off the road to look at me.

I scream and point at the curve coming up. She swerves just in time to make the turn, though a back tire hits the gravel shoulder and spins slightly. On the next curve she crosses over entirely into the opposite lane. Thankfully no one is coming our way, but I'm not counting on that kind of luck again.

I smack the power button of her stereo to turn it off. "What's wrong with you? Why are you going so fast?"

But she just laughs. "Abbey, chill out. Here, have a sip of this. It'll help you relax." She hands me her drink again, but I push it away.

"I don't want any of your damn Slurpee. I want you to slow down. I mean it."

She finally does what I want and applies the brakes on the final two twists before the road straightens out, then pulls over at the lookout area. "Sorry, I just wanted to have some fun. I didn't mean to scare you."

I'm sitting as far from her as possible to show my distrust. "Well, you did."

Her head falls forward on her steering wheel. "Sorry I'm such a screwup. I can't do anything right. You deserve so much more. I'm an asshole."

Now instead of being angry, I'm concerned. "Vi, it's okay. Just go slower, okay?" But I have a feeling we're not talking about driving anymore. "Is something else going on?"

"You wouldn't understand. God, you're so lucky your dad isn't around."

"He's dead," I say, then look away.

"Abbey, I didn't know...I didn't mean...I'm sorry." She reaches for my hand, but I pull it away. "All I wanted to do was be with you tonight, and now I've messed it all up. My dad is so right about me. I'm living a half-assed life. I'm never getting into UC Berkeley." And then she starts to cry.

I can't stand to see anyone sad, so I release my seat belt and hers and pull her over to me and hug her. "You're not a screw-up. You're wonderful. I mean it." I lift her head and wipe her hair back from her face. "I'm sorry your dad makes you feel that way."

"You should've seen his face when he saw my SAT scores. You'd think he was looking at a life sentence for murder instead of the results of a stupid standardized test. I missed my goal, or his goal, by four points, Abbey. Four." Vi drinks from her Slurpee again until it makes the all-gone sound.

"You have another chance, right?" I try to reassure her.

She nods, then wipes her face with her sleeve. "Yeah. Whatever." She shakes her head and then says, "It doesn't matter. Come on. I want to show you something." She opens her door and runs around to my side to open mine.

Before I can say thanks, she pulls me out of the car and drags me to the edge of the lookout point. She turns me around and holds me from behind as she leans against the railing. "Look up."

I do as I'm told and smile wide. "Amazing." Out here the stars look enormous, as if a magnifying glass is being held in front of our faces. It makes me think of my dad and the camping trips we went on. It makes me remember that night with Devin on the hammock in my backyard. But when Vi starts to kiss my neck, and her hand slips up my shirt, I close my eyes and only think of her.

"I want you, Abbey," she whispers in my ear.

I would respond, but as she starts to undo my jeans, I have lost the ability to form words. I turn around to face her. I want to look in her eyes. I want to remember everything about this moment. "Kiss me," I say softly.

She leans in to kiss me at the same time she attempts to move her hand underneath my underwear. Her mouth tastes strange and it's a sloppier kiss than I'm used to, but I disregard both things and pull her body into mine.

I don't want my bare bottom hanging out in the parking lot, so I suggest we go to her car even though I'm completely nervous and scared.

"Okay, my love. Let's go."

Love? Did she just call me her love? "Um, okay," I finally say because I'm about to have sex for the first time, and I think questioning her pet names right now might be kind of a buzzkill.

She takes my hand in hers and we jog back to the car as if time is running out. On the way, though, she trips on a rock and falls down in the dirt. Instead of swearing in pain, she starts to laugh hysterically. She tries to get up but can't. I laugh at first, too, but then my stomach sinks when I realize who she's reminding me of. She's acting just like Kate did, that night at the Halloween party and in the locker room. As much as I don't want to, I have to stop disregarding what's true. She's totally drunk.

I button up my jeans and stare down at her. When she finally realizes I'm not laughing anymore, she says, "Abbey, my love. Help me up."

"What did you put in your Slurpee?" I ask, feeling so stupid, and trapped, and more stupid. What's wrong with me? Wait. Me? What am I saying? What's wrong with *her*? "You could've killed us!" I storm off to her car. I hear her call my name, but I don't turn around. Instead I slam the car door and attempt to call my mom. I get as far as pushing send on my phone when it dies. "Are you freaking kidding me?" I yell at it. As much as I don't want them to, hot tears start to stream down my face. I turn the rearview mirror to check on Vi who has pushed herself upright and is sitting in the middle of the empty parking lot. She's crying, too.

"Abbey, I'm so sorry. I'm so, so sorry."

The drunk sorrys, like always, are making things worse. I grab a lock of hair, but then toss it aside. No more twirling, Abbey. Get in the driver's seat and take control.

With that, I march back out to Vi and demand her cell phone. She hands it over reluctantly, but not before adding a few more sorrys.

She's got plenty of battery, but no signal. "Really?" I yell up at the sky, hoping the universe will hear that I am quite done with its shenanigans. "Okay," I say mostly to myself. "I'm just going to have to drive us home. No big deal." I nod, then add, "I got this," channeling my inner Tai to help my courage grow.

I hoist Vi up and walk her to the car. I'm less angry than I am scared of driving the twisted roads home, so when she apologizes, I say it's okay. She finally stops crying.

"I'll drive you home." She tries to take the keys from her pocket but drops them.

"No, that's okay," I say as I pick them up. "You just try to sober up before I leave you at your house. I don't think your dad will want to see you like this. Just a guess." It's only nine, so maybe if we drive to the park near her house, there's a chance she'll pull it together before my curfew. A small chance, but I'll take it.

After I strap her in, I get myself situated in the driver's seat. Rearview mirror? Check. Seat? Check. Her car is newer than my Volvo, so it takes me a few seconds to figure out how to turn the headlights on. Once those are located, I start the engine and turn to Vi. "Tell me if you need to throw up. I'll pull over."

Vi responds with one last sorry, then reclines her seat until she is almost lying down. I guess I'm on my own.

"Okay, Abbey, don't screw this up," I say and put the car into drive.

❖

Thankfully my mom believed that Vi was too sick with the flu to drive me home. And thankfully she sent Tai to get me instead of coming herself.

We exchange *heys* after I get into the passenger seat of her Jeep, but I don't say more than that for the next five minutes. Then I turn to Tai, but instead of talking about my night, I ask, "What was up with Garrett visiting you?"

We pull up to a red light and Tai turns to look at me. "Why? Is there a problem?"

I shrug. "I dunno. She want to get back together with you or something?"

This time Tai shrugs. "I dunno. Maybe. It's complicated."

"You didn't, did you? I thought you were with someone." I tap her earring to remind her. I want Tai to be good, not like the rest. Her perfection is important to me for some reason. "Please say you didn't do it with my mom in the house, at least.

She laughs. "Well, she did go out and get groceries."

I scrunch up my face. "Well, if you ask me..." I stop because I'm used to everyone cutting me off at that point, but she doesn't, so I continue. "If you ask me, I think you're better off without her."

"Oh, really," says Tai. Long thoughtful pause. "So, anyway, what happened tonight? I'm not buying the flu scenario. You guys have a fight or something?"

"You didn't tell my mom, did you?"

"Nah, don't worry. So, what happened?"

I look out the window and consider telling Tai more lies, but that's not who we are to each other, so why start now. "She's just not who I thought she was." That's a truth, even if it's missing some concrete evidence.

"That really clears it up. Glad we had this talk." She shoves my head forward and laughs. "Come on, I'll tell you if you tell me."

"You're going to think I'm stupid, and I don't want you to get mad at Vi." For some reason I'd prefer that Tai think I was an ultracool sex goddess, not a nerd who gets all uptight about a little drinking and driving.

"Dude, she didn't hurt you, did she?" Tai glances at me intently to search for any signs that I'm lying.

"No, no. Nothing like that. It's no big deal. She got a little buzzed and I had to drive us back to her house and that's all. I think her dad is really stressing her out or something."

"That's all? You sure? I mean, that's messed up, but you're not hurt?"

There's no way I'm telling Tai I was hoping to go all the way with Vi tonight, and that I'm not only mad she screwed it up by drinking, but that I'm mad because sexual frustration is building up inside me and I feel like I might turn into the Incredible Hulk at any moment: Abbey horny! Arrrgh!

"So I take it you didn't get laid tonight?" Tai asks coolly, like my sex status is written across my forehead or discussed nightly on the Internet. Damn Garrett and her big mouth.

"That's private," I say and cross my legs. At least, I was hoping it was.

"Me, neither," Tai says and sighs. "I was just playing with you. She wants me again, but I'm not into her anymore. I've definitely found someone better."

I nod, but inside I'm relieved. For one, I'm glad she didn't have sex with Garrett in my house. If anyone's having sex with a girl in my house, it better be me. And, I don't know, I'm just glad she didn't fall for Garrett's tricks.

I pick up an imaginary mug off the dash and raise it to her. "Well, here's to celibacy until graduation."

She clinks her imaginary mug against mine, but adds, "Here's to love."

Oh yeah. Love. I almost forgot all about that piece in my quest for sex. Didn't I use to think they went together? Shouldn't they? Garrett says they don't have to, and she's proof of that. But Vi wanted to be with me tonight, so does she love me?

By the time Tai parks in my driveway, I have a headache from thinking too much. Maybe the answers aren't that hard, though. "Do you love her, Tai?"

"Who? Garrett?" Tai asks.

I shake my head. "No, Senorita Mysterioso."

"Yeah, baby D. I really think I do. Like, in a way I've never felt before."

I can't help but smile when she smiles. "What's it like?" I think I felt love with Keeta, but maybe that was just infatuation.

"It's"—she smiles even bigger—"amazing."

"That's nice. I hope it works out with this mystery girl 'cause then maybe I can meet her someday."

"Maybe. But for now, thanks for respecting my privacy. And

thanks for not telling G. It's nice to know you can actually trust someone in this world."

"No kidding," I say, and then we sit and listen to the crickets. "Well, she's lucky."

Tai turns her body so she's facing me, like what she's about to say is serious. "Abbey, you're a really sweet girl."

I look down. It's the nicest, most innocent thing I've been told in a long time.

"And I don't care what the bathroom walls say. I know you're a good girl." She laughs and shoves me.

This is what it must feel like to know someone will always be on your side. No matter what.

CHAPTER TWENTY-SEVEN

After I change my outfit three times and my hair four times, Tai, my mom, and I pile into the Volvo. This is the first time the three of us have been in the same car together and it's weird, but my mom insisted that Tai come so she could celebrate with us when I pass my driving test.

"If I pass," I keep correcting my mom.

But she just shakes her head and says, "Oh, Abbey," like I'm crazy.

My leg is bouncing up and down with nerves while we wait for my number to be called, so my mom finally places her hand on it and holds it down. As a result my other leg goes off—Tai presses her hand on it. And that's how we sit until my number is called.

"Number ninety-three."

Tai and my mom simultaneously push me out of my seat.

"Like a boss," Tai says and slaps my butt like we're on the court.

"Just take your time, Abbey Road," my mom says and gives me a thumbs-up.

I walk slowly to the DMV employee waiting for me in the doorway. She looks serious and cynical and stern and all other words that are not good things. "Ninety-three?"

I nod.

She looks down at her clipboard. "Abbey Brooks?"

I nod again.

"You can speak, right?"

I nod, but then add a quiet, "Yes, ma'am."

"Okay, let's go. You lead the way."

I walk out to my Volvo, and like we're on a date, I open the door for her. This makes her break her frown and temporarily stops my manic nerves from making me pass out.

Once I'm behind the wheel I go through my usual adjustments even though I was the one who drove over here. I fake adjust the mirror, then fake adjust my seat, and finally fake adjust the visor.

"This is a driving test, Ms. Brooks, can we get this show on the road?"

I nod and turn the key. The engine comes to life. In a last moment of desperation, I beg the ever-disappointing universe to please, just this once, give me a freaking break and let me pass. I put it in drive and away we go.

❖

"Let me see," Garrett says as she grabs my license from my hand. We're lounging on the bleachers waiting for track practice to begin. She wasn't on the team last year, and neither was Tai, but now that Tai has joined, Garrett has, too. She's either getting really desperate or really clever. "Not bad. Better than your school picture. At least you don't look like a twelve-year-old."

I yank it out of her hand so she won't drop it and proudly place it back in my wallet, in that special pocket with the clear plastic cover that is specifically made for driver's licenses. I want to kiss it, but I refrain.

"So, where did you go on your first-ever solo drive?"

I squint and look out on the field. A bunch of the pole jumpers are setting up the mats. I pretend I'm fully interested in the process and ignore her question.

"Abbey, you haven't gone anywhere, have you? God." She shakes her head.

"Yes, I did. I went to the corner store and got gas." I leave out the part where I accidentally locked my keys in the car and Tai had to drive over to give me the spare one.

She shoves me. "Why didn't you go see your girl? That's the first place I'd go. Speaking of my girl, you didn't tell her about me and K, did you?"

"No, why?" I say truthfully. It's not just because she asked me not to, but also because Tai and I are good friends now. If she knew I knew, she'd probably be pissed, and I do not want a pissed-off Tai in my house. But it's also because I'm embarrassed. Abbey couldn't finish the deal, so Garrett, like always, swooped in and did it better.

Garrett looks at me, then out on the field. "I dunno. She's just acting different."

"You mean, she's not taking you back," I accidentally say.

"What do you know about it?" Garrett says, glaring at me.

Great, now she's pissed off at me. "Nothing. I've just noticed that you seem into her again. You want her back, huh?"

Garrett, who is normally decisive and sure about everything, looks down and fiddles with her laces. "I don't know," she mumbles, "maybe."

"Is this a grass-greener kind of situation?"

She shrugs. "Maybe."

For a brief moment I feel bad for Garrett. But when I remember all the things she's done behind Tai's back, I shed my sympathy and renew my solidarity with Tai. "Well, you're the one who started it all that day on the courts."

"Thanks for reminding me," she says as we slowly clomp down the bleachers, then she turns to me. "You know, you can be a real bitch when you want to be."

In my head, I say, *I learned from the best,* but to her I say, "Sorry. I just mean, I thought that's what you wanted."

"Well, what I *thought* I wanted and what I *really* want don't always match or make sense, so sue me."

Finally, there's something Garrett says that I can totally agree with and relate to.

❖

"I'm going out," I say to my mom, who's at her easel, as usual. "I'll be back by dinner."

She looks at me over her glasses. "Where to, honey?"

I spin the keys around my finger and throw up my hand. "Here and there. You know, just want to go for a drive. You know, since I can, and everything."

"Well, aren't you proud of yourself?" She rinses off her paintbrush and smiles. "You need gas money?"

I pat my purse. "Nope, I still have some from my allowance. Need anything while I'm out?"

She says no and then gets all teary eyed, and I consider heading out, just leaving her like that. But I can't. "Mom, come on. Why are you sad?"

She wipes her eyes with the paint-speckled cloth she uses to clean off her brushes. "Not sad, honey, just…"

"Proud?" I say, hoping that's all it is and she won't bring up Dad. She nods. "Your dad would be, too."

I press my lips together to prevent my own tears from falling. It works. I make my exit before she notices.

After getting gas, my first order of business is to drive Sunrise all by myself. It takes me twenty minutes to get there, though, and by the time I turn left onto it, the traffic is horrible. I only go down for one stoplight because it's not fun, especially without Tai, who is currently out with a *friend*.

I take a few more lefts and rights, and I find myself pulling into Columbus Park. The courts are empty but inviting. "What the hell," I say to myself and park. I grab the ball I decided to keep in the back of my car.

I put my earbuds in and crank up a mix of Beatles songs, which always put me in a better mood. Not that I was in a bad one, but for some reason a lonely one. Vi has called and texted about a million times, apologizing and asking to see me. I'm still considering my next move, though. I mean, she could've driven us off the side of that road. She could've gotten pulled over and arrested. But at the same time, I really, really like her and was hoping to see if I could love her. We all make mistakes, right? I've forgiven every other person in my life for their mistakes. Why not Vi? Why all of a sudden am I the morality police?

"Yesterday" starts to play, but I skip over it. I don't need to be reminded of how all my troubles used to seem far away. "Revolution" blares in my ears and I'm energized once more. I shoot from the top of the key and make it. I try a bank shot next and make it. I dribble out to the three-point line, shoot, and… "No way," I say as it swishes in. I keep trying increasingly impossible shots thinking there's no way I'll make it, but they all swish in. *This must be a sign.* Then I dribble in for a layup, one of my most consistent shots, and totally miss. If this lucky shooting streak is a sign, then what does it mean that I missed the easiest shot of all?

Sign or no sign, I know where I need to go next on my mini road trip.

❖

"Sorry I'm late!" I yell as I run by my mom and Tai, who are setting the table. "Let me just wash my hands." It's six thirty-five, and I was supposed to be home at six thirty. As far as rebellious teenage acts go, this isn't a big deal, but I shouldn't have come home late from my first major journey out alone. It's bad form.

I run back to the kitchen and take my seat next to Tai. Out of breath, I say, "Hey, what's on the menu?" as I unfold my napkin and place it in my lap. "Tons of traffic out there," I say, starting off the night with a little white lie.

My mom serves us each a large helping of salad without asking if we want any. I pick out the onions and bell peppers and put them on Tai's plate.

"New necklace?" I ask Tai. "Nice."

My mom looks up and smiles.

"Thanks," Tai says and looks at me like I need to drop it, so I do.

"So," my mom says, interrupting our exchange, "what did you do? Where did you go?"

Tai looks over at me and smiles then asks, "Yeah, Abs, where did you go?" as if she already knows.

I take a large bite of salad and shrug, but they both wait patiently for my response, so I wash it down with milk and reply, "I went to the park to shoot around."

"By yourself?" Mom asks. "That seems lonely."

I don't want my mom to think I'm sort of a loner, so I let a little truth escape. "Then I drove over to Vi's house." The whole truth is I met her at the park near her house because she said it wasn't a good time to have company over. "And we hung out and listened to music." The truth here is that we listened to music in my car and had a very long makeup/make-out session in the parking lot until some creepers parked nearby and we got freaked-out. Tonight I learned that sober sorrys are a thousand times more enjoyable and meaningful than the drunk ones.

My visit with Vi seems to make my mom happy. "Oh, good. I thought you guys were maybe not dating anymore since I haven't seen her for a while. How is she? Good?"

I bite my bottom lip to prevent myself from grinning. Good? I would definitely say so. But I manage to say, "Yeah," without exploding.

Tai sees right through me, though, and clears her throat to indicate that fact. "Mrs. B., this chicken is incredible. Lemon and rosemary?"

My mom nods and adds, "Mark showed me how to make it. Not bad, huh? He's an incredible cook. In fact"—she puts down her fork and looks over at me—"I'd like to invite him over to cook us dinner soon. He'd really like to meet you, Abbey. You too, Tai. What do you think?"

"Sure. I guess. When?" I ask, as my mood free-falls from the heights of euphoria to the depths of depression. I keep on hoping this little fling with this stupid guy will end, but instead she's happier than ever. I even caught her dancing to Salt-N-Pepa while doing dishes the other day. She hasn't done that in years. What can she possibly see in him? No one is as perfect as my dad, so why bother?

"Next Saturday, okay?" she asks, like she's the teenager in the house.

I'm relieved to remember we have a track meet. "Can't. We have a meet at Tucson High." I look at Tai and she confirms with a nod.

"Well, those end by four, right?"

Darn. "Yes, but I have a date with Vi after that." This is a half-truth. We didn't quite get around to firming up any plans between the kissing and the apologies.

"Abbey, this is important to me. Can't you reschedule with her?"

Crap. I hate it when she asks me to do her a favor because she rarely does, which means I'd be a brat for not doing what she wants. "Yes. I guess so."

"Okay, great. You two will have time to shower after your meet. I mean separately, of course." She laughs. "I don't know why I said that." And then laughs again.

Tai saves the weird moment by saying, "Ew. I mean, no offense."

I say, "As if," back to her.

"Next Saturday it is, then," my mom says to move us along. "I'll call him after dinner." She smiles as she takes another bite. "Thanks, sweetie."

"Can't wait," I mumble to my plate, but she ignores my sarcasm, a skill she's mastered over the last couple of years.

❖

By the time Tai and I pull into my driveway, it's already five fifteen. Mark is expected at six, so my mom is in full-on freak-out mode when we enter the kitchen. "Where have you two been? Get in the shower." Then adds, "I don't mean together, of course," which makes me and Tai laugh a little.

"Sorry, Mrs. Brooks, the bus was late picking us up," Tai tries to explain, but my mom doesn't want to hear it.

"Showers, girls. Go."

"I'll take one in my mom's," I say to Tai as we head down the hall.

Then I stop and grab her shoulders. "You sure you don't wanna bail on this dinner? It's not too late. Save yourself."

"Showers!" my mom screams, and we both run into our rooms and do as we're told.

Tai gets away with wearing jeans and a T-shirt, but not me. I'm instructed to wear something *nice* and not so *sporty*. I'm tempted to call my mom on her hopefully unintentional homophobia, but because tonight is a special night, I let it go and slip on a pair of black pants, a dressy shimmery shirt, and flats.

"He's here. He's here," my mom says, as if we're as excited as she is. "How's my hair? This skirt look okay?"

"You look great, Mrs. Brooks," Tai offers, but I say nothing.

"Please be nice, Abbey," my mom says to my lack of response. "You promised."

"You look really good, Mom," I say because she does and I need to grow up, and like Tai said while we got ready, accept the fact that my mom has a heart, too, and everyone needs love to survive. I hate that Tai's right.

"Abbey, straighten out that pillow," my mom says, pointing to the couch. I do as I'm told. "No, I like it better the other way." I change it back. "Hmm, maybe a little to the…" I've never been so happy to hear a doorbell. My mom practically falls over herself as she hurries to answer the door. They hug and he presents some flowers to her. Then she takes his hand and leads him to the living room.

"Abbey, this is Mark. Mark, this is my daughter Abbey and her friend Tai."

Mark is now the tallest person in the house, and I don't think I like how that feels, but I smile and say it's nice to meet him and shake his hand like a good girl. Tai says the same and then we stand there in silence until Mark notices the piece my mom is working on. "Oh, Susan, it's better than the pictures."

He walks over to her easel and inspects the painting while I inspect him. Besides being tall, he's dressed in what seems to be an expensive suit and a tie that's my favorite shade of purple. His shoes are shiny, but he has just enough ease in his posture that his meticulous appearance doesn't make him seem like a dick. His hair is brown and freshly cut. He obviously put a lot of effort into looking good for my mom, and I guess I can appreciate that.

My mom is beaming as she describes the painting and her process.

She seems really, really happy. I try to hate her for it but can't. We all need love to survive, I repeat in my head.

"So, Abbey, your mom tells me you're quite a basketball star," Mark says as we sit down around the cheese plate I assembled for the night. "I played in high school, too. Not good enough for college, but I bet you will be. Any schools you're interested in?"

I frown. "Not really. I mean, I'm only a sophomore. But"—I pat Tai's leg—"Tai here has her sights on Grand Canyon University for volleyball." And like that, I've taken myself out of the conversation, which is where I prefer to be. I don't like that he knows anything about me. Besides, Tai is good at talking to grown-ups.

"Hey, you know, the GCU coach and his wife are becoming regulars at my restaurant. Maybe I can connect you two."

Tai nods appreciatively. "That'd be cool, thanks."

I fight with all my might not to roll my eyes, but instead, I ask, "Anyone famous ever eat there?"

He names a couple of politicians and other people I couldn't care less about, but then says, "And last week we had a couple of the starters from the Mercury come in. The center. Oh, what was her name?"

My jaw drops. "Brittney Griner?" I say after recovering.

"That's it. And another one. She's a guard?"

"Diana Taurasi?" Tai says, equally star struck.

"Yep, that's the one," he says and then reaches into the bag he brought. "In fact, I knew I was coming to meet you and thought maybe you'd appreciate this." He hands over a cloth napkin. On it are their two signatures, plus a message…to me: *Hope to see you at a game soon, Abbey! Thanks for your support!*

I put it carefully in my lap, worried that my sweatiness will ruin it. "That's really cool. Thanks."

My mom walks in with two glasses of wine and hands one to Mark. "I told you she'd like it."

Mark takes the glass in one hand, then helps my mom to the couch with his other.

"Well, I promised to make you all dinner, so I better get in there."

"Can we do anything to help?" I ask, trying to be polite and show a little gratitude for the gift.

"No, you two can hang out. Everything's all prepped, just need to know where all the tools are. Will you be my navigator, Susan?" he asks my mom, and she giggles. Lord, she has it bad.

❖

Why does this food have to taste so good? Even I'd marry him right now if it meant eating like this every night.

Tai and I finally come up for air after devouring another serving of the maple soy skirt steak and garlic mashed potatoes. Even his salad is worthy of another round, so I serve myself a little more. "This dinner is really good," I say for the tenth time before taking another bite.

"Glad you like it. I'm thinking about adding it to the events menu."

"For sure," Tai says, her mouth full. "I'd be happy to go to any party that had this on the menu."

Mark smiles and seems a little more relaxed now that the teenagers are happy and fed. My mom seems better, too, but that could be because she's on her second glass of wine, and since she hardly drinks, she's getting a little tipsy.

"Mark's restaurant is perfect for special events. The way they decorate for them—oh, it's just beautiful inside. I can't wait to show you sometime. It'll take your breath away."

"Especially the mural in the lobby," Mark says and rubs my mom's back. She gets bashful and looks down. It's kind of cute. I gag a little.

Everyone needs love, Abbey. Even your mom. I serve myself one more scoop of potatoes. Maybe it won't be so bad after all.

CHAPTER TWENTY-EIGHT

A few days after our dinner, Mark sent flowers—lilies, not roses, because lilies are her favorite—and a box of chocolates—dark truffles, not milk. Mom swooned, naturally, but the distance between them seems to be depressing her and she's been moping around the house all night playing one-woman Scrabble games. That's why I feel so guilty leaving her to go see Vi, but a you-know-who girl's gotta do what a girl's gotta do.

"Okay, I'm out, Mom," I say as I finish my snack. "Be home by curfew, 'kay?" I chug the rest of the soda and burp to bring attention to my accomplishment.

"Classy," Tai says from the living room, where she's elbow deep in scholarship applications. Since she got accepted at GCU, she's been scrambling to figure out how to pay for it since they only gave her a partial scholarship for volleyball and her dad hasn't contacted her once since she moved in. I wish we could help her, but I don't know how to ask my mom that. I can hardly get the nerve to ask her for extra gas money.

"Have fun, honey," Mom says as she digs through the letter bag until she finds an *M*. Wow, things must be pretty bad for her to cheat playing herself.

I look at the clock. Vi's expecting me at six. We're celebrating our four-month anniversary at Caruso's and then going to a movie. It's already five thirty, but I feel so bad for my mom. "Why don't you just call him, Mom?"

"He's working tonight." She lays *morose* down on the board and records her points. "Have fun." She pulls the other tray of letters in front of her and shuffles the tiles around.

In a last-ditch effort to feel less crappy for leaving Mom like this, I walk over to Tai, lean down, and whisper in her ear, "Would you please play Scrabble with my mom?"

Tai leans forward and looks at my mom then her watch. "One game, but then I'm leaving, too."

"Where are you going?" I ask, as if she needs my permission.

She laughs. "Out. Enough said."

Tai stacks her papers and gets up and walks into the kitchen. "Hey, Mrs. B., I need a break from those apps. Can I play a round with you?"

My mom says, "Sure," and quickly dumps the board's words into the bag for a new game.

❖

I'm halfway to Caruso's when my phone dings that I have a text message. As a promise to my mom, I keep my cell in the backseat, out of arm's length, so I'm not tempted to read a text or answer it when I'm driving. As annoying as it is, I've kept this promise because with the way kids are dying while driving and texting these days, it's fair to say my mom is on to something.

I pull over in the Circle K parking lot and do a contorted twist in my seat to reach my phone. When I see it's from Kate, I hesitate even opening it but touch the screen to reveal her message: *Abbey—can you please come over to my house. I really need to talk.*

I look at the time. It's already five fifty and she lives in the opposite direction of Caruso's and the opposite direction of where I really want to be, which is with Vi.

"Freaking Kate," I whisper and toss my phone into the backseat again. I pull out into traffic and head to her house. Maybe if I hurry, I won't be too late.

I wait for the green left turn arrow to appear. That's when I remember the emptiness she leaves me with and change my mind. As I make the U-turn, I think, *She's a big girl now. She can figure it out.* It's time I take care of me, and me wants to hang out with my girlfriend.

I pull up to Caruso's and park. Vi must've been looking for me because she walks over right away and opens my door. She holds out a rose, and I instantly forget about Kate and all other things that try to bring me down. I want to kiss her, but I know she's still too worried to do that in public. "Thanks, Vi." I smell it and smile.

She smiles bigger than me, if that's possible, and says, "I have a surprise for you, but you'll have to leave your car here, okay?"

I grab my cell from the backseat and follow her. It's all I can do not to skip as we walk to her Honda. "Where are we going?" I ask, even though I know she won't tell.

"Wait here. I ordered some food to go."

I do as I'm told and watch as she jogs into Caruso's. I flip down the visor to check my makeup and apply some lip gloss. If Kate could see me now, I think and laugh. She'd die knowing I actually applied mascara without the threat of torture. Then thinking of Kate makes me feel bad. No. She has other friends she can call.

I flip the visor back and get temporarily blinded by the SUV that's parking in front of Vi's car. When the lights turn off and I can see the driver, I almost duck down and hide. But there's no reason I should be afraid of Coach Alvarez now. It's off-season and we're off court. It's not like she's going to make me run suicide lines here in the lot. Still, I don't honk the horn and wave or anything. Why risk it?

She looks all dolled up and is definitely sporting some makeup, too. I guess us jocks clean up pretty nicely when we want to. She checks her face one last time before opening the door and heading to the entrance. Her heels are sparkly and her jeans are tight. Wow. Who knew that lady was a lady under her androgynous polo shirts and khaki pants? She must have a hot date. Good for her.

"It's busy in there," Vi says after placing the food in the backseat. I look back and notice that her sports bag is back there, too. Where is she taking me? "Sorry to keep you waiting."

"No problem. Can I pay you for some of the food?" She's never let me pay for anything, and I'm starting to feel bad. Garrett says I should embrace the hetero-influenced dynamic, but I'm beginning to think that not all of Garrett's advice should be followed.

Vi takes my hand in hers. "I'm taking care of everything tonight, Abbey, especially you." She kisses my hand then pulls me closer and kisses my lips. It was worth the wait.

We drive down Campbell until we hit Sunrise. I don't remember telling her how much I love this road and hope she and Tai haven't been talking about me, too. Just to make sure, I ask. "You and Tai talk lately?"

"Oh, hey, funny you should say that. I just saw her in Caruso's."

"No way. How funny. I knew she had a date, but I guess we never really told each other where we were going." Then I get excited. "Did you see who she was with?"

Vi speeds up a little for the dips in the road. I don't mind this time,

though, because, for one, I know she's sober, and secondly, I do the
same when I drive down this part. "No, she was sitting alone. But"—
Vi takes a left onto Ventana Canyon Drive, where only the richest of
Tucsonans can afford homes—"she acted totally weird when I said hi
to her."

"Like what?"

"She kept on looking over me to see if someone was coming, and
she acted like she was trying to get rid of me. What's that about?"

I shrug. "She's been really secretive about some girl she's seeing.
I don't…" I stop talking because I've just had a revelation, and it's too
big for me to handle.

"You don't what?" Vi asks as she looks over at me. "Dude, you
okay? What's wrong?"

Tai and Coach Alvarez? There's no way. It can't be true. Is that
even legal? I twirl a lock of hair between my fingers and squint into the
night like I'm trying to do algebra in my head.

"Abbey, you're freaking me out a little. Who is it?"

"Um, I don't know," I finally say, hoping Vi hasn't figured out my
tell. "Like I said, she's not telling anyone." Oh my God, oh my God,
oh my God. No wonder she hasn't told a soul. How could that even
happen? I'm racking my brain, trying to put all the pieces together.
Did Tai quit because of their affair or because of Garrett? Is Coach the
one who gave Tai all the jewelry? Is Tai the one who gave Coach that
hickey? I think I might ralph, so I roll down the window and take in a
fresh breath of warm desert air.

"Well, anyway," Vi says as she pulls up to a security panel and
punches in a code, "we're here."

Two giant iron gates slowly open and she drives through. The
mansions are so glamorous that I assume they're all owned by movie
stars. My mouth drops open as we drive along the winding road, and
I'm glad to be distracted from my grotesque possible-hopefully-not
discovery about Tai.

"That one has a five-car garage," I say pointing at the massive
light pink house with the lions standing guard in front of it. "Who has
five cars?"

"And it has two hydraulic lifts inside that garage, and two pools,
five bedrooms, a guest house, maid quarters, and for your stargazing
pleasure, a retractable roof in the master bathroom." Then she points
to the Mediterranean-looking one on the corner. "Now this one is a
beauty. Upon entering, you'll be blown away by the forged wrought-

iron glass-front doors that open to a grand foyer with a stunning twenty-two-karat-gold painted ceiling. And of course, there's the beautifully appointed living room with French doors, leading to one of many outside balconies. Or perhaps you'd like to snuggle up with a book in the library which features built-in cherry bookshelves and cabinets." She extends her hand as we drive by like she's one of those ladies on *The Price is Right*.

She makes me laugh. "How do you know this stuff?"

"It's my job. Well, one of many."

"I thought you just did computer stuff for your dad."

"Mostly, but I also write his descriptions. And in order to do that, I have to see these places."

"You've been in these houses? Wow."

"Well, not exactly. I usually just look at the pictures his photographer sends me, but sometimes"—she parks near the end of a long private driveway—"I get to go inside." She turns off the car. "Come on. I'll show you."

She won't let me carry anything, so I feel especially spoiled as we walk up the driveway and then to the huge front door of a more understated, but clearly just as elegant, home. "Aren't we going to get caught?"

"I know the codes. Don't worry. Nothing is going to spoil this evening." She punches a four-digit number into the box that holds the front-door key. "My lady," she says as she opens the door for me.

I walk in because I trust her. She would know more than me about how not to get caught in these places.

She enters another code once we're inside to disarm the security alarm. After she empties her hands of all the bags, she pulls me to her. "Finally. Just you and me and no interruptions."

As we kiss in the dark foyer of this empty house, I feel completely relaxed and uninhibited. As much fun as it is to sneak kisses in parked cars and dark theaters, this feels very freeing and very sexy.

She walks me over to the couch, but instead of joining me, she pulls away and says, "Wait here."

I do as I'm told.

She grabs the bags and races upstairs. I look out the picture window and see all of Tucson displayed before me. From up here, it seems so small, like I could drive all its streets in an hour. Then for some reason, thinking of driving makes me think of my text from Kate. I check my phone, but she didn't write again. See? I knew she'd figure it out.

"Okay, come on up," Vi yells from the top of the stairs.

As I ascend the grand staircase, feeling a little like Scarlett O'Hara from *Gone With the Wind*, I hear soft music playing and see small shadows dancing on the walls.

"What've you done, Vi?" I whisper even though I can see very clearly what she's done. The master bedroom's fireplace is on, and in front of it she's laid a blanket, our dinner, and her cell phone playing music. "Wow. This is beautiful." The only thing that's missing are the rose petals, but she makes up for it times a thousand when I see a box of my favorite chocolates on my plate.

"You like it?" she asks shyly.

I nod as I sit in front of her. "You're pretty amazing."

"I think you're pretty amazing, too." She hands me my plate, a napkin, and a fork. "Are you hungry?"

I look at the food. All my favorites are there—lasagna, garlic bread, and even tiramisu, but for once in my life, filling up my stomach isn't on the top of my list of to-dos. Instead of responding to her question, I move the dishes aside and then crawl over to her. "Yes, very hungry." And then I kiss her.

Vi leans back until I'm on top of her. It's the first time we've been completely horizontal with each other, and the feeling of my body pressing into hers makes me moan. Or it could be the fact that her lips are kissing their way down my neck and chest.

I sit up, straddling her, and even though the thought of someone seeing me naked with the lights on makes me freak out, the light from the fire seems more forgiving, so I say, "I'll be right back," roll off her, and run to the bathroom. I want to make an entrance and make sure I look perfect. Plus, Garrett always says that making a girl wait a little longer is always a good thing.

Once I have privacy in the bathroom, I take off all my clothes but leave on the cute matching bra and undies I secretly bought so she can admire them. Then I look at myself in the full-length mirror. It's usually easy to pick apart how I look, feature by feature, but when I see it all together as a whole almost-naked body, it's hard to imagine changing any part of it without changing all of it. I mean, my legs for days go with my long arms and my butt seems like the right size for my hips. My boobs, well, they could really use some meat, but my mom is one cup bigger than me, so maybe there's still hope.

After closer inspection, I notice the two hickeys on my neck. "Shoot," I whisper and lean into the mirror to look at them. They're light, but in places that are going to be hard to hide. Oh, well, it's not like I've never had to hide a hickey from my mom. Then I smile because I'm thinking about Vi and the way she makes me feel when we kiss.

If you like that, you're going to love what's about to happen, Abbey. If you would, you know, get on out there. I take a deep breath and reach for the doorknob. Here goes.

I open the door and she leans over on her elbow so she can look at me. "You are beautiful, Abbey."

Whether or not she means it, I'm feeling pretty in my purple lacy lingerie, so I don't argue with her and say, "Thanks," instead of shut up, like I normally would after a compliment is directed my way. And as much as I hate to think about Garrett at a time like this, part of me can't wait to tell her about the passport stamp I'm about to earn.

"Come over here," Vi whispers, and I crawl down to lie next to her. She brushes my hair away from my face and runs her fingers down my side. "Are you ready for this?" she asks as she kisses my neck.

In my head I'm screaming, "Yes! A thousand times yes!" But instead of saying a word, I pull her closer. In my head I'm singing her name.

But instead of kissing me more, she shoves me away. "No, no, no," she whispers and looks over her shoulder at the door.

At first my feelings are hurt, but then I hear the shouting, too. And like a possum, I freeze when danger is near.

"Violet Marie Bowersocks?" A man yells again, "You better have a good explanation for this."

Vi has a look of panic I've never seen on her before. She bolts up, grabs my hand, and drags me to the bathroom. "Stay in here. Lock the door." She slams the door shut. I do as I'm told and lock it, and then try to get dressed as quickly as possible.

"Dad, listen," I hear Vi say and realize why she was so scared. This is bad. Really bad. "I was just…"

"Violet. This is the last straw. It's one thing to screw up your own life, but don't you dare screw with my career." Then he yells, "What are you doing in here anyway? What is all this?" he asks, probably noticing our romantic spread. "Are you committing sin in this 2.1-million-dollar house? Do you just sit around thinking up ways to disappoint me?"

I want to go out there and defend Vi but still feel paralyzed with fear. That is, until I realize that I'm half-naked and continue to dress myself quickly.

"No one is here, Dad. I'm alone," Vi says, but he's definitely not buying it.

"Where is he?" I hear the sliding glass doors open to the balcony. "You get pregnant, you can kiss college good-bye. I'm not paying a dime for your bastard child."

"Dad, stop," Vi yells, but he continues his search.

When he tries the bathroom door and it's locked, he pounds on it. "You better get out here and show your face, young man," he yells into it.

I'm shaking, but with no cell phone and no way out, I don't really have a choice. I turn the knob and open it slowly. Instead of looking at him, I look at Vi to make sure she's okay. She's crying. When our eyes meet she mouths *Sorry* to me.

"Who are you?" he says to me, but I don't answer. Then he turns to Vi. "So it's true."

"Dad, I'm sorry," Vi says through her tears. "I'm sorry."

He takes a step back and seems to be in a different state—more shocked than angry. "Clean up this mess. Don't leave so much as a crumb. I'll see you both downstairs."

Vi and I don't say a word while we pack everything away. She won't even look at me when she hands me my cell phone.

Before heading downstairs, she leans in and whispers, "No matter what happens, I want you to know the only thing I regret is not having the chance to make love to you."

I nod and swallow down the lump in my throat because this feels like good-bye, and I was definitely not ready for one.

When Vi's dad orders me to call my mom or dad, I almost dial Tai to see if she'll fake being my mom but think better of it. No need to get her in trouble, too. As it is, I think she has her hands full with her own drama.

Vi's dad demands the phone from me as soon as it starts to ring. I obey and hand it over. He explains how the guard called him when he noticed a light on, and how he found us here—thankfully, leaving out the romantic picnic details—and requests my mom to come get me. After he gives her the gate code, he hangs up and we all wait in silence until she arrives. It's the longest twenty minutes of my life, hands down, and because I haven't eaten since noon, the smell of Caruso's is making my stomach make the most unsexy noises. But Vi's dad has no mercy on us. Instead he takes the food outside and tosses it in the garbage. He truly is evil.

My mom rings the doorbell, and we all jump.

"Mrs. Brooks," Vi's dad says after she enters. Then without giving her an opportunity to speak, he adds, "I could press charges. I hope you realize that."

My mom nods. "Yes, I understand." I can't read her face—that's usually a really bad sign.

"I'm not going to, but I hope you'll see to it that your daughter receives proper punishment."

She nods again and stares at me. "Oh yes, she will."

Gulp. It's very clear how she feels now.

"And I don't think our daughters should spend any time together anymore. They are obviously a bad influence on one another." Then he leans in closer to my mom and whispers, "And you should know I suspect some homosexual behavior has occurred this evening. Very sinful. You'll need to be sure you deal with that, too."

I think I see my mom hold back a smile. "Oh, my. Homosexual behavior?" She looks over at me, and I quickly look down at the expensive tile.

"Yes, ma'am. Best to nip these things in the bud before ideas start growing."

"Well," my mom says and then crosses her arms over her chest, I think to keep herself from slapping him. "Homosexual behavior would make a lot of sense since they've been dating for a while now."

Vi's dad turns red like a cartoon character. I half expect steam to start coming out of his ears. Then he points his big index finger at Vi. "Not my daughter, Mrs. Brooks. Violet is a straight A student and a volunteer at church."

"I assure you, Mr. Bowersocks, lesbians can get straight As and volunteer at church. And they can vote, and get married, and have babies, and they can even buy houses. And I can guarantee you they can get into UC Berkeley."

How does she know about Berkeley?

"You have a beautiful daughter, sir, and I hope you realize that before it's too late." Then she holds her hand out for me and, like it's a lifeline, I grab it and hold tight. "My daughter's a lesbian and I am so incredibly proud of her." I'm half-joyous because my mom is awesome and half-scared for Vi's life. What is she doing? How could she out Vi like that? Then she turns to my poor girlfriend and says, "Violet, honey, your mom really, really loves you. I hope you'll consider talking to her, especially after tonight."

And how does she know that? Has my mom been befriending Vi's mom behind my back?

Hearing this last statement from my mom makes Vi start to cry again. I want to hug her, but instead my mom drags me out the door and practically throws me in the passenger seat of her Jetta.

I have a million questions to ask her, like how she knows Vi's mom loves her, but I have a feeling I'd better let her do most of the talking right now.

"I hope you learned a valuable lesson tonight, Abbey," she says as we drive away.

I squirm in my seat and think, yep. If I want to travel to Belize with my girlfriend, use a very private jet to get there. But I keep this revelation to myself. Instead, I let her tell me what I should know.

"Trespassing? Breaking and entering? Is that the kind of thing you want on a police record?"

I don't want a police record at all, but I guess I wouldn't want it to say that if I did have one.

"Do you know how scared I was when he called me?" She turns to look at me. "I thought you were hurt, Abbey." She reaches out and grabs my hand. "I am so angry with you, but I still love you."

To keep myself from crying, I clear my throat and finally talk. "Mom, I'm really sorry. I didn't think—"

"Well, that's obvious," she says. "You and Vi are very lucky the cops weren't called."

I agree, but to help her remember how much she loves me, I say, "Thanks for sticking up for me, for us, like that. Do you think she's going to be okay?" I need her to tell me Vi's going to be fine, even if she can't back it up. "He was really mad, Mom."

She rubs her forehead like a headache has suddenly come on. "I shouldn't have said that stuff to him about Violet. I feel terrible. Just awful. Those meetings are confidential. It's her journey, and I took coming-out away from her."

I guess that explains how my mom knew so much about Vi's mom—PFLAG. To try and help her feel better, I say, "I think the secret was pretty much out. I'm sure she'll forgive you."

"Where's your car?" she asks, realizing she needs to drop me off to drive it home.

"Caruso's on Fourth."

She heads in that direction. "You know I'll always stand up for you, right?"

I nod. "I know, Mom." I look out the window and finally realize what lesson I actually did learn tonight: my mom is the greatest mom and I am the luckiest daughter in the world.

I almost turn to tell her this, but she says, "Just so we're clear, you're grounded for"—she slows for a red light and looks over at me—"a very long time."

Even the greatest moms in the world have to lay down the law once in a while, I guess. "I know," I whisper. "I'm sorry." Now look who has the case of the sorrys. Thinking this makes me think of Kate and her text. I look at my phone, but before I can put my password in, my mom snatches it out of my hands.

"Nope, this is mine."

"But, Mom, I was just checking—"

"If someone needs to reach you, they can call you at home." She parks next to my car. "I'll follow you home."

I almost protest the escort, but there's no point. As I drive home with my mom trailing behind me, I'm a nervous wreck and drive the exact speed limit for practically the first time since I got my license.

It's not until I'm home and in bed that I think about Vi and about the most amazing night I've ever had with anyone. I wasn't sure if I loved her before tonight, but now I feel pretty confident. And I think she loves me, too.

But does any of that even matter if I never see her again?

CHAPTER TWENTY-NINE

Still no word from her, huh?" Garrett asks as we warm up before our track events.

"Nope"—I pant—"not a word." We round the corner of the school and nearly run head-on into a group of girls from Amphi. We're at the Sabino Invitational, so the campus is packed with over a hundred athletes from twenty different schools trying to improve their chances to get to divisionals. Not me, though. I'm happy to report that my high-jumping abilities are less than impressive, so there's no pressure on me to place. Track is just a good way to work on my tan and stay in shape for our basketball summer league.

"Sucks," Garrett says. Then, as usual, she turns the conversation back onto herself. "I haven't heard from Tai either. Is she doing okay?"

At the mention of Tai my stomach tenses. I still haven't confronted her about my suspicion. Besides not being able to understand it, I think the less I know the better. That way, when they get caught, I can deny knowing anything at all. That seems like the safest approach since, knowing this school, they're eventually going to get caught. If, of course, my theory that they're dating is correct. I guess I could be wrong. There's hope.

"Well, is she?"

"Yeah, yeah. Good," I say, out of breath.

But then Garrett stops running and faces me. "What do you know, Abbey? You better tell me right now."

Just then, Coach Parker yells for us to check in for our events. "She's really busy with school. You know, apps and other senior stuff," I say as we walk toward the middle of the field, hoping she buys it.

"Yeah, I guess. It's just, I thought…" She stops talking once we meet up with our teammates. "Anyway, good luck. Jump high and shit." She slaps my butt.

"Thanks. You jump long and shit."

She laughs. "I'll pretend the pit is full of Coach Alvarezes. That should help."

I nod. "Great idea," I say and turn away before my face gives anything away. Lord help me if she ever finds out I knew before her—that is, if she ever knows.

Being grounded is not new to me, but last year when I was grounded, I could at least see Keeta at school. I haven't seen or heard from Vi in two weeks, and I feel like I'm going to lose my mind. At least I've used my prison sentence of solitude wisely this time. My grades are up, and I've even cleaned the bathroom twice without my mom having to ask me to do it. So, yeah, it's been a really, really boring two weeks.

Since I have to wait in between my jumps, I plug in my music to tune out the chatter of the girls also waiting. As Mary Lambert sings in my ear, I take a break from thinking about Vi and take some time to think about Mia. My mom does let me talk to Mia on the phone, but I can't tell her much since I'm not allowed to take the house phone into my room. So she *does* know why I'm grounded, but nothing else about that night. Not that she needs to. No one needs to know, which is why I haven't actually told a soul, not even Garrett. I almost told her, but then thought about how she'd take what was a beautiful night and quickly turn it dirty. I think Tai guessed what happened, or nearly happened, but didn't press me to tell her more. We seem to have a silent agreement between us. Don't Ask, Don't Tell may have been repealed, but it's in full effect in the Brooks household.

I look down to pick a new mix, but then a pair of hands cover my eyes.

"Guess who?" a girl says, trying to disguise her voice.

I pat the hands as if this will help me. "Grandma, is that you?"

"Hey," Kate says and shoves my head forward. "That's mean." She sits down next to me and knocks her shoulder against mine like we're still friends or something. "How's it going?"

I shrug. "Pretty good, I guess. What're you doing here?" She ran track last year but skipped out on it this year. She doesn't look pregnant, so hopefully it was just because she didn't feel like it.

She looks down and picks the grass. "I was hoping to see you. You never texted me back."

"Mom has my cell," I say, which is true. "I'm grounded."

"What did you do now?" She laughs.

I don't answer, but not because I hate her and not because I'm mad at her. I just don't feel much for her anymore, which seems a lot worse than the old days when we would fight and then make up after I apologized.

My name is called. "I'm next. Sorry, I gotta go." I get up and offer a hand to help her up. She doesn't take it.

"Yeah, okay. I'll see you around."

I bend down to stretch my hammies. "Yep, see you." I don't look up as she walks away. I regret it instantly. I think about calling her name but don't. Because then what? We'd go right back to where we were, where I'm not good enough for her as I am. I watch her make her way back to Ryder and remind myself of the words my mom said to me last year as I tried to secretly recover from my Keeta heartbreak. *Sometimes, in order to make room in our hearts for new people, we have to let some go.* I guess she was right, like always. Just like she was about needing to let love in again, which is what Mark is to her. A new beginning.

It's Friday night and I'm slumped down on the couch suffering from serious commitment issues.

"Abbey Road, I will throw that remote in the pool if you don't decide on a show in the next ten seconds."

I settle on *Cupcake Wars*. But now I want cupcakes. This is torture. "Mom, do we have any cake mix?"

She's still working on another piece for Mark's restaurant. I thought she'd be done by now, but for some reason she's taking an extra-long time on it. After she lifts her brush, she says, "You don't need a mix. Just follow a recipe online."

"Well, excuse me, Ms. Technology, but as you might recall, I've been banned from the twenty-first century."

She sighs. "Your phone is in my purse. Knock yourself out."

I spring off the couch like the cushion is an ejection seat and pounce on my mom's Mary Poppins–esque purse. "How do you not have a neck condition from carrying this stuff around?" I ask as I take out the larger items and feel around for my phone. "It's not in here, Mom."

"Yes, it is."

I dump out the entire contents on the kitchen table and it finally appears. I kiss it and start to scroll through its messages as if any of them are going to change my life, but there's only one from Vi, from the night we got caught. All it says is: *Sorry*. My heart sinks. I miss her so much. After that one, it's just a couple more from Kate asking if I'll call her. I don't know if it's the sudden sadness I feel about missing Vi, but I get all nostalgic and start missing Kate, too. Why do people have to change?

"Find it?" Mom asks as she refills her coffee. Then she notices the mess I made and hurries to clean it up like she's hiding something. She especially doesn't want me to see what's in a white paper pharmacy bag. I remind myself to snoop later. "Really, Abbey?"

"Sorry, Mom." I plop down in the dining room chair. What's the point of having my phone back if I have no one to call? Mia's still wrapped up in Maddy, Kate's wrapped up in whatever she's doing, and calling Garrett just means avoiding questions about Tai.

"You really miss her, huh, honey?"

I nod.

"I was going to wait until your punishment is over, but I might as well tell you now."

I look up at her.

"I called Vi's parents last night."

"If you're about to tell me some bad news, you should know that I'll have a level-ten breakdown right here at the kitchen table."

"I wanted to apologize to her mom, Debra."

"Uh-huh?"

"And to see if there was a chance they would reconsider letting you two see each other."

"Go on…"

"Debra was very sweet and accepted my apology."

"You're trying to kill me, aren't you."

She takes a deep breath. "And her dad said that as long as she can keep up with her grades and job and her volunteer work at their church, then it's okay with him. I guess Debra convinced him to go to a PFLAG meeting with her. He's had a change of heart."

I don't let myself get excited yet. "You're lying, right? This is a trick?"

"The same goes for me, Abbey. I want to see good grades and you staying on top of your chores and responsibilities. Got it?"

"You're not lying?"

"Give her a call and find out for yourself."

Every muscle in my body wants to leap in the air, run down the hall, and call Vi. Instead, though, I walk over to my mom and hug her tight. "I love you, Mom. You deserve everything you want."

"That's sweet, Abbey Road. Thanks." She holds me close and all is right in the world. Almost.

"Okay, Mom"—I break away from her—"need to call someone." I run down the hall to my room. The phone is already ringing before I slam my door shut. Happiness at last.

CHAPTER THIRTY

The smartest move Tucson Unified School District has made in the last decade is moving graduations to nighttime. Even though the sun has set, it's still eighty-five degrees, but at least we don't have to get third-degree burns while waiting for Tai to cross the stage.

"Mom, your balloons are attacking me again," I say and bat them away. "Why did you buy so many?"

"Oh, don't be a party pooper, Abbey, I'll put them on the end for now. Excuse me, Violet."

Vi moves her legs to let my mom pass. "No problem, Mrs. B. Do you want me to start unfolding the sign?"

"See, Violet knows how to have fun," my mom says as she unpacks the ginormous sign we made for Tai. It's about fifteen feet long and reads *Congrats, Taisha! We love you!* so it's a good thing we have the number of people we do to cheer her on.

Vi starts to unroll it and passes it along. I'm next, then my mom, then Ms. Morvay and Juliana, then Garrett, then Mia and Nicky, who have proven to be more on-and-off again than Rachel and Ross from *Friends*. I smile when I look down the line. As imperfect as they all are, they're what got me through this year and made it one of my best years ever. Nicky has a lot of leftover paper, so she scoots down so the sign doesn't sag, but then a man I've never seen before sits down next to her and puts out his hand to help.

I guess my mom has met him, because she leans forward to wave at him. Then she leans to me and whispers, "That's Tai's father." He nods back and takes the end of the sign. What kind of magic does my mom use on these guys to make them become decent human beings?

After we hear from the valedictorian and the salutatorian and the principal and the band and the choir, the reading of the names begin.

Tai's last name is Williams, so we have a long way to go until it's her turn.

"He came," I say to Vi. "Tai's dad." She looks down the bleacher and smiles. "See, dads come around eventually."

She nods and holds my hand. "Yep, eventually."

Ever since we've been reunited, things have been even better between us. We haven't attempted another night of lovemaking, but I know when we do, it's going to be the best night ever. I want to kiss her, but I don't because I've never kissed a girl in front of my mom, and I'm not sure Vi would appreciate the PDA either.

I'm too happy to sit still, so I take out my phone. "Smile," I say to my mom and snap a selfie of us. "You, too," I say to Vi. We lean in to each other and I take a shot.

"Another one," Vi says.

I hold the phone up, and right before I push the button, she turns my head and lays one on me. She giggles like we're in sixth grade and it's our first kiss ever.

"You are out of control, young lady," I tease and consider going back for more, but then look over at my mom and reel my naughtiness back in.

Being here in the stands reminds me that Vi's going to graduate next year. And as much as she drives me crazy, Garrett will be gone, too. One by one, these people are leaving my life. Why does it have to be this way?

We all jump up and scream when we hear Tai's name and hold up the sign that she could have seen from space. That lasts three seconds, then it's back to sitting bored again until Lori Zepeda's name is finally called.

"You okay?" Vi asks as we walk to the field to give Tai hugs and balloons.

"Yeah, I'm just"—I take a breath—"going to miss her."

My mom is beginning to lose it, too, and by the time we find Tai, Mom's full-on crying as she waits her turn for a hug. But we let Tai's dad go first. We try to give them space, but it's too crowded for that, so we all look in different directions and pretend not to listen in.

They hug and he tells her he's proud of her. He tells her to study hard in school and to be anything she wants to be. Tears roll down Tai's face and she nods while hugging him tight.

When they part, sooner than I think Tai wants, he shakes my mom's hand and says, "Thank you. For everything."

"She is a gift," she says to him, "but I think you know that."

He nods and then finds a hole in the crowd and disappears.

"Well, don't just stand there, hug me," Tai demands.

We don't know who she's talking to, so we all go at her at once and give her the biggest group hug I think that girl has ever had.

"Get in here, Nicky," Tai demands. "Don't think I don't see you."

Nicky bashfully joins in.

"Got room for one more?" a voice says from outside the circle.

We all look up and there she is, Coach Alvarez. The hug disperses and we all stare at her. I'm pretty sure I'm the only one who knows why she's here, but Tai quickly dispels any confusion when she pulls Coach to her and kisses her. Right there. On the football field. For the whole world to see. And I'm not talking a smooch. I'm talking a dipped, take-your-breath-away kiss.

When they finally come up for air, Tai is grinning from ear to ear. "Everyone, this is Ana, my girlfriend. Ana, this is Abbey and her girlfriend Vi."

Coach Alvarez shakes Vi's hand and winks at me.

"Abbey's mom."

My mom closes her mouth and waves.

"You know Garrett."

Garrett, who up until this point was pretty sure there was still a chance to win Tai back this summer, turns on her heel yelling, "Unbelievable!" as she storms off.

"Now listen, Ms. M., you can't get me or her in trouble. I'm eighteen, almost nineteen, and she hasn't been an employee here since our season ended."

"I wasn't, I mean, it's—" Ms. Morvay says, but Juliana comes in for the save.

"Nice to meet you, Ana."

That just leaves Mia and Nicky, so they introduce themselves.

"Those for me?" Tai says and points to the balloons.

"Yes, yes. Sorry," my mom says and hands them to her. "So, is this who you're moving in with this summer?"

"Yep, she just graduated from the U of A and got a job as a PE teacher at a middle school near GCU." Tai looks at Ana and smiles. They are really, truly in love, and not a single one of us can deny that.

Ms. Morvay and my mom exchange glances then decide telepathically that there's nothing to do but eat. "Who's hungry?" my mom asks.

Vi raises my hand for me and the rest of the crowd joins in.

"Okay, well, let's get going. We've got reservations at nine at Macayo's, and this mama needs a strawberry daiquiri."

"Make mine a double," I hear Ms. Morvay say as we head to the cars.

I ask if I can ride over with Vi since my mom needs an extra seat now for Coach, uh, Ana.

I get approval and jump in Vi's Honda. "Just you and me, babe," I say and lean in to kiss her. I'm happy she doesn't lean away even though some parents are walking by. Maybe Tai's bravery has rubbed off on her.

She ends our kiss by touching my cheek and saying, "I got you something."

"Me? But I didn't graduate." I don't put up more of a fight because I love presents, especially from Vi.

"Close your eyes."

I do as I'm told and wait with a big smile on my face.

She places a small box on my lap and I open my eyes. "Vi," I say because it's obviously jewelry, and I know I'm going to love it because I love everything she does for me. Maybe it's because I love her.

I turn to her. "Vi?" I say, then I add the "olet" to make what I'm about to say more serious.

She pushes my bangs aside and smiles. "Yeah?"

"I, I really…" I want to say it, so why can't I?

"Yeah? You really what?" She tilts her head and smiles. "You really want a chimichanga?"

"Well, yes. But I also really…" Soon, I decide, but not today. "I really like you. Like, so much."

She rubs my leg. "Yeah, me, too, Abbey Abs. Now, open it," she says and points to the box.

I do as I'm told. Inside is a silver charm bracelet. "Wow, Vi." I look at each charm carefully. "This is really beautiful."

She leans closer to me. "They represent things that are important to you. See?" She holds the paint palette between her fingers. "Your mom." Then holds the tiny microscope. "Your dad." Then she holds the basketball. "Well, we know what this one means." Then there's a heart. "This one is…" She pauses, so I fill it in for her.

"You."

She blushes. "Well, I hoped you might say that."

I hold it out for her to put it on for me.

"I love you, Vi," I whisper, thinking that I was going to say that I love *it*, but the *you* slipped out instead. I kiss her before she has a chance to respond. But I don't need her to. I've never been more sure about anything in world than I am about us right now.

Tai was right. Love feels amazing.

Author's Note

Abbey and her friends have had a quite a year and have had to overcome and deal with a lot of tough situations. If you or someone you know needs support dealing with the challenges that come up in life, please know there are people out there who want to help, and that you are never alone. You deserve to be safe, protected, and healthy. Here are some national resources that want to help and support teens, especially LGBTQ teens, live their happiest and healthiest lives.

The Trevor Project: www.thetrevorproject.org
If you're thinking about suicide, you deserve immediate help—please call the 24-hour Trevor Lifeline at 866-488-7386. This site also has tons of resources, including live online help.

The Safe Schools Coalition: www.safeschoolscoalition.org

GLBT National Help Center: www.glnh.org

The Gay/Straight Alliance Network: www.gsanetwork.org

PFLAG: Parents, Friends, and Family of Gays and Lesbians: www.pflag.org

About the Author

Annameekee Hesik grew up in Ojai, CA, on a healthy diet of Pippi Longstocking books, dipped ice cream cones, and Schwinn bikes. She came out when she was fifteen and has since become obsessed with rainbow everything. After surviving high school in Tucson, AZ, she went to college, where she changed her major five times. She earned her BA in English literature from UC Davis and her MA in education from UC Santa Cruz, and she is thrilled she finally decided to become a high school English teacher (with a background in anthropology, American Sign Language, world history, and environmental biology). When she isn't helping students enjoy the gift of literature, she spends her time in Santa Cruz, CA, walking her dogs, reading in her hammock, riding bikes with her wife, slurping down mocha shakes, and writing books that she hopes will help lesbian and questioning teens feel like they are not the only girl loving girls in the world. Her debut YA novel, *The You Know Who Girls: Freshman Year*, was awarded a Benjamin Franklin Book Award and is the first book in her You Know Who Girls series. Like her at facebook.com/annameekee.hesik, follow her on Twitter @youknowwhogirls, and check out her website to see her embarrassing high school photos, read her blog, and find what she likes to mix into her macaroni and cheese: www.annameekee.com

Soliloquy Titles From Bold Strokes Books

Asher's Shot by Elizabeth Wheeler. Asher Price's candid photographs capture the truth, but when his success requires exposing an enemy, Asher discovers his only shot at happiness involves revealing secrets of his own. (978-1-62639-229-8)

The Melody of Light by M.L. Rice. After surviving abuse and loss, will Riley Gordon be able to navigate her first year of college and accept true love and family? (78-1-62639-219-9)

Maxine Wore Black by Nora Olsen. Jayla will do anything for Maxine, the girl of her dreams, but after becoming ensnared in Maxine's dark secrets, she'll have to choose between love and her own life. (978-1-62639-208-3)

Bottled Up Secret by Brian McNamara. When Brendan Madden befriends his gorgeous, athletic classmate, Mark, it doesn't take long for Brendan to fall head over heels for him—but will Mark reciprocate the feelings? (978-1-62639-209-0)

Searching for Grace by Juliann Rich. First it's a rumor. Then it's a fact. And then it's on. (978-1-62639-196-3)

Dark Tide by Greg Herren. A summer working as a lifeguard at a hotel on the Gulf Coast seems like a dream job…until Ricky Hackworth realizes the town is shielding some very dark—and deadly—secrets. (978-1-62639-197-0)

Everything Changes by Samantha Hale. Raven Walker's world is turned upside down the moment Morgan O'Shea walks into her life. (978-1-62639-303-5)

Fifty Yards and Holding by David Matthew-Barnes. The discovery of a secret relationship between Riley Brewer, the star of the high school baseball team, and Victor Alvarez, the leader of a violent street gang, escalates into a preventable tragedy. (978-1-62639-081-2)

Tristant and Elijah by Jennifer Lavoie. After Elijah finds a scandalous letter belonging to Tristant's great-uncle, the boys set out to discover the secret Uncle Glenn kept hidden his entire life and end up discovering who they are in the process. (978-1-62639-075-1)

Caught in the Crossfire by Juliann Rich. Two boys at Bible camp; one forbidden love. (978-1-62639-070-6)

Frenemy of the People by Nora Olsen. Clarissa and Lexie have despised each other for as long as they can remember, but when they both find themselves helping an unlikely contender for homecoming queen, they are catapulted into an unexpected romance. (978-1-62639-063-8)

The Balance by Neal Wooten. Love and survival come together in the distant future as Piri and Niko face off against the worst factions of mankind's evolution. (978-1-62639-055-3)

The Unwanted by Jeffrey Ricker. Jamie Thomas is plunged into danger when he discovers his mother is an Amazon who needs his help to save the tribe from a vengeful god. (978-1-62639-048-5)

Because of Her by KE Payne. When Tabby Morton is forced to move to London, she's convinced her life will never be the same again. But the beautiful and intriguing Eden Palmer is about to show her that this time, change is most definitely for the better. (978-1-62639-049-2)

The Seventh Pleiade by Andrew J. Peters. When Atlantis is besieged by violent storms, tremors, and a barbarian army, it will be up to a young gay prince to find a way for the kingdom's survival. (978-1-60282-960-2)

Asher's Fault by Elizabeth Wheeler. Fourteen-year-old Asher Price sees the world in black and white, much like the photos he takes, but when his little brother drowns at the same moment Asher experiences his first same-sex kiss, he can no longer hide behind the lens of his camera and eventually discovers he isn't the only one with a secret. (978-1-60282-982-4)